K

"I am no virgin,"

Caroline whispered. "If I lie with you I shall be no better than a whore."

Her hand lay limp in her lap. Daniel raised it, turning it palm upward, then covered it with his own, lacing his fingers through hers.

"Ah, Caroline." He sighed. "If a man spoke thus about you, I would kill him on the spot. What shall I do with you?"

Caroline's pain felt beyond bearing; speechless, she shook her head. Releasing her fingers, Daniel drew her close to him.

He held her, unmoving, as her breath became regular. In time it deepened, and he knew she had fallen asleep. Still, he held her a bit longer, resting his cheek against her hair. Then he sat looking down at her face.

"Caroline," he murmured. "If we are given the time, I shall teach you about love. I give you my word on it."

Dear Readers,

As you may already have noticed, we have something a little bit different for you this month. The handsome gentleman on the cover of Kristin James's aptly-titled *The Gentleman* is one of two brothers whose stories we'll be bringing to you this month and next. Follow Stephen Ferguson from the East, where he's been brought up with wealth and gentility, to the rugged West, where he spent the first few years of his life. The family reunion that follows strikes sparks, but they're nothing compared to the flames that are ignited between Stephen and tomboyish Jessie Randall, who soon starts dreaming of being the kind of lady who could attract her very own gentleman.

And the excitement doesn't stop there, because next month, Dorothy Glenn's *The Hell Raiser* tells the story of Sam Ferguson, the brother who was left behind to make his way in the hard and dangerous Montana mountains. Sam is rough and tough—but even the toughest man can melt when he meets the right woman. Read *The Hell Raiser* and find out who she is!

In months to come we'll take you from East to West, Europe to America—even to China. Join us and watch the past come alive. It happens every month in Harlequin Historicals.

Leslie Wainger
Senior Editor and Editorial Coordinator

Summer's Promise

Lucy Elliot

Harlequin Books

TORONTO • NEW YORK • LONDON
AMSTERDAM • PARIS • SYDNEY • HAMBURG
STOCKHOLM • ATHENS • TOKYO • MILAN

To Ruthie Cohen from Burlington

Harlequin Historical first edition April 1990

ISBN 0-373-28644-9

Books by Lucy Elliot

Harlequin Historicals

Shared Passions #8
Frontiers of the Heart #24
Summer's Promise #44

LUCY ELLIOT

is a happily transplanted Easterner living in northern California with her husband, son, dog and any neighborhood cat who wants an extra meal. She has been making up stories for her own entertainment since earliest memory—full of romance, adventure and, of course, a happy ending.

Chapter One

Northfield, Massachusetts
April, 1745

The two wagons and the single rider creaked slowly north along the town's main street, passing shops and sturdy houses with neat, well-tended yards, and a group of boys playing marbles outside the one-room school. To the east were the low mountains rolling towards Boston, ninety miles off to the west, at the edge of the freshly plowed fields, the broad river. To the north—though the travelers could not see it beyond the town's steep roofs—lay the wilderness that separated the British colonies from those governed by France. Northfield was the last British bastion before that no-man's-land.

The flocks grazing in the wide street moved to give the wagons room, and barking dogs dodged their wheels, drawing the curious to their doorways for a glimpse of the procession. A half-dozen men gathered outside the blacksmith's shop, and their wives set aside their cooking to step into their yards, shielding their eyes from the afternoon sunlight to catch a better view. They counted three men and two women, and several young children, besides.

"New folks," they concluded, their seasoned eyes making a quick inventory of the wagons' contents—the barrels and the boxes, the spinning wheel and the churn, the iron plow and the harrow and the half-dozen straight-backed chairs, all crowded in together with sacks of grain and meal and something wrapped in feather ticks that might be a clock. "They must be come up from the south. Where do you suppose they are going?"

"Could they mean to settle in here?" one of the women wondered aloud.

"Could be," replied her neighbor, meeting her at the fence. "But, if so, wouldn't we have heard of them by now?" Settling in Northfield was not a thing casually done. New people had to make application with the town meeting and then undergo close scrutiny as to character and means.

"But, if not here, then where can they be bound?"

"North, perhaps? To the wilderness?"

The goodwives exchanged a look of incredulity. To be sure, other families had settled to the north in the past, drawn by the promise of virgin land and two decades' unbroken peace. But within the last year that peace had moved to the brink of collapse. In Europe, France and Britain had gone to war once more, which meant that hostilities would surely plague the colonies, as well. Fighting had already broken out on the eastern coast, and soon it was likely to spread inland. Perhaps even now the French governor in Quebec was whipping up his Indian allies, spreading anti-British hatred. And then the Indians would sweep southwards, with one goal in mind: to terrorize the British settlers all along the frontier.

"I wouldn't risk going north these days," said the first woman.

"Nor I," her neighbor agreed. "Not knowing the savages' fondness for violence and blood. There's trouble enough in this life without going courting it."

At the smithy, a red-haired man spoke up suddenly, pointing not to the wagons but to the man who rode ahead. "Wait a minute! Isn't that MacKenzie, who was up here last year? He came from down in Connecticut—New Haven, I think. Remember, he had a contract to cut timber in the wilderness?"

"Yes," said another, "and he had a grant of land, as well. He went up last summer to build his house, then returned

for the winter months. He said he'd be back in the springtime, but with the war I thought he would stay in the south.''

"He's a nervy fellow—and bringing his whole family!"

"Nervy, and mean, as well," responded the red-haired
man. "As I recall MacKenzie, butter wouldn't melt in his
mouth. He's probably too stubborn to give up good land
before the threat of war. He can't get much farther before
sunset.... I guess he means to stay the night. I pity Goodwife Willis, having to take him in. But whatever you think
of a man, you can't turn out his family when there's a room
for them.''

"Poor Goody Willis," another man said.

Ignorant of these comments, or perhaps only scornful of
them, Thomas MacKenzie guided his sorrel mare past the
blacksmith's shop. It was a good-sized mount, well muscled and fit, but it appeared a frail thing beneath Thomas's
brooding hulk. He slouched past the tidy houses with hardly
a sideways glance until he reached the one whose swinging
wooden sign proclaimed it the town ordinary, where a meal
could be ordered and a room had for the night. Drawing up
the mare, Thomas turned to wait as the two wagons made
their slow approach.

In the first rode Jonas Watson, Thomas's longtime em-
ployee, with his scrawny rat's face, and his sharp rat's wits,
as well. At his side rode William, broad backed and mild
eyed, whose heft would be invaluable in the cutting down of
trees. With a few grunted commands, Thomas left Jonas to
see to their things and sent William back to the second
wagon to help the women down. Thomas would see them
settled, and then he had business to do.

The men at the smithy watched the big-boned William
swing himself to the ground just as the second wagon pulled
up behind the first. Two women sat there. The first was
small and fair haired; her face was drawn and tired, and her
eyes darted here and there, giving her the appearance of a
small bird poised for flight. In her arms she held a child, a
baby fast asleep, and two others sat beside her on the high
seat. The wagon jolted as it stopped, and she pressed the
baby close to her, as if she would protect it from some new,

unknown threat. Her agitated movement roused the child, and it gave a cry of protest. She clucked to it, her smile tender despite her evident weariness.

At the child's cry, the other woman roused. The watching townspeople could see only that she was much taller, for her features were hidden by the heavy shawl she wore over her head. Coming up the main street, she had looked neither left nor right, but had kept her eyes straight ahead, as if Northfield's attractions held no shred of interest for her. Now, roused by the child, the woman shook herself, as if she were coming out of a deep sleep. Dropping the shawl to her shoulders, she looked about her for the first time. When she turned her head towards the smithy, the men in the doorway gasped.

"Well, I'll be!" they murmured, stepping down for a closer look, and the goodwives in the front yards stepped up closer, too.

The woman was beautiful. She had pure, milky white skin and coal-black hair and dark eyes whose almond shape gave her face an exotic cast. Her hair was tightly plaited into two long braids that had been pulled up and fastened close to her head, but the severity of the style only enhanced her striking looks. The first flush of girlhood had long since vanished from her cheeks; she might have been as old as thirty, but age had only served to refine the bones of her face. The good people of Northfield stared and muttered. Such beauty seemed strangely out of place on the frontier.

Caroline Fielding stared blankly at Northfield's broad main street, barely noticing the attention she attracted. Her body was numb and aching from the bone-jarring trip, and her mind was numb, as well—but that was from specific intent. In the two weeks since they'd left New Haven, she had retreated farther into the hard shell that had been her armor during these last eight years. The shell insulated her from the past, and from the present, too—and as for the future, she had no hope for it. The future belonged to her sister, Hannah, and to Hannah's children, beside her on the seat. For herself Caroline had no expectations, no dreams of happiness.

Caroline wasted no effort attempting to distinguish this town from the others through which they had passed. This one had the same wooden buildings, the same smug, complacent air, the same curious onlookers whispering among themselves. When she finally took notice of their staring faces, she felt her back grow stiff. Then she became aware of the baby crying in Hannah's arms.

"Here, Hannah," she murmured, turning away from Northfield's prying eyes. "You must be tired. Let me take her."

Smiling wearily, Hannah looked up at her sister. "It's all right, she's only startled. She'll quiet soon enough." Then, as if some new thought had come to her, Hannah's smile faded, to be replaced by an apprehensive look, and she raised her eyes from the child to Thomas's face.

Following Hannah's gaze, Caroline looked up as well, with eyes that were just as weary, but devoid of fear. Instead, her gaze held a disdain that was palpable even to the men at the blacksmith's shop. Her disdain was intended for Thomas; he recognized it, and his scowl beetled his heavy brows into a single dark line. At this Hannah shrank in earnest, but Caroline's chin only rose, answering Thomas's anger with a challenge.

"Don't, Caroline," Hannah pleaded, pressing the baby closer to muffle its cries against her breast.

Caroline saw Thomas's lip curl scornfully. For a moment her own lips tightened into a thin line, for she hated to give him satisfaction, even on a minor point. But a confrontation now would only upset Hannah more, and she was already agitated enough.

"All right," she murmured, releasing her breath in a sigh. Forcing herself to smile for Hannah's sake, she patted her sister on the arm. "After all, I've come along to lighten your burdens, so what sense would it make if I were to do just the opposite? Come, Tom, Elizabeth." She turned to the two older children, who were perched between them on the seat. "Look, William is coming to help us climb down." And, tucking her skirts about her, she prepared for the descent.

* * *

"So," said Goodwife Willis, who owned the ordinary.
"You've come back, Mr. MacKenzie, and brought your
family. And at a time like this."

Thomas MacKenzie's answer was a grunt of acknowl-
edgment, and a dark look, as if to tell Goody Willis that his
comings and goings were none of her concern—and perhaps, also, to warn her against being foolish enough to
alarm his wife in any way about conditions to the north.

Goody Willis had no liking for Thomas MacKenzie. Last
fall, when he had stayed here, he had disputed his bill, and
his man—the weasel-faced one—had cheated her out of a
sack of grain. For that alone she was tempted to bar him
from her inn, but his wife looked as though she would fall
if she didn't sit, and Goody Willis imagined the poor woman
had trials enough being MacKenzie's wife. Poor thing, she
hardly looked strong enough to survive the frontier. Her
heart went out to Mrs. MacKenzie, though her good wishes
stopped short of the other woman. Such beauty as hers, she
thought, was a sin before God.

"There's just the upper chamber," she said, nodding towards the stairs. "The women and children can stay there
and the men in the stable loft—unless you yourself would
prefer a cot in the spare pantry."

"Ah, keep your extra pantry!" Thomas MacKenzie
growled, drawing a mirthless smile from his sister-in-law. It
wasn't, Caroline knew, that he lacked the coin to pay for the
extra room. Thomas did well in all his businesses, licit and
otherwise. Rather, he was unwilling to part with any coin he
owned. That was the reason they had brought no serving
girl. The servants had stayed with the house in New Haven
when it had been let. Thomas saw no use in spending money
on hired help when he could get the same work out of his
own family. Besides, that was the stipulation he had ex-
acted from Caroline for having allowed her to come. She
hated to have Thomas best her, but she had no choice in
this, for she could not allow him to drag Hannah off alone
to the discomfort and danger that must surely lie ahead.

Besides, she was responsible for Hannah's having married
him.

"And, as for the meal," Goodwife Willis continued, ignoring Thomas's retort, "we've good pork and mutton, and
fresh-baked bread, as well. I'll have the girl show you up to
your chamber and fetch linen for the bed."

"So you're from Connecticut?" The maid, red cheeked
and buxom, dropped the linen on the chest that, with bed
and table, made up the room's furnishings. Caroline looked
about her, realizing yet again that eight years in New England had not accustomed her to its Puritan ways. In Surrey there would have been curtains and a rug upon the floor,
and perhaps even a picture hanging on the wall.

"Yes," Hannah said, nodding. "We've come from New
Haven." Hannah had less interest in the room's furnishings than in her two daughters, who were playing on the
floor, six-year-old Elizabeth amusing the baby, Hetty, with
a bit of string. Young Tom was, as always, nowhere to be
found. He was probably off in the stables, bothering the
men. "From New Haven, most recently, and from Surrey
before that. My father was estate agent to Sir Edmund
Bredon at Harrow Hall."

As she spoke, Hannah glanced nervously at Caroline,
knowing how she hated to hear Sir Edmund's name. But
Caroline appeared not to have heard. She stood in the
doorway, looking about the room with the vague indiffer-
ence that was so often on her face. Sometimes Hannah
could not match this blank-eyed sister of hers with the
glowing, vibrant creature she had idolized as a girl. Caroline, the elder daughter, so dashing and devil-may-care.

"I don't know much of Surrey," said the girl, unfurling
the sheet. "But my own great-grandfather came from New
Haven. He came here when Northfield was founded, in
1672, but of course he didn't stay long, just three years at
first."

"Why did he leave?" Hannah asked, turning towards her.

"Why, indeed!" The girl clucked. "Because the Indians
came, that's why! And seized every poor soul who could not

get away. Tore out their tongues and burned them alive at the stake! Great-grandfather was lucky. He managed to escape. But that was the end of Northfield, at least for a while." She spoke in bursts as she smoothed the sheet. Reaching for a quilt, she added, "And they did worse things at Deerfield when they attacked there. They murdered the babies in front of their mothers' eyes."

"Goodness!" quavered Hannah, her hand rising to her throat, her eyes moving to her children, full of trembling fear.

Her tone awakened Caroline from her reverie. "What is it?" she asked, frowning.

"This girl has just been telling of the terrible things that occurred right here in Northfield when the Indians attacked!"

"What have you been saying?" Caroline asked harshly of the girl.

"Only the truth!" she retorted, stung by Caroline's accusing tone. Then she saw Hannah's face and she relented. "Though, to be sure, those things happened many years ago. There's been no Indian problem since way before I was born. Nonetheless, I wouldn't trust them—not with the war and all."

"But," Caroline responded, speaking for Hannah's benefit, "the war has not come here. If we are lucky, it may not come at all. And, even if it does come, now there are the forts that the governor has had erected all along the frontier. Fort Dummer is only a half-dozen miles from our land, and at the first sign of trouble we shall seek shelter within its walls."

"If you can reach it in time," the girl said with another cluck, leaning down to draw a sheet over the trundle bed. "Those Indians sneak up mighty sudden in the night. Then, all at once, they're on you, before you know what's hit!" She caught herself and grinned sheepishly. "But, as you say, that may not happen this time. Perhaps the war will miss you and you will farm your land in peace until you're old and gray!"

"Oh, we don't mean to stay that long!" Hannah's eyes widened at the very thought. "No, indeed, I don't think we'll live there for more than a few years. My husband is no farmer. He has a contract to cut masts and spars for the King's Navy. We will only stay north until the trees are cut. Then my husband will return to his business in the south. He has a factory and a ropewalk, which my father is running for him."

"Well, I guess you'll find no dearth of trees where you're bound!" the girl said with a laugh. "Though, for myself, I'd miss the company of town. Well, to each his own. I guess I'd better get down to help with the meal. We'll call you when it's ready. Good day to you." And, dropping a quick curtsy, she turned and left the room.

Her footsteps retreated down the steep flight of stairs. "Mamma," Elizabeth asked, her forehead creased with a frown, "will the Indians really come to get us in the night?"

"Of course not!" Moving to the children, Hannah bent and scooped the baby into her arms. "There won't be any Indians... will there, Caroline?"

"Of course not!" Caroline said, keeping her voice cheerful, and her face, as well. She knew that Hannah was longing to have her add that Thomas would not expose them to risk, but, despite her love for Hannah, she could not speak such words. For her own part, she wondered just what Thomas really thought. Neither she nor her parents had been surprised in the least when Thomas had announced that he had won the contract to supply the King's timber. What had surprised them was his announcement that Hannah and the children should go along, for they had expected him to leave the family behind. Her parents had protested, as had Caroline, but, pressed for a reason, Thomas had retorted that it was a man's right to pick his family's choice of home. From which Caroline had concluded that, even on the frontier, he wanted the comforts that only a wife could provide.

Did Thomas see the risks towards which he was leading them? Or was he too blinded by thoughts of the profits he could realize? Or was he perhaps right in his assessment of

such fears as exaggerated? Not for the first time, Caroline
wished she knew the answer.

But, though her thoughts were troubling, for Hannah's
benefit she kept them from her face. Instead, she smiled and
said, "Besides, you know our troops are sailing north at this
very moment to attack the French fort at Louisbourg, off
the Canadian coast. I've heard it said that if we are victo-
rious the French may well end the war."

"Yes, indeed!" Hannah nodded. Her eyes, above the
baby's head, lit with a ray of hope. "So let's have no more
talk of Indians or terror in the night!" Smiling weakly at
Caroline, she shook her head. "It's all so far from Surrey.
Do you ever think of it?"

"Never!" The denial was torn from Caroline, and she felt
a stab of anger at herself when she saw Hannah flinch.
"That is," she added quickly, seeking to control her voice,
"there is so much else to consider, what with this new life....
Why don't you rest until dinner? I will unpack our things."
And, without waiting for Hannah to answer, she turned to
the chest, where she had left the bundle that she had carried up.

She unwrapped it with trembling hands, struck as always
by the power the memories still retained. Did she ever think
of Surrey! Indeed, when did she ever not? When did a day
go by that she did not see Edmund, so smilingly arrogant,
and herself as she must have been, starry-eyed with her
dreams. Not a day went by that she did not regret the fool
she had been to let Sir Edmund Bredon have his way with
her. Had she really believed that he would marry her—he,
the lord of the manor, and she, the daughter of his estate
agent? Had she been so vain? If so, she had been punished
for her vanity. She was being punished still.

"Aunt Caroline!" Elizabeth's startled cry shattered
Caroline's thoughts, and she turned in time to see Hannah
take a faltering step towards the bed.

"Hannah!" she cried, springing forward to snatch the
baby from Hannah's arms. Half leading, half carrying, she
managed to lay Hannah down. Then she knelt beside her

and began to chafe her hands. "You are ill! Hannah, what is it?"

"No, no, I am fine. It is only—" Hannah paused, glancing at Elizabeth.

Caroline understood the look. "Not again!" she cried with dismay. "Is it his intention to sire a battalion through you?"

"Caroline!" Two discs of hot color flared in Hannah's pale cheeks. She glanced at Elizabeth, relieved by the innocence she saw on the girl's face. "Thomas wants another boy. You know how men are."

"Men!" exclaimed Caroline, ignoring Elizabeth. "Is it not enough to make this journey, to face what lies ahead, without bearing this added burden? Does he know of this?"

Hannah nodded. "I told him. But only after the plans were made. In any case," she added, her lips curving with pride, "he wouldn't have left me behind."

"No, of course not," Caroline agreed. "Thomas likes to keep all his possessions close at hand. And what under heaven would you have done had I not insisted upon coming along? And to think that, knowing of your condition, he would still have turned me back if he could have!" Then she caught sight of Hannah's anxious eyes, and her own anger faded, to be replaced by regret.

"There now," she murmured, stroking Hannah's hair. "Rest is what you need now, not some heavy meal. I'm sure that the kitchen will yield a cup of broth. William can watch the children while I bring you up a tray. Likely Young Tom's been with him this last hour, dogging his footsteps and asking about everything!"

"Dear Caroline!" Hannah's eyes were filled with gratitude. "What would I do without you?"

What, indeed, thought Caroline, turning her eyes away. But for me, you'd still be in England, likely married to some good man with a pretty little cottage on Sir Edmund's estates. Pushing back the pain, she smiled for Hannah's benefit. Then she gathered the children and herded them down the stairs.

* * *

Clouds like mounds of copper and violet shot through with golden light hung suspended over the meadow and the mountains beyond, caught and returned by the river, to be carried away to the south. On the banks, newly sprouted willows dipped lemon-colored boughs into the placid flow, and new grass silenced Caroline's step as she crossed the meadow from the town, drawn by the river and the yearning for solitude.

Hannah was resting comfortably after a bowl of good beef broth, and William, steady William, was keeping an eye on the children. That meant that Caroline had a few minutes to call her own, for almost the first time since they had left New Haven. She'd thought to stretch her legs with a stroll along the town's main road, but no sooner had she set out than she had felt the inquisitive eyes. So instead she'd sought the solace of the river's banks.

And solace they did provide, though they also touched her memory with their likeness to home. If she ignored the mountains and the style of houses behind, if she concentrated on the colors and the water's flow, she could almost imagine herself back in Surrey, in the village below Harrow Hall. Even the same birds were calling as had fluttered about in the yard as she had stood at the gate of her father's house, watching the fine coach draw to a halt.

The coach had been Sir Edmund's, bearing him home after two years in London to claim his dead father's estate. In the time he'd been gone she'd grown into a young lady. Sir Edmund had grown, too; he was taller and more handsome, his stance full of an arrogance that seemed to advise the world that he had come to assume his rightful place as the master of Harrow Hall. Caroline had curtsied, then glanced up, just in time to see the interest in his eyes. The coachman had been waiting for the order to drive on, but Sir Edmund had stayed him, his eyes lingering on Caroline. Then he had smiled, and she had smiled back, and the consequences of that smile had changed her entire life.

* * *

"It is beautiful, is it not, this ending of the day?" The words, softly spoken, came from just behind, and Caroline nodded, still lost in the past.

"Yes, it is," she murmured. For a moment she could almost have believed that the speaker was Edmund, come from her past to haunt her, and she turned, her eyes soft with wistfulness, but also shining with desire.

A last ray of sunlight shone over the horizon, coming from behind Caroline to illuminate the man standing at her side. In the light's first brilliance, she thought he wore a wig, but then she saw it was his own hair, caught back in a thin thong. It was not powder that made his hair so pale, but the sun's gleam, which turned it to a shade somewhere between silver and gold, the same hue as his lashes, which grew thick as ripe wheat. She was not in Surrey, but in America. And this man was not Edmund, but a perfect stranger.

The moment called for speech; she knew it, even willed it, but no words came. Instead, she stared, her eyes fixed upon this strange man who stood perfectly still, his gaze locked with hers. Something about him compelled her, for, although he did not move, she felt a tension about him, a watchful wariness, as if he were listening closely for something just beyond. He brought to mind a lithe cat that watched, always poised. In her mind, she saw him reaching out to her, as Edmund had done so long ago, felt his hands touch her shoulders, drawing her towards the warmth she could almost feel from here, relieving her hunger with soft and hungry lips.

He spoke again, his voice lower than the calling of the birds. "Yes," he said, "it is beautiful, but it is also dangerous."

"Dangerous?" she repeated, the words echoing in her mind. The sun had disappeared now, though the shadows remained.

The stranger nodded, a half smile touching his lips. "There is a war in this country—or have you not heard?"

His clothing was peculiar, like none she had ever seen. Instead of a coat and breeches, he wore a long tunic, made of what looked like buckskin and reaching to his knees. The seams of its sleeves and its hem were adorned with a deep leather fringe, and the belt that held it gathered about his slender hips was sewn with colored beads. A sort of leather legging was wound about his calves. On his feet he wore moccasins, and at his waist a knife. A hunting rifle rested against his side, the end of its barrel reaching to the tail of the peculiar hat he now placed on his head. This looked like a small animal crouched upon his hair, its legs tucked beneath it and its tail trailing down just behind his right ear. The sight struck her as so funny that she smiled in spite of herself.

The stranger saw the smile, and his own lips twitched in answer. Then his eyebrows rose. "*Mademoiselle* finds war amusing?" he wondered.

War. Danger. The voice of reason spoke sharply in Caroline's ear. The spell broke. Shivering, she stepped back.

"Yes, of course I've heard, but the war is to the east. And the forts will stop the Indians long before they get this far."

His shrug easily encompassed the breadth of her excuse. "And if the Indians want war they will come to the forts to fight? Is that what *mademoiselle* believes? But that, I regret to inform you, is not the way of the woods." Pausing, he added, "You are not from here."

It was not a question. *Mademoiselle.* Then he was French. And Frenchmen came from Canada, which was the enemy. Stepping back another pace, Caroline wondered what a Frenchman was doing here. It was a question that did not require the nicety of a response, for she knew even as she posed it that he could intend no good, lurking about in the shadows at the edge of town. He had spoken of danger and Indians.... Had he been warning her? Or was he amusing himself with a game of cat and mouse, even now intending to signal to some hidden savages who would dart forward from the shadows and seize her as their prisoner?

Another shiver shook her as she recalled the words of the maid, and her own brusque response. Evening had fallen, and the shadows were deep. The meadow was no longer bright green, it was dark, and the distance to the houses long. Caroline doubted she had the speed to outdistance

him, not when he stood ready, and coiled like a spring. And
he had a gun.

Drawing herself up, she faced him. "What do you want
with me?"

"Want?" She saw him straighten as she had done, and
even the growing darkness did not hide his surprise. "Why
should I want anything?"

"Because you approached me, as I was standing here."

"To share the appreciation of the end of day," he replied, spreading his hands. "And to satisfy my curiosity as
to why a single woman would venture out on her own so
close to dark. If you have finished with the sunset, I will see
you back."

Caroline opened her mouth to protest, but before she
could speak he had turned away from her and was walking
back towards the town. She stood where she was for a moment, wondering whether she ought to follow him or not.
She could cut away from him, to the left or the right, but
either would be awkward, since it would lead her through
the fields, whereas he was following the path that led between. From the darkness behind her, an owl moaned
plaintively. Drawing her shawl closer around her, she set off
after him, holding her skirts with her free hand in order to
quicken her step.

He glanced at her when she caught up, and she thought
she saw him smile, but she could not be sure. In any case,
she had to hurry to keep pace with him, for he walked
quickly, though his step made no sound on the earth. Moving, as standing, he reminded her of a cat. He had the same
fluid motion, the same center of gravity. Other men she
knew walked erect, with their chests thrust out, but this one
kept his shoulders still and his center low.

The fringe on his tunic rippled with every step he took,
and the tail of his hat, as well. Glancing up at that hat again,
she caught the sheen of his hair, as fine and shining as
moonlight on a snowy field.

A massive chestnut tree grew at the edge of the meadow,
at the far boundary of the first house's yard. The stranger
stopped in its shadow, and she stopped uncertainly at his

side. Across the yard a door opened and a shaft of light appeared, silhouetting the form of a man, who crossed to the barn. A dog barked sharply in the darkness, paused, then barked again.

Caroline looked at the stranger, straining to see his face. Behind them, the moon had risen, a curving thumbnail of light. She stood close enough to him to inhale his scent, smoke and warm leather and sweat and pine needles. Suddenly, without warning, her hands began to shake.

She pressed them together. "Why do you stop?" she asked, her voice unnaturally loud in the seamless dark.

She heard rather than saw the same half smile as he replied, "Does *mademoiselle* require an escort to her very door?"

"No, of course not," she said, stepping away from him. "Thank you for your trouble."

"It was no trouble. Good night."

"Good night," she said to the darkness, and turned away from him. She took two steps into the yard, then turned back. "I don't know your name," she said, hearing the perplexity in her own voice. Why was she asking? What did it matter to her?

"Daniel Ledet" was the answer that came from beneath the newly leafed branches. For a moment she strained to see him, but the obscurity was complete, so much so that she had the impression that he might not be there at all. She was tempted to step closer, to reassure herself, but if he was there she would feel foolish, would not know what to say. So, forcing herself to turn away, she walked instead towards the house, and the ordinary, where Hannah was no doubt waiting up.

Daniel watched her go, his eyes, after years of practice, picking her out easily in the darkness of the yard. Who was she, he wondered? Even more, he wished he knew what she had been thinking of as she had stood at the river's edge. Or, rather, not of what but of whom, for a man had been in her mind, of that he had no doubt. Again he remembered her eyes when she had turned, the way her lips had parted, the timbre of her voice. When she had stared at him, she had seen someone else. Lucky man, thought Daniel, to possess such a jewel.

Where was that man right now? he wondered, intrigued by the thought. His mind, schooled by necessity to puzzle things out for itself, addressed the question. This woman was not from Northfield, of that he was fairly sure. He knew most of the Northfield women by appearance, if not by name—and one of such striking beauty would surely be known to him. Of course, she might have settled here since his last visit, but he tended to doubt that, as well, for anyone with whom she lived would have cautioned her against going alone to the river at dusk. Northfield folks were cautious by nature and by history.

That meant she was passing through, either coming from Boston or heading that way. She could not be heading south, as there were hardly two dozen women in all the north country, and he knew them all. And, as for heading north—that was more than unlikely. What man in his right mind would want to go north now, let alone bring a woman to face the threat of war? He wondered if she was on her way to join her lover, or if she had left him behind. Something in her expression made him think the latter the case. Her eyes had been wistful when she had turned to him, and they had held none of the eagerness he would have expected had she been looking forward to meeting her lover at her journey's end.

Her lover. The words sent a thrill through him as he imagined what she would feel like in his arms. There had been a moment, just after she had turned, when he had half thought that he might know. A pity, he thought with a sigh. Perhaps once in a lifetime one met such a woman. Recalling her beauty, and the longing in her eyes, Daniel could not help but wonder if she had not been real, if she had been one of the wood spirits in which the Indians believed. Perhaps he had been living alone for too long.

He smiled at the idea, his eyes resting thoughtfully on the lit windows of the town. He had had business at a trading post to the west, and had detoured to Northfield to visit a certain widow, whose back door would open quickly at his discreet knock. The extra thirty miles had meant little to him; he made his own hours and chose his own trails. It had been several months since he had spent the night beneath a woman's roof, and he had been waiting only for darkness to cover his approach. Now, his eyes lingering on the darkness of the yard, he found he had changed his mind. He would spend this night, too, alone in the woods.

And what of the woman, the one after whom he watched? Would she think of him tonight, as he would surely think of her? Or would she think of the one she had left behind? A moment more he lingered, and then he turned away, moving off silent-footed into the encroaching night.

Chapter Two

"But there is nothing," Hannah said, her eyes, wide and bemused, moving from left to right. "Nothing," she repeated. "It is as though, after Northfield, life has simply stopped."

"What do you mean, Mother?" Young Tom asked with a laugh. "Life hasn't ended! There's plenty of life right here. Trees and stones and the river—and animals and birds. Lots and lots of things to see!" He swept the air with one hand while the other maintained its grip on the barrel upon which he rode perched in the wagon's bed. Elizabeth was settled beside him in the valley between two chairs, and the baby, wedged in her cradle, was slumbering peacefully.

Young Tom looked about him with great satisfaction. He hadn't been happy to leave his friends back in New Haven, and he had been bored in the wagon for these past two weeks, for none of the towns they had passed through had held a candle to New Haven. But, now that they were in the forest, things were looking up. He wondered, peering into the shadows, if there would be Indians. He hoped there would be. Not enough of them to really hurt anyone, just a couple that he could help capture or kill—once he'd learned to shoot a gun. He wondered if William would teach him. He thought perhaps he would, so long as they didn't tell Mamma, who would faint at the very idea. Poor Mamma, thought Young Tom, turning to her again. She was still looking about her with that scared, baffled expression.

"But there are no houses," she said. "No towns, no people . . . not even so much as a field. Just miles and miles of forest. I had not expected it. Not quite so soon, in any case."

"That is the thing," agreed Caroline, "how soon after the town it all stopped. A few farms, an orchard, then nothing but woods. Not even a proper road!"

The road had vanished abruptly at the north end of the town, shrinking from its former grandeur to a narrow, rutted track that sometimes hugged the river and sometimes the woods.

"Be glad it's not gone completely, or the going would be slower yet." William came up beside them on the mare, which he was riding today, while Thomas sat with Jonas in the first wagon. "I guess this land's got attractions, the same as any other. I've heard that when the salmon run up here the river turns silver with them, and the pigeons fly so thick that the Indians knock them down with clubs."

"I'd like to see that!" Tom exclaimed, and William smiled.

Hannah returned William's smile, and so did Caroline. Both of them had thanked God when William had agreed to come north with them—and especially after Thomas had decided to take Jonas along. In New Haven, Jonas did Thomas's dirty work, such as spying on other merchants. But, though Jonas was wily, he was small and without much strength. He would be of little use when it came to cutting timber or raising what food they would need. Thomas said that Jonas would be useful even in the north, but Caroline suspected that Jonas knew too many secrets to be trusted alone back in town.

William, by contrast, was worthy of anyone's trust. Big boned, fair haired and open faced, William was strong as a workhorse and clever with his hands. In New Haven he had tended the equipment of Thomas's factory. In the north he would not only cut trees, he would also fashion whatever they needed and had not brought along. Even Thomas acknowledged William's worth to him, while the children adored him for his unfailing kindness to them, and Hannah and Caroline were glad of his help and his unthreatening company. William's natural integrity made it difficult to regard him as a servant, for all his deference. Sometimes Caroline found herself wishing that Hannah were married to William, factories and ropewalks notwithstanding.

Elizabeth squirmed up out of her nest. "William, why do the Indians hate us?"

"Because of the French," said Young Tom. "The French hate the English, and the English hate the French."

"But why?" asked Elizabeth.

For a moment, no one spoke. There was no simple reason. It was a complex web reaching back hundreds and hundreds of years. For centuries, the kings of England and of France had coveted each other's lands—and the vast expanses of the American continent and the riches it held had only escalated that conflict.

"I suppose," said William, "because the French don't want the English claiming this wilderness. They would rather let the Indians have it and buy the furs they trap."

"Does it belong to the French?"

"Sometimes they say it does, and sometimes they say it belongs to the Indians. But in truth the English claimed it a long, long time ago. The deed the governor gave your papa came from the Indians."

Young Tom leaned forward before Elizabeth could speak again. "William, do you think there will be Indians? On our land, I mean. Do you think they will attack us?"

Hannah gasped. "Tom! What a thing to ask! Of course there will be no Indians! Your papa has told you so! If there was real danger, we wouldn't be going north."

"Well, if there are any," Tom continued, ignoring his mother's protest, "I bet they'll have tomahawks. All Indians carry them. I've heard that if you're quick enough you can catch a tomahawk someone's thrown and throw it back again. Do you think you could do that, William?"

"With practice." William grinned. "But I reckon we'll have other business to keep us occupied. Like planting and chopping wood. Are you glued to that barrel, or would you like to ride for a spell?"

"You mean on the horse, with you?" Tom's face lit up. The Indians were forgotten.

"If your mamma has no objection." William glanced at Hannah, who shook her head. "And afterwards we'll give Betsy her own turn," he added, winking at Elizabeth, whose forehead had puckered in protest. William helped Tom out of the wagon and onto the horse's back.

"He is so good to the children!" Hannah sighed gratefully as the horse with Tom and William fell behind again, for here the trees pressed too close to allow it alongside.

"He is," Caroline agreed, though her thoughts had long since moved from William to what Young Tom had said. *The French hate the English, and the English hate the French.*

The words stirred an echo of a deep voice saying *"Mademoiselle,"* and she felt herself shiver, although the day was warm. Again she saw the silver flash of bright hair beneath the moon. *Daniel Ledet.* The name rose and fell in her mind, softened by the accent with which he had spoken it. Last night she had fallen asleep thinking of him, and this morning she had watched for him as they had ridden out, and had felt sharp disappointment when he had not been there. But he was French. Did he hate her? Did she hate him?

Up ahead, in the first wagon, Thomas and Jonas were conversing. The murmur of their voices carried back to where Caroline sat, and she watched Thomas make an expansive gesture with his arm. "Thomas appears in high spirits," she said wryly, wondering what had happened back in Northfield to put him in such a rare state.

"Oh, yes!" Hannah nodded. "He found a man in Northfield to carry his logs to the south, all the way to the ship that will take them across to the English yards." Shaking her head, she added, "It does seem like such a lot of bother to go to for some trees, but of course the Royal Navy cannot do without masts." Nor could England supply her own, her own great forests having long since been exhausted. So every new grant of land in the colonies reserved the tallest, straightest trees for the Crown and now

Thomas had won the contract to cut and ship those trees. Other merchants had bid against him, but, with Jonas's able assistance, Thomas had won easily.

"But," wondered Caroline, "how many trees will there be? William is resourceful, but he is only one man. And Jonas will not be much help."

"Oh, Thomas plans to have a good deal more help than that! He plans to use the soldiers from the garrison at Fort Dummer. He says that the soldiers at the fort must be awfully bored, stuck up there all winter with only themselves to talk to and no Indians to fight. After all, they're not really soldiers, but only militia boys who were mustered into duty when news came of war. Thomas says that they'll be only too glad for a diversion—and for the extra pay. Thomas has thought it all out!"

"I'll bet he has," Caroline replied. Trust Thomas to see those poor, lonely militia boys not as valiant soldiers but as a pool of cheap labor. Likely he already had the costs figured, down to the shillings and pence. Shaking her head, she wondered just what else Thomas had up his sleeve.

They had come out of the thick trees and into the meadow again. The sun shone warm upon them, flashing bright on the river that flowed beside them. Caroline thought of what William had said about the attractions of the land. Perhaps it was empty, but it was peaceful, as well. The melodies of birdsong were a sweet relief after the constant pressure of the curious, prying eyes that had met them at every farmhouse and followed them through every town. Most of the time, Caroline had hidden beneath her shawl; whenever she had removed it, the reaction had been the same—that gasp of admiration and that sniff of disdain. In the more tolerant cities beauty might be esteemed, but here in the Puritan countryside it was frowned upon as a sin.

Beauty, she thought with a sigh. What was it to her? Some called it a blessing, and she had once felt the same. But now, after what had happened, she considered it a curse. What else but her beauty had attracted Edmund's eye? She, dazzled by his flattery, had believed that he loved her for her soul. But she had learned—how harshly she had learned—

never to trust her beauty, never to rely upon it. She had learned to turn from men's admiration before it blinded her to the truth. In New Haven, many men had paid her court, but she had rejected them all, mistrustful of their true motives. Still, after all these years, she bore the pain of Edmund's betrayal.

But here, she thought, looking up into the tangle of trees, here there was no need to hide herself beneath a shawl. Here there would be no temptations, no flattering male regard. Here there would be nothing but Hannah's familiar company and enough work to keep her busy by day and eager for rest at night. True, she had joined this odyssey for Hannah's benefit, but in it she had also seen the hope of a safe haven. Here, in this wild northland, at last she would be safe. Here she might possibly find some measure of peace.

Lost in her thoughts, Caroline had not felt Hannah's gaze upon her; nor had she seen Hannah's expression of puzzled sympathy. For a time, Hannah hesitated, but then, finally, she spoke. "Dear Caroline," she murmured. "How I wish you were not alone!"

At Hannah's words, Caroline shook her head. "But why should you say that, when I have you and the children for company?"

"Yes, of course," said Hannah. "But I was thinking of men. You won't have the sort of company that you had in New Haven."

Caroline shrugged. "In New Haven I stayed at home with Father and Mother. They were my company, except when you came to visit, or I visited you."

It was true, Hannah thought, for she knew without having to be reminded how Caroline had turned away from male companionship. She had collected suitors simply by showing her face in the street, but, though she had been courted by eligible and handsome men, she had never shown the slightest interest in any of them. Her eyes resting on her sister's lovely face, Hannah felt the familiar mixture of perplexity and frustration.

"Perhaps," she ventured softly, "if you met the right man, then you would fall in love."

The look Caroline flashed her held a frustration all its own. "There is no right man, Hannah. Not for me, anyway."

"Yes, of course," Hannah said quickly, distressed by Caroline's bitterness. "But even so...." she added, with an involuntary sigh that brought a tolerant smile to Caroline's lips.

"Dear Hannah..." Caroline patted her sister on the arm, as though it were she who required comforting. "Don't worry. I shall be fine. We shall be snug and cozy in our little nest, and I shall be content. Look, the baby's awakened and is crying for you."

Indeed, little Hetty had begun to wail, and Elizabeth was clamoring for her turn on the horse. Caroline watched the bustle the rearrangement caused, her own words still echoing in her mind.

There is no right man, Hannah. Not for me, anyway. Yet, even as the words drifted through her consciousness, she saw the expressive face of Daniel Ledet. This time, however, she shook her head sharply, as though she could drive the image of him away. Why should she think of him as any different from the other men she had known? Why should she think of him at all? He had come in the nighttime, and he had disappeared back into it, hardly more than an apparition, a vision in the dark. Soon the memory of him would vanish, just as he had himself. Yet even as Caroline lectured herself, she felt her body shiver again at the memory.

The day stretched wearily. Once or twice, just for a little variety, Caroline climbed down to walk, but the track was uneven, and the ground was still spongy from the winter thaw, so the going was difficult. They had brought food from the ordinary, and they ate without stopping—cold meat and bread washed down with cider that had long since begun to ferment. William gave Young Tom another turn, and then Elizabeth. When he returned her, he took the baby from Caroline's arms. Though Hannah protested, in the end she could not help but laugh at how Hetty waved her chubby fists and gurgled with delight. The sun, having passed its

zenith, slipped down to the west, and the shadows were
lengthening when they passed through a stretch of woods
and emerged in a meadow at whose far end stood a farm.

The sight was disconcerting, after the miles and miles of
wilderness, the hours without a sign of human life. Caroline stared at the neatly fenced pasture, struck by a sudden
pang of fear. It was as though she were seeing something
that was not quite real.

But the fence was real, as were the man and two boys who
were repairing it when the wagons appeared. They stopped
at the first sound, and Caroline saw the man reach out to
raise a rifle. But when Thomas called out a greeting, the
man put the gun aside and stepped forward to meet them,
the boys following behind.

"Mr. MacKenzie! I didn't recognize you at first. We
hadn't heard any word of more soldiers for the fort, and as
for families heading north...well!" He stopped, catching
sight of the women and thinking better of his words. Nodding a greeting to Caroline and Hannah, he gestured towards the house, saying, "You are welcome to stay the
night. My wife will be glad of the company. She has precious little of it. And, Mr. MacKenzie, you'll be wanting to
inspect the trees. We might as well do it now, while there is
still light." He turned to the boys. "Edward, run and tell
your mother that we've got company. Gideon, you can help
the men with the animals. Now, Mr. MacKenzie, if you'll
step this way..."

Caroline watched Thomas move off with the farmer, then
turned her attention to the house they were approaching. It
resembled neither Northfield's homes nor its outlying farms,
being fashioned less as a farmhouse than as a small stockade, built of rough-hewn logs, with a door of hewn planks.
The first story had no windows at all, while the second,
which overhung the first by perhaps a foot, was cut with
three portholes.

"To shoot at the Indians," explained Young Tom, aiming an imaginary gun. "Or, if they put up ladders, to throw
down scalding water. That's why they build the second floor
out like that, so they can't climb up the side."

"How do you know?" asked Caroline, surprised by this sudden wealth of frontier lore.

"The girl in Northfield told us," Elizabeth replied. "The one who made the beds. She said that her grandfather was living in a house like this when the Indians came. She said—"

"Hush, Elizabeth," Hannah said automatically. The door to the stockade swung back to reveal the younger boy, followed by a woman with unkempt gray hair, who wiped her hands on her rough linen apron before greeting them. Her eyes, Caroline noted, were wary and eager both, as if she at once feared and craved their company.

"Please," said the woman, beckoning to the open door. "Won't you come in and rest and have something warm to drink?"

"Thank you," replied Hannah, handing Hetty to Caroline so that she could climb down. Young Tom had already vanished, followed by Elizabeth, but she trusted William to see that no harm came to them. A cozy hearthside cup of tea sounded heavenly.

It took their eyes several minutes to adjust to the dimness of the house. Except for a few long, narrow slits in the walls, the only source of light was the fire roaring on the hearth. They had come into a big room, a kitchen and hall combined that ran the full width of the house and half its length. A second chamber lay across the central hall, and would be warmed and illumined by the same vast chimney. At the back, a flight of narrow steps led up to the second floor.

"Won't you please be seated?" the woman said, gesturing towards a trestle table that stood in the middle of the room. She herself moved about the chamber, gathering tins and crockery. Her movements, Caroline saw, were slow and deliberate, like an old woman's, although her face looked not much older than her own. Glancing about the chamber, Caroline saw that the furnishings were meager, most of them hand-hewn, except for a low carved chest, which they must have brought when they'd come. There were neither wardrobes nor closets, and implements and clothing hung from pegs driven into every wall.

"Of course," the woman continued, busy with her tasks, "when Mr. MacKenzie came last year he said that he would be returning in the spring with his family. But, what with the war starting, I thought he might change his mind."

"Oh, no." Hannah shook her head, glancing at Caroline. "My husband found no reason to alter his plans. He believes the fighting will stay in the east, for the Indians will be put off by the soldiers at the forts. He says Indians only fight when their numbers are superior." She paused, then added, "What does your husband think?"

"The same, more or less," said the woman, turning to regard them with an expression that was at once hopeful and sad. "He says there's no point in giving up what we've worked so hard to build before there's real cause to leave. One thing's for certain—the Indians will soon work mischief on an empty house."

"Do you think Indians are near?" Hannah's eyes widened with fright, but the woman only shrugged.

"Most likely," she said. "They've always been around these parts, hunting and trading, doing odd jobs for a meal or a bit of wool. They've only made themselves scarce since word came of the war. Faded back into the woods, or gone up to Canada."

"Were they French Indians, then?" Hannah asked, but the woman shook her head.

"They weren't either, I guess," she said. "Though I suppose the French could win them by selling them guns. My husband says that's why they go with the French. The French tell them that it's the English's fault that they've lost their lands. They fill their heads with popery and then they give them guns and send them down south after English scalps." Seeing Hannah shudder in reaction to her words, she added, with another shrug, "But I don't reckon the Indians around these parts to be the fighting kind. More likely they'll just lay back and bide their time until the danger's past. In the meantime, they'll support themselves with petty thievery."

At the hearth, the kettle was steaming. She took the lid off the teapot and reached for a hide bag, then paused. "We haven't any real tea, only dried blackberry leaves. You get used to the taste."

"It sounds just fine," said Caroline, but Hannah shook her head.

"If you'd prefer real tea, we have some with us."

"Have you?" Eagerness lit the woman's dull brown eyes. Then reservation quenched it, and she shook her head. "Thank you for the offer, but you'd best keep it for yourself. There's no telling when you're likely to see more—and there's plenty of things we're needing more than we need tea."

"Oh!" said Hannah flushing. "I didn't mean that we'd sell it to you—I meant it as a gift." She had seen the woman's look, and she had seen the rough, unfinished room. Handing Hetty to Caroline, she rose from her chair. "I will fetch it from the wagon. I know just where it is. And, as for us running short," she added, lest the woman object, "then we'll drink blackberry leaves, just the way you do!"

"It's awfully good of her," the woman muttered as Hannah left the room. Then, after a moment, she added, as if to herself, "Not that it's likely that you'll be lacking in real tea. There isn't a grant in this country that doesn't reserve the best trees for the King. Your brother-in-law's a sharp one, getting the contract for himself."

"That he is," Caroline agreed, exchanging a look with the woman that said far more than words could have.

The woman shook her head. "At least you'll have your sister's company, and she'll have yours—though I can't say you'll find much with which to amuse yourself. Except for the soldiers, there's hardly a single man in these parts, and most of them are farm boys, scarcely old enough to shave."

"I have no interest in soldiers," Caroline said. "Farming or otherwise."

Her eyebrows raised, the woman replied, "Then I guess you won't mind."

They drank the tea from wooden cups, and the woman brought out maple sugar, tapped from the trees of the farm, to sweeten it.

"How long have you been living here?" asked Hannah, her eyes taking in the dim room.

"Five years," replied the woman, looking where Hannah had, but with the expression of one searching for something lost. If she was, she did not find it. She looked back again, adding, "Seven for my man. He came up first to build the house and put in a crop so that we'd have something when we first came. My man says that we're lucky to have this place up here. He says soon enough folks will be hungering for this land, just as they did in the south. God willing," she added, "that the war doesn't spread."

Her eyes moved to little Hetty, who was nestled in Caroline's arms. The heat from the fire had lulled the child to sleep. Her head was tucked in Caroline's elbow, and one plump arm was thrust out. At the sight, the woman's eyes softened. "She's a pretty one, isn't she? Mine was hardly older when we lost her two years back."

Tears sprang to Hannah's eyes. "I'm so sorry!"

The woman looked as though she might cry, too. "Lost my big girl, as well, she that was just getting past six. The fever took them both. The baby went quickly, but my girl lingered on . . . and the ground too frozen to put them in till spring." She sighed heavily. "I miss the girl most of all. She would have been good company, while the men are gone."

"I *am* sorry," Hannah whispered, reaching out to lay her hand upon the woman's arm.

At her touch, the woman's lower lip began to quiver. Then she straightened her shoulders. "Well, no matter," she declared. "What's done is done, and no good comes of brooding over it. I'm not the first it's happened to, nor will I be the last. If you'd like to put her down to rest, there's a bed in the other room. I used to keep a little cot in here by the fire, but my husband took it out so I wouldn't have the reminder of what had been. As if a mother needs reminding of the babies that she's lost . . ." Sighing again, the woman made as if to rise. "I'll show you the bed."

"Don't bother yourself," said Hannah, rising as she spoke. "I'm sure I can find it myself." And, taking Hetty from Caroline's arms, she left the room.

Caroline heard her fussing about in the next room. Hetty must have awakened for she was singing her back to sleep. The woman was sitting in silence. She was listening, as well, and Caroline could imagine what was going through her mind. But, even as she thought this, the woman looked up and, leaning closer, said in a low voice, "I didn't want to upset your sister, her seeming so delicate, and perhaps time will prove our men right.... But, all the same, it does no harm to take precautions. Against Indians, that is. Her husband will likely be out cutting down his trees, which would leave you unprotected in case of an attack. Take care to leave the door bolted and the children close at hand, for they are the first to suffer in an Indian attack."

"Yes." Caroline shivered, recalling what the girl in Northfield had said. "We shall take precautions. Thank you for your advice."

"It's a hard life." The woman sighed. "Good luck to you both."

There was no farm the next evening, so they made their camp in the woods. The children were ecstatic at having such an adventure, and, despite the discomfort, Caroline felt relief. The pall of the dim farmhouse and its mistress still hung over them, and, after the claustrophobic darkness of the farm, it was good to eat supper in the open air. Even Hannah seemed not to mind the rough surroundings, while Thomas's good mood had endured a second day—most likely, thought Caroline, because he'd been totting up the profit he'd make from last night's farm. He'd contracted with the farmer to cut down thirty trees, and to haul them to the river, where they'd wait until wintertime, when teams of oxen could drag them south over the ice. He was assured of ten guineas' profit per tree, after expenses. No wonder he looked so pleased as he chewed his bread and meat.

After dinner, Hannah settled the children for the night while Caroline went to wash the dishes at the river's edge. The water was ice-cold, but clear and full of fish; she could hear them jumping as she knelt upon the bank. There was no sunset to admire, as there had been two nights before, no mountains of purple and gold to woo her admiring eye. Instead, the evening was overcast, as the day had been, with a dampness in the air that deepened the green of the willows and of the new grass into the lush emerald she remembered from her English childhood. The green brought back another evening, much warmer than this one, with air soft as cotton wool and the grass beneath her bare feet scattered with bright buttercups....

She sat in the meadow above Harrow Hall, her heart ringing like a hammer on an anvil as she fought to catch her breath. Six weeks had passed since Sir Edmund's return from London, six weeks of chance encounters—and not-so-chance ones, as well. Of course, Sir Edmund had not been openly courting her. That would have attracted too much attention and caused too many tongues to wag, including that of Sir Edmund's mother, who would hardly have applauded such a match. Yet, at the same time, Sir Edmund had made it clear that he took an interest in her, though that interest had been unstated until this afternoon.

This afternoon! Just the thought of it made her heart race and her breath come fast again. She had been working in the garden when he had passed the gate and had stopped, as always, to pass the time with her. As always, they had had little privacy, for at the sight of Sir Edmund her mother had stepped out to pay her respects.

"In all the time since I've been back," he had said when her mother had gone, "I don't believe we've had five minutes in which to talk alone." Pausing, he dropped his voice. "Have you ever noticed it?"

"Perhaps." She had nodded and then ducked her head to hide the light shining in her eyes.

"Perhaps!" He had chuckled, and the sound of it had thrilled her. Then he had added, "Then perhaps it might be arranged. Do you know the beech tree at the top of the meadow above the hall? It is a lovely spot from which to watch the sun setting. Perhaps this evening we could watch together. Perhaps at eight o'clock." His voice had grown lower as he had spoken. Then he had stopped and waited.

"Perhaps," she had repeated, and, flashing him a quick look, she had run into the house, her cheeks flaming, her whole soul on fire.

So now she sat waiting beneath the ancient beech, her eyes growing tired from searching the meadow for him. The sun, sinking lower, dipped beneath the hills, and the shadows grew dark. Her racing heart gave way to a chilling doubt. What if he was not coming? What if he had never meant to come? Then the branches rustled, and there he was at her side.

"Sir Edmund!" She sprang to her feet. "Where have you come from?"

"From the hall, my little goose. And you have come, as well! I wondered if you would."

"And I you," she said, looking down.

"I am late. I apologize. Guests came at the last minute. I thought they would hold me back!" His breath, too, came quickly; he laid his hand upon his heart. "Whew! I am winded— Come, let us rest." Taking her hand, he pulled her down with him on the grass. When Caroline resisted, at first he laughed at her. Then he raised his brows, asking, "What's this? You don't trust me?"

"Oh, no, sir . . ." She was all but melting from the tenderness of his smile.

"Edmund!" he said.

"Oh, no, Edmund—that is, yes. Yes, I do trust you."

"Well, then, if you trust me, you should know that I would never cause you harm. Caroline, I love you—I have ever since the day that I came back from London and saw you standing at your gate. Would you believe me if I said I wanted to marry you?"

"Oh, sir— Oh, Edmund!" Her eyes came up then, bright with incredulous tears, and through the blur he was smiling, nodding in affirmation of her deepest, her wildest, dreams.

"But your mother," she said, her voice faltering. "She would never allow such a thing! She would never give her consent."

"Won't she?" Edmund tossed his head. "Then I'll marry you without it! What can she do, disown me? She does not control the estate. I am Sir Edmund Bredon! I can do as I wish! Wait," he added, searching the ground at their feet. Reaching down, he plucked one of the buttercups and, tying the stem into a circle, raised her left hand. "Caroline...with this ring I do thee troth." Lifting her hand higher, he pressed it to his lips, which lingered briefly before moving down the soft skin of her arm.

"Sir!" she whispered, trying to pull away. "Edmund, you must not!"

But he held her fast. "Do you not trust me, Caroline? Ah, Caroline, you must!"

Though her heart was pounding more with panic than with desire, Caroline feared that if she stopped him he would stop loving her. So long as he did love her, it could not be wrong, and in the end they would marry—that was the crucial thing!

"Marry! Oh, God!" Caroline's groan cut through the still evening air, bringing her back from Surrey to this American riverbank. "Oh, God," she repeated. "What a fool I was!" Would these memories never release her? Would they never leave her in peace? Would they haunt her in this north country as they had in New Haven?

The kettle full of washed dishes stood waiting at her feet. Bending, she raised it and turned back towards the camp. But she had not taken more than a dozen steps when the murmur of voices caught her attention. They came from a thicket of spruce trees a few yards to her left. A thrill of fear shot through her. Indians! she thought, ready to fly. Then her nose caught something it had missed before, a whiff of the tobacco Thomas smoked in his pipe. So it must be Thomas hidden in the trees. To whom could he be speaking? Jonas, most likely—explaining some new scheme that had come into his mind. How very like Thomas to steal away—as if any of them posed a threat to his plans! She took another step. Then, hesitating, she glanced back towards the thicket. It might be interesting to know what those two discussed when they were alone. Laying down the kettle so that it would not give her away, Caroline drew her skirts close and crept nearer to the spruce.

The voices were indistinct. Straining her ears, she managed to pick out several words. "Pelts," and "ammunition," and something that sounded like "Albany." She crept as far forward as she dared, hoping to hear more, but now the interview had ended, and the participants were walking off in the direction of the camp. Caroline stayed where she was. She would give them time to get back to the wagons, lest they see her and guess what she had been about. She stood, concentrating until the steps had disappeared. She would wait another minute, and then—

Her breath caught sharply when a hand clamped about her arm, another over her mouth, yanking her body backwards, against a man's hard chest. Her scream was stifled by a rough-skinned palm.

A voice spoke in her ear. "I will release you, *mademoiselle*, if you give me your word not to scream."

She nodded, knowing she had no choice, intending to break her word as soon as she could draw breath. As if its owner had read her mind, the hand lingered where it was. Then, suddenly, it was removed, and she felt cool air on her skin. She filled her lungs quickly and had already opened her mouth to scream when she realized that he had called her *mademoiselle*. And the scents of smoke and warm leather were familiar, as well. Closing her mouth, she turned to face Daniel Ledet.

He swept off his funny hat in a half-mocking bow. "Mademoiselle," he said smiling. "So we meet again."

He had kept his voice low—thinking of Thomas, no doubt—and she replied in the same tone, "What are you doing here?"

"Conducting business with your brother-in-law—as you no doubt overheard."

She opened her mouth to deny it, then changed her mind. "How did you know that Thomas is my brother-in-law?"

He shrugged. She found herself wondering how his hand would feel on her arm, not grabbing her as he had done, but touching lightly instead. She shivered now in the shadows, as she had done when she had imagined his presence.

"Information is one of the goods in which I trade," he said.

"You are a spy?" As a Frenchman, what else would he be doing here?

"I am a *coureur de bois*. Literally translated, that means one who runs through the woods. I am a trapper by training, a trader by circumstance. I barter the white man's goods to the Indians in exchange for their pelts."

"French goods?" she asked him, her tone accusing, but he only shrugged. Watching, she could not help but wonder at the exact color of his eyes. She remembered them as gray, but the memory was uncertain. Surely, with hair so light, they must be a shade of blue.

"British, by preference," he said. "The Indians prefer them, especially the copper kettles and the bright red cloth. For some reason, the French seem unable to make cloth as bright as the British, or kettles as strong." He spread his hands to emphasize his words, and, as before, she found herself imagining their touch upon her skin.

Putting the thought out of her mind, she tried to concentrate. "But it is illegal for the British to trade with the French. Which makes what you do smuggling. You could be caught," she concluded, wondering at the alarm the thought struck in her breast. Was her fear of him, or was it on his behalf?

His glimmering smile flashed in the dimness. "And who would catch me?" he asked. "The French? But they hunger for British goods as much as the Indians, while the British crave the beaver that will keep them in top hats. Everyone is happy, and so the trade thrives, and so, *coureur* that I am, I scurry back and forth."

She saw his smile flash again at the image he drew of himself. "What business have you with Thomas?" she asked, and the smile disappeared.

"Quite to the contrary, *mademoiselle*. It is he who has need of me."

"Need of you?" she repeated, wondering what it could be. "You don't mean that Thomas has hired you to help cut his trees?" She could not imagine it. She had no doubt that the man was capable, despite his slender build, but somehow she could not imagine him wielding an ax for pay. He was too proud and free to be any man's servant.

A muffled wheezing shook his shoulders and the fringe of his buckskin shirt. He was laughing, she realized, and felt her color rise. Wiping his eyes, he answered, "Perish the very thought! Had I wished to be a peasant, I should have stayed in Montreal.

"No, *mademoiselle*," he continued, shifting to lean against his gun. "I have no connection with Mr. Mac-Kenzie's famous trees. But, you see, your *beau-frère* is a man of broad interests. He means to have his finger in every northern pie. He is considering starting a trading post up here in the north. I would supply him with pelts from the Indians, and he would trade them for British goods. When peace comes and the land is settled, he will have many customers. In the meantime, he would settle for the soldiers at the fort."

Caroline listened, startled both by his frankness and by the substance of his words. No wonder Thomas had insisted on Hannah coming along. He intended to settle here for more than several years! And how very like him not to have said a word.

The wind, rising suddenly, whispered through the trees, tugging loose a dry twig and sending it spinning downwards. The twig landed on Caroline's shoulder, caught in the wool of her shawl. Daniel reached up to free it, and she shivered at his touch. She felt his hand freeze for an instant, and then it fell to his side again. For a moment they stared at each other. Then she shook her head. "How did you come here?" she wondered. "How did you know we were here?"

He spread his hands in answer. "In the way such things are known in these woods. Your *beau-frère* had heard of me last autumn when he came north. In Northfield and elsewhere, he left messages for me. As I happened to be passing, I thought I might stop for a chat." Glancing about him, he added, "Hiding in the bushes was your brother-in-law's idea. He seems to be a man who enjoys secrecy."

She could not help but smile at how well he seemed to have grasped Thomas's ways. "Will you trade with him?"

"Perhaps, perhaps not. It depends on what the future brings. Your Mr. MacKenzie strikes me as a man to hold at arm's length. For the present, I can trade with the soldiers well enough on my own."

"Even with the war?" she asked, envying him the coolness with which he could speak of Thomas's strength.

"The war does not concern me. I am a trader, and trade continues despite the war. The same happens also in England, or did you not hear of it there?"

"How did you know I came from England?"

He chuckled in the dark, coming one step nearer, as if to see her reaction. She thought she ought to step back, but she stayed where she was, and the nearness of his body lit a slow fire in hers.

"I learned from the girl at the inn at Northfield. She was filled to the brim with news. It spilled from her, like beer from a well-filled jug." He gestured with his hand, and Caroline forced a smile, pushing back the sharp prick of jealousy she felt at the thought of him speaking with that girl. Had he smiled at her as he was smiling now? Had he stood as near—so near that she could feel the warmth of his breath on her cheek and the heat of his body through the wool of her skirt? Had her heart beaten as quickly? Had her face grown cool, as if her very skin were longing for his touch? Then she forgot about the girl, forgot because she was lost somewhere in his eyes.

"I want you," he whispered. Or had she imagined it? Her eyelids fluttered closed as his hand rose to rest against her cheek. Without even thinking, she turned her face into it, until her lips tasted the salt of his palm and she heard him catch his breath. For a moment, his palm lingered; then it was withdrawn, and she felt her own fingers caught and raised as his had been, pressed against his rough cheek and then to his lips.

"Caroline!" Hannah's voice, coming from behind, held a note of alarm. Caroline felt Daniel move backwards, felt her fingers released. Still, she stood staring, unable, unwilling to move.

Trained to live by his wits, Daniel recovered first. "You are missed," he murmured, nodding towards the camp. "*Mademoiselle*, you must go."

"Yes..." Still dazed, she turned away. She took a step towards the wagons, then turned back again. "What about you?" she asked.

His smile flashed in the dark. "That depends. What did you have in mind?"

He had meant it as a joke, but he saw her brows come down and heard the sharp hiss of her breath. What magic had existed evaporated in the dusk.

"You're all the same," she hissed. "Oh, how I hate you all!" And Daniel felt the trees stir as she whirled away.

He stood, watching her go, letting the cool evening air still his racing pulse. Her last words still echoed in his mind, just as the touch of her lips still burned upon his palm. He must have been mistaken in his first impressions, for a woman who condemned all men in a word, as she had just done, hardly pined for a lover on a riverbank. But then, did such a woman act as she just had? Did she seek out the warmth of a man's hand with her own soft lips? Once again he remembered the yearning that he had seen in her eyes, and he felt his response stirring deep within him.

She was English, but that made small difference to him. If anything, Daniel preferred the English to the French. He admired their independence and their energy. The French king held Canada for profit and profit alone, the governor and his cronies milking the people dry to send furs back to France, there to be turned into treasure for King Louis's court. To be born poor in Canada was to toil as a serf on the narrow strip of river that had been colonized.

Life was very different in the British colonies. For all that the King might want to keep the people in his thrall, English self-reliance and factionalism at home had combined to create a freedom unknown in Canada. English towns took root and expanded, the countryside bloomed. The English had a vitality lacking in the French. A young man in the British colonies could raise himself above what his father had been, while in Quebec the only route to freedom lay in flight to the woods.

Daniel had gone to the woods. He had lived the half-legal life of a *coureur de bois* since he had turned eighteen, tolerated by the governor for his usefulness in trade. He had lived among the Indians and had learned their ways. Some men, like MacKenzie, sought riches when they traded for furs, but Daniel sought the satisfaction of the life itself. He had become one of those men who baffled their own countrymen by caring more for the wilderness than for the company of other men. He had lived so long in the open, with no more than a gun and his wits and perhaps a blanket to keep him alive, that by now the four walls of a house seemed like a prison to him.

The life he had chosen was a hard one, but it was a good one, as well. It had shown him things that he would have missed had he stayed in Montreal. He had seen mountain peaks of a natural majesty that surpassed the grandest cathedral. He had walked on handmade snowshoes across the vast frozen expanse north of Lake Superior. He had seen eagles nesting and panther cubs being born. He had walked through country where no other white man had trod.

At moments he had been lonely, but the moments were few and far between. For the most part, he had not missed the lack of companionship, and when he felt the lack he knew how to satisfy it. He had known the pleasures an Indian maid could give, and besides the widow in Northfield there was one at a post in New York who was glad to see him whenever he passed through.

But this woman was different. This woman who had left her path marked upon the new grass, she could not be forgotten for months at a time. This was a woman whose touch would burn upon a man's skin long after she had withdrawn, and who could fill a man with a longing that pushed all else from his mind. He could tell himself stories and pretend he could turn away, but he knew that, sooner or later, he would have to see her again.

Sooner or later, he thought, his eyes following the path to where it turned and vanished in a stand of white-limbed birch. Her skin was as perfect as the underside of birch bark when it was peeled away from the main trunk just after the winter thaw. And her hair, bound up so tightly, had the dull sheen of black silk. He knew what that hair would feel like spread upon his palms; he could imagine its heavy softness slipping through his open hands. He wondered what would have happened if her sister hadn't called.

Caroline. That was the name that the sister had called. Caroline. He repeated it in his mind, lingering on each syllable as her lips had lingered on his palm. He wondered at MacKenzie, at his bringing the women along. He had put the question, and MacKenzie had replied that he liked all the comforts of home. Then he had added, with a smile Daniel had not liked, "Do you like the dark one? Perhaps something can be arranged."

MacKenzie was taking a risk, coming up north just now. He would surely suffer in a full-scale war. But even Daniel could not say whether the war would come, for the Indians grumbled and the French plotted even in times of peace. If MacKenzie could hold on, in the end he would be rich. The English were too vital to be held back for long, and the French were too static to hold them at bay, even with Indian help. Sooner or later, English settlers would pour into this land, and Thomas MacKenzie would be ready and waiting for them.

Caroline. Daniel recalled her expression when he had told her of MacKenzie's plans. Clearly, she had not known before. He wondered if she would repeat what he had said to MacKenzie. He doubted it. She seemed the type to keep her own counsel. Again he felt her body start at the touch of his hand. Again he felt her soft lips pressing against his palm.

A bird cried, mocking him from above. Night was falling, and there was no point in lingering. Shaking himself soundlessly, Daniel turned from the trees and moved off, picking his path through last summer's fallen leaves, where his silent moccasins would leave no trail behind.

Chapter Three

Although the morning had been chilly, the midday sun was warm on Caroline's shoulders and back. The earth beneath her bare feet was yielding and warm as she paused to bend over the next tiny hillock, counting the seeds automatically. Three from the pouch of corn kernels and two from that of pumpkin seeds; she dropped them into the cup-shaped depression in the top of the mound, then watched them disappear when Young Tom added a handful of dirt. Keeping pace with each other, they moved on to the next tiny hill.

Around them, in all directions, stretched the freshly turned field. William had had to plow it three times before it had been fit, while Thomas had twitched with impatience for him to begin cutting trees. But, soon enough after the plowing, the lumbering had begun, with the men away most days from dawn until dusk and the women and the children tending to the farm.

"William says this is the richest soil he's ever seen!" Young Tom's voice rang out in the quiet morning air. "He says we're lucky to have such good, rich land."

"Oh, he does, does he?" Caroline turned her face so that he would not see her smile. William had become Tom's idol since New Haven. Tom had followed him up the furrows when he had plowed the field, bothering him with questions and collecting the smaller of the stones that the land yielded up in a seemingly endless supply.

"He does," Young Tom said. "He says the crops will shoot up in soil like this. And," he added firmly, "William says that once they do we'll have to keep a close lookout for critters sneaking in to steal a meal." At this, Tom's eyes moved towards the split-rail fence, against which a light rifle leaned.

The rifle belonged to him. It had been a present from one of the soldiers at Fort Dummer. The MacKenzie party had spent their last night on the road within the shelter of the fort's stockade, and within the first hour Caroline had seen how right Thomas had been in assessing the soldiers' mood. The fifty-odd men who composed the fort's garrison had greeted them with open arms, weary to death from the winter's boredom and ready for a change. Before taking leave the next morning, Thomas had hired a dozen of them to work for him cutting trees in such free hours as they were allowed.

The soldiers had also come calling at the farm. At first they had come for Caroline, but, eliciting no response, they had shifted their interest to the rest of the family. Most of them had come from farms of their own to the south and had spent the winter yearning for their own families. They did odd jobs for Hannah and played with the children for hours. One of them had produced the light rifle as a present for Young Tom.

Hannah had protested that the gun was dangerous, but Thomas had silenced her with one look. "This is not the city! Weren't you yourself raised in the country, where boys know how to shoot?"

"But, Thomas, he is only a child."

"He is a boy!" Thomas had roared, and, seizing the rifle, he had stomped off to teach the boy how to shoot. But Thomas was impatient, so in the end William had stepped in, and now Tom could hit a rabbit perhaps six times out of ten. At first he had carried the rifle with him everywhere, but it had been unwieldy, so now, when he was working, he left it close at hand.

"William promised to take me out after deer," Young Tom said, his eyes still on the gun. Then, sighing, he added,

"If he ever gets the time. Aunt Caroline, why does King George need so many trees?"

"Why, you know, Tom. To make masts and spars for his ships."

"Then I wish there was no navy!" Tom kicked a clod with his bare foot. "Then William would have time for something besides cutting trees!"

"But, if there weren't a navy, our soldiers could not have sailed up the coast to attack Louisbourg." Last year the French had attacked the English in their colony near Louisbourg, and now troops from New England were seeking their revenge. The ships had sailed from Boston early in the spring, but as yet no word of their landing had reached the frontier.

"But, if we do win at Louisbourg, I've heard that that might end the war."

Tom's tone was disappointed. Caroline looked up. "Why Tom, you sound positively disheartened by the idea. You sound as though you were pining for a battle in this very field!"

"Well," the boy admitted, with a sheepish look, "I wasn't thinking of anything really serious. But what's the point of being up here if we see no Indians? What will I tell the fellows back in New Haven?"

"That you were fortunate!" Caroline laughed, and shook her head. "And I hope you know enough to keep such sentiments from your mother's ears!" Straightening, she turned her eyes towards the house, where Hannah and Elizabeth were working, preparing the noonday dinner at the big fireplace. The door to the house was open, and through it came the sound of Hannah's voice raised in song. These days, Caroline reflected, Hannah sang all the time—most likely because Thomas spent so much of his time away.

Scanning the stout walls, with their slitted openings, she recalled her reaction when she had first seen it. Somehow she had expected their farm to be different from the one in which they had stayed their first night out of Northfield. How her heart had tumbled at the sight of the grim stockade, with its tiny slits for windows and its thick, ugly walls!

Standing in the dimness, looking about the inner rooms, she had felt herself in a prison.

And yet, she thought, her eyes returning to her task, how malleable humans were. Even in that first hour she had begun to adapt, and by the time they had had the wagons unloaded and the furniture arranged she had begun to consider the stockade home. She was still unused to how dark the kitchen was, but the upper chamber she shared with Elizabeth had two windows for light, and when the weather was fine she spent most of her time out of doors.

Three corn and two pumpkin seed, then move on again. They had been working since morning and were not yet halfway through. And when they had planted the corn and pumpkin, they would go back again to plant the rows of beans in the valleys between the hills. It was the way of the Indians—or so William had explained—and when Young Tom had objected William had only smiled, commenting that it was a wise man who learned from his enemy.

"William says this north land is worth as much as gold," Young Tom went on. "He says we'll get sixty bushels of corn from this one field." Pausing, he looked down the row, then about the field, trying to measure the glory of a bumper crop against that of a successful fight. William thought the crop was important, but William was not a boy, and Tom's friends back in New Haven would hardly be impressed by tales of raising corn. Whereas a half-dozen Indians would make him a celebrity. His eyes moved again to the rifle, and then back to his aunt.

"You don't mind it, do you, Aunt Caroline?"

"Mind what?"

"Doing this kind of work? You don't find it tedious, after New Haven?"

"Not at all." Caroline smiled. If anything, she found it soothing to the nerves, despite her aching muscles at the end of the day. Here, she had found a peace that she had not known in years.

"When I was a girl, in Surrey," she explained to Young Tom, "we lived in a village completely surrounded by fields. They planted wheat and barley, and oats and hops and rye.

You should have seen it in August, when the crops were ripe—acres and acres of shimmering gold rippling beneath the sky! Of course," she continued, as they moved down the row, "we weren't farmers, so we didn't work the fields, but when it came time for harvest we all would lend a hand.

"It was hard work, I suppose, but we never remembered that part from year to year. What we remembered was the celebration that would come just afterwards. Dancing and feasting that would go on until dawn..." Brushing her hair back from her forehead, Caroline recalled how it had been: the merriment, the laughter, the courting, the jokes. She had danced with Edmund at the last festival, her head full of visions of the future they would share, despite the nagging worry that had been growing in her.

"But when shall we marry?" she had asked him later, when he had managed to sneak her away for an embrace in the dark. "When will you speak to my father?"

"Soon, soon," Edmund had said. "I shall speak to him tomorrow. There, will you kiss me now?"

And, sure enough, the next day, Edmund called her father to the hall. He stayed there a long time—or so it seemed to her, as she waited beside the gate. But at last she saw him coming and ran to meet him in the lane.

"Father! Sir Edmund—what did he say to you?"

"In fact, we spoke of marriage," her father replied, looking at her with a confusion in his expression that she did not understand. "Sir Edmund introduced me to a friend of his—"

"A friend?" Now it was her turn to be confused.

"An acquaintance," her father amended. "A fellow from London who's moved to the colonies. A man called MacKenzie—he's done quite well over there. Got a couple of factories, and half interest in a ship. Sir Edmund has spoken of your character, to which I have added my word. Thomas MacKenzie strikes me as a man who will go far."

"But," she asked, frowning, "what has that got to do with me?"

"Caroline," said her father, "Thomas MacKenzie wishes to marry you."

"Marry!" She stared at him in shock, unable to make sense of this wild tale he was telling her.

"Of course," her father continued, frowning at her reaction, "it would mean your emigrating, to Connecticut. But many have done it and found it agreeable. The climate is not so different from what we know here, and I have heard that life presents more opportunity—especially for one with Mr. MacKenzie's means. Our life here is not uncomfortable, but I believe that in New Haven..."

But she heard no more, for she had already spun away and started up the lane. He called out in confusion, but she paid him no heed, running like a wounded creature, uphill, towards the hall.

The shortest route led through the park and across the lawn that spread out below the graceful stone terrace. She came across the terrace, meaning to go around to the front, but she heard Edmund's voice coming from the house. One of the long windows stood slightly ajar. She moved in its direction, listening as she did.

"...so, as you see, the father will make no objection. And, as for the girl, she's high-spirited, but she's tameable—and her beauty you've seen for yourself."

"Yes, yes," said a rough voice that she did not recognize. "But I recall you saying that you'll make this worth my while."

"Of course. Very much so." Even from the window she could hear the distaste in Edmund's voice. "Two hundred, as I've told you, and an extra two hundred if she's out of the country within the month."

"You're in quite a hurry."

"I am to become engaged, and I wish my fiancée to be spared any unpleasantness this girl might try to cause—not that it is any affair of yours. Four hundred total. A fair price for a good wife."

"Make it five and you've got a deal. Three hundred to marry and two hundred for speed."

For a moment, Edmund was silent. Then he said rapidly, "All right, then, five hundred. Come, let us shake on it. You'll not regret coming back for an English wife. Though

I would have thought the colonies might produce beauties of their own.''

"And stiff as a starched shirtfront—Puritans one and all! I prefer a wife who answers to my rule, as well as God's.''

"Or over God's rule, eh?'' Edmund chuckled at his own joke. ''Well, Caroline is no Puritan, on that I can give my word!''

Sick to her very soul, Caroline stumbled away from the open window. Groping like a blind woman, she reached the stone balustrade and leaned upon it for support, unmindful of the passing of time until she heard someone whistling.

Edmund! He must have seen his guest off at the front of the house, for now he came around the side, jaunty in his stride—like a man who had just disposed of a thorny problem. He stopped when he saw her, and the whistle died away.

"Caroline!''

"Edmund! What does this mean? You gave me your word of marriage. You trothed yourself to me!''

"I—'' For a moment he faltered, and she saw his guilty flush. Then she saw his lips tighten, saw him take hold of himself. Stepping towards her, he laid his hand on her arm. ''Now, Caroline . . .''

She shook off his hand. ''You're trying to sell me to this man MacKenzie! I heard what you said!''

He hesitated, then spread his hands, one towards the house behind him, the other towards the sweeping lawn. ''Caroline, please understand. People depend upon me. I've got a name to preserve.''

She could have protested, could have reminded him of every promise he had made. But, in a blinding flash, she saw how futile it would be. Edmund's word was law on his estates, and even her own father would not help. What she had lost to Edmund could never be restored. Watching him now, she realized that everything was lost. Or almost everything.

"Very well,'' she replied, drawing about her the remaining shreds of her dignity. ''Very well,'' she repeated, ''you may break every vow, but you cannot force me to marry against my own will. You can't ship me off to America just to soothe your guilt. I may live forever with the shame of what you have done, but I won't relieve you of the memory!''

But Edmund had won in the end, and he had hurt her in a way even she could not have foreseen. Edmund had paid MacKenzie to marry Hannah, instead, and to bring the entire family over to New Haven. Lured by the promise of position in America, Caroline's father had gladly given his consent, while Hannah, always docile, had offered no protest. Shattered by Edmund's rejection, Caroline had been slow to learn of the plan, and by the time she had learned it was too late to change it. Her ticket, with the others', had already been paid; when the ship sailed from Southampton, she, too, was aboard. Stone faced and dry-eyed, she watched England slip away.

Three corn and two pumpkin. The seeds fell in her shadow, which was very strange, since at this moment she was facing the sun. And what was even stranger was the fact when she moved to the next hillock her shadow remained behind. Then she saw the moccasined foot planted between the rows, and in the same moment both she and Young Tom gasped.

Even before she raised her eyes she thought of Daniel Ledet, and all thought of the past vanished from her heart. She had not seen the Frenchman since that evening in the woods, but she had thought of him often, with both a frown and a smile, and with the shiver of pleasure that came with the memory of his touch. She had told herself that it would be better if she never saw him again, for he represented a temptation that she would do better without. But that resolution, which worked well with other men, had not seemed to affect her feelings for Daniel Ledet. If she had feared his coming, she had hoped for it, as well. And now, at last, he had come! The beginnings of a smile played around her lips as she raised her eyes from that deerskin shoe that, since their first meeting, she had associated with him.

Then her smile shattered, for the man who stood so close was not the blond-haired Frenchman. It was an Indian, who met her look of astonishment with dark, impassive eyes. Time hung suspended.

Then she felt Young Tom move. He whirled away, towards the fence, and in the same instant she knew why. The gun! In her mind she saw the swift, flashing flight of a tomahawk and heard a sickening thud as it encountered flesh.

"Tom, no!" she gasped, turning as he did, and then she gasped a second time. Even Tom stopped, frozen in mid-stride. For, where he had left the rifle stood a man, a white man with bright hair. The Frenchman, Daniel Ledet. In one hand he held Tom's rifle, in the other his own.

He leaned against the fence, one leg crossed over the other, in a posture of unconcern that was so at odds with what she felt that Caroline could do nothing but stare, first at Daniel himself, then at the Indian again.

He, too, was watching Daniel, his lips a long, unyielding line beneath the high beak of his nose. She saw now that he, too, held a rifle between his two hands, a long-barreled rifle that gleamed in the midday sun, gleamed as did the bronze skin of his muscular, bare chest.

What could all this mean? Her mind raced through the possibilities, seeking to make sense of them. Daniel had never harmed her in the past. But why was he here with an Indian? And why would he take Tom's rifle, if he meant them no harm? But, if he meant to harm them, why did he only stand? And what of Hannah and the children? She glanced towards the house, then back, as Daniel pushed away from the fence.

She watched him come towards her, hardly able to breathe for the pounding of her heart. Part of her feared him, and part of her only recalled the times he had stood before her in the gathering dusk. But it was not dusk now, it was full daylight, and his expression was as unreadable as the Indian's.

He stopped, less than two feet away from her, and she waited to hear what he would say. But, before he could address her, Young Tom moved again—this time to launch himself at Daniel's midsection, reaching for the short rifle and trying to wrestle it from him.

"Leave her alone!" he cried. "I'll kill you if you lay a single finger on her!"

Although Daniel had every advantage over the boy, he was made awkward by trying to maintain his grip on both rifles at once. The Indian came to his aid. Shouldering his own gun, he grasped Tom from behind, pinioning the boy's arms and body against his chest. Immobilized, but undeterred, Young Tom kicked out, and Caroline heard the Indian grunt when a heel caught his knee.

"Let me go, you red bastard!" the boy cried, struggling.

"Thomas!" exclaimed Caroline, shocked by the curse. The boy ignored her, continuing to kick and squirm, but Daniel threw back his head and laughed.

"Is cursing not permitted when a man fears for his life? That seems a bit extreme." Shaking his head, he turned to Tom. "May I have your promise that you will stand still if you are released?" But the boy's only answer was another kick.

"He thinks you mean to harm us," Caroline explained. There was a question in her voice.

Daniel shook his head. "I thought you knew me better."

"I don't know you at all," she replied, trying to ignore the thrill his words raised in her. For all that there were Young Tom and the Indian to worry about, still all her awareness was focused upon him, and had been since she had first seen him at the fence. "And what about the Indian?" she said, turning away to look instead at the red man, who still held his prey.

"He is Iroquois," Daniel said. "The Iroquois are friends of the British—despite the fact that they buy their arms from the French. But you must not hold that against them, as they would buy from the British, if only the British would sell. A mistake on the part of the British, since to the Indian mind there is no greater act of trust than to sell a man a gun. They call the French their true brothers."

"But they do not fight with them?" she asked, distracted from Young Tom's predicament.

Daniel shook his head. "The French want their lands, and the French are bound to the Algonquian, who are the Iroquois's enemies."

"But this one is with you."

"I am an exception to the rule—though that may change with the next kick. Will you tell the boy to be still?"

"Tom, be still!" she said, and saw the boy subside, though his eyes, fixed on Daniel, remained mutinous. Even so, he made no movement when he was released.

Ignoring Tom's expression, Daniel held out the short rifle. "I believe this is yours."

"It is." Young Tom grabbed the gun, but Daniel raised it out of reach.

"A gun is only useful if it is at your side. It becomes the greatest danger in your enemy's hands. Had I wished you or your aunt any harm, you would either be dead now or successfully kidnapped. I hope this has taught you a lesson that you will never forget."

"Yes, sir," Young Tom muttered, his eyes dropping to the ground.

"Good." Daniel nodded. "Now tell me something else. Do you think that your mother would like a basket of quail eggs?"

The boy looked up, confusion in his eyes. "Sir?"

"A basket of quail eggs, to boil and to eat."

"Oh, yes, sir," Young Tom nodded. They had a half-dozen chickens that they had brought up with them, but the trip had upset them, and they were not laying well.

"I know where you can find one, very close to you. Turawah will show you," he added, glancing at the Indian. Young Tom looked at Caroline, who opened her mouth to object, but Daniel forestalled her. "He is perfectly safe," he said. "I would trust him with my own child." He addressed the Indian in a guttural tongue. The Indian replied briefly. Then, grinning, he bent to rub his knee. "He says he thinks the boy will be a great warrior someday. Turawah's own father is a well-respected chief."

"Does he?" Tom's face lit up. He looked to Caroline.

"All right, you can go," she said, but he hesitated still.

"What about the gun, sir?"

"I'll hold it here for you. After all, you'll need your hands to carry back the eggs."

Caroline watched them walk away, Young Tom taking four steps to the red man's one. "Is that what he really said?"

"More or less." Daniel smiled, his eyes shifting to her. She had changed in the weeks since he had seen her last. She had lost that closed-in city look, and her face had filled out. He had watched her working in the field for some time, long enough to know that this was not the first field she had sowed. Not that he cared for farming—perish the thought—but he liked a woman who loved the land. "More literally, he said that if a man had kicked him thus he would have broken both his legs. I see that you have been making progress here."

He meant the field. Nodding, she looked around. "It took some time to plow, but it wasn't all that bad, considering this is the first time it has ever been cultivated."

"But it isn't." He turned back, and she saw that his eyes, which she had thought were gray, were really a mixture of gray and blue, sometimes more one color and sometimes the other. Just now they were the color of the morning sky when the sun has risen just behind the clouds. "The Indians have planted crops in these meadows for hundreds of years. Or used to plant them—until the white man came. At first they thought the white man only wanted a turn with the land, and by the time they found out otherwise, of course, it was too late." He shrugged.

"But I thought that they sold the land away. The General Court had to pay the Indians for this land."

"Yes, they paid the Indians, but the Indians believed that the payment was for use. They have no concept of land ownership. They know only using and taking turns on land. Now, too late, they are beginning to understand. They are slow learners in some things. Other things, such as shooting guns, they learn with admirable speed." He handed her the rifle that he had kept from Tom. "What about you?" he asked.

"I?" She looked down at the gun. It was warm from the sun, and from his grip, as well.

"Do you know how to shoot?"

"I know where to put the ball, and where the powder goes." She had watched men load guns all her life, though she had never tried to load one herself.

"Well, that is something," Daniel said with a nod. "Let us see if you prove yourself to be as quick as the Indians."

"Quick?" she repeated, looking up to find that Daniel had turned away and was walking across the field. "Where are you going?" she called after him.

He paused and turned back. "To teach you to shoot that rifle. Are you coming or not?"

She had to hurry to keep up with him, and yet his pace was easy, and his movements were relaxed. Her own progress was awkward over the uneven ground, for she had to hold her skirts in one hand and the rifle in the other. Taking time to glance up at him, she tripped upon a rock. He reached out to catch her arm, and, after he released her, still the warm pressure of his touch burned upon her skin. Until she had seen him she had not been conscious of having missed him. Now she was conscious of little else.

"The men are away."

He did not quite ask it, but she nodded anyway. "Yes, they are most days, off cutting Thomas's wood. He has most of the soldiers cutting, also, in their free time."

"He is an enterprising man—and also a foolish one, to leave his women alone, protected by a boy."

"I suppose he would take precautions, if there was a threat. But no one has seen any sign of the Indians."

"Perhaps not." The fringe on his tunic swung as he walked. At first she had found it peculiar, but it had become a part of who he was. "But, by the time a sign is seen, then it will be too late. You leave the front door open."

"To let in light and air. And there are the soldiers—"

"Who are also cutting wood. Had I desired, I could have entered your house and taken scalps or made prisoners of you all."

"Thus you have taught me the same lesson you taught to Tom." She stopped and faced him, tired of his peremptory tone. "Perhaps we have been careless, but that does not give you the right—"

"I claim no right," he said, interrupting her. "I offer only a friendly suggestion, which you may take or leave." He started moving once more, and, although again she hesitated, in the end she followed him.

He set down his rifle in order to climb the fence, springing up and over as though it were nothing at all. She would have climbed after him, but he reached back for her, and in a breathless moment she found herself swung over the fence, rifle and all, and set down at his side. For a moment his hands lingered upon her waist, long enough for all her thoughts to rush back to their last meeting. But, even as she recalled the coolness of the evening air, he released her and reached for her gun instead.

"Nine-tenths of successful shooting is a steady arm. If your arm is not steady, find something to rest your elbow on. This fence, for instance, or a windowsill. Or, if you happen to be lying down, the ground will do very well. Have you ever used a sight?"

"Not really." She shook her head, still struggling to drag her mind back to the business at hand. He seemed to suffer from no such distraction, raising the gun to examine the sight himself, then handing it to her.

"It's not difficult to learn. You just fit the bead into the notch, and keep it that way until it's aimed at your target. Here—" He raised the gun in her arms; then, moving behind her, he held it to her shoulder so that her eye looked along the top of the barrel. She saw the notch and bead that he had described, saw them come together, then drift apart again as his arms came around hers, his head so close to hers that she could feel his breath stir her hair. If she leaned back just a fraction, she would find his chest, warm and hard as it had been when he had held her against him among the spruces at the river's edge. If she turned her head, she would feel his cheek against her own.

"Fix upon that tree trunk, on the knot, you see?"

"I think so," she murmured, pointing at the blur. If she turned her head, she would also find his lips. She remembered the fleeting moment when they had touched her fingertips. Then she felt him move.

"So there you see," he said. He released her and stepped away, and she would have dropped the rifle if he had not maintained his grip on it.

He held the gun before her. "This is the flint," he said, pulling back the cock to show her. "When you let it forward, it strikes against the frizzen, here, making sparks that light the powder in the pan, which send fire through the touchhole and into the barrel, here." He pointed as he spoke. "So the first thing is to be sure that your flint is good. Then," he said, opening the horn he wore over his right shoulder, "you need to prime your pan. Here, you do it." He held out the open horn.

"Me?" she repeated, dazed from the spate of instructions and still shaken from when he had stood so close.

She saw his mouth twitch. "In case someone else isn't there when you're loading up. That's it, just a tiny pinch, then you snap the frizzen shut. Now we pour a bit more down into the barrel, and a bullet afterwards." He handed her one from his pouch. "Then you ram it down."

Having recovered the better part of her senses, she did as he said, while he watched critically. "Firmly, that's right," he said, "but a bit more slowly. That's it, and then the thing is to keep the barrel up so that the ball doesn't roll out and ruin all your work. All right, that's good enough. Now let's see you set your sight."

Then, for the second time, she was in his arms, but this time she was conscious of the rifle that she held. She hardly knew him, and yet, from what she knew, she could tell that this lesson was not a joke to him. So she trained her concentration on the bead and the notch, setting one within the other, then moving them both towards the trunk of the tree, which stood twenty paces off.

"On the same knot again?"

"Whatever you like," he said. "Wait until you've got it, then squeeze the trigger as smoothly as you can. And keep your eyes open. That's it, take your time."

It was harder than she'd thought. Even as she had it, the knot swam away, and the longer she held it the heavier the gun grew. "I'm sorry," she murmured. "I just had it now, but then I lost it again."

"That's all right. Take your time," he said, with an ease he did not feel, for his body was responding to the warmth that rose from her. It took every bit of his concentration to hold his own arms still. Since the last time he'd seen her, he'd been to Montreal and New York. His last stop had been Albany, and from there he should have gone west, but he had found some pretext for coming back this way.

She'd been in his mind all these past weeks, coming to him in the evening as the shadows grew, whispering to him at night. He'd told himself that the wise thing was to stay away from her, and then he'd told himself that it could do no harm to see her in passing. Perhaps he'd built up her beauty these past weeks in the woods; perhaps he'd be disappointed when he saw her again. But of course he had not been. Standing in the shadows of the trees that flanked the field, he had felt the warmth of desire as he had watched her work. Now his mind imagined how it would be to turn her around, to crush her close against him and feel her yielding warmth.

The knot swam into view. Forgetting his instructions, Caroline closed her eyes and squeezed. Something exploded in her face, while what felt like a mighty fist slammed into her chest, thrusting her back against Daniel so hard that she heard him grunt, and she would have fallen if he had not held her up.

The impact of the recoil had knocked the breath from her lungs. She slumped like a rag doll, her mouth working noiselessly. At first, Daniel held her. Then he lowered her to the ground and, coming around beside her, peered into her face with a mixture of anxiety and surprise that made her want to laugh.

"Are you all right?" he asked.

"I think so," she gasped, finding breath at last. She drank in the air in loud, thirsty gulps while he held her hand. The sharp tang of gunpowder tickled in her nose. "I guess I missed," she said.

"I guess you did." He laughed. "It was a good first try. Next time, try to remember not to close your eyes and not to let go of the gun."

"Oh. Is that what happened?"

"That's what happened," he said, just as a cry came from behind them, from the direction of the house.

"Caroline!" It was Hannah, her face white as chalk, running along the edge of the field.

"Oh, dear, the shot. Here, please help me up. It's all right," she called, waving, with Daniel supporting her. "No one has been hurt."

"Tom! The gun!" Hannah gasped, reaching them at last, her eyes moving from Daniel to Caroline's powder-smudged face. Then her eyes widened when she heard Tom call out and, turning, saw him running from the woods with an Indian.

"Mamma! Aunt Caroline! Has anything happened?" he called out as he came.

"No, nothing," called Caroline. "I was only learning to shoot. It's all right, Hannah, really, it's all right," she repeated, taking her sister's hand, which was cold as ice. Hannah was trembling, her eyes on the Indian.

"It's all right, Hannah. This man is an Iroquois. He was showing Tom where to find a nest of quail eggs."

"Quail eggs?" Hannah repeated weakly.

"Yes, Mamma, here they are!" Tom thrust it out to her. "There are eight in all. You can boil them for dinner. My, won't they taste fine!" Then, looking at Caroline, "You've got powder on your face!"

"Yes, I shot the rifle—though not very well. Mr. Ledet showed me how. Hannah, this is Daniel Ledet, he's an—an acquaintance of Thomas's."

"How do you do, pleased to meet you," Hannah murmured, her eyes, completely baffled, moving among the
group.

"I am sorry if we scared you," Daniel said, addressing
her. "We should have thought to warn you before the gun
went off."

"Yes, well, as long as no one was hurt…" Hannah smiled
weakly, reaching out for Tom and pulling him close to her.
"Would you—would you care to stay to dinner?" she asked
doubtfully, her eyes moving to the Indian, then back to
Caroline.

Daniel shook his head. "Thank you, but we cannot. It
was a pleasure to meet you."

"Yes…" Hannah's voice trailed off. "Well, there is
Elizabeth and dinner to see about. Tom, come along."

"Yes, Mamma. What about the gun?"

"Remember what I told you." Daniel handed it to him,
and Young Tom nodded as he followed his mother towards
the house.

Caroline lingered, though she could think of no reason
why she ought to stay. The shooting lesson was over, and
Hannah would think it strange if she stayed behind. And
then there was the Indian, who stood at Daniel's side.

"I should go back with them."

"Yes, of course," he said. "Is there someone besides
MacKenzie who could teach you to shoot?"

"There's William," she replied.

"Who's William?" he asked, though he knew it was no
affair of his.

But she answered readily. "He's Thomas's man. But he's
not like Jonas. He's…kind to the children."

"Then he'll do," Daniel said, stifling a pang of jealousy
towards this man he had never met.

"Shall I tell Thomas you were here?"

"I'll tell him myself."

"But he is out in the woods somewhere…."

He grinned. "Then I'll have to listen for the sound of his
ax." He nodded towards Hannah, who had paused to glance

back at them. "Your sister is worried about you, hobnob-
bing with the enemy."

"Yes, I'd better go.... When—when will you be back this
way?"

"Is that an invitation?"

"I just wanted to know."

"Oh, well...in that case, I can't say for sure." But, as he
spoke, he smiled, and she smiled back at him. On impulse,
she held out her hand, and he took it in his. He held it for a
moment, and when he let it go she turned away, towards
where Hannah was waiting for her.

Daniel also turned away, and he was almost to the trees
when he heard her calling and turned back again.

"I'm sorry, I didn't hear you."

"Thank you for teaching me to shoot."

"Let's see if the next time you remember to hold the
gun."

"And keep my eyes open," she added, laughing as she
turned away, and that was the image he carried of her for the
next weeks, barefoot and laughing, standing in the newly
plowed field.

Chapter Four

June faded and July bloomed, fragrant and sunny and hot. The corn in the field now reached to Caroline's knees, and the pumpkin vines spread their broad leaves over the sun-baked earth. The first of the beans would be ready to pick in a week or two. Rows of neat bright green marched through the kitchen garden, and the slip of rose that Hannah had brought from New Haven was already showing new shoots. Elizabeth was enthralled by all the new growing things. She counted the bean pods and poked under the pumpkin vines until Caroline told her, laughing, that she'd worry them to death.

"Remember?" she asked Hannah. "Remember when we were young, how it was in the springtime, when everything first began—when Papa brought home young hare and Mamma let us go without our shoes?"

"I remember." Hannah smiled, then sighed and closed her eyes.

They were sitting side by side on the rough bench William had built on the side of the barn, facing north. They had made soap that morning, melting down the rendered fat before adding the ash, then stirring the seething mixture in the biggest iron kettle over a fire built in the yard. It was hot work, and tiring, and now that it was done and the soap cooling in pans they felt they had earned a rest. The sun having crossed its zenith, the bench lay in the shade, though the dusty earth beneath their bare toes was still baking-hot. They leaned back, luxuriating in the coolness and the warmth, watching the three children playing tag in the yard. Hetty, the baby, could not run fast, so Tom and Elizabeth took turns letting her catch them. Hetty laughed triumphantly when her sticky hands seized their legs.

"And the new lambs," continued Caroline, still following the same train of thought. "Remember how sweet they were on their wobbly little legs? Remember the little black one that almost died that year? You nursed it like a baby, and in the end it lived."

"I'd bring it up to sleep with us when Mother couldn't see!"

"Yes, and it would squeak and you would pull the covers up!" The sisters laughed together at the memory. "What was the name you gave it?"

"Rosepetal," Hannah said.

"Yes, Rosepetal." Caroline closed her eyes, rubbing an itch on her shoulder against the rough barn wall. Then, the itch abated, she leaned back with a contented sigh.

Hannah watched. Her lips were still curled with laughter, but her eyes held surprise. This was the first time since they had left Surrey that Caroline had mentioned it—mentioned it in any way, let alone nostalgically. And that wasn't the only remarkable thing. Now that Hannah studied her, she saw how Caroline had changed. Her skin was brown and glowing, and her jaw had lost the stiffness that had clenched it all these years. And her eyes no longer glittered like obsidian, but were soft again and sparkled, as they had in the old days. That is, Hannah amended, as they had in the days before Sir Edmund had taken his pleasure with her and then broken her heart.

Perhaps life was finally turning happier for Caroline. She deserved some joy in her life, joy such as she herself had been blessed with. Caroline might think Hannah to be pitied, with Thomas as her husband, but he had given her her children, who were the true joy of her life. Her hand moving to circle the growing swell of her stomach, Hannah smiled as she felt the magic stirring within. She knew that Caroline disapproved of this pregnancy, but, though it made each day longer and each task more burdensome, still she welcomed it.

Poor Caroline, she thought, her smile softening, to grow through one's womanhood without ever knowing the joy of feeling one's own child warm against one's breast. But perhaps it was not too late. Of course, there were not men here, as there were in New Haven, but perhaps among the soldiers there would be a man to catch her eye. Or perhaps down in Northfield, if it could be arranged. Wouldn't it be wonderful if such a thing occurred—if Caroline found a husband whose children she could bear? Six months ago—even two—she would have thought it impossible. But now... Her eyes upon the red-faced, tousled children, Hannah rubbed her stomach, beaming at the thought.

Caroline was smiling, as well. She was thinking of the expression on Daniel Ledet's face as she had sat gasping on the ground after the kick of the rifle had knocked the air from her lungs. Of course, her own face must have been twice as amusing, with powder smudged everywhere and her mouth working like a fish's. She remembered, too, his expression when he had bidden her farewell, his eyes holding the promise that had been missing from his words. And, of course, the way he'd held her while she'd aimed the gun... Remembering those minutes now, Caroline hugged herself, running her hands along her arms, bringing back his touch.

These days, she found herself thinking often of Daniel Ledet. What a change, after all this time, to have a man to think about with something besides bitterness and cruel longing in one's heart. How sweet, after all these years, to feel that weightlessness again, and the sense of something lying ahead instead of everything lying behind. At night now, when she lay looking up at the stars, she no longer had to brace herself against the pain, but could relax and welcome the images that came.

Now she had things to remember that brought a smile to her lips, and a quivering within her that she had thought never to feel again. She had the time they had met near the

spruce trees and he had cupped her cheek with his hand, and
her lips had touched the rough skin of his palm, and he had
kissed her fingertips. She never smelled the scent of spruce
without thinking of him—thinking of him with pleasure and
with a thrill of anticipation.

After their last meeting, she had felt some fear at first.
She had worried that she was falling into the old, bad ways.
Her experience with Edmund had shown her her weak-
nesses; indeed, she had dwelled upon them all these long
years. Other women could meet temptation and manage to
turn away, but she had submitted once and might do the
same again. And, while she might tell herself that the last
time she had been misled, she knew that she could never
again use such an excuse. A girl who lay with one man might
be called a fool, but there was a far more cruel name for a
woman who lay with two. Caroline had avoided men these
past eight years, in part from the bitterness that Edmund
had left in her heart, but also in part from the fear that she
might learn the worst of herself. Were Daniel to court her as
persistently as Edmund had, would she have the strength of
will to resist her attraction to him?

But, when one week had passed, then another, and then
a third, she felt the fear decreasing as a new idea took form.
Unlike Edmund, who had always been within reach, Daniel Ledet was a trader who ranged far and wide through the
wilderness. Most likely she would not see him for weeks or
months at a time, and then always among the family, with
small chance for more than the flirtation in which they had
engaged thus far. In Surrey there had been ample chance for
secluded rendezvous, but here in the wilderness women did
not wander off on their own; nor did they wander off with
men they knew only casually. Thus it seemed that Daniel
Ledet might be just the thing for her—a man about whom
she could daydream without the fear of disaster that had tied
her all these years.

Young Tom's short rifle stood propped against the bench;
the sight of it brought a new smile to Caroline's lips. She had
continued her shooting under William's tireless guidance,
and had mastered the art of loading, not to mention that of

remaining on her feet after the gun had discharged. She still could not be certain of hitting anything smaller than a house, but she knew that with practice she was sure to improve.

She ought to practice now, she thought, though she hated to move. She would never touch the gun when Thomas was around, knowing well the condescension with which he would greet her attempts.

But Thomas was gone today. He was out with a crew of soldiers, lumbering near the fort. These days, the soldiers were plagued by an extra restlessness, which came from waiting for the outcome of the fighting at Louisbourg. News of the successful landing had come just after Caroline had finished planting the field, followed a few weeks later by word that the fort was under siege. But news was so long in making its tortuous way to the north that for all anyone knew Louisbourg was already taken and the British troops sailing west to Quebec. No one ever mentioned the possibility of a British defeat, though of course they considered it. It added to the tension, and to the soldiers' restlessness.

"I think I'll practice with the rifle," she said, straightening.

At her words, Hannah shuddered. "I hate you shooting that thing. I'm always afraid that it will explode in your face."

"I should think you'd be more anxious about my shooting one of you by accident," Caroline replied with a chuckle. Hardly had she spoken when she heard voices rising from the trees beyond the field. She recognized Thomas's among them.

"Oh, dear," Hannah said, her expression reflecting her true thoughts. Then fear flooded her eyes. "I hope that nothing's happened . . ."

"It's nothing bad, at least," Caroline replied, for even from this distance it was plain that the voices were raised in joy and not in alarm. A moment later they burst out of the shade and into the open meadow, a throng of perhaps a dozen, with Thomas in the lead, one arm slung about the

neck of the soldier at his side, the other waving his gun in
time to the garbled words he sang.

"My goodness!" Hannah exclaimed.

"It must be news of Louisbourg!"

"The news must be good!"

They watched the men come towards them, skirting the
edge of the field. The children left off playing and ran to
welcome them. Caroline saw William swing Hetty onto his
shoulders and give Young Tom his hat. Even Jonas, she saw,
had a smile on his thin lips. Then she saw Daniel Ledet,
walking just behind. She knew she was smiling, and she
knew she could not stop.

"What are you staring at, women?" Thomas roared,
coming into the yard. Caroline could see from his red face
that he had been drinking already. "Get into the kitchen and
bring us out some ale! Louisbourg has fallen, and the way
to Quebec is ours!"

"Hip, hip, hurrah!" cried the soldiers, and one, tipsier
than the rest, pointed his musket at the sky and issued a
booming discharge. "God save the King!" he cried. The
children were ecstatic, except for Hetty, who held her ears
at the sound of the gun.

"Quebec?" Hannah gasped. "Will it really fall?"

"It will if they press ahead," replied the soldier, turning
to wink at the sister-in-law. Perhaps it was the whiskey they
had drunk at the fort, but it seemed she was looking even
handsomer than when he had seen her last. She was smiling, and he couldn't recall having seen her smile before. The
sight of that smile was enough to make him willing to risk
MacKenzie's wrath to steal a victory kiss from her. But she
wasn't looking at him, so she didn't see his wink. Her eyes
were on the Frenchman, and his on her, as well, and there
was no mistaking the welcome in her look. Why, the lucky
devil! thought the soldier to himself, just as a thump on the
back from a comrade almost sent him sprawling on his face.

"Ale!" cried Thomas, "and be quick with it, for I've got
a terrific thirst, and much to celebrate!"

The bustle spilled into the house. While the women gathered up the ale and the tankards, and the bread and meat,

the men brought the trestle table and the benches out into the yard. The children, overwhelmed by so much company, rushed about, ecstatic and everywhere underfoot. And Thomas was in such high spirits that he did not even fuss when Hetty tripped and skinned her elbow and cried most lustily.

"Poor baby!" Hannah said, clucking, when Elizabeth carried the child to the kitchen, where she was setting meat on a trencher while Caroline filled the jugs. "Elizabeth, sit with her until the men are served. Then I will see to her."

"No, go ahead." Caroline turned, a half-full pitcher of ale in her hand. "We've just about done, anyhow, except that this barrel is dry. I'll fetch a new one from the cellar, and then I'll be out, as well."

"Yes, all right." Hannah nodded, scooping the sobbing child up from Elizabeth's arms. At her mother's touch Hetty subsided, hiccoughing sulkily. Hannah and Caroline exchanged a smile. "Isn't it wonderful!" said Hannah. "Now perhaps the fighting will end. Perhaps now the war is won!"

From outside came the men's rising voices, competing to tell the tale, for their own enjoyment and as sauce for the meat. When Hannah had gone out to join them, Caroline paused to listen for Daniel's voice. Then she caught herself. Of course he would not be jolly over Louisbourg's fall. Daniel was a Frenchman. It was his side that had lost. Frowning, Caroline wondered what he thought of the defeat. And she wondered what the soldiers thought of his presence here.

Thomas kept his barrels in the shallow cellar beneath the trapdoor in the kitchen floor. Caroline had the door open and was bending to raise a new keg when a hand touched her shoulder and a familiar voice spoke at her side.

"Let me," said Daniel, kneeling on the rough wooden floor. It was the first time they'd been close since the day he had taught her to shoot, and she felt her body responding to his proximity. A sharp twinge of excitement shot up through her, and the coolness rising from the cellar brushed the heat of her face.

Straightening, she faced him. "Do you mind very much?" she asked.

"Mind?"

"About the battle?"

"Oh. Not really." He smiled. "You ought to see Louisbourg. A godforsaken place. It's no prize they've won."

"But what of Quebec? Everyone is saying that they'll go on to there."

His smile twisted wryly. "It's a long way from Louisbourg to Quebec, and one that the British have failed to cross before. In any case, the main force has returned to the south. It only remains to see how the French will bear the loss."

She watched the play of his muscles as he leaned forwards, grasping the sides of the barrel to haul it up onto the kitchen floor. He turned, his breathing quickened by the exertion.

"You say 'the French,'" she said, trying to ignore the rise and fall of his chest. A pulse beat strong and steady at the base of his throat, just above where the leather thong held his tunic closed. Her eyes upon it, Caroline imagined the rough heat of his bronzed skin beneath her lips.

His eyes, too, were upon her. "What should I say?" he asked.

"You could say 'we,'" she ventured. "You are French, aren't you?"

"By birth, at least. In any case, it seems to make a difference to you."

"Not such a difference," she said. Then she flushed at her own words. Her skin was tingling, and she felt the stillness with which he watched her.

A burst of hearty laughter split the silent air, and, rising above it, Thomas's raucous cry: "Woman! We need more ale!"

Caroline jerked back, as though Thomas were there with them. She heard Daniel exhale; then he, too, leaned back. Rising, he lifted the barrel and carried it to the table, where the pitcher stood. Caroline followed him.

Daniel leaned against the table, watching as she poured. He'd heard the news of Louisbourg from a trapper to the east and had carried it to the fort along with the six dozen beaver pelts he had brought to trade. He knew that Mac-Kenzie would have liked the pelts for himself, but Daniel had been trading at the fort for years and saw no reason to make MacKenzie his middleman.

In any event, MacKenzie had been in the woods beyond the fort and, in a moment of uncharacteristic expansiveness, had invited his whole lumbering party back to his place for a drink. Not exactly the conditions Daniel had been hoping for, but still he had tagged along, caring less about the news than about seeing Caroline.

A strand of her black hair hung down her neck, silken against her skin. He longed to touch its softness, and yet he held back. Part of him was content to feast his eyes on her, while at the same time his body tingled with eagerness. Coming here to see her was a treat he had promised himself all these past weeks, and the thought had only grown sweeter with every day's delay. Perhaps if he lingered after the others had gone there would be time with her alone. Perhaps there was somewhere in the shadows where he could feel her in his arms.

Caroline was conscious of him watching her, and it took a great effort to keep the stream of ale directed into the ewer's mouth. Still, she could not resist the temptation to glance up at him. She found his eyes upon her, their expression obscured by the dimness of the room. From outside came more laughter; she watched him turn his head.

"So," he said, turning back, "how does the shooting go?"

"Better, much better. I've injured no one yet!"

"So long as you weren't aiming for an injury," he replied, his lips curving in a smile.

The pitcher was brimming. Her hand had begun to tremble, so she set it down. Daniel's hand was resting on the barrel's rim; without any effort, she could imagine it on her skin. Without the slightest effort, she could imagine herself in his arms, his cheek pressed against hers, rough skin against smooth. She saw his fingers tighten, as if he had read her thoughts, and then his hand left the barrel, moving towards her arm.

"And just where, in the devil's name, has that ale gotten to!"

They sprang apart as quickly as if they had been shot, turning to the doorway, where Thomas's broad hulk loomed.

At the sight of them, he grinned. "Well, now," he said, his eyes moving between them, "perhaps I should beg pardon for interrupting this!" He made no effort to lower his voice—if anything, he pitched it so that it would carry through the door. Caroline, cringing, heard a loud guffaw. She felt her body stiffen, and felt Daniel's stiffen, as well. Even through her anger she felt his lack of fear.

Daniel was smaller than Thomas, and far beneath him in weight, and yet she knew without pausing to think that he would accept a fight. The knowledge gave her fierce pleasure, but she felt apprehension, as well, for if Thomas lost a fight, he would sulk for days, taking out his ill-humor on his entire family.

Daniel was coiled like a cobra and ready to spring. He was waiting, she realized, for a sign from her. It made her feel like weeping, from frustration and from gratitude, but if she wept he would spring. So instead she straightened, brushed the loose hair back and, ignoring the pitcher, swept out of the room. At first she thought that Thomas would not let her by, but at the last minute he moved to give her room.

MacKenzie turned his head to watch Caroline pass. Then, turning back to Daniel, he said, "I'd apologize, *monsieur*, but I doubt I've deprived you of much. She may be a looker, but she's got no use for men. Likely all I've saved you is a slap across the face." Then, his lip curling, he added with a sneer, "You should have known her back in England, where she felt otherwise!"

Daniel knew what he meant. MacKenzie, when drunk, had a loose tongue, and such stories traveled quickly along the gossip-starved frontier. Daniel had heard the sordid tale about Caroline and the lord who had thrown her over. It didn't surprise him, given what he knew of the aristocracy; nor did he think to hold it against Caroline. Whatever might have happened, he had no doubt she had suffered enough without MacKenzie throwing the past in her face.

He saw MacKenzie squinting, judging his reaction. For his own sake, he would gladly have taken MacKenzie on, but he knew that whatever pain he caused would only be passed on to Caroline. So, controlling his breathing, he forced a shrug. "Thank you for your advice," he replied, taking the jug from where Caroline had left it when she had turned to him. The warmth of her fingers still lingered upon the handle.

As he had done for Caroline, MacKenzie let him pass, and Daniel had to clench his fists to keep from pitching the ale into his face. Coming out into the sunlight, he felt all eyes upon him. Though his would have gone to Caroline, he managed to resist. Instead, he smiled and raised the pitcher in his hands, saying, "I hope you'll excuse the delay. It's been such a long time since I've been in a house, I have trouble finding the door!"

The soldiers at the table laughed, and what could have been a tense moment passed and was lost in the celebration. The soldiers toasted Louisbourg and her victors again and again, and wondered at their chances of being home by the fall. Perhaps it was unlikely, but this was a day for high hopes. Tomorrow MacKenzie would surely regret his ale, for he was as closefisted a fellow as any of them had ever met. But today the ale was flowing and the sun was bright and spirits were soaring up into the clear blue sky.

For Daniel, the moment remained, and he could not but believe that Caroline felt the same. One day, Thomas MacKenzie, he thought, struggling to harness the rage seething inside him; one day you will venture too far, and someone will kill you for it. Then again, he reflected, that probably was not true. It seemed that the worse the man the longer he was bound to live. Take King Louis, for instance, both this one and the last; think of the misery they had caused, and yet look how well they survived. MacKenzie might have cause to hope for immortality.

His eyes moved down the table to where Caroline sat. As he had expected, she did not look up, but instead kept her own eyes fixed on the table, black and impassive as onyx. Gazing at her white face, Daniel felt a surge of pity for her. But she would not want his pity; that he knew well enough. She had not challenged MacKenzie just now in the house; nor had she surrendered her pride to him.

Daniel doubted now that he would linger after the others had gone. As much as he wanted to be with Caroline, he knew that such a sight would only egg MacKenzie on, and he knew that she would avoid him for the same reason. But the fight was not over; the fight had just begun. Someday, somehow, he would make Thomas MacKenzie pay for what he had said today.

Chapter Five

News of the fall of Louisbourg buoyed up frontier spirits. Although, with most of the troops headed back to Boston, it seemed unlikely that there would be any further assault on Canada, still the mood was optimistic, matching the weather, which was hot and fresh and clear. The restlessness that had plagued the soldiers at Fort Dummer was not relieved by the news, but rather seemed to infect the settlers, as well. People were not satisfied to sit home alone with such good tidings; the fall of Louisbourg was a story to be told and retold. So it was decided to have a party at the fort so that everyone could gather and celebrate to their hearts' content.

News spread through the wilderness, carried by the soldiers and by the very summer air, until there was not a family or settlement that had not heard. They knew of it across the river at Ashuelot and Fort Number 4; they'd heard down in Northfield, and everywhere in between. The MacKenzie family had been among the first to hear, and they were up before dawn that morning to see to all the chores before leaving for the fort.

Although in the past months the men had traveled far and near in the quest for wood, the women and the children had not left the farm since their arrival. Thus, this trek of seven miles was a source of great excitement. The children had thought of little else since they had first heard, and Caroline and Hannah shared their eagerness.

Caroline's first thought upon rising had been of Daniel Ledet. She had not seen him since the day Thomas and the soldiers had brought the news of Louisbourg—the day Thomas had insulted her in front of Daniel. How well that day had begun, and how badly it had ended—he masking rage with wit, and she so stiff with embarrassment that she could not meet his eyes. She would have avoided him when the time came for leave-taking, had he not sought her out. He had spoken her name in a way that had made her look up at him, and so she had seen that his expression held friendship and respect—not a trace of pity, and not a trace of humiliating lust. Taking her hand in parting, he had said simply, *"Au revoir."*

Au revoir. Until I see you again. And today would be the day, she had thought, springing up from her bed to gaze out over the meadow and the misted river beyond. The air held the same promise she felt within her breast, a promise of blue-skied brilliance and hot sun and dazzling wildflowers. For the first time in many years, she dressed herself with care, choosing a skirt of deep blue with a matching bodice and a cream-colored chemise. As she brushed out the heavy mass of her unbraided hair, she was tempted to wear it loose. Then she thought of Thomas, stomping about below, and, with a sigh of regret, she braided and pinned it again.

"Caroline, you look beautiful!" Hannah exclaimed as she came down the stairs, and the children forgot their porridge to gape in admiration.

"Come now," Caroline said, at once pleased and embarrassed. "This is but a plain frock."

"No." Hannah shook her head. "It is not the dress but the wearer whom the children admire, for they have never seen you claim your own beauty."

Claim her own beauty. Yes, she knew what Hannah meant. For had she not sought to disown that very beauty all these last long years? But today, though her mind might tell her to disown it still, in her heart she felt a pleasure that had been absent for too long.

William had harnessed up the wagon, and he helped Hannah and Caroline into it as though they were royalty. He drove the wagon while Thomas and Jonas rode; Young Tom and Elizabeth sat on William's two sides while Hetty sat in the wagon bed with Hannah and Caroline and basins and heaping platters of food that they were bringing to share.

The fort stood at the southern end of the Great Meadow, which spread for several miles along the river's western bank. The fort itself was built on the bank of the river, in the same stockade style as the MacKenzie farm, its walls of stout hewn timber, locked at the four corners. In recent years an outer picket had been added, of posts a foot in diameter and twenty feet in height. These had been driven deep into the ground, then sharpened at the upper ends, with spaces left between them so that guns could be fired out. There were also battlements mounted with swivel guns so that the fort could be defended from attack on every side.

On Caroline's only previous visit, the massive gate had been closed, and Thomas had had to shout his name and his intentions up to the soldiers on watch. Today the gates were open and the parade ground filled with wagons and horses and milling holiday crowds. Compared to New Haven, the congregation might be sparse, but, after the seclusion of the past months, it seemed almost overwhelmingly large.

A number of houses had been built along the fort's inner walls. The earliest were quite rudimentary, only one story, with a one-sided roof slanting down from the wall behind. The newer ones, however, were quite comfortable, being two stories and well constructed. Today their doors were open, and people passed in and out, and with them drifted the rich smell of cooking food.

The MacKenzie party was welcomed with shouts of joy. Willing arms reached up to hand the children down and to receive the food and drink that they had brought to share.

"My goodness!" exclaimed Hannah, gazing about her. "It seems the whole world is here. Look, there is that woman at whose house we stayed."

Glancing around, Caroline saw the woman standing apart, her work-roughened hands clasped over her apron.

"Poor thing," Hannah murmured, touching her swelling stomach with superstitious fear, as if the memory of the woman's loss would bring her bad luck. "Oh, do watch, Tom!" she cried, distracted. "You'll drop the berry pie!"

Caroline caught the berry pie on its way to the ground and passed it to a soldier who was standing at her side. Passing out a basket, she scanned the parade ground, searching unsuccessfully for Daniel. Although the celebration had not been promoted as a fair, any gathering in the north country was a good time to trade. A few Northfield merchants had brought cartloads of goods that were displayed on the parade ground, to which the settlers and soldiers added what stock or crafts they had produced: a few chickens, handmade chairs, wooden bowls and baskets woven from river grass. Would not Daniel also want to trade his furs? Yet, though an occasional fair head glinted in the crowd, none of them was his.

The drink had been settled on two stout plank tables that had been set out along the northern wall. Kegs of ale and cider crowded each other for space. There was tea for the ladies, and later there would be rum to warm the men's spirits in the night to come.

The women bustled about the hall of the largest house, arranging the platters and kettles that arrived with the guests. There were roast quail and smoked venison and two dozen pigeon pies, made from the passenger pigeons that roosted so plentifully that a man could knock them from the trees with a club in April and May. There were pickerel from the river, and pike and salmon and shad, pickles made from green walnuts and pears and nasturtium buds. There were wheat bread and corn bread and five different kinds of fruit pies, and bowls of grapes and chokecherries, and sweet, tiny wild strawberries.

The children were everywhere. Barefoot and half wild, they nosed about the tables, keen as hungry wolves, until their mothers shooed them out into the sun again. Everyone was brimming with happiness and good cheer, for such a celebration was rare and wonderful.

The wrestling began. A settler from Ashuelot, across the river, challenged all comers. He was a black-haired giant with forearms the size of hams, brawny and forbidding but for the twinkle in his eye. One of the soldiers took up the challenge, and his comrades applauded his bravery. Stripped to the waist, the two men circled each other, pawing the air like bears. The soldier lunged forwards, bringing his opponent down with a grunt amid a cloud of dust and applause from the soldiers, calls from the settlers. The men rolled on the ground, their arms locked around each other, each with one hand free and groping for a new purchase. Then they sprang free and were up and circling again.

The air was alive with calls of encouragement. The soldiers cheered their champion, and the settlers theirs. For the sake of this sporting contest, two sides had been drawn, but Caroline had noticed that this was the exception to the rule. All were united in fighting the common enemy. It was not as it had been in England, where soldiers were professionals. These men were militia, farm boys and artisans. They might all have been brothers, and, in a real way, they were. The ribbing was as good-humored as the encouragement.

Now it was the Ashuelot giant who felled his opponent, catching him by forearm and thigh and flipping him into the air. The look of surprise on the soldier's face when he hit the ground brought roars of laughter from the crowd. His breath was knocked from him, and for a moment he lay where he was. Then the victor, leaning forwards, extended one beefy hand to help him up again.

"Next victim!" the crowd shouted, as the conquered was led away to be consoled with a pint of ale.

The wrestling continued for the next hour. The giant downed his next foe, but was beaten by the third, and soldiers and settlers alike gave him a rousing cheer as he left the ring.

Caroline clapped and cheered with the rest, but her eyes were automatically scanning the crowd, still hopeful of a glimpse of Daniel's fair head. She had not seen him yet, but the crowd was pressing close, and if he had come in this last hour he might be in the back. Perhaps if she moved a little to one side she could have a better view, but even when she did so she could not see him.

The wrestling ended, and the shooting began. The target was a walnut dangling from a string. The string was attached to the end of a four-foot pole driven into the stockade, and the contestants had to hit it from fifty paces back. All who were successful would then try again, from twenty paces more, and so on until there remained only one. The prize was a belt of wampum, such as the Indians made, which was the closest thing to money in frontier trade.

The contestants lined up amidst much good-natured bantering. The soldiers were at a distinct disadvantage, for most of them had left their rifles at home and brought only the muskets the government issued to them. Because a musket loaded quickly—up to three times in one minute—it was the preferred weapon in a war. Rifles, however, had a longer range and a greater accuracy and were thus favored by the settlers, who used their guns to hunt. This disparity, however, was soon resolved by the settlers' sharing their guns with the men from the garrison.

Most of the men were fair shots, but the target was small, and many of them had already sampled the whiskey and the ale. Of the forty or so who took part in the first round, hardly more than a half dozen passed successfully to the next. Now the line was moved back by another twenty paces, and the crowd pressed closer as their excitement rose. The first marksman, a soldier, registered a hit, but the second missed, as did the third and the fourth. As the next man stepped forward, a murmur rippled through the crowd, which drew apart to let a newcomer through.

It was Daniel Ledet, his head and shoulders almost hidden by a huge bundle of pelts that he now dropped to the ground. Straightening, he brushed the dust of travel from his buckskins and reached for the rifle slung across his back. Caroline's heart leapt at the sight of him, but Daniel did not see her. Instead, he was looking at the nut dangling from the string.

"Has he come for the shooting?" asked a man beside her of his companion.

"If he has, he'll find he's come too late, for he's missed the first round."

"Oh, let him try his hand if he wants. After all, it's only sport" was the answer.

This appeared to be the general feeling. The contestants, all in good humor, admitted him to their ranks. Stepping back, they beckoned him up to shoot next. Caroline held her breath as Daniel loaded and aimed; then he squeezed the trigger, and the walnut disappeared. Caroline felt Hannah's hand sneak into hers. Turning to her sister, she saw her smile.

In the end, there were three of them left, Daniel and a farmer and a man from the garrison. The captain of the garrison moved to stand at the stockade. Reaching into his pocket, he drew out another nut, calling for the first of the men to take aim. It was the soldier, who was shooting with a borrowed rifle. All noise died away as he raised his gun, and when he gave the signal the captain threw the nut. The barrel of the rifle followed the path of the nut; the soldier fired, and the crowd held its breath. Not a moment later, the whole nut fell to earth.

A groan passed through the crowd.

"Better luck next time!" someone called, and the soldier shrugged and grinned, returning the rifle to its rightful owner.

The second was a settler. Again the nut was tossed up, and again it was missed.

"What will they do," Hannah wondered, "if they all three miss?"

But they won't, thought Caroline, her eyes on Daniel's face. I know he will hit it, and he knows it, as well, I can tell from how still he is. She watched him raise his rifle, find his sight and sign. For the third time, the captain tossed the nut high into the air. With the rest of the onlookers, Caroline watched it rise until it reached its apex, then turn back to earth again.

Why did he not shoot? Had he given up, or was something amiss? Taking her eyes from the nut, she glanced to where he stood, just as he pulled the trigger and the shot rang out.

"Bull's-eye!" someone shouted. "Hit it right on the mark! Followed it up and down, took his own sweet time!"

"Hurrah!" The cry went up as the captain knelt to retrieve a fragment of the shattered shell. Daniel disappeared in a throng of well-wishers. Without thinking, Caroline took a step in his direction, and heard a malicious chuckle behind her.

"That's it, girl," Thomas said mockingly. "You'd best be quick to claim him, if that's what you intend, or you'll find yourself replaced." He jerked his chin towards the crowd around Daniel, which included women, as well as men. "Learn from experience, eh?"

He moved away then, but Caroline did not move, and Hannah, who had been racking her brain for something comforting to say, shrank before the unspoken rage she saw in her sister's eyes.

After the shooting the tables were brought out from the houses so that dinner could be served and eaten on benches placed in the open air. Everyone had made a point of bringing the best they had, and the bounty of the feast spread on the tables added to the sense of joy, confirming the goodness of the land and its ability to sustain. This thought was reflected by the garrison's chaplain in his grace. He offered up thanksgiving and prayed that the French might sue for peace.

"Do you suppose he means me?" Daniel asked, coming up behind Caroline. She stood beside a table, helping the other women serve. He spoke quietly, so that only she would hear, his warm breath brushing her ear.

"Who would you sue?" she answered, turning to smile at him, glad to have him near her, glad to see him, to hear his voice.

"Your *beau-frère* perhaps—though perhaps on other grounds," he replied, his eyes steady upon hers. He stood there a moment, and then he moved away, to another table where there was still space to sit.

She did not mind that he went. Somehow, with those few words, he had erased the hurt, turning Thomas from a source of torment into a secret they could share. In his words she found confirmation of what she had believed. She knew that he understood that Thomas would continue to torment her if he lingered at her side; nevertheless, he had let her know that she was in his thoughts. She had not seen his eyes turn to her during the contest, but now she realized that he must have seen her there, and Thomas just behind. She felt as if a burden had been lifted from her arms. She realized that she was smiling as she leaned forwards to retrieve an empty platter that would have to be replaced with a full one from the house.

Darkness was falling by the time they had eaten their fill, and, though the older children were still at their games, most of the younger ones were nodding in their mothers' arms. The mothers carried them into the houses to put them down to sleep, while the men lit torches and lanterns until the night was ablaze. Then they pushed aside the benches, and the music and dancing began.

Fifty years before, at the end of the last century, such public celebration would have been prohibited as a sin. Indeed, there were still many in New England who considered dancing the devil's way; virtually every town and city included its fair share of rock-ribbed Puritans. But those who had the spirit to conquer the wilderness were generally more understanding of the importance of amusement. If they weren't when they arrived, they became so soon enough. After the isolation of the long winter and the uncertainty of the war, even the most rigid soul among them was yearning for relief. And among the soldiers the only lack was of partners. The last dancing party had been months before, and feet were tapping eagerly before the music began.

The orchestra consisted of two fiddles and a mouth harp, the musicians standing on a plank table. They played lively galops and more sedate quadrilles. Those who had skill at dancing showed it, and everyone else improvised. Even the children who were old enough to have escaped being sent to bed whirled about like bright tops, bonnets hanging forgotten, curls flying free.

Hannah's condition prevented her from joining in, so she sat on the side with another woman who was pregnant and one who had a new infant. Caroline sat, as well, her hands folded demurely, though a tumult ruled her breast. In her years in New haven, she had attended parties, but it had been no hardship to sit on the side, for her ears had been as deaf to the music as her heart had been to the joy. Then she had wished for nothing but to remain invisible; now she fought a silent war against her own desires.

She wanted to dance with Daniel, to smile and laugh with him, to feel his fingers around hers and to match him step for step. Her soul was torn between the yearning and the icy fear of what would happen if she dared stand up with him—a fear of Thomas's comments, and of herself, as well. Ever since dinner Thomas had been gone, off in one of the houses with some of the men, who were drinking and playing cards. Likely they were gambling, and that would keep him occupied, for Thomas would put nothing before the chance to gain a coin.

She wondered if Daniel knew where Thomas was. Glancing up, she saw him dancing with a girl with light brown hair. The sight stabbed her with a pain that was almost physical. Perhaps he would not ask her, for her own sake. Of course it would be better, and yet she knew she could not survive watching him partner every woman but her.

So absorbed was she in her struggles that she failed to see the soldier approaching until he stood at her side.

"Miss Fielding," he said, bowing. "May I have the pleasure of this dance?"

"Oh!" She drew back, surprised. Her thoughts had been so fixed on Daniel that it had not occurred to her that another man might seek her as his partner. She shook her head automatically, and saw his face fall.

Hannah's hand touched her arm. "Oh, Caroline, do!" she urged her. "After all, the poor men do outnumber the women so. It is almost your patriotic duty."

"Just so!" the soldier said. He was curly haired and freckled, with the eyes of a friendly pup. His eyes asked nothing but that she share in a little harmless fun.

"All right," said Caroline, and his brown eyes shone. Laying her hand in the soldier's, she followed him onto the floor.

She danced a galop with him, breathless from lack of practice, but hardly had the music ceased before the band struck up again and another man stood ready to claim her as his partner. She danced the next five dances without a single break, and if her legs grew tired and her lungs sore for want of breath, her spirit was lighter than it had been in years. All the joy she had denied herself these past years rose up, and with it the carefree youth that had been cut short.

She had never dreamed that she would ever feel so light-hearted again. Perhaps it was unseemly for a woman of her age to act and feel thus, but she saw no disapproval in the eyes of her partners. A night like this was about nothing more than having fun, and finally, after eight years, she was able to take part.

The fifth dance ended. Laughing, she closed her eyes, and when she reopened them it was on Daniel himself.

"May I?" he asked, bowing with a natural grace, and for her answer she gave him her hand. In truth, she could not have spoken had she thought of words to say, for her heart had ceased beating momentarily. Now it raced on ahead, and it was all she could do to keep pace with it.

They faced each other for the opening bow. Daniel held her hand, and held her eyes, as well. He had not wanted another confrontation with MacKenzie, so he had not asked her at first, but he had been conscious of her ever since the music had begun. He had seen the soldier approach her where she sat, and he had ached with longing to be the one at her side, the one at whom she smiled, the one whose hand she held. His eyes were used to the forest, to picking his prey out of the maze of twisting branch and leaf; they had had no trouble tracking her through the patterns of the rounds.

He had watched her through five dances, and he had seen the fire grow; watching her had been like watching a flower bud, then burst into full bloom. In the loveliness of the woman he could imagine the beauty of the girl. He could imagine her as she must have been, dancing at the village fairs, and he could imagine the lord watching, yearning for her. He could almost forgive the man for lying to possess her.

As the dances had passed and MacKenzie had not appeared, at last he could no longer resist the temptation. And he knew, from the smile with which she had greeted him, that she had been waiting, as well.

They were dancing a quadrille, not as it was danced in Paris or even in Montreal, but with the good-natured roughness that was part of frontier life. Daniel did not dance often, but his life was a physical one, and his body was accustomed to following his commands. He doubted that Caroline had danced often in New Haven, yet she followed him through the steps as though she had been born to it. It was a pleasure to see her move away from him and a greater pleasure to see her return, and each time they faced each other her eyes lit anew. Her cheeks were flushed with pleasure, her eyes flashed pure black, and the dress she was wearing reminded him of the sky on a perfect autumn day.

It had not occurred to him that the dance would end. Somehow he had imagined it would go on and on, but the fiddles were giving a final flourish. They faced each other, clapping, both of them smiling. Then he saw her falter. Before he could turn to see why, a voice spoke in his ear.

"You fancy my sister-in-law? Indeed, I understand that she is worth what trouble she may give. Perhaps a little rusty, but that will soon work out."

Thomas made no effort to speak above the noise of the crowd, but Caroline heard his words, and the room blurred before her eyes. Then something moved quickly, and a hand shot out. She heard the grunt of the impact and saw Thomas pitch backwards to the ground. For a moment, Daniel stood looking down at him, and the tension in his body made Caroline think he might strike again. But, when the moment ended, he spun away instead, pushing his way through the crowd that was already gathering.

Without thinking, she followed him, but he was faster, and her eyes were still blurred. She lost him amidst the forest of jostling shoulders and arms; twisting and muttering apologies, she pushed her way through. Then she was past the dancers and the surrounding throng, and she caught sight of him, still striding beyond the last circle of light.

She meant to call out to him to wait, but she had not the breath, so instead she lifted her skirts and began to run. He had reached the wagons now. They stood in a neat row where they had been parked this morning, when everyone had arrived. She saw him pause, listening, and realized he must have heard her running after him. She reached him just as he turned.

His breath came as unevenly as hers, and his eyes glittered in the dark. For a moment, they faced each other, unspeaking. Then she felt something snap, as if a slender filament had been cut within her breast, and in the next instant she was in his arms, her body pressed against his, her lips eager and open beneath his devouring kiss.

Had she had breath left to be stolen, it would have been snatched away by the raw passion of the kiss. Everything she had buried and denied these past eight years rose up to engulf her, and to merge with the hardness and fire that he brought to her. She felt his hands in her hair, then pressed against her back; her own gripped him everywhere, claiming everything at once. They clung to each other as though waiting to be torn apart. What she had known with Edmund had nothing to do with this.

The bright flame of Daniel's anger became the heat of his desire. He pressed her closer, his mind too chaotic for thought, all his senses drowning in the passion of her embrace. He wanted to taste much, much more than her lips; he wanted to taste her soul. He wanted to possess her, to make her part of him, to fit her within him, to feel her in his blood. He wanted to make love to her, and never to have that love end. He pressed her against him and felt her response. She would not deny him. She was ripe for him—he had seen it in her dancing, in the sparkle of her eyes. She had held back too long to hold herself back now.

But even as he thought this he felt a hesitation. She moved in his arms, and he knew that she had been touched by the same thought as he. He could have her this one night, because she was weak, but forever after she would be lost to him, buried and swept away in the darkness of her shame. What he meant to give her she had shared before, while what she really needed he did not possess. He could give her passion, but not a husband's love, and not the home and family she had been denied once.

They tore apart and faced each other, their breath as ragged as before. Behind them, the sounds of voices and music blurred into a haze, the noise of another world. Caroline saw Daniel as if from across an abyss, as clear as moonlight on water, and as impossible to hold. For a long, unspeaking moment, her gaze locked with his; then, with a sob, she turned and fled blindly into the night.

Daniel stood listening to the echo of her steps, his hands empty, and his soul, as well. If he stood here long enough, in time the sun would rise and another day would begin. He knew that it was so, and yet it seemed impossible. It seemed impossible to imagine going on from here. Only Caroline was real—his lips were still throbbing from the pressure of hers, and his hands from the heat of her skin.

How could he live without her when he ached this way, and yet what choice had he? She needed a good husband, not a lover who owned nothing but a long-barreled gun. Could he change for her? Despite the tension of the moment, Daniel had to smile at the image of him trying to survive on a farm. After only hours, already the stockade's walls seemed to press in upon him. He needed the forest, it was his world, his life. He knew that in the open he would find balm for his soul.

And as for Caroline... His heart trembled at the thought of her name. What balm would life offer her? With a sudden, vicious fury, he wished he had killed MacKenzie just now, so that at least he could leave her with a gift she could

use. She did not need a lover, but she needed a friend....
Could he be that for her? Staring at the light beyond whose
rim he stood, Daniel pondered the question as a new dance
began.

Chapter Six

The celebration ended at the break of day, and the families went home, calling out to each other with weary good humor as their wagons creaked across the meadow beyond the fort. Perhaps we will have another celebration after the harvest is in, they called. Perhaps if all is well. As they reached the edge of the forest, they all turned to wave at the soldiers who stood on the battlements and in the open gate. It had been a fine party, except, perhaps, for the Frenchman's striking MacKenzie. And, as to that incident, most seemed to think that MacKenzie had deserved such a blow and more.

Some among them murmured that the Frenchman might be a spy, but others, who had known him for a half-dozen years, scoffed at such an idea. There were merchants in Northfield and over in Albany who would vouch for his character. And who could forget how well he had shot? Yes, they would savor the memory of this party in the weeks to come, and perhaps, if all went well, there would be other parties to come. Perhaps, if they were lucky, the war would not come here after all. Then they would be free to expand their crops and improve their farms. These were good neighbors, and the land was rich. They could go far together, if only the war would stay away. The creaking of the wagons seemed to echo the hope: if only, if only....

But the war paid no heed. Within a week of the party, one of the settlers lay dead, his scalp decorating an Abenaki Indian belt. William Phipps was hoeing corn in his field up the

Great Meadow from the fort when he was attacked by a party of Indians. Two of the Indians dragged Phipps into the woods, while the rest went on. Phipps, who was a big man, managed to knock one of his captors down and to shoot the second with the first one's gun. Though wounded in the encounter, he set off for the fort, intending to spread the alarm and to seek help for his family. But the Indian he had knocked out soon came to again and alerted the rest of the party, who caught up with him before he reached the fort. This time they killed him outright and scalped him where he lay.

Phipps's body was discovered by a group of soldiers out to cut wood for Thomas. They sent a runner back to the fort, and by the time they arrived with the body the garrison had been split into three parts. The first and largest party would remain to guard the fort, while the other two would go out to warn the settlers of the attack and, if possible, catch the Indians who had caused Phipps's death.

The Indians escaped. The patrols found no sign of them, though they must still be near, for why would they come all this way for only one scalp? The high spirits of Louisbourg vanished in the late-summer dust, to be replaced by days of anxiety and nights of fear. Everyone braced for the next attack, but a week passed, and then two, with no sign of the savages. Even so, the pressure was too much for some to bear, and a number of families packed up and headed south. The majority, however, dug in to see what would happen next. They recognized the danger, but they hated to give up after all the work they had put in, with their crops so near to harvest. These fields and houses were their homes. As had the first settlers in Northfield the century before, they determined not to be defeated by fear alone. Perhaps, they said bravely, Phipps's death had been a fluke. Perhaps he had done something to anger the Indians. But anyone who knew Phipps knew this to be unlikely. And, besides, what had the Indians been doing on Phipps's farm?

Hannah panicked at the news. Her lips bloodless, her eyes dilated with fear, she begged Thomas to leave.

"Oh, my poor children," she moaned, rocking herself back and forth, while William bustled the little ones away to bed. "Oh, my poor baby!"

"Hush." Caroline sat with her arm around Hannah, stroking her hair. "You know that the soldiers found no trace of the Indians. Chances are that they're already on their way back to Canada."

"They aren't!" Hannah insisted, shaking her head violently. "They're here, in the forest, watching us even now! Can't you feel their eyes upon us?" she asked, shivering as she looked around. "Perhaps they have been watching us come and go all these last weeks, thinking of how pretty our scalps will look upon their belts."

"Hannah!" exclaimed Caroline, shocked by her sister's morbidity.

"It's true." Hannah clutched at Caroline with ice-cold hands. "And you know as well as I do that scalping is not the worst! You've heard the stories of how they torture their prisoners—how they make them walk through fire and how they murder little babies just because they cry!"

"Hannah!" Caroline cried. "Those are all old stories of things that happened years ago. I know they killed Mr. Phipps, but they didn't torture him. Perhaps they didn't mean to and that's why they ran away."

"They didn't run," moaned Hannah. "I know that they're still here. They mean to kill my babies, and the rest of us, as well!"

"Oh dear." Caroline sighed and stroked her sister's arm. She knew that Hannah was right about Indians' cruelty, but somehow she could not believe that this was the end. She could not imagine deserting the crops standing in the fields; all her country upbringing rebelled against such waste. Her thoughts returned to the celebration at the fort, and she felt again the sense of the power of the community. If the Indians were still here, as Hannah believed, then most likely they were waiting to see what the settlers would do. Perhaps, if they saw that the settlers would not flee, they would give up and go back to Canada. Surely it was at least worth waiting to see.

Hannah shivered at her side. Reaching for a blanket that hung on a peg, Caroline draped it across her shoulders, though the room was warm. She pitied her sister and knew how she was longing to be gone from here. Yet, for all her pity, still she could not add her voice to Hannah's plea. Hannah had a house waiting in New Haven, and a life that she could resume. What did the northland offer that she could not have there, and what did it promise instead? Uncertainty and danger and the hard winter to come... No wonder Hannah was moaning to be gone.

It was different for Caroline. For Caroline, New Haven offered nothing at all, nothing but the bleakness of the past eight years, whereas this new land offered a ray of hope. She had felt joy here, and the resurgence of life, and those things were too precious to be given up quickly. Going to New Haven would mean giving Daniel up, turning her back on him for the rest of her life. That she could not do. Not yet, not so soon.

Ever since the party at the fort, he had dwelled in her thoughts. Even now, glancing at Hannah, she saw his face instead, his eyes dark and glittering, as they had been that night, full of the same pain and longing that battled in her breast. Once she had feared that what had happened with Edmund would happen to her again, but until she had kissed Daniel she had not understood what it was she had to fear. She had allowed Edmund to take his pleasure with her, but what she had found with Daniel went far beyond permission. For all that she had dwelled upon Edmund year after year, she had little memory of his caresses. After the first thrill of danger had passed, his touch had become a burden to be borne on the brighter promise of what was to come.

By contrast, Daniel's touch was a promise fulfilled. Even now, its memory burned like a brand on her soul, wiping away all thought, save of the moment itself. The passion they had shared had been born of both anger and joy, wedded to strong emotions and building upon that strength to explode with frightening power at the meeting of their lips. That night, she had wanted Daniel beyond reason; she was still not sure if he had released her or if she had broken away.

But there was more than that. Her longing for him went beyond the force of that embrace. It went to how he had addressed her as she had served the meal at the fort, and his leave-taking of her the day of the news of Louisbourg. It went to his showing her how to shoot, and to how he had struck Thomas down for insulting her. It went to his compassion, to his friendship and respect—to his caring not just for her beauty, but for her feelings, as well. She ached, not for his caresses, but for his companionship, and in the depth of that aching she saw the breadth of her loneliness. Daniel had already made a place for her in his heart, but she knew that he could not do the same in his life. After what had happened at their last meeting, she knew the danger inherent in their meeting again, and knew Daniel recognized it, as well. Yet, even so, she believed that if she were in danger here Daniel would tell her to go.

And if he did tell her? If Daniel were to come here and order her to leave, would she do as he said? Would she return to New Haven on the strength of his command? The thought lay like lead upon her heart; nor could she find comfort in the fantasy that he might come with her. There was no more place for him in her life than there was for her in his. She knew that if she went south she would never see him again.

She hung suspended in a strange limbo. As much as she longed for Daniel, she feared seeing him, as well. The passion that had sprung up that night at the fort still dwelled within them both; it was a low flame, but it was constant, and it was ready to flare bright at the least provocation. Even now, sitting here, stroking her sister's arm, she saw what would happen if that passion was set free—how quickly it would burn out, leaving behind only disillusion and a new burden of guilt. Would Daniel still want her after he'd had her once? Perhaps for a while, the way Edmund had, or perhaps he would turn away from her in disgust. And how long could she hold back the flood of her own shame? But could she have his companionship in any other terms? That she did not know. So she hovered in limbo, unable to go forwards and unable to retreat. She resisted Hannah, and she waited for Daniel to come.

In the end, Hannah agreed to stay at the farm under two conditions. Firstly, if there was another attack, they would all leave right away, and secondly, in any case, the children would go south as soon as possible. Thomas was too busy to leave his trees, but once the wheat was harvested William would take it to Northfield to be milled. The children would go with him, and he would send them on by stage, as far as New Haven, where they would spend the winter with their grandparents. If spring came with no further problems, then the children would return. And, of course, if the war ended, the children would not go.

In the meantime, the MacKenzie farm joined the rest of the frontier outposts in strengthening the community's defenses. Some of the families whose farms were less secure had taken shelter in the fort, and the men went forth daily to tend their fields. Other families remained in their homes, but the fort sent out soldiers to guard them by day. Most nights two or three men from the garrison slept at the MacKenzie farm, and Hannah slept better for knowing they were there.

August ripened and began to fade. Once again, the leaves of the willows turned to bright yellow and drifted down to the river, which bore them away to the south. The first of the birches had begun to turn, and the red of the sumacs blazed bright against the green. The woods were alive with the scurrying of creatures, who ate both night and day, storing up the nourishment that would see them through the snows. The absence of further attacks in the passing weeks fed the flame of renewed hope. Panic slowly faded, to be replaced by a dreamy calm. The words *if only* crept back into men's thoughts.

They harvested the wheat. William and Jonas and Thomas moved in a line across the field, scythes moving back and forth in a slow, steady rhythm as the golden grass fell away. Hannah's belly was too big now for her to help, but Caroline and Young Tom followed behind the men, gathering up the sheaves. Two of the soldiers stood at the edge of the field, their eyes scanning the forest, their muskets in their hands.

But for the soldiers, they might have been in Surrey again, helping the farmers bring in the crop. Stopping for a drink of water from the bucket Hannah brought, Caroline looked with pride at the cut rows behind. Then, of their own volition, her eyes rose to the trees, searching—as always—for Daniel.

When she saw Caroline looking, Hannah's eyes filled with anxiety, and she turned, as well, to search the shadows of the woods. "Did—did you think there was someone?" she asked, knotting her hands.

"Someone?" Caroline turned quickly, her skin, beneath the sun's flush, coloring with embarrassment. Could Hannah be so observant—and so tactless, as well?

"Indians," said Hannah, glancing at Thomas, for she knew how he hated for her to show disquiet.

"Oh!" Caroline almost laughed with relief. "No, I wasn't looking for Indians."

In her relief, she had forgotten Thomas. He was at her side, awaiting his turn to drink. Since the day of the party he had in the main left her strictly alone, perhaps in deference to Hannah's already overstrained nerves, but certainly also because of his own preoccupation with his wood. Now that the soldiers were busy with their patrols, he had only William and Jonas to help him with the trees. Then there was the added delay of having to harvest the crops—and, too, the constant danger of an Indian attack.

Like everyone else, Thomas was praying that attack would not come, but, despite his assurances to Hannah that they would leave if it did, he had no intention of abandoning his wood. For a distance of thirty miles above and below the farm, his trees lay neatly stacked on the river's banks, awaiting only the time and the means to be hauled downstream. They would bring him enough money to buy additional lands in the north, and to stock the trading post he meant to open here. Thomas had no great love for the woods, but he recognized that so long as England held America in thrall, the possibilities for a merchant's success in the cities were limited. Frontier trading, by contrast, offered great opportunities, because so much of it was carried on outside the law. The war was an inconvenience he meant to outwait. Soon enough, there would be a great deal of money to be made right here, and he meant to lay claim to the lion's share.

Now, at Caroline's laughter, Thomas lowered the dipper and said, "She's looking for no Indians, but for that French lover of hers. Well, you'll not find him here, for he's already served his purpose and gone back up north."

"What purpose?" asked Hannah, frowning at her husband's words.

"Spying, of course, woman! Passing word to the Indians, so they'd know where to strike. Most likely he's got Phipps's scalp hanging from his belt."

Caroline whitened with rage, but before she could answer he had turned back to his work.

Hannah snatched Caroline's hand. "Don't listen to him," she said quickly. "He is only put out about what happened at the fort."

"It's nothing," Caroline replied, tossing her head as she turned back to her work in order to hide from Hannah the misery in her eyes. How was it that Thomas had such an unfailing knack for pointing his arrows at her most vulnerable points? Fully four weeks had passed since the party at the fort, and, for all her faith in Daniel, still he had not come. Could he really have been here just as a spy? Reaching out for the next armful of golden wheat, Caroline wondered if his interest in her had only been as an access to the settlers. And she wondered what she would do if he did not return.

William took the wheat south. The morning of his departure, Hetty woke with a high fever. Caroline suggested that they wait until she was well, but Hannah was afraid that Thomas might change his mind and keep Young Tom and Elizabeth, as well. Besides, it might be two weeks before

Hetty was well enough to go. So Hannah decided to keep Hetty with her. After all, she reasoned, everyone said it was safe.

Tom didn't want to go. "I'll miss everything! And I could help with the shooting if the Indians do come."

"Hush!" Caroline glanced in Hannah's direction. "Anyway, there won't be any Indians."

"If there won't be Indians, why do we have to go? New Haven is boring, and we'll have to go to school."

At that Caroline could not help but smile. "Think of the fun you'll have with William driving down to Northfield—and just think of all the stories you'll have to tell the boys!"

This last mollified Tom, who gave up his complaining and immediately set in to composing a stirring version of the past five months. Thus distracted, he submitted to his mother's embraces and allowed himself to be bundled up to the wagon's seat.

Six soldiers rode with them. They would pick up other wagons as they made their way south. The whole convoy would be guarded to Northfield and back, for if there were indeed Indians, what more tempting plunder could there be than the wheat upon which the settlers were counting to sustain them through the coming months? As they drove off, Hannah closed her eyes and uttered a silent prayer for their safekeeping and for a joyful reunion. Then she turned back to the house, where Hetty was awake and crying out for her.

Two days after William left, the weather turned very hot. A patrol passed in the morning on their way west, and Thomas joined them, taking Jonas, to see about some trees. Caroline, with Hannah's help, began bringing in the corn. Hetty's fever had broken late the night before, and she lay sleeping in the house, listless in the heat.

"How long do you think it will take them?" Hannah asked as they worked. She picked the high ears and Caroline picked the low, as Hannah could not bend. The sun beat down upon them, and upon the soldiers guarding them. Overhead, no clouds stained the pale blue sky.

"A week?" said Caroline, wiping her brow with the back of her arm and leaving a smear of dust. "To come and go, that is. They'll be there tomorrow sometime."

"Yes," said Hannah, also wiping her brow. "You think that they'll be all right?"

"They'll be all right," said Caroline, ignoring the twinge she felt. Perhaps they were in danger, perhaps even now. She wanted to disbelieve it, yet she felt some impending distress in her bones. Or was it only her uneasiness because Daniel did not come? She wished it were cooler, though she knew she should be happy so long as it didn't rain until the corn was in.

Thomas should have stayed to help them with this field, she thought, casting her eye over the motionless stalks. At the pace they were working it, it would take them all week. It would help if the soldiers were working with them, too, but she knew that Hannah would not stand for them to lay down their guns. "They'll be fine," she repeated, wiping her brow again and moving on to the next stalk, with its bulging ears.

She slept badly that night, tossing and turning on the bed she shared with Hannah when Thomas was away. When she slept, she had awful nightmares of fires and screaming for help. Daniel was in the background, she could see him and she struggled towards him, but just before she reached his side he disappeared in the flames and she woke, disoriented and sweating, her heart pounding against her ribs.

The room was stifling. Hannah's body radiated heat like a fire-heated brick. Upstairs in her own room it might be just as hot, but at least there was a window through which to see the stars. Rising, she slipped on her dress, buttoning it as she passed into the hall from which the stairs rose. Across the way, in the kitchen, two of the soldiers slept. Another slept leaning back against the door, his head nodding on his chest, his musket across his lap.

Caroline turned away from him, took one step towards the stairs and stopped. Now that she was standing, she didn't feel tired at all, and she had no inclination to spend the next hours in her own bed, struggling against her nightmares and waiting for dawn to come. As a child, when she couldn't sleep, she'd gone outside into the yard, or even walked in the meadows, meadows all silvery from the moon. What a blessed relief it would be to walk in the meadow now, away from the soldiers' snoring and the closeness of the house.

Crossing to the mantel, where the guns were hung, she took down the light rifle and a powder horn and a bullet pouch. Then she moved silently to the door.

The soldier was leaning against it. She had to rouse him in order to leave.

"What's wrong? What's the matter?" he muttered, springing up at the sight of her holding the gun. He was young, hardly into manhood, and he blinked like a tired child.

"Shh! There is nothing!" She laid her hand over his mouth. "It's only that I'm not tired and thought that I would step out."

"Oh, no. I can't let you. It is too dangerous."

"I won't go far, and besides, I've got a gun. If I see anything, I'll come back, or I'll fire off a shot. And no one has seen an Indian in almost two months."

In the end, he let her go, unable to dissuade her and unwilling to wake the house. He watched as she crossed the yard. Then she heard the creaking of the door as he shut it after her, and despite her relief at being out of doors she could not help but shudder at the sound of the bolt.

It was a lovely night, as soft and warm and balmy as Midsummer Eve. The sky was clear, but there was no moon to light the fields, and there was a ghostly stillness about them that made her shiver again. Grasping the rifle tightly, she made her way towards the riverbank, stopping beneath a willow whose branches reached almost to the ground.

She sank down on the soft earth, which was still warm from the heat of the day, breathing in the smell of the river and of the cool earth of the bank. The sound of the water lapping soothed her restlessness; she leaned back against the rough trunk and, sighing, closed her eyes. A light breeze stirred the branches, setting the leaves to rustling and touching her skin with its warm breath. Sighing again, she smiled, but in truth she was already asleep.

The wind was rising now, swaying the branches. It lifted them from the ground, and their soft leaves trailed across her face and arms. She murmured in pleasure, turning her cheek into their caress. Then she heard a low voice whispering her name.

"Caroline."

It was Daniel, kneeling at her side. It was his hands, and not the willow, that were stroking her skin. Nestling closer, she felt him sink down and slide his arms around her, drawing her closer to him. Her eyes still closed, she felt his lips upon hers, not harsh, as they had been that night at the fort, but as soft as his caressing hands. She was as willing as he. They traded kiss for kiss, tasting and touching, while his hands ran up her arms and under the sleeves of her dress. Then there was no dress, and his hands were on her skin, running the length of her body, which rippled beneath his touch.

Was it wrong? she wondered dreamily. Ought she to stop him now? But his touch held a drugging wonder that left her unable to move, except to stretch and purr like a cat beneath his roving hands. But something was nagging at her, that twinge she had felt before. She was afraid of the Indians—but why should she be, now that Daniel had come? Now that he was here, she could ask him if she was really safe. Opening her eyes, she found herself looking into Edmund's face.

She sat bolt upright, her heart hammering. She was alone in the grayness, with yellow leaves all about her, and something was upon her lap—Good Lord, it was a gun! She wet her lips, blinking, and slowly she remembered where she was. She had sat down under the willow, and she must have fallen asleep. And then she must have dreamed.

Her heart quieted, but the dream stayed with her, and so did her strange disquiet. Rising, she climbed down to the river to bathe her face. She wondered why she shivered when the water touched her skin, for it was not especially cold, and the air was warm. Shaking herself, she climbed back up and set out across the wheat field in the direction of the house.

Then, suddenly, she stopped. Something was wrong, she sensed it in her every pore, though it took her another moment to realize what it was: a pillar of dark smoke coming from the direction of the house, and the smell of wood burning, suspended in the still air. Caroline began to run, holding the gun in two hands, her skirts whipping about her legs. The wheat stubble cut into her bare feet, but she did not notice it, nor the fact that for the first minute she did not breathe at all.

It had seemed, from where she was, that it was the house that was burning, but as she came nearer she saw that it was the barn. That gave her a moment's relief that ended abruptly when she came around the side of the house and into the front yard and saw the front door open and the body on the ground.

"Hannah!" she cried—or didn't cry, for she had no voice, only a little squeaking sound that came out in a wheeze. But even as she sank to her knees she saw that it was not Hannah, but rather one of the soldiers, who lay in a pool of blood. She knew that he was dead even before she touched his face and stared, her eyes wide with horror, at the bloody mass of his head where his scalp had been cut away. She tried to say something, gagged, then turned away, rising to run towards the open door of the house.

Here she found the second corpse, the body of the soldier who had slept against the door. He lay with his arms outflung, his blood a spreading dark stain on the rough wooden floor. She did not bother to kneel beside him, but rather stepped past him and into the house. She stopped for a moment when she saw the wreckage that greeted her, everything upended, cast upon the floor—all of Hannah's linen, the pots, the crockery. The clock was dashed forward, its cabinet smashed and gaping wide. She gagged at the sight of the cabinet as she had at the first man's missing scalp and, hardly knowing it, vomited on the floor. Pressing her apron to her mouth, she moved across the hall.

Hannah and Hetty were not there; nor was the third soldier. It took her some time to be sure that they were not, for she saw images of their bodies lying in every room, shattered and running with blood. But their beds were empty, and they were neither downstairs nor up. Looking down from her room, she saw the flames leaping through the roof of the barn, yellow and orange and red. Like the leaves, she thought distractedly. Like the changing leaves. It was an easier concept to grasp than this reality.

She tottered downstairs on shaking legs. At the foot of the steps, she paused, uncertain what to do. As she stood there, the body at the door stirred.

"Water!" it croaked. "Water, for God's sake!"

Her hand was shaking so badly, she spilled half the dipper on the floor, but she managed to raise him so that he could drink. He gagged on the water as she had gagged before, and once again she felt her gorge rising in her throat. But she managed to swallow as she laid his head in her lap. His eyelids fluttered; then his eyes opened into hers, unfocused with the approach of death.

"Indians! Dozen or so of them. You can catch them if you hurry—can't have gotten far." Coughing, he closed his eyes, and Caroline realized that he mistook her for one of the men from the fort.

"My sister," she said, bending over him. "Mrs. MacKenzie—what did they do to her?"

At first, she thought that he did not mean to reply, but after a moment he croaked, "Took her—her and the baby both. Tried to stop them, but they knocked me down. Tell the captain to send a patrol right away. Tell the captain—" He stopped then, and with a sigh he died in her arms.

"Oh God!" Caroline stared down at him. Blood was already staining her dress. When she raised his head to move it, she felt it warm and wet on her hands and thought that she would faint, but the smell of smoke brought her to her senses again. She remembered that the barn was burning, and wondered if the house would catch.

Standing, she looked about her, wondering what to save. The cooking utensils? The chairs Hannah had brought north? The man lying at her feet? Then her eyes fell upon a chunk of bread lying on the floor, where someone had dropped it. No matter what happened, she would need food to eat. Moving towards the kitchen like a sleepwalker, she began to save what she could, before the fire spread and the house went up in flames.

She had cleaned out the kitchen and finished with the chairs and was bringing out the biggest quilt when Thomas rode into the yard. By then, the barn was blazing and the roof of the house had caught. Dawn had come and passed, the heat of the sun adding to the heat of the fire so that her dress was plastered to her body and her face was filthy with soot. Thomas pulled up the gray mare and paused, staring down at her, standing before the pile of his possessions.

Caroline opened her mouth, intending to explain, but words would not come. In the end, she gestured, saying only "Indians."

"I know." Thomas dismounted. "We met one of the men coming through the woods. He told us everything. He wasn't sure about what had happened to you."

"I was at the river. I fell asleep down there. When I woke up, the barn was on fire and they were already gone. What happened to Jonas?" she asked, looking around.

"He went on to the fort. To bring the soldier's body and to sound the alarm."

"Body?" she asked blankly. "But I thought you said—"

"They'd scalped him and left him for dead. He managed to save his horse, though they took the other two. He must have been heading for the fort, but he didn't make it there. We found him lying on the ground, his horse standing nearby. He only lived long enough to tell us what he knew."

Caroline shuddered at the thought of his death. Then her eyes opened wide and, seizing Thomas by the hand, she said, "We must go after them!"

"We?" Thomas looked at her in surprise. "The two of us together against two dozen savages?"

"There are only a dozen of them," she said, recalling what the soldier had said. "They can't have gone very far—We can catch them if we hurry."

"And what do you propose we do after we've caught up?"

"Rescue Hannah and Hetty! We've got to try!" she said, increasingly aware of how hysterical she sounded. "We can't stand here and let them be taken off! Who knows what is happening to them right now?"

"The soldiers will go after them," said Thomas, moving past her now.

Caroline turned to follow, pleading with him as she went. "Then the soldiers will join us, but we will have the trail. You know what everyone says about tracking Indians—if you let them get ahead of you, you'll never catch up. We really have to go!"

But Thomas was not listening. He was walking faster now, striding across the wheat field towards the river's edge, an expression of deep anger growing in his eyes. Confused, Caroline turned to the river now, and then she saw what Thomas must have seen before. There, drifting in midstream, were a half dozen of his logs, like a school of giant salmon making their way towards the sea.

Thomas uttered a curse. "Those red bastards must have set them loose. If nobody stops them before they reach Turner's Falls, they'll break up on the rocks—unless someone sees them and claims them as his own," he added, spitting on the ground.

"Trees!" she cried, in her disbelief forgetting her fear and weariness. "You're thinking about your trees when Hannah and Hetty are gone?"

She stood, rigid and incredulous, her eyes burning into him. Thomas's gaze left the river and returned to her; for a moment he stared, as if he were considering a reply. Then, with a grunt, he turned away and headed towards the house.

"Where are you going?" she called out.

"To get the horse," he said. "There's a ferry down below the fort. If I get there soon enough, I can stop them there."

"You can't!" She grabbed his arm, torn between her hatred and her desperation. "You have to think of Hannah! You have to think of her! If you won't go with me, I'll follow her alone!"

They had reached the yard again. The mare stood waiting where Thomas had tied her to the fence. The barn was beyond saving, and the house soon would be, too. For a moment, Thomas stood gazing up at them. Then, turning to Caroline, he raised his shoulders in a shrug.

"Do what you like," he muttered. "It's your life, after all. I'll send soldiers from the fort." Then, without another word, he swung into the saddle and turned his horse down the meadow in the direction of the fort.

Caroline watched him go, half of her wanting to curse him, the other to call out for him to stay. Somehow, for all these past years, for all that she had hated him, she had not thought that Thomas MacKenzie would rather save his money than his own flesh and blood. Suddenly, all her weariness dropped away, and her heart filled with a blazing hate. When she had emptied the house out she had set her gun aside, and it leaned nearby against the fence. Moving to it quickly, she raised it to her eye, but by now he was too far off for her to hope to hit him.

She would have if she had been able. She would gladly have killed him in cold blood, and even then his death would not have paid back the misery he had caused. And where was Daniel? she thought irrelevantly. Why had he not come? She had trusted him to save her, and he had let her down.

"Damn you!" she screamed. "Damn the lot of you! If you won't save Hannah, then I'll save her myself. Before God, I will!"

She looked around the yard. There was the food she had salvaged, and a blanket and a sack, and her stout winter shoes, which would protect her feet. She gathered them together and tied them in a pack. Swinging it onto her shoulder, she added the gun, then turned to look at the house. It would be gone by nightfall, nothing but a smoldering heap, and probably the things she had pulled out would burn in the end, as well—and all the standing corn. The thought of the corn drained away some of her fortifying rage. Turning away quickly, before more of it could dissipate, she turned her face north. Of course it was madness, but she didn't care; she'd rather die trying than have to stay here. Probably the soldiers from the fort would overtake her before night—

"Damn all men!" she cried, readjusting the weight of the pack as she moved towards the river and the trail leading north.

Chapter Seven

The gun was heavy. She had not noticed that yesterday, had not noticed very much of anything. Propelled by her anger and numbed by her shock, she had hardly noticed the distance that she had walked, and she had stopped only when darkness had hidden the trail from view. She had slept in a clearing, cushioned by soft grass, with hardly a thought for her own safety, nor for her survival. She had fallen asleep from exhaustion as soon as her cheek had touched the ground, and had awakened in the gray dawn, stiff and uncertain until she had remembered Thomas and his outrageous greed. Then a new wave of anger had set her on her feet and propelled her forward anew.

But the wave had not lasted long. Her legs were sore from the distance she had traveled the day before, and her feet were already blistered from the chafing of her shoes. She took them off and added them to her provisions; it served only to increase her awareness of how heavy her bundle was. And then there was the gun. She recalled that Daniel wore his strapped to his back, but hers had no strap. Her eyes on the trail, she began to inventory her stock, testing each possession for its suitability for conversion to a strap. But, even as she busied with this task, her mind was aware of the thought from which she was trying to hide. That thought concerned Daniel, and his role in this.

She could not help herself. Again she remembered Thomas naming him a spy, and saying that she would never see him again. It's not true, Hannah had said, but where was

Hannah now? Captive of the very Indians she, Caroline, had said were not to be feared, trusting in Daniel to save them all from harm.

No, she could not believe it of him. She could not believe that Daniel could do such a thing. Perhaps he had lied about his loyalty to the French, but she could not believe that he could bring about such a thing. Once again the image of the dead soldiers rose in her mind, and she had to push them away before she became ill again.

And, even if Daniel was somehow responsible, still it was she who was to blame for Hannah's captivity. Had she joined Hannah in insisting they return to New Haven, perhaps Thomas would have been swayed.... At least she might have gotten Hannah safely to the fort. But instead she had opposed Hannah's all-too-logical fear because she had been obsessed with her daydreams of Daniel Ledet. If she died following Hannah, she would only be getting what she deserved.

But she must not die. Somehow she must find Hannah, and somehow set her free. For, whatever she felt now, she had to consider how much worse Hannah must feel. Why, even now they might have her tied to a stake and be torturing her with fire. Perhaps they were torturing Hetty, instead. All the old, horrible stories came flooding back, stories of how the Indians killed their captives by pulling them apart slowly, bit by bit, so that the agony of dying lasted days, even weeks. Of the priest whose hand they had cut off, then forced him to eat. Of the helpless babies— That was the very worst.

"Oh, Hetty!" Caroline murmured. "Oh, Hannah!" she moaned. And Hannah was so pregnant. How would she survive?

The sun beat down on her. The light layer of fog that had hung over the river at dawn had long since burned away, and, although it was not yet midmorning, the day was blazing-hot. The heat shimmered on the water, shimmered on the grass. She longed for the cool of the water, longed for the cool of the woods, but she could not afford to take the time for such luxuries. If she hoped to catch up with Hannah, she could not stop to rest.

Yesterday she had pressed on with no real plan or goal in mind, but today, as her mind cleared, she considered both. In leaving the farm, she had naturally struck out to the north, following the path that led along the river. For a while, she had been able to see the prints of the soldiers' horses, which they had taken along with them. But, even after the prints had disappeared, still she had continued. She knew that the Indians were good at hiding their trails, and she had lived in the northland long enough to have at least a rudimentary knowledge of what lay to the north. She knew that the major trail to Canada lay along the Connecticut River, with minor ones branching off along the rivers running from the west. Thus, she was fairly certain that the Indians would follow the Connecticut until they reached the first of the lesser streams that fed it. She knew, as well, that she must reach them before they did, or she would have no way of knowing whether they had continued north or turned off to the west. And, if they had crossed the tributary, how would she cross it herself?

And where were the soldiers from the fort? When she had set out yesterday, she had expected them to overtake her before nightfall. But she had walked for hours yesterday, and today, as well, and as yet the soldiers had not caught up to her. This was strange, since she was walking, and she knew they would come by horse, at least to the southern bank of the first stream. Once again, she considered the possibility that for some reason they would not come, but she could not accept it—she would not let herself. The thought was too overwhelming, vast as the wilderness that spread away from her in every direction. If she paused, she could see how very small she was, and how very insignificant in the greater scheme of life. But she must not pause. She must keep on going and trust in the soldiers to come.

Shifting her bundle from shoulder to shoulder, she forced her weary legs ahead, trying to take comfort from the river flowing so steadfastly at her side. A snatch of Scripture came to her now.

"By the rivers of Babylon, there we sat down, yea, we wept, when we remembered Zion."

She recalled the text. It was about the harshness of captivity, and the loneliness, as well. It was about homesickness. It brought to her the evening she had stood on this river's bank, thinking about Surrey and longing for the past. Was this, then, her punishment for her selfishness? Had she turned away from God, and He away from her? But even if God would not lift His hand for her, would He not take pity on Hannah, who had done no wrong?

"Dear Father," she murmured through sun-parched lips, "I ask nothing for myself, but only help me to lead Hannah and the child back to safety."

Could God have been listening? Could He have heard her prayer? She had prayed before without answer, yet how else to explain that in the very next instant she saw the handkerchief?

She could easily have missed it. Certainly, she was paying small heed to her surroundings, and it was hardly obvious. But, even in her discomfort, still her eye was drawn to the lady slippers blooming beside the trail. She loved those little flowers, so frail and delicate, and could not but wonder how beauty could continue to grow when there was so much cruelty and suffering in the world. Perhaps the beauty of flowers was meant as a message of hope, she thought, her eye lingering on the blooms, and just at the last moment she saw the fragment of white.

Even so, she almost passed it by, for she hated to break her momentum. She knew she ought to stop to see what the fragment was, but she was afraid that, if she stopped, her tired body would refuse to move again. For a moment, her mind debated and her legs continued to move, and she was past the flowers before she stopped and turned. Setting her bundle on the ground, she reached out with her hand—and as soon as she touched the fabric she knew what it was.

Hannah's handkerchief. She uncrumpled it, heedless of the hot sun, of the sweat snaking down her back, of the flies that gathered, attracted by the scent. Bending, she smoothed the linen against her dirty, wrinkled skirt, then held it up again. What was that dark stain on one corner? Blood! Her weary heart froze. But there was little of it. The wound it had stanched could not have been more than a scratch.

Hannah's handkerchief, and she had almost passed it by—would surely have missed it, but for the glorious blooms! Then, abruptly, a thought came to her. What if Hannah had not dropped the handkerchief by accident? What if she had left it here by intent, hoping that someone's eye would be caught by the flowers, and then by the handkerchief. Her heart beating faster, Caroline let her eyes survey the surroundings, passing from the meadow to a stand of birch some twenty feet away. Had the grass been trampled, or was it her imagination? Retrieving her bundle, she made her way towards the trees and discovered, in their center, the remains of a recent camp. This, then, must be the place where Hannah had passed the night.

A wave of elation swept up and over her. She was on the right trail—and not only that, she had found a sign! The wilderness might be vast, but she was not without wits—and Hannah, too, was working towards her own rescue. Perhaps Hannah had feared that whoever might come after her would not find the camp, and therefore had left her handkerchief on the trail. Then she must still be alive and hopeful of rescue!

But, even as Caroline's heart drew strength from the revelation, her weary shoulders slumped as she realized how far behind she must be. If they had reached here the first night, where must they be by now? But she could not dwell on that. She must look on the bright side, must dwell on the thought that she had found a sign from Hannah and that she was on the right trail. She had asked for God's guidance, and He had shown her a sign. As long as she kept going, somehow she would succeed.

The handkerchief carried her through the worst heat of the day. When she felt her spirits flagging, when her feet ached unbearably, she took it out and held it and found renewed strength. She ate some bread and salt pork, chewing as she walked, for she feared that if she sat down she would not get up. At some point, the trail left the meadow to enter the woods, offering sweet relief from the burning sun. The shade restored her spirits and raised her hopes further. Buoyed by her success in tracking the Indians, she set aside the problem of Hannah's rescue. Cross one bridge at a time, she thought to herself—and the thought was ironic, for it was then that she came to the stream.

It was more a river, really. In the spring, when the winter snow melted, it would reach twenty yards across. Now it was close to that, and fairly deep, as well. From the bank on which she was standing, she could not see bottom farther out. Of course, that could be the result of the lack of sun. The afternoon was waning, and the stream was in the shade. Perhaps, once she reached the midpoint, she would find it not so deep.

Caution dictated that she test the waters unburdened, for she could afford to lose neither gun nor food. So, laying down her burden at the edge of the bank, she hitched her skirts above her knees and stepped into the flow.

Ah, but it felt good! Cool and clean and refreshing... How wonderful it would be to strip off her hot clothes and enjoy a leisurely bath. Leaning over, she splashed her face and neck, shivering as the rivulets ran down her skin, softening the stiffness of her sweat-starched clothes. She splashed her face again, and her arms, one by one, feeling the weariness wash away in the first moment. She saw a flash of silver as a school of trout flicked past, felt her mouth water at the thought of how good fresh trout would taste. But she had no fishing line, and no time to prepare a meal. Straightening with a sigh, she moved out into the stream.

It was very deep. She waded out until the water was at midthigh and still had a good ways to go. Clearly, at this point, she would have to swim, which she thought she could manage, but for the pack and gun. As much as she hated to waste time in a search, she would have to search upstream for a suitable ford. Wading back to the bank, she retrieved her gun and her bundle, then turned her steps westward, along the shaded bank.

She had gone a half mile when she came to a long, flat boulder rising in the stream's midpoint. A tree had fallen from the other bank, and the tip of its trunk just touched the boulder's far side. If she could reach that boulder, she could use the tree trunk as an anchor the rest of the way.

If she could reach the boulder. Once again, she probed the near shore; the stream was no less deep, but there were rocks underneath that allowed her to reach the boulder with shoulders and waist still dry. She waded back to retrieve her things from the bank.

It was more difficult loaded down, for the rocks were slippery, and the current tugged at her skirts. She had tied her bundle around her neck, but the gun she had to carry as she made her way. Once she almost fell, and, though she regained her balance, the bundle had gotten wet, and the weight of the water increased her burden. But at least the gun was dry. Only three steps farther and she would be safe. Only two steps now—

And then disaster struck. Her right foot slipped beneath her. Though she fought with all her power to keep herself erect, the current was against her, and so she went down, choking and thrashing, pulled down by the bundle's weight. She knew that she could not afford to lose what the pack contained, but on the other hand she knew that she would drown beneath its weight, which was tugging her to the bottom with a relentless drag. And to untie the knot she had to release the gun. For a moment, she struggled, refusing to let go, but already her lungs were bursting from the lack of air. Well, she thought to herself, opening her hand, perhaps if I am quick I can catch it downstream.

She was anything but quick. On the other hand, she managed to hold on to the blanket, though she lost all of its contents. Bedraggled and water-soaked, she clawed her way onto the rock, hoping that it might give her a clearer view of the bottom, but, though she strained her eyes in every direction, she could see no gun. Again she lowered herself into the water, exploring the bottom, using her toes to probe, but to no avail.

What should she do? What chance had she in the forest
with neither gun nor supplies—and yet what good did it do
to remain here? The sun was setting, the shadows were
deepening. She had already wasted precious time trying to
ford the stream. If she stayed much longer, she might never
find the trail. If it came to starving, she could find nuts and
berries to eat. And as for the gun—

The gun. Her shoulders slumped, she thought again of
Daniel, saw in a flash the late May afternoon when he had
taught her how to shoot. She felt the warmth of his body,
the strength of his arms around her—it all came so clearly
that for a moment she was there, leaning back against him,
sheltered and secure. But then the moment ended and she
was in the stream, her skirts swirling about her, her feet
benumbed by the cold. Slowly and with an effort, she
groped her way about the rock and, with the tree trunk for
guidance, to the opposite shore.

Stooping, she wrung out her skirts and the blanket. Then,
straightening, she stood, gazing back at the darkening flow.
She could gain nothing by lingering here, but, by the same
token, it was difficult to leave. Working her hand into her
pocket, she felt a sodden mass. For what it might be worth,
she still had the handkerchief. With weary persistence, she
turned to the east and made her way back along the bank to
where the trail resumed. She traveled into darkness, until her
strength gave out. Then she sank down at trailside, seeking
oblivion in sleep.

A light rain had been falling since before dawn. It had
penetrated her clothes, down to her very skin. The heat wave
had finally broken, and the rain was cool. Pressing closer to
the tree trunk, Caroline drew the blanket close, but it was as
wet as her body and offered little warmth. It was morning,
light enough to go on, and likely Hannah's party was already traveling. She ought to rise, she knew, but instead she
stayed huddled where she was.

The tree was a yellow pine, whose branches filtered the
gray sky overhead. Just the sort of tree Thomas would have
claimed, she thought, but felt no responding flicker in her

breast. Even the thought of Thomas could not warm her chilled bones. That, more than anything else could have, told her how low she was.

She had to drag herself up, to force her body to move. She would never find Hannah sunk here beneath this tree. But, her beaten spirit responded, would she find her at all? She had already fallen at least a day behind, and when she had been at her strongest she could not keep up. Therefore, exhausted and footsore, how would she make up time? How would she ever catch them before they turned off the trail?

Perhaps they had already. Perhaps they had chosen to follow the stream. Yesterday she had not considered the idea, for the stream was too small to climb to the watershed that divided the two sides of the great mountains that marched towards Canada. But what, she now considered, if the stream led to a river that in turn led north? Perhaps she was already too late. Perhaps she had lost them for good. What would become of Hannah? What would become of her?

And then, because she was low, the other thought came as well. What did she mean to do if she did catch up? Had she ever really intended to rescue Hannah? Perhaps she had, with her gun. But now, unarmed and bedraggled, the idea seemed ludicrous. More likely she would only end up being captured, too. Well, she reflected, at least then Hannah would not be alone, and she would be able to offer the comfort of companionship.

What was the alternative? Turning back at this point? But what would be waiting for her? The smoldering ruins of the house, and Thomas and his trees? Returning to New Haven to tell Tom and Elizabeth that she had followed Hannah and then given up? Spend the rest of her years blaming herself for Hannah's fate? No, it would be better to perish here in the wilderness.

An owl hooted somewhere above. The mournfulness of the sound sent fear shuddering through her. What if she *did* perish here? What if she missed Hannah's trail and blundered into the woods to lose herself in the wilderness and slowly starve to death? What if she met death at the jaws of

a wild animal? Closing her eyes, she heard the echoing of
her own shrieks. The panic she had known so briefly yesterday swooped back upon her now, and she let it come,
feeling the forest looming, hostile and threatening. Surely
she would die here, one way or another.

The owl hooted again, its call disappearing amidst the
steady drip of rain from leaf to leaf above. Opening her eyes
with an effort, Caroline watched the mist rise from the
ground, swirling about the tree trunks like the smoke plumes
of a witch's fire. One thing was certain: she would die here
where she sat if she did not force herself up and on her way.
Drawing her legs beneath her, she made herself stand up,
though every muscle, every joint, every inch of her, protested.

The tree in whose scant comfort she had huddled for the
night was some twenty-five feet off the main trail. Now she
picked her way back through the forest on bruised and half-
numbed feet, her clothes plastered to her body, her hair
plastered to her face, dragging the weight of the blanket
along after her. Brush reached out with thorny fingers to
catch her sodden skirts, pulling her this way and that. She
pulled back weakly, striking her already bruised shin on a
rock. Pain seared up through her, bringing tears to her eyes.
Sniffing them back, she plunged forward and promptly
tripped over a root, landing sprawled face down on the forest floor.

Damp leaves clung to her cheek as she raised her head.
When she wiped them away with her hand, she left a smear
of mud. She let her head fall back, her right cheek resting in
the wet and dirt. What was the point in trying? She would
only fail. What was the point in getting up, only to fall
again? What comfort could she bring Hannah when she
could not care for herself? Everything was her fault, everything was her doing. She was lying there, too heartsore even
for tears, when she heard something rustle the leaves on the
trail.

Danger! Fear propelled her nerveless body, pulling her up.
She knelt, crouched in the underbrush, her eyes strained
towards the trail. *Indians* was her first thought, but then,

with a soaring hope, she thought of the soldiers coming
north from the fort. Bent over and listening to the thundering of her heart, she wondered if she had perhaps been mistaken about the noise, for she saw nothing, heard not a
single sound.

The silence made things worse; she felt the skin tingling
on the back of her neck, and saw in her mind's eye the dead
soldiers. Dear God, she prayed, if they kill me, please let it
be quick. She dug her nails into her palms and nausea rippled through her stomach. She was dreaming, she must be,
life could not hold such terror. She would open her eyes and
see that she was at home in bed.

"Caroline." A hand touched her arm. Oh, yes, she'd been
dreaming, and Hannah was waking her.

"Caroline?" But the voice was too deep for Hannah's.
She thought of Thomas, of William—and then she knew
who it was. Her eyes flew open and, raising her head, she
saw him kneeling in the leaves, the fringe of his tunic stirring as he bent to her. And in his eyes was the expression she
had dreamed of all these weeks.

"Caroline?" he repeated, and she drew a breath.

"Oh, Daniel!" she heard herself sob, and then she was in
his arms.

Where did the tears spring from? Her mind was exhausted, her body was spent, but still the tears flowed and
the racking sobs welled up, and it was as if they would never
stop. He held her and stroked her, murmuring in her ear,
sounds that had no meaning, words in a foreign tongue. She
wanted him to hold her and never let her go. Perhaps, if he
held her tight enough, it would all disappear, the dead men
and the fire and Hannah being gone. Perhaps he could
smooth away the last days as he smoothed the tangles of her
hair back from her dirty face. Since she had been a child, no
one had soothed her this way, and she would have given
anything for it to never end.

Again he spoke her name, gently, but now with firmness
in his tone. His fingers were firm, as well, straightening her
shoulders so that she was facing him. "Caroline. Caroline,

you must calm yourself. Try to take a deep breath. There, that's a good girl."

Reluctantly she obeyed, and, as his warmth deserted her, she felt the sodden damp of her clothes, and once again the weariness stole back into her bones.

"The Indians came," she said, allowing him to wipe her face with the edge of her apron, which could not have been much cleaner than her skin. "They killed two of the soldiers—three, in the end—and they took Hannah and little Hetty with them. Thomas—" She stopped then, too weary to endure the wrenching anger that she knew the memory would bring.

In any case, he spared her. "I know," he said briefly.

"You know!" She stared at him, but he paid her no heed. He pushed back her damp hair, tucking it behind her ears so that he could clean the worst of the dirt from her face with the hem of her apron. She watched, but he paid no heed, completely absorbed in his task, his forehead wrinkled, his lips pursed in concentration. Beneath his ministrations, some of the numbness abated, and the tightness began to unwind.

"Thomas said it was your doing," she said, and his fingers stopped, though his eyes remained upon her cheek.

"What was?"

"Everything. Even the death of William Phipps."

His features were unmoving, but the stillness was artificial. "And did you believe him?" he asked.

"I didn't know what to believe. At first I knew he was lying, but then I didn't know. I blamed myself for believing that you would warn us if we should leave."

"You believed—" he began, looking up, but she did not hear, her mind once again returning to the scene at the burning farm.

"It was terrible," she said. "Horrible. Horrible. They had all just been living, and then they were dead. The barn was already burning, and then the house caught, as well, and I couldn't save everything. And I was so scared for Hannah, and Thomas would not help."

Her eyes looking back on the terror, she missed the change in his face. The stillness dissipated, and his features relaxed. Shaking his head, he touched her cheek with his forefinger. "You need no more challenge. It was thought-less of me to ask. This is scarcely the time for playing guessing games. I had nothing whatsoever to do with the two raids. I was in the Iroquois country when William Phipps was killed. I did not hear about it until several weeks afterwards, when family business called me to Montreal. Then I learned that there would be more raids. I feared for your safety, and came as soon as I could get away—but I came too late. I reached Fort Dummer yesterday morning. I have come right from there."

"The fort!" She sat up straighter. "Then you have brought soldiers with you!" she said, looking about her now, as if to find them hidden in and among the trees. But the trees held nothing but a measure of the gray morning light. Her eyes returned to Daniel, and she saw him shake his head.

"No, no soldiers," he said. "Most of the men were ea-ger, but the captain held them back. It was his opinion that if there were to be more attacks the bulk of the force would be needed to defend the settlements. He was afraid of being drawn away and into an ambush. He has sent for reinforce-ments from the south, and he promises to send a party in pursuit of you and your sister as soon as they arrive."

"But that could take days!" she cried, hardly able to be-lieve her ears. "By then the Indians will be long gone! Doesn't he realize?"

"Perhaps." Daniel shrugged, relinquishing her apron and sitting back on his heels. "It may be of some consolation to you to hear that the captain was equally deaf to your brother-in-law's demand for a party to save his wood. Nor were the soldiers sympathetic to his cause, being of the opinion that he should have tracked his wife. The last I saw of him, he was headed downstream with his man."

"I hope he drowns," she said. "It would only be just."

"Life is not just."

"No, it's not." Her eyes came up to meet his. "And what did the captain have to say about me?"

For the first time, Daniel paused, and at the flicker in his eyes Caroline's brow drew down.

"You have held something back."

"I had considered it," he said, wondering if he had done so for her sake or his own. "There was some confusion about your whereabouts. MacKenzie's man said that the soldier seemed to think you were safe, but when MacKenzie came later he said they had taken you, as well. I suppose he didn't want to appear too much of a cad for having let you go off alone."

Caroline shook her head. "Thomas wouldn't give a damn of how he appeared. Likely he was worried that the thought of a woman wandering about on her own might send the men off to rescue me, at least. And he hates me. Then," she asked, as the thought came into her mind, "how did you know the truth? Or did you—?"

"No, I knew," he said. "I didn't trust MacKenzie, so I put the question to him again. In private," he added, "and with some persuasion." Closing his eyes, he remembered the killing rage that had washed over him, remembered how his fingers had tightened about MacKenzie's neck until MacKenzie's voice had been nothing but a thin gurgle. He would have killed him then and there if Jonas hadn't pulled him off—and even then he might have done it, had he not realized that if he killed MacKenzie they might keep him at the fort and Caroline would be left on her own in the woods. Turning his head, he spat on the ground, as if the very thought of Thomas left a bad taste in his mouth.

Caroline watched, knowing just what he felt. "I believed he loved her," she said. "Despite how I felt about him, I believed that he did love her. But when he had to choose between her and money he chose the money. If I had known how he felt, I would never have let her come. I would have kept her in New Haven. I would have kept her safe. It is my fault that she came here. It is all my fault."

"No, Caroline." Daniel took her hand, but it lay slack within his, and he saw her shake her head, refusing his comforting words. Then, in the next moment, her fingers returned his grip, and her eyes, coming up, lit with new purpose.

"But you are here!" she said. "You are here, and, together, surely we can save her."

"Together?" he repeated.

She nodded vigorously, ignoring the doubt in his tone. "Did you think I'd turn back just because you're here? Of course I mean to continue. Surely I can be of help."

"I can't say that you would be," he replied. "I don't know how much help someone would be who doesn't know that owls only call at night."

"Owls?" she repeated. Then she remembered the calls she had heard when she had huddled beneath the tree. So that was Daniel! Flushing, she set her jaw. "I won't make that mistake again, and besides, don't you think it would be just as risky for me to try to make my way back alone?"

"Absolutely. I will take you back to the fort myself, then go after the Indians."

"Take me back!" She stared, dismayed. "But that makes no more sense than the captain's reinforcements! You will lose whole days, and we're already well behind!"

"I'm not concerned about the time. If they haven't killed them thus far, they don't intend to. I can get you back to safety and still catch up with them."

"Perhaps. Perhaps not," she said, standing now and brushing at the mud and wet leaves that clung to her skirt. Her blanket lay a few feet away. Retrieving it, she shook it out, then slung it over her back.

Daniel had risen with her, and he stood watching her preparations. "What are you doing?" he asked.

"Going after Hannah," she said, brushing past him towards the trail. She felt his fingers close over her arm, snapping her back to where he stood.

"No, you're not," he said.

"Oh, yes, I am," she retorted, twisting to free her arm, "and you can't stop me, either. If you tie me up and drag me back, I promise I'll try to escape. It's no use, Daniel. I've made up my mind."

"Caroline—"

She shook her head. "Hannah is my sister. She's all I've got in the world. She's almost eight months pregnant.... Even if you get her away, she can't go very fast. If anything happens to her, I mean to be there. I mean to," she repeated, her voice rising, betraying her. She clamped her jaw down hard, trying to choke back the threatening tears. She'd spent the last month in limbo. At least now she knew what she must do.

For a moment, Daniel watched her, arguing with himself. Of course, it was madness to think of taking her along, but, on the other hand, he knew that she would fight him if he tried to take her back, and he had no weapons with which to change her mind. Fear would not deter her, for she did not care for her life. He knew that he cared for her more than she cared for herself. It was strange, their standing here. How often in these past months had he imagined her with him in the woods, walking just behind him, so that he could turn and see her face...lying with him in the darkness, only a heartbeat away? But that had been a dream and this was reality, and reality was composed of things like sore feet and scalp-hungry Algonquians, not to mention the distance to be traveled and the rescue itself. Still, as she herself had pointed out, what were his alternatives?

Caroline watched as his eye moved over her, from her tangled hair to her filthy, bare feet. Though she was braced for a refusal, still she gaped at his next words.

"What are you wearing beneath your skirt?"

"Beneath— A petticoat," she said.

"Good. Please take it off." And, when she did nothing but stand, gaping still, he added, "Please, quickly. We have no time to waste."

So she did as he asked, turning her back to him to untie the string. She handed it to him and watched as he tore two narrow strips from it. The rest he rolled up and stuffed into his pouch, exchanging it for something he offered to her.

"What is it?"

"Dried meat. When was the last time you ate?"

"Sometime yesterday." She put the meat in her mouth, bit into it and chewed automatically. She didn't think she was hungry until she tasted the meat on her tongue; then she found she was ravenous, so much so that she didn't notice when Daniel dropped to one knee and drew his knife from its sheath. She didn't realize his intent until she heard the material rip. Looking down at him then, she almost choked on the meat, for he had ripped her skirt in two as far up as her knees.

"What?" she cried in disbelief, her jaw hanging slack. She could not imagine what he was about, destroying her only dress when she had nothing else to wear.

He stilled her protests with a shake of his head. "You'll see," he said briefly, moving around to slit the back of the skirt as he had the front. She watched, chewing slowly, as he gathered the halves one by one, wrapping them around her legs to make crude leggings, each of which he tied with a strip of the petticoat. When he had finished the leggings, he reached into his pouch once again, this time for a pair of moccasins much like his own, only decorated on the tops with brightly colored beads.

"For me?" she said, staring down stupidly at the shoes. "But where did you find them?"

"In Montreal," he said. "I meant them as a present, but they'll do well enough."

"A present," she repeated, unable to take it all in. He had been coming to see her, bringing a present with him. Had it not been for the Indians, he would have brought her these at the farm. She watched with wondering eyes as he put them on her feet and tightened the drawstrings so that the fit was snug.

Rising, he inspected his handiwork and nodded. Then he glanced about them. "MacKenzie thought you might have a gun."

"I did," she said, looking down. "I lost it fording a stream."

In the moment that followed, she thought that he meant to rebuke her for the loss. But he said only "Come. We'd best be gone." Then, turning away, he set off along the trail. And she had to hurry just to keep up with him.

Chapter Eight

Caroline's back was breaking, and her legs, as well. Every step sent a hot flash of pain shooting through her knees. The rain was still falling, and her pretty moccasins were already covered with mud from the times she'd missed her footing and slipped on the trail. Her hair had come down again and was straggling in her face. She'd have to braid it again when they stopped—if they ever stopped.

Up ahead, Daniel moved with the low-shouldered gait that she'd noticed that first night at Northfield, when he'd walked up from the river with her. He was moving quickly— almost running, it seemed to her—and he seemed never to tire, though she was dead on her feet. Every bone in her body was crying out for rest, and she had to bite down on her lip to keep from crying out herself. She knew he would stop, or slow his pace, if she asked him to. But she didn't want to ask him. She wanted to show him that she could keep up. She wanted to show him that he had been wrong about her coming along. Even so, she wasn't sure how much longer she could last, and she knew she would be starving if her bones weren't so sore.

Then, just when she thought that she must drop, despite her resolve, Daniel came to a sudden stop. She would have bumped into him had he not turned sideways, holding one hand out straight to halt her as she came. When she opened her mouth to question him, he laid a finger on his lips. Turning away, he lifted his head into the air, sniffing like a hound. Caroline watched him, fatigue overcome by curiosity. When he moved off the trail, she followed behind, crouching forward as he did and taking care to put her feet where his had trod so that she would make no noise.

They walked perhaps thirty yards, past an outcropping of granite, to a clearing in which a fire had been made sometime in the past. All that remained was a black circle of charred wood. Stooping to retrieve a stick lying on the ground, Daniel prodded the fire's remains. Then he leaned down to touch it with his hand.

"Here," he said, gesturing for her to do the same.

The cinders were warm. "They camped here last night," she murmured, feeling the same excitement she had felt upon finding the handkerchief. She could not be sure of the time, for there was no sun, and her body felt as though she'd been walking for hours and hours. But it was not twilight, of that she was sure—and that meant they were keeping up. She turned back to Daniel. He had straightened once again and was looking about the abandoned camp. Seeing the tilt of his head, she recalled how he had sniffed the air back on the trail.

"You mean you could smell them here?"

"Of course," he said, plainly amused by her incredulity. "Humans have the strongest scent of all the animals— And then there was the fire." His brows rising, he asked, "Why do you look at me that way?"

"I was just wondering how long I would have lasted alone."

"They say that necessity is the mother of invention," he said with a smile. Reaching into his pouch, he drew out another piece of meat, and she took it readily.

She raised the meat to her lips, then paused. "And Hannah?" she said, hesitant to speak what was in her mind. "What will they do to her?"

"Take her to Montreal and sell her to the French, who will ransom her in turn."

"But in the meantime, while they are traveling…how will they treat her? After all, she is pregnant, and Hetty has just been ill."

Recalling how she had sensed it when he had held back earlier, Daniel looked away. He hated to lie to her, and yet he knew that, for all her stamina, she had enough to bear without him adding to her fears. In truth, there was no answer to any of her questions, for, unlike the British, who dwelled snug in their towns, the Indians depended upon nature and even luck. Then, too, the captives' treatment would depend on their master—on the specific Indian who had actually taken them and who would therefore claim them as his slaves. If the tribe had meat, then the captives would eat, as well, and if the master was a good one, they would be well treated. But if the tribe was hungry, or the master cruel, then things would not go so well. And if the baby came early, or the child fell ill again... There were too many possibilities to guess which one would occur. It wasn't a question of lying, but rather of hoping for the best.

"She will be well treated," he said, a note of finality in his voice. "After all, they want her to fetch the highest possible price. So they will keep her healthy—her and the child both."

"Then they will not be tortured?"

"To what purpose?" he asked. He nodded towards the meat she held uneaten in her hand. "If you're not feeling hungry, I suggest we eat on the trail," he said, and turned away before she could respond, leaving her no choice but to hurry after him.

They stopped at dark, in a clearing just off the trail. Daniel offered her more meat, but she was too tired to eat. The rain had stopped, but the grass was still wet, as was her blanket. She was about to spread it out when something touched her arm.

"Here," said Daniel, offering her his blanket, which, having been rolled up in a hide, was almost completely dry.

"Oh, no, I couldn't."

"Take it," he said. "I'm used to the damp, and you won't be of any use if you catch pneumonia."

So, in the end, she accepted, too weary to resist. Wrapping the blanket around her, she lay down on the grass, and in the space between two breaths she was fast asleep.

Daniel knelt, watching her. Her face was exhausted and, despite his ministrations, very far from clean. She had a scrape on her forehead, and another on her cheek. Her braids were still pinned to her head, but curls of her hair had come loose and fallen in a tangle across her face. Reaching down, he tucked one back and felt her stir in her sleep, her lips moving gently as she muttered wordlessly. His breath caught in his throat. Even dirty and bedraggled, she was beautiful to him.

She slept on her side, her knees drawn up and one hand tucked beneath her cheek, as a child would sleep. He thought of her expression when he had ripped her skirt, and he smiled despite himself. She had spirit, he had to grant her that. He could just imagine her confronting MacKenzie— and once again he regretted not having choked the bastard to death. He knew that the day's pace had been too much for her, but she had not complained. Perhaps she would be able to keep the pace until they found the Indians, and then perhaps he would manage to free the woman and the child. His intention was to strike a bargain in goods, but there was always the possibility of out-and-out escape. It would be a challenge—in fact it would be almost impossible—but it was challenge that made life worthwhile.

For a moment more, he watched Caroline. Then, rising, he shook out the sodden weight of her blanket and, spreading it around him, settled himself on the ground, grunting with satisfaction as his muscles relaxed. Unlike Caroline, he did not sleep curled up, but with one hand on his rifle and the other on his knife. All his instincts told him that the Indians were ahead, but he had survived this long by never trusting the night. And there were always animals to be wary of. He closed his eyes, drew one deep breath, and was asleep, as well.

The dawn had already broken when Caroline awoke, though raindrops still trembled on the needles of the pine beneath which she lay. Dew had dampened the blanket, but it still gave warmth. Drawing it up, she stretched, then groaned when her limbs protested. She wondered if Daniel had slept as well in her wet blanket. Propping herself up on one elbow, she looked about her to see where he had slept.

He was not there. Sitting up, her heart pounding, she felt fear rising in her throat. Had he gone on without her, in order to leave her behind? Would he do such a thing? Then she saw his things, gathered neatly on a rock a few feet away. Shaking now with relief, she pushed the blanket back and, rising on stiff legs, looked down at herself.

She looked a fright—at least what she could see, and she could imagine the rest. Raising her hand to her hair, she felt nothing but matted snarls. It would be impossible to braid it again without a comb or a brush, and all she had to work with were her fingers. She unpinned both braids, pinned them back again and was weaving the loose strands wherever they would fit when Daniel reappeared.

"Good morning."

"Good morning," she said, dropping her hands from her hair to smooth the wrinkles of her skirt. But she had forgotten that her skirt was a skirt only to her knees, and then breeches beneath. The material was filthy, and the leggings, as well, and her bodice was a fright. She opened her hands, overwhelmed.

"You look fine," Daniel said, his eyes still dazzled by the way the light came from behind, illuminating her profile, and the curve of her arms when they had been raised above her head.

"You are polite," she replied. "Where have you been?"

"Reconnoitering. Here, you need to eat," he said, delving into his pouch and then handing her bread and meat.

It was corn bread. He must have gotten it from the fort. She ate over a low rock, crouched on the ground. She tried to make herself chew, but she wanted to gobble it down. She felt him watching and looked up. "You are not eating?"

"I ate earlier."

"I have held you back," she said, making as if to rise, but he waved her down.

"We will catch them eventually. This is their hunting season, and their grounds lie to the north. Their families will be waiting for them there in a camp. Then, when the hunting is over, they will take their captives on to Montreal."

"But won't they be worried about someone coming behind?"

Daniel shook his head. "They don't expect pursuit. They know the English better than the English know them. They know that it will take the English more than two assaults to screw up their courage enough to take on the woods. The English prefer to see their woods plowed under to make into farms."

"Your tone is bitter."

He shrugged. "It shouldn't be. After all, there are plenty of woods to go around. It would take more than my lifetime for even the English to bring them all under the plow. The Indians are not so lucky. The English push them north into the arms of the French, who fill them with hatred, then send them back south again. In the end, the two countries will make peace and divide the land between them, and then the Indians will have no more value—not even to the Jesuit fathers, who are so eager to save their souls in order to claim their arms for the King."

Caroline shook her head. "I don't understand," she said. "You are French and a Catholic, and yet you speak against both your King and your religion."

"In England there are many who speak against the King. Why, then, not extend the same right to me, especially given the self-indulgent spendthrift who sits on the throne of France? And, as for religion, I would call myself a Catholic—it is a crime to do otherwise—but my mother raised me Huguenot, as her mother raised her."

"But I thought the Huguenots were thrown out of France years ago. I thought they were all in England."

"England and Germany. Most of them. But there were the exceptions...my grandparents among them. My grandmother was pregnant when King Louis ordered all Protestants to convert or be burned at the stake. With the rest of their family, my grandparents packed and prepared to leave, but on the way to the border my grandmother's labor began. A kind family took them in and cared for my grandmother. My grandfather was a clothier, and he was soon offered work. With one thing and another, they set down roots and remained.''

"But they never converted.''

"Not my grandparents, though they made a show of it. My mother was christened in the Catholic church. But she learned her religion at home. It is an interesting story, but we are pressed for time. If you have finished your breakfast . . .''

Caroline nodded, but she did not rise. The story of his grandmother had brought a new worry to mind. "And when we reach them,'' she wondered, "how will we get them away? How will we outrun them, with Hannah so very pregnant?''

"Perhaps we shall not,'' he said. "Perhaps we shall not even try.''

"But—'' She frowned, bewildered.

Daniel could not help but smile at her naiveté. Was that what she had intended in pursuing her sister—that she would somehow spirit her off and back to the south? Two women and a child outrunning Abenaki warriors?

"The most likely solution is that we shall bargain for them—as in this country one bargains for all things of worth.'' He watched her face as she absorbed this new idea.

"But, if you mean to bargain, what will you offer them?''

"Wampum.'' He shrugged. "Or blankets. Rifles, if they prefer. I have some things with me, and can get more at the northern posts.'' He failed to add that he had brought these with the idea in mind that she, too, might have stumbled into Abenaki hands.

"And they will give you Hannah, in exchange for your goods?''

"Why not?'' he asked. "After all, it will spare them the trouble of carrying her all the way north. And, if the price is high enough . . .''

"I will repay you,'' she said, misunderstanding him. "Whatever it costs for their freedom, I will repay it to you.''

"I am not worried about repayment," he said, turning away so that she could not see the uncertainty that darkened his eyes. He had greater worries than being repaid the cost, not the least of which was the possibility that the Indians would refuse a trade. Captives gave a tribe a status that trade goods did not, and often tribes that had been depleted through warfare and disease chose to adopt their captives in order to swell their ranks. Children, especially, were taken for adoption, and a pregnant woman and a child would be a rich prize indeed. But there was no point in adding that knowledge to Caroline's burden.

"Then it is that easy. I didn't know," she said, shaking her head in wonderment.

"All that remains is to find them. All," Daniel repeated, stifling the twinge of guilt that came with the deceit. Rising, he picked up a branch that lay upon the ground and, breaking off a single bough, swept the ground where they had slept.

Caroline watched him. "Why are you doing that, if no one will follow us?"

"Habit," he replied. "The same way you make your bed when you rise in the morning."

She nodded, seeing in the bough's movement the distance between their lives.

As he had done yesterday, Daniel walked in front. Today it seemed to Caroline that he did not walk as fast, or perhaps it was only that she was accustomed to the pace now. They had been moving for several hours when he stopped and, bending down, showed her a peculiar depression just beside the trail.

"They have a horse," he said.

"Yes, from the soldiers at the house. They ought to have three."

"That may be so. They tie squares of leather over each of its hooves in order to mask its print. Likely your sister is riding—and likely the child, as well."

"Do you think so?" She looked up, hope blazing in her eyes, for if Hannah was riding, the trip would not be so hard.

Daniel nodded. "That would explain their speed."

That afternoon, they came upon the place where the Indians had camped the night before. Caroline was ecstatic when she saw how much ground they had gained. Exhilarated by the knowledge, she forgot her fatigue. Now nothing could stop them! But she rejoiced too soon, for, hardly an hour later, they came to the river. This was no stream, as the last had been, but rather the first of the tributaries that ran from the northwest. This was the first major branch of the trail north to Canada.

The river was broad, at least two hundred yards across, and far too swift to swim. The day had been sunless, but now, as they stood on the near bank, the clouds began to break. A flood of sunlight poured through an opening above, turning the trees to emerald, the water to glittering gold. The scene was breathtaking in its beauty, but Caroline could not see that; she saw nothing but the obstacle lying across their path.

"You don't think that they turned here?" she asked, but Daniel shook his head. His full attention seemed to be taken by a tree, or, more precisely, by a deep gash in its trunk. "Then what will we do?" she wondered.

"Cross it," he replied.

"But how?"

"How good a swimmer are you?" he asked. His lips curved in a smile as he turned from the tree to look at another that grew a few yards away. This one was a mighty spruce; its trunk towered over them. Laying his hands on the trunk, Daniel ran them up and down it. Then, while Caroline watched, mystified, he unsheathed his knife and sank the blade into the bark.

He made an incision, running up and down, from as far up as he could reach to three feet from the base of the tree. Then, swinging himself up onto a low branch, he continued the incision until it extended a distance of at least ten feet. Slipping the blade into the cut, he began to work the bark free from the tree.

"What are you doing?" she asked, drawing near. From the way his head jerked up, she knew that he had forgotten her in his concentration. It was the same concentration she had seen yesterday, when he had cleaned her face with the edge of her apron.

Now he paused in his work to look down at her. "You'll find some vines growing just beyond those trees," he said, gesturing. "Cut two lengths at least twelve feet each, and two more of just less. You ought to be able to break them— if not, I'll give you the knife."

She did not mean to protest, nor even to debate; still, she was left standing when he turned back to his work. For a moment more, she watched him; then she turned away, moving in the general direction in which he had pointed her.

The vines were hard to break, but she managed to tear off the lengths he had described. When she got back to Daniel, he had peeled the bark back to a distance of some three feet and was still working with his knife. He had stripped off his tunic in the time that she had been gone, and sweat shone bright on the smooth skin of his back.

Caroline stood watching, feeling her blood tingling, for she had never seen a man so perfectly made as he. He reminded her of a classical statue she had seen as a girl, but that had been of a boy, while this was a man's body, hardened by a life out of doors, all excess flesh stripped away.

Sensing her presence, Daniel glanced around, raising one forearm to wipe the sweat from his eyes. "Good. I need your help. If you can hold the bark out, I can get inside the rest."

She stood behind him, between the trunk and the bark, which curved around them like a tube-shaped shell. She stood nearer the opening, with her back to Daniel, who worked with his knife, so close that he touched her each time he drew breath. The smell of his sweat mingled with the strong odor of spruce, intoxicating her senses so that she could not concentrate, all of her mind homing in on the memory of their kiss the night of the dance at the fort.

"Whew!" He let his hands fall to his sides. Leaning against the bare trunk, he turned his head towards her. She watched his chest heaving as he caught his breath, watched the rivulets of sweat trickling down his skin. She felt the heat rising from him, and from herself; when he looked down at her, their eyes met and held. Slowly he raised his fingers until he was cupping her chin. Her eyes were open as she received his kiss.

This time, his lips were gentle, savoring, tasting the sweetness of her mouth, and, when her lips opened, she tasted him as well. If she let the bark go, it would trap them against the tree, yet her fingers tingled to touch his skin, to trace the patterns in the sweat on his muscled back. For a long, timeless moment, they lingered as they were. Then Daniel raised his head, drawing a long, shaken breath.

"We'll never cross the river with distractions like that. Are your arms too tired, or can you help some more?"

She nodded in answer, incapable of speech. She felt that she would shatter if air touched her skin. She felt that her very chemistry had changed. But it was just a feeling, for still she stood with her hands pressed flat against the resisting bark. Daniel, for his part, seemed once again to have forgotten her, his whole being focused on his work.

After a few more minutes, he relieved her of her task, holding the bark open so that she could slip free, then slipping out himself. Moving around to the farthest point where the bark had been worked free, he made another cut, the same height as the first, and then horizontal cuts to release it from the tree.

When the bark was completely free, together they pulled it off and laid it on the ground, with the ends curling up. Daniel weighted the bottom with heavy stones, then cut three branches to fit inside at intervals as ribs. The branches were supple enough to curve with the bark, yet at the same time they provided enough pressure to hold the sides open. With his knife he made a series of holes at either end, and then he and Caroline used the vine she had cut to sew them together. They did the same to secure the ribs.

Another spruce tree stood beside the first. Rising, Daniel went to it, and, following, Caroline saw two deep gashes cut in its side. The tree, healing its own wounds, had produced gum to fill the cuts. Now Daniel scooped this gum out and, returning to the boat, smeared it over all the places he had sewn, in order to seal the holes. The result was a canoe.

"Crude but serviceable" was his verdict as he stood back, inspecting it.

"I think it's wonderful!" Caroline exclaimed. "To be able to build a whole boat, out of nothing, just like that!"

"It wasn't out of nothing," he said, amusement in his eyes again. "And, besides, you helped me."

"I . . ." She gestured vaguely with her hand, all thought vanishing as he moved towards her.

He rested his hands lightly on either side of her waist, leaning away just slightly in order to study her face. Shaking his head, he smiled again as he had before. "If I show you all my secrets, what will I have left?"

"Have you shown me all?" she murmured, hardly knowing what she said. She felt like swooning at the animal scent of his sweat. Slowly he drew her to him as he had done before, and her lips were open when his reached them. This kiss, too, was languid and dreamlike. His hands moved slowly up her back, one to cradle the nape of her neck, the other, open palmed, to draw her to him.

This time, her hands were free to run the length of his back. His skin was satin, it was marble yielding up the sun. She felt her fingers open, reaching and reaching for more. Through her chemise and bodice came the heat of his chest as he held her to him gently. He moved without rushing, yet the very slowness of his movements fed the flames. Then, also slowly, the kiss ceased to be, and once again he held her gently away from him.

"Caroline," he murmured, "sweet, sweet Caroline. If you do not stop me, I shall devour you."

She leaned back against his arms, her thighs resting against the length of his. They fit perfectly together, two halves of a whole. He had spoken the word *devour*, but his tone held no threat; his voice was the same deep velvet as his embrace. And Caroline wanted nothing more than to be devoured by those hands, those lips. Tomorrow did not matter, nor even today, nothing mattered but probing the depths of this desire, following wherever his touch led her. Pulling herself closer, she laid her cheek against his, closing her eyes and drinking in the very feel of him.

Then, suddenly, she was floating as he lifted her in his arms and carried her without effort to a place where the grass was soft.

He laid her down and then knelt beside her, drinking her in with his eyes, as if she were cool water and he parched with thirst.

"I have wanted you," he whispered, "since that first night we met. Beside the river. Do you remember?"

She nodded, her eyes open now. Her heart had begun to beat irregularly. Though she resisted it, the feel of the grass beneath her brought back the memory of Edmund. For the first time, she remembered her dream beneath the willow tree—how Daniel had turned into Edmund, and how both had disappeared, leaving her dazed and yearning.

Daniel's eyes were a pure blue as his fingers reached for the top button of her dress. She felt herself trembling as he undid the first catch, and the second and the third. When she felt his fingers through the cotton of her chemise, the last of her nerve caved in. With a jerk, she pulled herself up and away from him, drawing her knees up close as if to fend him off.

"I can't!" she gasped. "I'm sorry, but I can't!" Unable to meet his eyes, she turned her head away. There was a moment's silence. Then she heard his breath release.

"Why are you sorry?" he asked.

She jerked her head around, for, whatever she had expected, surely it was not that. His eyes held no anger. They held desire, but also the compassion she knew so well.

"Because I made you think that you could...that I would..." She could not speak the word. Dropping her eyes, she said, "You have been so good to me."

"You made me think nothing," he said. "And I expect nothing, least of all this, in exchange for whatever I have done. I told you to stop me, and that is what you have done. Why apologize?"

An ache was growing in her chest, an ache she did not understand, as if too many tears were swelling within her and if she tried to release them she would explode into nothingness. It was a misery that was total, and yet it contained the seeds of hope. She raised her eyes to his.

"I am no virgin," she whispered. "If I lie with you, I shall be no better than a whore."

Her hand lay limp in her lap. Daniel raised it, turning it palm upward, then covered it with his own, lacing his fingers through hers. "Ah, Caroline... If a man spoke thus about you, I would kill him on the spot. What shall I do with you?"

The pain was beyond bearing; speechless, she shook her head. Releasing her fingers, Daniel drew her close to him.

It was an embrace without desire, an embrace that offered only warmth and shelter from all care. Caroline did not know for how long he held her, but slowly the pain subsided. The comfort he gave her infused her, and she let it come, closing her eyes and resting her weary head against him.

He held her, unmoving, as her breath became regular. In time, her breath deepened, and he knew she had fallen asleep. Still he held her a bit longer, resting his cheek against her hair, before he laid her back, gently, on the soft grass. Then he sat looking down at her face, as he had the night before.

"Caroline," he murmured. "If we are to be given the time, I shall teach you about love. I give you my word on it." Rising, he fetched a blanket with which to cover her; then he went to check the newly made boat in the last of the dying light.

Chapter Nine

The smell of roasting meat tugged Caroline awake. Blinking, she turned her head in the direction from which it came. Daniel crouched at the fire, where two rabbits roasted on spits, his back to her. He was still shirtless, as he had been last night; the pale morning sun highlighted the bone and sinew moving beneath his skin. She watched the play of muscle and bone as he tended the meat. Drowsily she recalled the feel of that bare back beneath her open hands, and how gently he had held her as she had sunk into sleep. But her calm was short-lived, for the memory brought a rush of emotions, too many for her to sort through. Pushing back her blanket, Caroline sat up, pausing out of habit to take stock of her appearance.

It was a habit, she quickly realized, that she would do well to break in the days to come. So far as her personal appearance went, her need for improvement was outdone only by her lack of available means. Her clothing was already showing the rigor of the past three days, mud-stained and fraying where she had caught it on branches and twigs, while the repeated drenchings and dryings had left it wrinkled and without shape. Still, and again out of habit, she ran her palms over her bodice and skirt. Then, with a sigh, she raised them to the tangled mass that was her hair.

She had not lost all the hairpins that held her hair in place, so what was left of her braids still clung valiantly to the crown of her head. But curls and locks that had come undone straggled everywhere, snagged and snarled and knotted and stuck through with twigs and burrs. Without either comb or brush, she could make little difference, but still, automatically, she began to make repairs. Delving with her fingers, she managed to find the pins; when she withdrew them, the two plaits tumbled free to hang along her back, reaching almost as far as her waist. She drew one forward and began to undo it.

Hearing Caroline stir behind him, Daniel turned from the fire, watching as she worked her fingers in and out of the coils. She did not see him watching, being too intent on her work, first freeing the three strands, then rebraiding them in a routine as timeless as the woods themselves. How many times had he watched Indian women braid their hair just this way in the first light of the sun? He recalled his own mother sitting as Caroline did, her arms soft and graceful, her head tilted to one side, her eyes soft and wistful, staring off into space.

What did women think of when they braided their hair? Did they dream of a lover whose magic would change their lives, or only of the tasks ahead in the day to come? He knew well enough a man's thoughts at a moment such as this. A man thought of the weight and warmth of that fall of hair, how soft it would feel beneath his lips, how fragrant to his breath. A man imagined the silken curtain drifting across his bare chest; he imagined running his fingers up the velvet skin of those arms.

Last night he had been master of his appetites, but now, as he watched her, he felt a stirring within his loins. He felt his heartbeat quicken and his skin begin to burn. If she were to look up now, he would go to her. If her look was welcoming, he would take her in his arms, not swiftly, but gradually, until he felt the softness of her breasts pillowed against his chest. Then he would tilt her head back to taste her lips, lips that would be as sweet and full and open as they had been last night. He would lead her slowly into the corner of paradise that must have been created especially for them.

But she did not look up, and the sound of fat sizzling in the fire brought his head around. The rabbits were burn-

ing, and he turned them on the spit. Behind him, he heard
Caroline rise and put her cover aside. He heard the crunch
of her step as she went down to the stream. In his mind he
saw how she would kneel at the edge, supporting herself
with one hand while she dipped the other into the clear water to bathe her face. He imagined how she would shake her
hand, shaking off the last drops before she dried it on her
skirts. Though the image was prosaic, that did nothing to
still the ache within him. He heard her returning, heard her
approach, then hesitate—and that moment's hesitation cut
straight to his heart, easing the knot of desire and filling him
with the same peace he had felt last night.

The first of the rabbits was cooked. Leaning forwards, he
moved it onto the rock at his side before he turned to her,
giving himself time to chase all but plain friendship from his
smile.

"Good morning. I trust you slept well."

"Yes, very. And you?" she replied. Unable to meet his,
her eyes shifted to the meat.

Seeing this, he smiled, struck by how simple life could be.
He could not banish her nightmares yet, but he could at
least fill her stomach with hot food. "I thought we could use
a change from jerky. Once we cross the river, we can't risk
either the gun or the scent of cooking meat."

"It smells wonderful," she said, and she meant it. Her
mouth was watering. But still she was all too conscious of
the expanse of his bare back. Over the fragrance of the rabbit came the smell she recalled from last night, of pine pitch
and hot sweat, and she dug her nails into her palms, trying
to chase it away. When he handed her her portion, a shaft
of light fell on his arm. She felt her breath catch, and
warmth surge up through her. Strange, that such a small
thing could make her feel so much. She took the meat and
found a seat on a nearby log.

The meat, the first she had tasted in four days, was hot
and savory. She ate with purpose, completely absorbed in
the meal. But, as her hunger abated, her consciousness
shifted to him, and again she felt her gaze drawn irresisti-
bly. She scanned the clearing for something to distract her

thoughts, and finally settled on the towering spruce from which they had cut the bark. Yesterday she had thought only of the canoe, but now, looking at the tree, she saw the wound that they had caused. The whole lower portion of the trunk was left raw and running with sap.

Following her gaze, Daniel saw her wince. "It looks sore, doesn't it?"

"Very." She shuddered. "Will it recover?"

"The tree? Oh, yes. It will recover, and more. Trees are like people—when they've been cut, they grow a second skin, thicker than the first."

As I did, thought Caroline, her eyes upon the tree. But it had not been without cost. She had grown a skin like armor, a skin that nothing could penetrate. And yet, last night, when Daniel had touched her, she had felt him well enough. Felt him and more, she thought now, as it all came sweeping back. She felt her skin begin to tingle—and firmly thrust the feeling aside.

"But," she said, frowning, turning to him, "if the Indians crossed here, they must have made boats, too. But, if they did make boats, then where are the trees they used?"

"On the other side," he said, gathering up the bones from his meat and tossing them into the fire. "They brought them over when they came down and hid them in the woods. Then, when they returned here, the boats were awaiting them, requiring only a bit more gumming to carry them."

"The gash in the tree! They must have made that in order to get pitch to seal their canoes!" Her eyes lit up as the final piece fell into place. "I thought that it was only a sort of trail marker."

Daniel shook his head. "The Indians hardly need to mark their trails. But canoes of spruce bark, though quickly constructed, are not as watertight as birch. Speaking of which," he added, rising as he spoke, "if we mean to leave soon, I'd best see to ours."

She felt another pang of desire as he moved off, supple and athletic, to kneel beside the boat. This time, the morning sunlight fell on his head and back, filling her with a longing so complete and powerful that to endure it without

shattering she had to turn away. This deep, wrenching desire reached beyond the memory of last night, beyond reason and comprehension, to embrace the fire before which
she sat and the rich taste of the rabbit still lingering on her
lips. It included the river, the earth, and the trees and the air,
but mostly it was Daniel, kneeling by the boat, his hair a
dazzling crown above the lithe curve of his back. She
thought of Hannah and their purpose in being here, but
even the grimness of those things could not dim the sun.

Overhead, a crow cawed, swooping down to the grass,
tottering two steps towards the aroma of the meat. It
glanced at her with bright eyes, paused, then advanced. The
sun glinted on its back, too, which seemed as hard and black
as coal. The longing swelled in Caroline; then it burst and
was gone. For a moment more, she sat, staring at the crow.
Then, sighing, she rose and turned away, moving not towards Daniel but along the river's rocky shore, where piles
of leaves and driftwood lay scattered at random. Behind her,
the crow crept closer, to claim whatever scraps she might
have left.

The sun was warm on Daniel's back as he smoothed the
coat of resin along the last seam, his fingers working on
their own while his thoughts ranged ahead, to the day's
journey. Beside him the river flowed, its water sparkling,
while the wind played sweet music in the trees overhead. His
stomach was full of good meat and his body was warm and
loose, ready to respond to whatever the day might bring.
Raised on a mixture of Catholicism and Calvinist teaching,
Daniel had never found religion inside a church as strongly
or as surely as he had in the woods. Here, at such a moment, he felt very close to God. He felt that he was playing
his appointed role in life. The river was his cathedral, the
sighing wind his choir, the pitch beneath his fingers his own
private prayer.

He loved his life. At times like this he felt the depth of that
love and felt a profound gratitude for having been granted
it. How would it be, he wondered, to have to spend one's life
strangled by the city or chained to a struggling farm, always moving backwards and forwards over the same worn

path, a path that was narrowed by obligation and by neighbors' wagging tongues? How would it be never to know a moment such as this, never to stand atop a mountain and see sunrise above the clouds?

He thought of Caroline. They were alike in some ways. They had both chosen solitary lives, but while his was rich with pleasure, hers was bleak and closed. She lived penned and isolated while he ranged far afield, facing nature's dangers and drinking in its gifts. But for her sister's capture, Caroline would never have come here. She would have spent her whole life dwelling within the known, all the mysteries snatched from her by the ax and the plow. And, while he could not thank God for the tragedy that had brought her here, still he could not turn away from the gift of this time. Nor did he mean to let her turn away from it.

He had confidence in his ability to match wits with the Indians, but life in the woods had taught him that nothing was guaranteed. Even if he and Caroline did survive this adventure, in the end they would part. But, in the meantime, there were things he could share with her. He could share with her, for instance, the secrets of this land; he could teach her to trust it as she could not trust a man. And perhaps he could teach her to trust herself, as well. Then, after he had left her, she would still have a friend.

He heard her step behind him as his fingers reached the last stitch. Lifting his head, he saw her coming along the rocky bank, dragging along behind her two lengths of driftwood. The one she held in her right hand was almost as tall as she, the other somewhat smaller. Both of them were flat rather than round in shape.

"For paddles," she explained, coming to a stop a few feet away. Leaning them against her, she drew her hand across her brow. Then, shrugging, she added, "Unless you've got something else."

"Not a thing." He smiled and saw the quicksilver gleam of her gratitude. Yes, he thought, his heart lifting, he could do those things for her. Perhaps there would be time enough to show her everything.

He carried the boat to the river, balanced above his head, while Caroline followed, towing the paddles and the blankets. Lowering it to the water, he pressed down with his full weight, his eye scanning the bottom for signs of a leak. Finding none, he let up and held the boat steady for her.

"Have you ever been in a boat before?"

She nodded. "Many times at home. In Surrey we lived near the river. We had an old rowing boat."

"All right, then. Let's go."

Caroline moved forward to stow the paddles and the blankets away. Then she hesitated, her lips caught between her teeth. "Are you sure that it will hold us? That it won't dump us in?"

"That depends upon what you were planning to do in it," he said, and he could have bitten his tongue when he recalled how she had taken offense at such jokes in the past. But today she seemed to draw comfort from the joke. Throwing him a quick, nervous, smile, she stepped into the boat.

That is, she tried to step in. Unprepared for the extreme buoyancy of the craft, she leaned too far forward, failing to balance her weight. Hardly had her first foot touched the canoe's bottom before the boat gave a violent lurch. It would have shot out into the river, but for Daniel's steadying grip. The motion pushed Caroline back. She tried to regain her balance, but it was no use. With a grunt of reluctance, she sat down in the stream.

Busy with the boat, Daniel heard the splash of her fall and turned to her, words of contrition on his lips. But, at the sight of her in the water, he laughed in spite of himself. "It's not a barge, you know. You've got to hold both sides and keep your body low."

"You might have told me that in the first place!" she grumbled, struggling to her feet, water pouring from her clothes.

Her bodice clung to her body, as did the breeches he had fashioned for her. Through them, he could see the heavy swell of her breasts and the curve of her hips. Daniel caught himself staring and shook his head to break the spell. "It never occurred to me. You seem to take so naturally to everything else.''

He had intended no flattery, yet Caroline could not help but flush. Shaking the worst of the water from her streaming clothes, she stepped forwards once again, and this time managed to keep her balance climbing in, though the boat bobbed like a bit of cork with her every move. Daniel, however, left her no time for second thoughts, but sprang into the stern and, catching hold of one of the crude paddles, pushed off into the stream. He angled them upriver, against the current. With each stroke of the paddle, the craft shot forwards, hovered, then shot again.

Caroline sat frozen in the bow, afraid to attempt more than maintaining her seat, holding her breath for fear that she would upset the boat, which seemed to react to every ripple in the stream. The second driftwood paddle lay close at hand, but she made no move to lift it, instead clinging, white knuckled, to the rough sides of the craft.

The last of the early-morning haze lingered still over the water, while the trees on the opposite shore dipped forwards, dark and mysterious. A pair of wood ducks, startled by the passing of the boat, rose up, their wings pumping, their creamy underfeathers gilded by the sun. Caroline's eyes rose to follow them, and she felt her hands relax as the beauty of the moment eased her fears away.

For it was beautiful here, in the newness of the morning, with the mountains rising beyond. Skimming across the water, the breeze in her hair, Caroline had to force herself to remember that this was not a pleasure trip. She doubted that Hannah, making this same crossing, had noticed the gleam of the water or the warmth of the sun on her arms. And, if she had felt terror at the boat's unsteadiness, what must Hannah have felt—pregnant and with Hetty, tense and exhausted and surrounded by enemies. It was all very well for Daniel to explain to her that there was nothing to fear, but she doubted that the Indians had done the same to ease Hannah's mind. If she had not been tortured yet, how was she to know that the next hour did not hold such a fate?

She wondered how long it had been since Hannah had crossed this way. She and Daniel had lost little time in building the canoe; they couldn't be far behind Hannah and her captors. Perhaps they would catch them tomorrow... She wondered what they would do then. She wondered if Daniel had a plan. Behind her she heard the steady dipping of his paddle. Releasing the gunwales, she raised her own, adding what she could to their speed.

The other shore was near. There were rocks in the water; stowing her paddle, she leaned forward to pick their way, directing Daniel so that he could steer them safely in.

"Be careful getting out," he cautioned, and she could hear the chuckle in his words.

Tossing her head, she replied, "I'm not a total fool," and promptly lost her step, only saving herself from going down by grabbing an overhanging limb.

"Not total," he agreed, leaping out with a grace that put her own disembarkation to shame. His foot, landing on the bank, hardly made a sound. She shook her head admiringly, but he took no notice, turning instead to the business of hiding the canoe in a hollow log twenty feet from the river's edge. She helped him to carry and stow it and to conceal the hiding place. She would have spent a moment admiring their work, but, as before, Daniel lost no time in setting out. He carried his gun and the blankets and she followed behind.

At first she thought that he must be walking blind, but then she realized that he was following a trail, though one far more narrow and faintly marked than the one they had tracked thus far.

"Did the Indians come this way?" she asked, wondering how the horses would have managed some of the lower growth.

Daniel shook his head. "It's more likely they followed the main trail. By taking this one, we shall gain some time on them." She noticed that he kept his voice low, and that his eyes moved back and forth even as he spoke. As always, she was struck by how well he knew the woods—and by how slim the chance was that she would have survived without him.

They walked until night, stopping only once, and then only for as long as it took them to chew their food. They spoke only very rarely, but Caroline found the silence anything but oppressive. Daniel's presence gave her comfort, and demanded nothing in return. From his manner, his demeanor, it was almost as though last night had not occurred, as though they had never kissed. And yet she sensed that he recalled those minutes as clearly as she.

They stopped as the light failed. Tonight he made no fire, though the air held a chill.

"It could be seen," he murmured, once again keeping his voice low. In the gloom, she saw the flicker of his moving eyes.

She shivered. "You mean we are that close?"

He nodded. "We ought to be. We ought to come upon them by tomorrow night."

"But, if we are so close, why are we stopping now?"

"Would you have us blunder on them in the dark? Surprise is our only advantage. I'd rather keep it in reserve."

She knew that he was right, and yet, despite her fatigue, it was difficult to rest, knowing that Hannah had come within reach. Hugging her knees to her chest, she stared into the growing gloom. Part of her wanted to urge him to go on, while the other part was grateful for his wisdom and his restraint.

"What would I have done," she wondered, "if you had not come after me? I could not have crossed the river—if I had managed to reach it at all."

"If I had not stayed so long in Montreal, perhaps your sister would be safe at home even now," he said, and wondered that he could speak such words without feeling guilt. For, if he had managed to avert the attack, he would not be here at this moment, with Caroline so close.

But Caroline's thoughts had moved in another direction. "What took you to Montreal?" she asked. "You spoke of it before."

"My father's death," he replied. "I had to return there to settle his affairs."

"I'm sorry," she said quickly. "Did you love him very much?"

"I loved my mother more. I felt real sorrow when she died. The ties with my father were the ties of blood. I loved him as a child does."

"Does every child love his father?" she wondered, staring into the dark. "I don't believe I do. Perhaps I did at one time, but I don't think I have since—" She stopped.

"Since what?" Daniel murmured, his voice wrapped in the gathering night.

His tone was not demanding, and yet she felt herself respond, felt a growing yearning to confess to him. Warring factions struggled within her breast; the desire to tell him, and the awful choking shame, the knowledge that he must turn from her when he knew—that she would lose the chance of his love before she had ever known it. But what was the value of a love bought by deception? She recalled the compliment he had paid her after she had almost capsized the boat, and then, with wistful longing, the way he had held her last night. Were she to answer his question, she would surely forfeit both, for how could he respect her after he heard the truth? And yet, all that had happened to Hannah was in a way her fault, so perhaps it was only her due to be punished by the loss of Daniel's respect. Still, she lingered a moment longer before she finally spoke.

"It is a long story, but I will tell it all to you. Then you will know the sort of woman to whom you have been so kind."

"I believe I know the woman."

"You know nothing at all. Nothing." She shook her head. "A woman who would sell her virtue, and her sister's, as well . . . vain and proud and selfish and willful to a sin—"

"Caroline—"

"Let me be! Hold your protests until you have heard what I have to say. And then I fear that you will hold them forever. There was a man," she continued, before he could interrupt again, "where I grew up, in Surrey, a rich and powerful man. At the time, I thought I loved him, but now I see that I did not, but rather coveted his power, his title and his wealth. I coveted them so much that I was willing to trade my virtue for his empty promises.''

"What promises?" Daniel asked.

"Marriage, for one," she said. "He said that he would marry me if I gave him his way. Fool that I was, I believed him, blinded by my greed."

"And not by his promises?"

"What difference does it make?" she asked bitterly. "I knew what I was doing, and I chose to sin. I chose to believe that a lord could love a village girl."

"And why not?" Daniel asked, her words awakening the old anger buried in him, the anger he felt toward Canada, with its graft and peculation, where status served to excuse the grossest excesses. "Does status make a man?"

"Status and wealth," she said. "Although this man might choose to take his pleasure with me, when it came time for marriage, he chose within his class. He wanted to be rid of any embarrassment I might cause, so he paid a man to wed me and take me to America."

She stopped, hugging her knees closer, seeing it all again: her shock, her humiliation, her anger, her disbelief. She was scarcely aware of Daniel, so silent at her side.

"I went to my lover," she said, her voice hardly louder than the whispering of the wind. "I told him that I would have no part in this plan of his. I told him that he would never be rid of me that way, that I would remain in Surrey, an emblem of his shame. He sought to mollify me, and, when he found he could not, he paid Thomas MacKenzie to marry Hannah instead."

Daniel's head came up at her last words. This was something he had not known, but, even as she said it, he saw how it all fitted. His mouth tasted bitter with disgust at the ways of men. Again he felt MacKenzie's nose beneath the hard bones of his fist.

"And I let him," said Caroline, unaware of Daniel's re-action. "I let him marry Hannah, when I might have married him myself."

"You refused the marriage. Could not your sister have done the same?"

"It was not in her nature. Oh, how I begged her! How I implored her to reject Thomas MacKenzie's suit!"

"But she was pleased to accept."

"She was pleased to honor my father—and he pleased to allow her to."

"Perhaps." He paused. "And, having accepted the marriage, you believe she has suffered for it."

"She has had to live with him."

"Yes—to live with him, in her own house, with her own children. While you have allowed yourself to live with nothing at all. Except, that is, for your guilt."

"I have deserved nothing!" Her voice rang out, and two doves, alarmed, rose up from the underbrush.

Daniel ignored them, his full attention focused on the struggle for her soul. "For a mistake you made as a girl? Do you think Hannah regrets her life one-tenth as much as you regret yours?"

"She deserves no regrets at all."

"No, you're wrong," he said. "Everyone has regrets, no matter how high or how low. It is part of human nature. But regret must be balanced against forgiveness."

"I cannot forgive," she whispered, into the night. "Not now, not with Hannah afraid and perhaps in pain. How can I forgive now?"

He stared at the shimmering paleness that was the oval of her face. He wanted to reach out for her, to teach her to know the truth. But one night would not undo these years full of knots. Tonight he could do nothing but add to the weight of her guilt. But he could not resist asking, "How can you forgive later, if you cannot now?"

The question was rhetorical. He spoke it with a sigh. Standing, he unrolled the blankets and handed the warmer of the two to her. "Here," he said gently. "The hour is growing late."

"Thank you," she muttered, turning to spread it on the ground.

For a moment, he watched in silence. Then he spoke her name. "Caroline?"

"Yes?"

He sensed more than saw the eagerness in her look, and, as had her hesitation of this morning, it went to his heart. Reaching down, he caught one of her hands in his and, turning it upwards, as he had the day before, touched his lips to her palm. Before he gave it back to her, he curled her fingers up, pressing them in gently, as if to hold his kiss.

"Good night, Caroline," he murmured.

"Good night," she whispered back, feeling the first of the hot tears burning their way down her cheeks.

This night she cried alone, silently, so that he would not guess that she wept. She had told him her worst secret, and he had not turned away. She felt the warmth of his comfort lying close at hand, but she would not allow herself to reach out for it. She did not deserve it, she told herself sternly, but even so she felt a surge of gratitude. The strength of his protection enveloped her, soft and light and welcome. After all these years, someone stood between her and the world. Tomorrow, when she woke, he would be there for her. It seemed too much to ask for, and yet it was true. Closing her eyes against the tears, she drew a long, deep breath, and before she had released it she was fast asleep.

Daniel lay on his back in the darkness, listening to the sound of her muffled tears, every fiber of his being longing to reach out and draw her close to him. He told himself that at least she had confided in him. Surely that proved she was beginning to trust. Still, it was difficult to let her cry alone when he could have kissed away each diamond tear. He lay with his eyes open, and heard when at last the tears stopped and she fell asleep; then he lay a while longer before sleep came to him, as well.

"Close your eyes," he said.

They were standing in the forest, beneath the canopy of the trees. It was after midday, though how long after she could not tell, for they had been walking since morning and had hardly spoken a word. When Daniel had stopped just now, she had thought that he meant to eat, but instead he had stood frowning at the trees for a long moment. Then he had told her to close her eyes.

"Close my eyes?" she repeated.

He nodded his head. "Give me till thirty. Then you can open them."

"Hide-and-seek?" She stared at him in amazement. Had he lost his mind?

But Daniel only smiled. "Oblige me in this one thing."

So, shaking her head, she seated herself upon a log. Laying one arm across her eyes, she began to count aloud. She heard the briefest rustling, then nothing but her own voice.

"Twelve, thirteen..." She wondered whether to be charmed or worried by his boyishness. "... twenty, twenty-one..." Finally: "Twenty-nine, thirty... There. Now, what is required—ready or not, here I come?" As he made no answer, she stood and looked about her. He had left his gun beside her, and their blankets and the pouch. Apart from these items, she was as alone as she had been before he had appeared.

Tentatively she looked, taking a few steps in one direction and casting her eye about. The forest, which had seemed so companionable when he was near, suddenly seemed very quiet, and very, very big. She didn't like the sensation, and she shivered in spite of herself.

"Daniel?" she ventured. "I don't want to play anymore."

"We aren't really playing." His voice came from overhead. Looking up, as he had done, she searched the trees for him.

"Where are you?"

"Up here."

She could hear him very clearly, but she could not see a thing. "Where? I can't see you."

"Just as I thought," he said. She heard another rustling, and saw a branch stir. Then a foot appeared, followed, a moment later, by the rest of Daniel. He jumped from the lowest branch, landing lightly at her side.

"That ought to do well enough."

"Do well enough for what? Are we to play another game?"

"Hardly." His tone was dry. "It will do very well for your hiding place, while I'm scouting the trail ahead."

Frowning, she looked up. "Why can't I come with you? If it's only a matter of bargaining, why can't I be there?"

"Because only a fool would walk into a war camp without reconnoitering first. Besides which, I'd rather be spared the challenge of explaining your presence."

"But I want to come," she insisted. "I won't betray you to the camp. And, when you go in to bargain, I'll stay hidden in the woods." Then she added, "Besides, if you think I plan to spend all afternoon perched up in some tree, with Hannah just up ahead and likely needing me..."

Chapter Ten

Caroline arched her back away from the unyielding trunk, twisting from side to side as much as her perch allowed. She had no idea how long she had been sitting in the tree. With no company but her thoughts, it seemed hours since Daniel had left. She wondered for the hundredth time what his absence meant, whether he had found the Indians and was spying on their camp, whether perhaps even now he was bargaining for Hannah's release. She wondered how he would do it, and how long it would take. Perhaps, at this very moment, he was leading Hannah and Hetty back. Forgetting her discomfort, she imagined the joy with which she would hear Hannah's voice calling from below. From what she had heard, the Indians were as devoted to ceremony as French royalty. She hoped that they would not keep Daniel listening to speeches all night. She doubted that her back would survive so long in this eyrie.

A bird landed on a branch nearby. Catching sight of Caroline, it cocked its head, instinctive fear battling with curiosity. In the end, fear triumphed, and the bird flew away, leaving Caroline and her troublesome thoughts behind. Perhaps Daniel had not yet found the Indians. Perhaps he was still tracking them. Perhaps he had been wrong about their hunting camp, and they were still moving north—which would mean that they were losing time at this very moment. The worst part of waiting was not being able to know.

Caroline shifted again. To Daniel's credit, the seat was as comfortable as a perch in a tree could be. The branch on which she rested widened where it joined the trunk, forming a shallow depression just wide enough for her. It allowed her to relax without worrying about her balance, and for the first little while she had been almost comfortable. The view was pretty, as well: a sea of green and yellow and the beginnings of red and orange, and overhead the domed sky, which was turning from blue to pink. She had not been mistaken; it was drawing towards evening. Daniel had been gone for some hours. She wished he would return.

She peered down through the leafy depths at the ground below. He had told her to stay where she was until she heard his call, but he could not have intended to leave her here all through the night. What if something had happened? What if the Indians had found Daniel before he could find them? For the first time since he had left, she felt fear, the same icy stab she had felt earlier, when she had opened her eyes after counting and found herself alone. Once again, she had the sensation of the woods stretching endlessly, dwarfing her importance until she became irrelevant, a speck of dust to be brushed away with the back of a hand. If Daniel had been captured, what was she to do? Fear turned to panic, rising bitter in her throat.

Stop, she told herself. All this will lead to no good. Daniel will not be captured, he knows the woods too well. And, anyway, she added, chiding herself for her fear, why would they capture a Frenchman whose vocation was trading with them? No, Daniel would not be captured, he would return to her.

He would, she thought, recalling what had happened last night. She had told him about Edmund, and he had not turned away. If anything, he had seemed too willing to excuse her. She still could not believe it, though it must be true, for this morning his manner to her had not changed. He had treated her with the same friendliness mingled with respect. What was it he had said? That she must forgive herself. Well, perhaps it would happen once Hannah was safe. He had given her a glimpse of what life would be like if the awful weight was lifted from her shoulders at last. Perhaps, if they saved Hannah, she would throw off the weight. And then perhaps, somehow, she and Daniel could find the way.

An owl hooted mournfully, drawing her attention to the failing light. Caroline drew her shawl closer, trying to ignore the sound, but her effort met with failure, for the owl hooted again, sending a shiver of apprehension down the length of her spine. Then, suddenly, she sat straighter, the fear dropping away. Of course! It was Daniel—calling as before!

"I'm here!" she called back. "Have you found them? Have you got Hannah with you?" Scrambling from her position, she began her descent, but her legs had so stiffened from the hours in the tree that she had to go very slowly in order not to fall.

"I'm coming!" she called out. "It's only that my legs are stiff. Perhaps you'd better stand back, in case I fall on your head!"

Chuckling at her own joke, she peered down through the leaves, but the shadows were too dense for her to see the ground clearly. She thought she glimpsed him, but then she was not sure. Nor did he call back, though she heard the leaves rustle as he moved. She wondered if he had brought Hannah. Shivering with anticipation, she picked her slow way down.

She came down branch by branch until she reached the last, some six feet off the ground. Daniel would have to help her, would have to catch her as she swung. Relinquishing her handhold on the branch above, she crouched on the branch, slipping her hands down the trunk to maintain her balance.

"Here I am!" she declared, turning her eyes to the ground, to where four sets of stony black eyes stared back up at her.

Indians! For the first instant, she was frozen. Then fear set her blood to racing, filling her with sudden energy. Uncoiling, she reached upwards, but just as her hand grasped the branch she felt the iron grip of a man's hand close tightly around her calf. For a moment she was tempted to try to shake it off, but in the next she realized how little sense that made. What was her intention—to scramble back up the tree? And what would she do when she reached the topmost branch, leap to the sky like a bird? And besides, there were four of them, and likely every one more adept at climbing up through a tree than she. Still, she could not bring herself to accept the fact of her capture, until she heard a word uttered in a guttural voice.

"Vite!" a voice commanded, as the hand that gripped her pulled with a force that almost sent her tumbling from the tree. Somehow she managed to keep her balance still, but in the next moment she felt herself being pulled to the ground. Then she was on her feet, surrounded by the Indians.

There were four of them, all bare chested, clad only in breechclouts and moccasins, their chests smeared with paint, whose colors she could only guess at in the failing light. Their faces were painted, as well, jagged bands of color across the flat planes of their broad cheeks and down their high, beaked noses, turning them into apparitions summoned by her fright.

One of them was her height, though broad and muscular; the other three were all at least a head taller. The man who had pulled her from the tree was the tallest of them all. Unlike his three companions, who all wore their hair down, he wore his pulled in a topknot and lashed with a leather thong. One of the others wore a scalp dangling from his belt. The sight of it filled her with a sudden nausea, and she swallowed in desperation, praying that it would pass.

They circled her as she stood, poking and prodding and talking in a language she did not understand. Part of her was so terrified that she thought she must faint dead away, while another part was deadly calm, even dispassionate—as though she were watching this whole thing happen to somebody else. Daniel said they kept captives for money, but Daniel was not here now. Bits of terrible stories jangled in her mind: how the Indians ripped out fingernails and bit fingers off with their teeth; how they drove sharpened spikes of hickory up their victims' arms; how they flayed them and burned them and cut them, and laughed at their agony. And the things they did to women— No, she couldn't think of it. She would go mad and start raving, and they would slay her where she stood. She must hide her fear from her captors, and from herself, as well.

They had stopped speaking now. The one with the topknot grabbed her and, thrusting her ahead, uttered a command that she understood to be an order to start walking. Because she had no alternative, she did as he said, though her knees were so weak and shaking that she stumbled with every step. This angered Topknot, and he prodded her from behind, speaking again in that harsh, guttural language. Then another of the group passed her, pulling ahead to set the pace, leaving her no choice but to keep up with him.

They walked in silence, moving in single file. Were they taking her to the encampment? Had Daniel sent them, perhaps? Yes, perhaps the bargain had taken longer than he had expected and he had sent them back through the forest to bring her to the camp. How else would they have known where to look for her? From her shouting, her mind replied. Anyone within three miles would have heard her shouting in the tree, and she had come down so slowly that they could have reached her easily. And, if Daniel had sent them for her, why did they treat her thus? A cold chill grew in her stomach, as did the certainty that something had gone wrong.

The Indian before her set so rapid a pace that she had almost to run in order to keep up. Her legs were no longer shaking, but she was weak from her fright, and the rapid motion gave her a stitch in her side. When she slowed to ease it, Topknot prodded her from behind, so she had no choice but to go on, though each breath was a searing pain.

She hoped that the camp was near. Perhaps they would meet Daniel before they arrived. But what good would that do? All her captors carried rifles, and, if the camp was near, would they not alert the others by firing their guns? Then another thought struck her for the first time. What if these men were not of the party that had attacked the farm? What if these were some other Indians? What if the direction in which they were moving led not to the camp, but rather towards Canada? But, even as her heart froze on this new fear, she saw the first flicker of light ahead, and two minutes later they were in the camp.

It was not much of a camp: a couple of fires amidst a scattering of fallen trees on which a handful of warriors sat eating their evening meal. Others reposed upon the ground, their blankets wrapped about them against the evening's chill. And, on a blanket a few yards to her right, Caroline saw Hannah, with Hetty asleep at her side.

"Hannah!" she cried out. At her cry, Hannah raised her head, her eyes wide and disbelieving. Caroline flew to her. "Oh, Hannah, you are alive!" she sobbed, throwing herself pell-mell into her sister's arms.

"Caroline?" Hannah's voice was as incredulous as her gaze. Though Caroline's arms were around her, for a moment Hannah's hung limp; then her hands rose slowly to touch Caroline's back and head. "Am I dreaming?" she wondered, but the back she felt was warm, and the arms tight around her her own flesh and blood. "Caroline, my sister! Oh, Caroline!"

They clung to each other, their tears mingling on their cheeks. Then, without warning, Caroline felt herself ripped free with a force that would have sent her sprawling on her back, had the hand that had seized her not maintained its grip.

It was Topknot, his face rigid with anger. Pointing to Hannah, he shouted at Caroline in his native tongue. Caroline, still shaken, saw his hand draw back. She heard Hannah's strangled cry just before the pain exploded in her left ear. This time, she did fall, the rough ground rushing up to meet her outstretched hands. Her head throbbing, her hands and forearms scraped, she lay where she was. Even as she lay there, she heard him shout from above, and, though she did not know his language, she knew what he desired. Slowly, painfully, she raised herself to her knees, and then to her feet, brushing the dirt from her clothes to delay, if only for a moment, the time when she must confront that arrogant dark face, with its unyielding eyes and its tight, cruel lips.

Topknot was not alone. His rage had brought the others from their evening's repose to stand in a circle about her, murmuring to themselves as they studied her with eyes that were no friendlier than his. This must be a nightmare, she thought, her gaze passing from face to face, searching for relief that she knew she would not find. *Daniel left me in the tree, and I must have fallen asleep. If I make an effort to open my eyes, I'll find that I've been dreaming, and all this will go away.* But, make what effort she might, she could not change a thing. If this was a nightmare, it was a stubborn one.

She heard a rise in the murmuring and turned her head to see the circle part, admitting a broad-shouldered man whose pitch-black hair was shot through with lines of gray and whose tightly coiled topknot was pierced with an eagle's feather. For a long moment he studied her; then, grunting, he nodded his head and folded his arms over his chest, as Topknot began to speak.

He was, she soon realized, recounting the tale of her capture. She heard the hoot of the owl, and his imitation of her own cries. While he spoke, Eagle Feather listened, his face impassive. *What could he be thinking? What power did he have? Did they mean to hurt her?* Daniel had told her that they would not, but Topknot had already struck her, so perhaps Daniel had been wrong. *Had they hurt Hannah?* She had hardly glimpsed her sister's face before she had thrown herself into her arms, and now the gathered Indians hid Hannah from her view. *If Topknot had struck her, had he or somebody else also struck Hannah? Had they struck Hetty, as well? Oh, Lord, where was Daniel? Why did he not rescue her? Why did he not do something to snatch her from this dream?*

Topknot had finished, and now Eagle Feather spoke. His words must have been pleasing, for Topknot grunted in satisfaction. Reaching out, he gripped Caroline's arm once again, pulling her roughly toward a tree that stood nearby. One of the others gave him a length of stout rope, one end of which he fastened to her right wrist. Then, shoving her back against the tree, he pulled on the rope until the roughness of the bark cut into her right arm. In the next moment, she felt her left arm seized, as well, pulled back as her right was and fastened with the rope, so that she was pinioned securely to the tree.

The position was painful. The rope bit into her wrists, and her shoulders ached. She thought of her resentment at being left up in the tree and, in a flash of bitterness, thought that this must be her punishment for having complained so easily. Now she would be taught what real discomfort was. She looked about for Hannah, but her hair was in her eyes, and tossing her head to move it only made the bruise from Topknot's blow throb more.

Nearby, someone was roasting meat on a fire. At the smell, her stomach rumbled, for she had not eaten since this morning, and she had come a long way. Oh, Daniel, she thought wearily, where can you be? How can you let this happen to me? Has something happened to you, that you cannot help?

Clearly satisfied with his handiwork, Topknot moved around the tree to stand before her once again, his arms crossed over his chest. As much as she wished not to, she raised her eyes to his and forced herself to resist the hostility she saw glittering in them. Then his eyes left hers to prowl with slow deliberation down over the rest of her, dwelling so long upon her breasts that she felt the heat rise in her cheeks. At the expression on his face, she forgot her aching arms, forgot all discomfort before the horror of this new threat. Dear God, she prayed silently, please do not let him. Her mouth turned to ashes, and her heart ceased to beat. She watched in frozen horror as Topknot raised his hand to her bodice. Then from somewhere behind her branches snapped and harsh words rang out.

Daniel had spent several hours watching the camp. From the numbers of Indians left to guard the hostages, he had guessed how many must be out scouting and hunting for food, but because numbers were crucial, he wanted to be sure. Mrs. MacKenzie and the child looked well, though frightened and worn from the trip. When six braves returned with a brace of freshly killed wood pigeons, he was glad to see one of their number bring her some of the meat. The man must be her master, he who had first laid hands on her, and the fact that he thought to serve her spoke well of her condition. Despite the value of hostages, often they were abused, either from the master's inbred cruelty or from his lack of care. Caroline would be relieved to hear that her sister was well.

She would not be happy to hear his conclusions as to the likelihood of escape. After several hours of scrutiny, using his knowledge of the terrain, Daniel had concluded that the risks of attempting to spirit Mrs. MacKenzie away were too great to take. Most likely, Mrs. MacKenzie would sleep surrounded by the men, but even if she slept alone he feared that she or her child might be frightened and give the alarm if he tried to wake her. And, in order to have a real chance of outrunning their pursuit, he must seize the horses, too, and doing all that in perfect silence was too much to hope for. An Abenaki brave might sleep deeply at home with his family, but a brave on the trail slept lightly, and with his senses awake. If they apprehended Daniel trying to steal their horses and hostages, not only would he suffer, but so would Mrs. MacKenzie and the child—and Caroline would be left on her own in the woods.

He had decided instead to bargain for them with goods. He had seven belts of wampum hidden in his pouch, along with some silver jewelry and a small pot of the red dye that the Indians loved so well. Beyond this, he could offer a voucher to be exchanged at the posts near the Indian villages south of Montreal, where his credit was always good. Together this should be more than enough to pay for the two hostages and the horse that they would require to bring Mrs. MacKenzie home. Of course, there was the danger that her master might refuse a trade, but in the wilderness risks were a part of life. In Daniel's favor was the general belief that turning down a Frenchman was bad luck for an Indian.

At this point in his ruminations, he had thought of Caroline. To bargain for her sister would take a goodly amount of time, for such things required suitable ceremony. He was fairly sure the Indians would want him to spend the night, in which case he could not leave Caroline perched high in her tree. A better plan would be to return to her now and come back in the hour before dawn. This decided, Daniel left the camp, but he had not walked five minutes when he heard the rustle of footsteps up ahead. Concealing himself in a thicket, he saw the four braves, with Caroline, their prisoner, prodded along in their midst.

His shock was momentary. By habit he vanquished it in order to keep his mind clear for the action required. But what to do? Shooting was out of the question, with the camp so close, and, if he managed to wrest Caroline from these four, he would be declaring himself as their enemy— after which he could not hope to bargain for Mrs. Mac-Kenzie's return. And she would be more closely guarded than she had been before.

While his mind continued working, his body kept silent pace with the Indians. Listing again the value of the trade goods that he possessed, he tried to imagine the workings of the Abenaki mind. What if he claimed Caroline to be his own hostage? He wondered where they had found her. If she had still been in the tree, he could tell them that he had left her there to protect her from wild animals while he had gone to hunt for food. But then they would wonder why he had left her unbound. He could say that he had bound her, but that she had escaped. And, if she had been his hostage, their honor bound them to give her back. Then, maybe, he could bargain for her sister, as well. It all depended upon the Indians' intentions, and their present mood—and whether they would trust him. Some tribes favored traders, and others did not. He hoped that this one was among the former.

Another thought came to him. He had rejected the idea of escape because Mrs. MacKenzie might give him away in her surprise if he appeared. But Caroline would be watching for him to rescue her, and wouldn't she tell her sister to watch for him, as well? The Indians had three horses; with cloth over their noses and their hooves, perhaps they could be silenced long enough to be drawn off. Perhaps, with Caroline helping, escape was possible.

The Indians had reached the camp. Crouching in the bushes where he had hidden before, Daniel watched the reunion between Hannah and Caroline—and saw Caroline thrust onto the ground. At this he sprang forward, caution forgotten, but then he caught himself. He froze in a crouch, his heart pounding with fear that he had been perceived, but the Indians had been too busy watching the spectacle to hear him in the brush.

His pulse throbbing with hatred, Daniel watched as the brave began to recount the tale of her capture to his fellow warriors. When the brave hooted, then cupped a hand to his ear in surprise, Daniel realized what must have occurred: an owl must have hooted, and Caroline had taken it for his call. She must have called out and come down to welcome him, finding instead her captors, who must have been fully as astonished as she.

Then, his story over, the brave seized her once again, prodding her like a swine towards the tree, where he bound her so tightly that Daniel's own wrists burned in sympathy. Attempting to calm the rage swirling in his chest, Daniel reasoned that if they bound her, perhaps they would leave her on her own and he could approach near enough to call out to her without being overheard. He watched her captor survey his handiwork, then watched him move around to survey Caroline herself. With a growing sickness, he watched the change in the swarthy face. When he saw the bronze hand reach out towards her, the sickness exploded and his control broke.

"Halt! What do you do there?"

He called out in the Indian's dialect, crashing through the underbrush and into the startled circle surrounding Caroline. He came to a halt behind her; even in his anger he knew that it was better not to risk his own reaction to the sight of her face, for he feared that the sight of her horror would push him past the brink.

Her tormentor turned to face him, fierce anger in his eyes. "What right have you to assail me?" he demanded, his voice harsh.

"The right of a master. This woman belongs to me."

"Yours!" The dark eyes glared. "But I have just found her, alone and in the woods. This woman belongs to Eshtan!" Angrily he jabbed himself on his painted chest.

Governing his temper, Daniel shook his head. "You found her where I left her when I went for food. When I returned, she was missing, so I tracked her here."

There was a rustle behind him as the circle drew apart to admit a man whose eagle-feather headdress proclaimed him chief.

"What trouble?" he asked.

The enraged brave, Esh-tan, spoke out. "Ho, Ti-sha-wa! This man says that the white woman is his! He says that he left her when he went for food. But, Ti-sha-wa, I ask him, why was she not bound? Why did she come forward so freely when we passed beneath?"

Daniel shrugged. "Perhaps she thought you were I. And what need to bind her? Where would she run, all alone in the wilderness?"

Esh-tan's eye swept him contemptuously. "Ha!" He hawked and spat.

Ti-sha-wa turned to Daniel. "Can you prove what you say?"

Daniel nodded. Looking into the chief's shrewd eyes, suddenly he saw not just the explanation, but his plan, as well. He wondered why he had not seen before. "Yes," he said, "I can prove it. But these are not matters to be shouted to the winds." He glanced towards the fire.

Ti-sha-wa understood. "Very well." He nodded. "Come, let us sit."

Ti-sha-wa turned away and moved towards the fire, but, as Esh-tan did not follow, Daniel held back, as well. He knew that Esh-tan was looking at Caroline, and, though he feared his own reaction, he longed to look, as well. Standing so close, he could hear her breathing, could hear the stir of her dress when she moved. Submitting to his weakness, he glanced up at her face.

As he had feared, her reaction was swift and violent. Her whole body stiffened, and her eyes filled with tears. Daniel could see that she was trying to control herself, but, between her capture and abuse and his appearance, her defenses had been laid low. Her eyes were wide with terror, and a silent, desperate plea. She longed for reassurance, but he did not trust himself to speak. Then he saw the bruise purpling on her cheek and thought for one raging moment that he would kill Esh-tan here and now, regardless of the consequences to her or to himself.

At his side, Esh-tan uttered a grunt. "Ti-sha-wa is at the fire! Do you make him wait for you?" Turning, he stalked away. For a moment longer, Daniel's eyes lingered upon Caroline. Then he followed the brave.

They settled themselves on the ground, Daniel and Esh-tan on either side of the chief. The last of the pigeons was roasting on a spit. Now the chief removed it and offered it around. Daniel accepted some out of politeness. He hadn't eaten since early morning, but he chewed without appetite, thinking of Caroline, who must be as hungry as he, and easily as nauseous with stomach-knotting fear. Esh-tan also took some pigeon and chewed on it noisily, tossing the bones in the dirt.

"I am Ti-sha-wa," said the chief. "And this is Esh-tan, brother of my first wife."

"I am Daniel Ledet. I am a *coureur de bois.*"

Ti-sha-wa nodded. "I have heard of you. You trade with the British."

"I trade with the Abenaki, as well."

Ti-sha-wa nodded. "So, the meat is good?"

"Very good," said Daniel, knowing that etiquette prevented the chief from rushing him into his explanation. But he was grateful for delivery from the food. Setting the bones aside, he drew breath and began.

"I have come from the south," he said. "From the farm above the Great Meadow from which you took the woman and child." He nodded across the clearing, to where Hannah and the baby sat. "There, her husband offered a good ransom for her return. I agreed that I would find you and offer you his price."

Ti-sha-wa's lips curled in a smile. "And keep something for yourself?"

"To pay for my time." Daniel shrugged. "I will pay you better than will the governor in Montreal when you present them to him. And I will relieve you of the burden of their care."

"We feel small burden," said Ti-sha-wa. "As you see, we have horses, so the woman rides. And you see, there is meat to eat."

"And the second woman?" Esh-tan put in. "Why does she come with you? Perhaps to keep you warm at night on the ground?"

Daniel felt his muscles tighten at the sneer on the brave's face, but he forced himself to shrug. Addressing the chief, he continued, "MacKenzie had told me that she was taken, as well, but I found her wandering in the woods. She told me that she meant to rescue her sister alone."

"Ha!" snorted Esh-tan, but the chief only smiled.

"So you took her as hostage," he said. "Why did you not lead her back to claim MacKenzie's price?"

"How much would MacKenzie pay for one so quickly found? Besides, I knew that she would fight me," Daniel said, with another shrug. "She was determined to save her sister's life. When I told her that I meant to get her sister back, she went along easily. She is strong," he added, "and did not hold me back."

"And so," finished Ti-sha-wa, "you left her in a tree while you came to bargain with us. Are you sure that you and the woman did not mean to steal our hostages away? I have heard that you do business at the British forts."

The question caught Daniel off guard, but he thought quickly. "I am a trader, not a thief," he said, meeting the chief's gaze. "I will pay well for the woman and child. What would you ask for them?"

Ti-sha-wa glanced at Hannah and Hetty. "As you say, they are worth a good price. The woman is with child. That is something to keep in mind. And you would need a horse."

"I would pay for the horse, as well. Five belts for the woman, and two for the child. And for the horse I have jewelry, and perhaps some red dye."

Returning his gaze to Daniel, Ti-sha-wa raised his brows. "You offer a good bargain. This MacKenzie must be rich."

"He would have his child born beneath his own roof."

"Ah! What father would not? We ourselves have lost many children and women in the past years. The white man's plagues have struck us and carried many away. Perhaps we shall take the woman and her children into our hearts. They would swell our numbers and give us happiness."

He meant adoption, making them part of the tribe. Daniel shuddered within at the thought of what Caroline would say to this. Outwardly, he only shrugged, saying, "They will, if they survive. A British woman is not like an Abenaki squaw, especially one with child. She could sicken and die from a hundred causes on the trail. Upon learning she will not be ransomed, she might pine away. And it would seem a pity to lose the ransom and the hostage both."

Ti-sha-wa spread his hands. "There is a risk in all things. We may lose our captives, or they may be stolen from us. By you, by another— You know how these things are."

"The French and the Abenaki are brothers," Daniel said evenly.

"As you say," Ti-sha-wa agreed. "And, because we are brothers, I have a suggestion. Why not trade your hostage to us, instead? MacKenzie will be angry when you come back with only this one. Perhaps in his anger he will pay no price at all, and then you will have gone a long way for naught. As I have said, we have lost many women, and our braves are left without brides. Perhaps Esh-tan would take that one as his wife."

Ti-sha-wa gestured in Caroline's direction, and Daniel saw Esh-tan's head come up at his words. Without even looking, he caught the gleam in the warrior's eyes.

"I would offer a dozen fine beaver pelts for the woman," Esh-tan announced.

Daniel tasted the bile of hatred rising in his throat, but he managed to swallow it down. "Your offer is most generous. But she is not for sale."

Had his voice betrayed him? He felt Ti-sha-wa's eyes studying his face. Then, slowly, the chief smiled. "Is she not?" he asked. "Well, perhaps we shall persuade you to change your mind. Or perhaps you will even change ours. In the meantime, you shall travel north with us. You shall come as our brother and our honored guest."

As their prisoner, he meant. "Thank you for your offer," Daniel said carefully. "But I believe I will take the woman back for what ransom she will yield."

"Do not cheat yourself, my friend. As you say, the ransom will grow the longer she is gone. And what comfort for her sister to have her close at hand! No, it is decided. We shall travel as one. We shall guard your hostage as though she were our own."

It was decided. The chief had cast the die, and Daniel had no choice but to accept the throw. Did Ti-sha-wa doubt his story about Caroline's status, or did the chief suspect him of being a British spy? Either way, he was bound to travel in their midst, and with Caroline as their captive, guarded both night and day.

Bowing his head, Daniel answered, "My people and yours are brothers. I am honored to travel with you."

"Good," said Ti-sha-wa. "Then let us smoke the pipe!" Reaching for the clay pipe that lay upon the log, the chief happened to notice the remains of the pigeon lying in the dirt. Pausing, he gestured, saying to Daniel, "Perhaps you wish to give this to your hostage to eat. Unless you have better for her."

The words were a warning, a test. The Indians treated their captives harshly, and the French did the same. Besides, the British were their natural enemies. If Daniel showed himself too kind in his treatment of Caroline, would he not confirm what Ti-sha-wa might already have guessed? Their best hope for freedom lay in his gaining Ti-sha-wa's trust, and if cruelty would gain that, then he must be cruel. And Caroline's reaction would only help their cause. Scooping up what was left of the pigeon from the dirt in which it lay, Daniel rose from the fire and moved towards Caroline, silently begging her forgiveness for what he must do.

Caroline watched him come, weak in the knees and almost fainting from relief. It felt as if she had been watching him at the fire for hours, and in all that time he had not so much as glanced at her. In fact, but for the moment when he had first appeared, he had seemed almost single-minded in ignoring her. Cold, aching and frightened, she had told herself that he was only playing a part, yet, as the minutes had passed, she had felt her heart sink. She could not even draw reassurances from Hannah's being near, for Hannah was across the clearing from her, blocked from her vision by the men gathered at the fire. But now, at the sight of Daniel coming to her at last, she felt her spirits rising again. With new hope, she raised her head. Now Daniel would tell her what was going on. The sound of his voice, speaking, would be sweet balm upon her soul after the harshness and cruelty of the Indians.

Her eyes went to his as he neared, but she found no sign of feeling, no compassion, in them. He looked to her like a man walking in his sleep. Fear, puzzlement, exhaustion, pounded in her head. Her lips groped for a question that her mind could not phrase. In any case, he passed her, moving behind the tree, and she understood quickly that he meant to set her free.

The bonds had been done tightly, and her hands were almost numb. She cried out at the sudden pain when the rope tightened momentarily before she was released. She staggered one pace forward, then felt herself caught roughly. His hand closed around her arm and lowered her to the ground. He towered above her. She looked up dizzily in time to see him drop something in her lap. A pile of half-gnawed pigeon bones. She stared at them in shock.

"It is your dinner. Eat it!" His voice came like a shot, and she felt her body jerk in reaction to its sting. She waited for him to say more. "Then you must go to sleep. Tomorrow will be a long day," he said harshly.

Stunned beyond reaction, she watched him walk away. She must be dreaming, for she could make no sense of this. It was as though a stranger had stepped into Daniel's skin. Without thinking, she called out, "Dan—Mr. Ledet!"

He paused, as though considering whether to turn or not. For a moment, she feared he might not, but in the end he did.

"Yes? What is it?" His face was in the darkness, so she could not see his eyes, but his voice was impatient and lacking in any warmth. She had never heard him speak in such a voice before. Had her senses left her? What had changed him so?

He was waiting for her to speak. The other men in the clearing were waiting, as well, staring intently at their faces to glean from their expressions the meaning of their strange words.

"Yes?" Daniel barked, in the same impatient tone.

One of the men muttered something in their guttural language, and another snickered in response. Caroline felt her back stiffen, despite her sinking heart. Looking down at the bones that lay in her lap, she swept them away with her hand. "I'm not hungry," she said, setting her jaw firmly against the hot rush of her tears.

For a moment, he stood silent, but then she saw him shrug. Again he turned to the fire, moving away from her.

A little while later, one of the men came to retie her hands and to give her a blanket that she recognized as her own. He must have gotten it from Daniel, who was still at the fire, laughing and chatting with the men. He'd paid no more heed to her after he'd untied her bonds, acting as though he were glad to be done with her.

Two of the men lay down beside her, one on either side, and both were soon fast asleep, snoring noisily. She lay in the darkness, trying to comprehend what had happened to her over the course of the day. It seemed a lifetime since last night, when she and Daniel had sat in the dark, she murmuring her confession and he forgiving her. How sinless and unburdened she had felt afterwards, how disbelievingly relieved. Had it been just this morning that she had risen with a light heart?

It seemed years ago. Worse, it seemed a dream, buried beneath the nightmare of the forced march through the woods, the blow, the cruelties she had suffered since. Last night, even Hannah had seemed close at hand, while now, when she was really only a few yards away, Caroline felt as distant from her as though she were on the moon. She wished she could understand.

Her stomach was growling with hunger, and her head was throbbing with pain. Her hands were again half numb, tied back behind her back, and her legs were hobbled and fastened to one of the men to keep her from trying to run off while he slept. And where would she run to, all on her own in the woods?

Why had they not set her free? What had Daniel told them, when they had talked by the fire? She'd thought that he would give them some reason for their being in the woods. She wouldn't have minded if he'd told them that she was his woman—anything in order to get her away. But, although the fireside conversation had seemed amiable, it had resulted in nothing but a pile of dirty bones and Daniel's chilling words.

Why had Daniel acted thus? What had happened to change him, to make him appear so friendly to the Indians and so hostile to her? She had thought her mind empty, but now she heard Thomas's voice, saying, "Spying, of course, woman! Passing word to the Indians, so they'd know where to strike. Most likely he's got Phipps's scalp hanging from his belt!"

No! Her soul rebelled, just as it had before. No, he cannot be a spy! He is a good man! I know him to be gentle, and honorable and kind! He would not betray me, I will not believe it! But, aching and heartsore, she felt nagging doubt eroding her convictions with harsh facts. Had the Indians not found her where he had left her in the woods, and had they not taken her directly to the camp where Daniel had seemed contented to see her a captive? What if his intention from the very first had been to lead her north and deliver her to the tribe?

Why should he do such a thing? demanded her outraged heart. Her weary mind replied: in order to gain their trust. No, she would not believe it, could not believe it true. The memory of these past days would not let her believe—not after the way he had held her, the promises he had made. But Edmund, too, had promised, and look what had come of that.

Daniel was different. He was honest and courageous; he would not betray her. She was no longer the starry-eyed girl she had been at Harrow Hall. She was a mature woman who could judge a man's worth. She knew Daniel's character; she would stake her life on it.

Then how to explain today? And the way she lay right now? And the growling in her stomach from lack of decent food? Round and round her thoughts ran, like a dog chasing its tail, until she was too weary to ponder anymore. She fell asleep aching, heartsick and confused, to dream of owls and fires and Thomas's sneering face.

Chapter Eleven

The party moved swiftly and silently, the men spread in a loose line, walking hunched forward, both hands hanging free, ready to reach for tomahawk or rifle at a moment's notice. Their moccasined feet broke not a twig and stirred not a leaf on the ground. For the most part, they did not speak. Watching them, Caroline could not but note the contrast between this group and the one in which she had traveled north from Connecticut. The Indians moved as stealthily as the animals in the woods, while the wagons had rattled along, making more noise than a herd of cows at milking time.

Hannah rode up ahead on the young soldier's bay mare. Caroline would have been glad to ride, as well, but the other horses were already burdened down with the booty the Indians had taken from the farm. The spinning wheel from the kitchen rattled against a tin washtub and the pewter ewer that had been her grandmother's. The sight of the ewer brought a stab of anger to Caroline, and made her grateful that most of the plunder was hidden away, bundled into blankets and quilts stripped from the beds. Sometimes Hetty rode perched before Hannah on the mare, and sometimes the Indians carried her hanging from their backs in slings fashioned from the red blankets they all seemed to have.

In the two days since Esh-tan had separated Hannah and herself so forcibly, Caroline had not spoken one word to her sister, had not spent a single moment at her side. In camp they were kept apart from each other, and while they were traveling Caroline was not allowed even to walk near Hannah's horse. The reason for this, she concluded, was simple coldheartedness, for the tribe could hardly suspect that they would plot to escape—two women and a child, surrounded by two dozen armed men! Even Caroline, in her misery, could see the hopelessness of it.

Today, the trail they followed hugged the side of a creek, sometimes along the damp earth and sometimes over the rocks. Mostly it was uneven and hard to negotiate. Mistaking her footing, Caroline suddenly tripped. She felt herself pitch forward and struggled to save herself before she hit the ground. She was lucky this time. The last time she had stumbled she had bruised her knee badly. The man behind her had not helped her in any way. Among the tribesmen, she had noted, Hannah's master alone was kind. The rest of the men shared the cruelty of an insensitive child. They did not lend a hand when she stumbled, instead laughing at her. Except, that is, for Esh-tan, who continued to glare, as though he would yet reclaim that of which he had been deprived. At least her status as Daniel's hostage protected her from Esh-tan. It was perhaps the one thing for which she felt gratitude—that, and the fact that she knew that Hannah was alive and well. But this separation from her sister lay like a weight on her heart.

The trail steepened, descending jaggedly. The horses had to be led on a more serpentine path through the woods, and Caroline hit her knee again making her way down. Reaching the bottom, she saw that the stream had descended, as well, forming a series of pretty falls over the rock outcropping. The water splashed invitingly from ledge to ledge, forming rainbowed showers and deep pools at the base.

This was obviously a stopping place, for the men threw off their burdens and splashed beneath the falls, crying out in pleasure as the cool water washed their skin. Looking around, Caroline saw Hannah seated a few yards off, not far from where the horses were tied. She saw, too, that Daniel had not joined the men, but had instead found a soft spot in the shade of a spruce tree, against whose trunk he had settled, apparently for a nap. His hat was tilted forward, and his eyes were shut.

The sight of him gave her pain, a sharp pang that shot through her heart. In the two days since her capture, he had hardly looked at her, and when he had spoken his tone had been the one that had shocked her so that first night. She continued to struggle to understand the change. Again and again she heard Thomas's voice taunting her, but still she resisted naming Daniel as a spy.

Was he playing a part? *Was he?* She longed to believe he was. Sometimes she watched him, hoping for a clue, but his face, once so gentle, now gave nothing away. Last night, however, she had thought she sensed a change. She had been ordered to gather firewood for the camp, and she had been stooping to retrieve dry branches from the ground when she had sensed him behind her. Pausing, she had looked up. Although it was already dark—for they had traveled until the light had failed—she had sensed the presence of the old gentleness in his eyes. His hand had stirred beside him, as though he had meant to reach out to her, and her hand had moved in response.

But, in the next moment, his hand had snapped back, and his voice had cut her cruelly. "Do you work so slowly? How will you cook your food? You will sleep hungry tonight!" And he had moved away from her without another word, to converse with Ti-sha-wa, who stood a short way off, leaving her to add this contradiction to her tortured thoughts.

The men frolicked like puppies in the deep pools and the falls, droplets beading their slick backs. The water was inviting after the heat of the march, and Caroline's feet ached for the relieving cool. But, in order to enjoy it, she would have to subject herself to comments that she did not understand and snickering that she did. Glancing once more at Hannah, she found her sister looking at her with an expression of longing that brought tears to her own eyes. The men were busy with their amusement, and Daniel's eyes were closed. Slowly, very slowly, Caroline rose and began creeping towards where Hannah sat.

From beneath his lashes, Daniel watched her go, keeping one eye on the water, in case someone else saw her. Then he would have to leap up in order to catch her first, to save her from a chiding more severe than his. And yet he, too, would have to be severe. He would have to hold her arm so that a bruise appeared, for Ti-sha-wa would be watching, watching, as always. In the two days since they had been detained at the camp, Daniel had not been given a moment alone with her. Instead, he had felt himself tested constantly. After two days of constant trial, he wondered how much more it would take to gain Ti-sha-wa's trust.

He had almost lost it last night. He had sent Caroline off to gather wood, hoping that if she moved away from the rest of the men he might have a moment with her. When he had assured himself that the other men were busy with their own concerns, he had moved off after her. Approaching her, he had felt his heart contract with pain at the sight of her servile stoop. He had longed to raise her to stand at his side, to smooth back her tumbled hair, to soothe her still-bruised cheek, to hold her gently to him, murmuring words of love. Yet he could submit to no such temptation, not with Ti-sha-wa so near. But perhaps he could talk to her. It would take only ten seconds to tell her the truth, to lift the extra burden under which she trudged.

He knew the moment at which she sensed him behind her, and a pang struck him when he saw her flinch. But, when her eyes came up to his, he forgot the pang, and forgot his resolution. He began to reach—but, just at the last moment, his forest-trained ears caught the almost-soundless tread of moccasins on bare earth. Stopping himself from reaching for her, he chided her instead, forcing himself to ignore the way she flinched again. And, turning, he had seen Ti-sha-wa, not five feet away. Watching, always watching. Watching him for a false move. Then, he supposed, the wily chief would take Caroline from him and give her back to Esh-tan, who wanted her for a wife.

It wouldn't last much longer. Tomorrow night, they would arrive at the next river, on the far side of which the rest of the tribe was camped. There they would stay for hunting and the ritual celebrations. Those things would offer a diversion, and perhaps cover for an escape. He might not be able to manage the sister, but he would take Caroline as far as the first settlement at which she would be safe. Then he'd go back alone. He would think much more clearly when he knew that she was safe. But, in the meantime, he must continue to pass Ti-sha-wa's tests. With a sigh, he watched her reach her sister's side; then he turned his attention to the men at their play. He hoped she would be granted at least a few minutes of peace.

"Caroline!" Hannah gasped as Caroline dropped down beside her. She returned her sister's tight embrace, clutching Caroline to her, then pushing her away. She darted an anxious glance from the men in the stream to Daniel, then to Hetty, who crouched a short way off, following the progress of a black beetle in the dirt.

"They're busy," murmured Caroline, taking care to keep her voice low. "I couldn't stand it any longer. I had to talk to you!"

"Yes! Until I saw you, I feared that you were dead, somewhere back at the farm. But how comes Mr. Ledet to have taken you prisoner?"

"He didn't," said Caroline. "I fell asleep by the river and didn't wake until after the raid. When I found out what had happened, I came after you. Then Daniel found me, and we came together. He said that he would free you—"

Hannah gasped. "He tricked you!" She was still feeling the shock that had come two nights ago, at the sight of Mr. Ledet holding Caroline hostage. Although she had heard Thomas proclaim him a spy, she had not believed it. But she had seen the proof here. "Then Thomas was right," she said, following her own thoughts.

"No!" Caroline started at the violence she heard in her own voice.

"But you are his prisoner."

"Yes, I know," she said. "But I believe he may be acting, for our benefit. Perhaps he must prove to the Indians that he is on their side, so that he will be able to spirit us away."

Hannah frowned, trying to take in what Caroline said. "But is it necessary? If we try to escape and they catch us, I fear what they would do to us. This way, I believe they will take us with them to Montreal to be exchanged by the governor for a ransom Thomas will pay."

At the mention of Thomas's name, Caroline remembered the scene at the burning farm, when she had gone after Hannah and Thomas had gone after his trees. Her expression must have betrayed the sentiments in her heart, for Hannah gripped her arm tightly.

"Thomas!" she exclaimed. "There is something you are hiding! Has some ill befallen him? You say that you were coming after me alone? Why did Thomas not come, as well?"

"No." Caroline shook her head. "No, Thomas is well. And, as for his not coming...he had gone to the fort to alert the other men. I sneaked off on my own." She knew she had to lie to save her sister pain. But, she vowed in silence, *if I get you home, I swear by all that is holy that I will tell you the truth. I swear that Thomas will not benefit from what we are going through. I will change your future, if I must do it with my own bare hands.* "And you?" she asked, pushing Thomas from her mind. "You are treated well?"

"My master is kind, as you see. And they carry Hetty when I cannot bear her weight."

"She is worth money to them. They want to protect her worth," Caroline retorted, but Hannah shook her head.

"Perhaps. But they could refuse. At first she cried, from her illness and from fear of so many strange men. They said that if she did not stop they would put her to death. I feared that they would. But finally she stopped." Hannah's haggard look reflected the trials of that time.

"Poor Hannah," murmured Caroline, "to have suffered so much alone."

"But now it is better," Hannah said, with a wan smile. "Now it is you who suffers."

"No—" began Caroline, but her words were suddenly cut short by Daniel's outraged voice, rising from just behind.

"What is this, woman? Will you not obey? You are told to keep away from your sister, and yet you sit with her!"

Caroline's head jerked around.

"Will you flout my authority before all the world? I will teach you to be obedient!" he cried, seizing her arm. Caroline felt herself jerked bodily from the ground and dragged along the rough rocks towards the edge of the stream. Her eyes blinded by the pain of his grip upon her arm, she thought that he meant to throw her into the nearest pool. Instead, he stopped at the stream's edge, forcing her down upon the bank.

"Take off your shoes!" he commanded.

"My shoes?" She stared blankly at him, all her senses reeling.

Instead of repeating his command, he knelt and, rough handed, pulled off her moccasins. Taking her right foot in his hand none too gently, he raised it, sole upward; then he thrust it away.

"Covered with blisters!" he said, as though she were somehow to blame. "Soak them in the water, then wrap them in wet oak leaves. They will draw the infection off." And, before she could question or even absorb this command, he whirled away from her and stalked off, back to his tree.

The men were watching her from the pool. She could feel their mocking eyes fixed upon her face. She hated to have to move closer to where they were, but she feared that, if she did not, Daniel would rage at her again. Her arm was throbbing from where his fingers had gripped. Why had he cut short her precious moments at Hannah's side? His voice, his grip, his reaction, all bespoke real hatred. Was he only acting, or was that how he felt? And, if so, why? Shaking her head sadly, she raised herself up and moved to the edge of the first pool, seating herself on a flat stone and lowering her feet into the water.

She could not help but sigh with satisfaction as the coolness engulfed her throbbing feet. He was right about her blisters; they had caused her increasing distress. She wriggled her toes in the water, feeling the muscles relax, lowering her legs farther, until the water reached her knees. The water was clear and dark; through it she could see down to the bottom of the pool. She moved her feet back and forth, watching the current flow. Then her breath caught and froze when a hand gripped her calf.

She knew who it was before she looked up. Esh-tan, his dark eyes gleaming with a malevolence that caused her to shiver as the water had not. Slowly, very slowly, the hand loosed its grip and the fingers moved up her leg to the soft flesh beneath her knee. She tensed herself to keep her leg from trembling with fear. Esh-tan felt the movement, and it made him smile. With the same deliberation, he flicked his tongue along his lips as his fingers crept up past her knee.

Please! Caroline prayed. Please, do not let him dare. Oh, does not Daniel see what is happening? Will he not rescue me? But, even as she prayed for Daniel to come to her aid, Esh-tan's hand released her, and he turned away, moving back to the other men, leaving her pale and shaken, her stomach heaving with fear.

The whole thing had taken less than a minute, but that had been long enough to open her eyes to a whole new fear. Hannah might be content to wait for her freedom until they reached Montreal, but could she herself last that long? How long would it be until Esh-tan approached her again?

They reached the wide river next evening at dusk. From the far bank, across its width, plumes of smoke rose up from the trees. Caroline stood on the rocky beach with Hannah and Hetty while the men went to retrieve the canoes they had hidden on their trip south. They left Daniel behind, as well. At first, Caroline wondered why they had not taken him, but then she realized that they must not want him to know of their hiding places. She noticed that they had left a brave behind, as well—presumably to guard them, though in fact he seemed more interested in gazing across at the camp with longing eyes. And Daniel seemed equally lost in admiring the colored clouds piled high in the sky.

Caroline glanced over to where the horses were tied. What if she and Hannah managed to get to them? What if they rode off quickly—could they get away? Coming north, there had been places where the trail had been overgrown and the horses had had to ride wide. But those spots were farther down, as she recalled. For the first several hours of riding, they would have a fairly clear trail. Could they go faster than the men could in pursuit? She thought that they could.

She glanced over at the guard. The beach was strewn with rocks of all sizes and shapes. Bending, she raised one that fitted within her palm. Brought down with enough force, it would stun a man. But what of Daniel? Her eyes moving towards him, she thought of something else. Was it worth the gamble? She thought that it was. And escape would only be harder once they had crossed to the river's far side.

"Hannah," she whispered, "can you mount a horse on your own?" In their travels, the Indians had helped her up.

Hannah turned, bewildered. "I don't know. Why do you ask?"

"Because I am planning for the three of us to escape."

"What—now?" Panic froze Hannah's face. "But, Caroline, it is madness! We shall never succeed!"

"And I think we might," she replied. "I will knock the guard unconscious. You be ready to mount when I give the sign."

"And Hetty? What of her?"

"I will take her with me. Leave her on the ground." It was something she had not considered, but she would manage somehow. Leaving the ashen-faced Hannah behind her, Caroline moved away, not towards the contemplative guard, but to where Daniel stood.

She wondered if he sensed her coming up behind him. She could not believe that he did not, trained as he was in the ways of the woods, and yet he did not turn. Touching him on his fringed sleeve, "Mr. Ledet?" she said.

For response, Daniel nodded his head. That sixth sense he had for trouble alerted him, and he had seen her pick up the rock from the corner of his eye. He wondered if she meant to strike him, or if it was meant for the guard. She obviously had not seen the brave hidden behind the bush, nor the other behind the tree—sentries that Ti-sha-wa had posted to spy on him, lest he submit to the temptation to try to get away. Though he saw no humor in the chief's continuing lack of trust, he could not but view with bitter amusement Ti-sha-wa's low opinion of his own spying skills. If he could not spot such a sentry, he could not have survived this far.

He was prepared to seize Caroline's hand should she strike, but that was not her intention. Instead, she moved to his side, speaking in a low voice and choosing her words carefully.

"Mr. Ledet. Daniel. I don't know what has happened to cause this change in you. Thomas would say that you had always been in league with them, but I can't believe it is true. Whatever you feel about me, I beg you to help me now. I want to take the horses and go with my sister. If you have been acting these last days, then come away with us. If not, I will give you money to allow us to get away. Whatever price you desire will be waiting for you in the south. Only please do not betray us. Please..." Her slender fingers closed upon his arm.

Although it took all his strength, he pushed her hand away. Raising his voice, so that the guard turned, he demanded, "What is this foolishness? Why do you come to me with this wild babbling? I thought I had told you to stay there on the beach? Will you never listen? Now go, as I have said!" And he pushed her sharply along the rocky beach. As he did, he felt the stiffness of her anger and hurt. One day, perhaps, he would be able to tell her how he had just saved her life.

"It is better," whispered Hannah, when Caroline rejoined her. "We could not have been successful, and we would have suffered for it."

Caroline made no response. Indeed, there was none to make. The promise of escape had already slipped away, to be replaced by the greater shock of Daniel's reaction. She had pleaded with him, begged for his compassion. How could she believe in him after he had betrayed her this second time? And how could she survive the future, knowing that he had?

A few minutes later, the men appeared from the woods, four of the braves together carrying a single canoe. The craft they launched in the river were very different from the one that Daniel had made in one evening. These were fashioned of creamy birch bark, with curved maple gunwales and their inner portions reinforced with thin cedar strips. They were larger, as well, twice as long or more, so that four men could paddle each, still leaving space for the captives, and all the loot, as well.

The horses swam behind, their leads tightly secured to the man closest to the rear. Despite the drag the horses created, the ride was swift and smooth. The braves stroked in unison, their bare backs straining as they leaned forward, their paddles flashing silver in the dying light.

They paddled with their eyes fixed on the opposite shore, and as they reached midstream one brave rose to his knees. Cupping his hand to his face, he gave the cry of a northern loon. The call rang out and echoed across the stream and back, and hardly had it died away when lights appeared along the shore. Little points of light strung in an uneven line—women and children, watching their men from the shore. Seeing the flickering line of lights, the men broke into song, a chanted song whose steady rhythm matched the paddles' strokes.

It was a lovely night, with the stretch of sparkling water beneath the mild evening sky. Despite the tumult of her feelings, Caroline could not help but notice the beauty of the scene. As the canoe drew nearer, she watched the lights grow and expand into the silhouettes of people standing on the shore. Then she remembered once again that she was a captive, and the beauty disappeared.

Unable to watch any longer, Caroline turned away. The canoe that carried Ti-sha-wa and Daniel was farther back, but Hannah's canoe was directly behind the one in which she rode. Catching Hannah's eye, she managed a reassuring smile, unwilling to show Hannah the fear she really felt. At least, she told herself, ready to grasp at any straw, now there would be women. Surely the women would be less cruel. And women would care for Hannah as the men could not.

The flaring pine brands that the women held aloft cast fantastic shadows on the shore, turning the women's faces into strange satiric masks as they came forwards into the water to wave the men ashore. Caroline heard the cries of pleasure with which they welcomed their heroes' return, and felt their sharp eyes upon her, measuring her worth. She forced herself to hold her head high and her eyes straight ahead, so that they would have no cause to suspect her fear.

Her canoe landed first, and hardly had she heard the scrape of the bottom on the shore before strong hands were raising her, pulling her from the boat. She landed in the water and waded to dry ground, where she was immediately surrounded by the chattering, gesturing throng. Then she became aware of Esh-tan speaking nearby, recounting yet again the story of her capture. The women turned to listen, admiration lighting their eyes, but when he reached the point about Daniel the women's faces fell. One woman in particular seemed to be expressing her disgust. Planting her hands upon her hips and spitting to one side, she gave Caroline a hard look that resembled Esh-tan's own so closely that Caroline felt her heart sink.

In the next moment, the group was distracted by the cries of pleasure that greeted Hannah's and Hetty's canoe. Most of the women drew apart in order to welcome it, but the woman who looked like Esh-tan remained behind. Taking the pack that Esh-tan had deposited on the beach, she thrust it at Caroline so roughly as to almost knock her down. Signaling with one arm, she ordered her to carry the pack up the bank and to the camp. For a moment, Caroline hesitated, her eyes returning to the boats, but then she remembered that Daniel would offer no relief. Seeing her hesitation, the woman grunted with displeasure, her face darkening. With no one to defend her, Caroline dared not refuse. Tightening her grip on the pack, she turned towards the camp.

This shore, like the other, had a flat, rocky beach, and a steep embankment that was still slick from the last rain. It was, in fact, too slick for Caroline to scale with the pack in her arms. At first, she struggled without success. The Indian woman made no move to come to her assistance, but watched from behind, her eyes as hard as before.

Setting the pack on a nearby rock, Caroline slung the strap across her chest, as she had seen the men do. The burden was awkward, for the strap was too long for her, but though its weight dragged her backwards, at least she had the use of her hands. Clawing, sliding, scrabbling, she finally reached the top.

She found herself in a small field, less than an acre across. Beyond it, through the twilight, she saw a line of spruce trees and a circle of bark huts beneath it that comprised the camp. Caroline took one step towards the camp, looking backwards as she did for the Indian woman. But, to her surprise, the woman was no longer at her side, but rather down upon the beach, welcoming the canoe that had borne Daniel and Ti-sha-wa both. Caroline found herself searching for the familiar bright silver head; then, again, she remembered what had happened earlier. The weight of his desertion, added to the weight of the pack, was too much. She sank down in the rough grass to await the next blow, wondering dully whence it would come.

As the canoes landed, the women received their cargo. Then they pulled them onto the shore, and the whole tribe gathered around, cheering and chattering. Caroline saw Hannah standing at her master's side and, with another pang, saw Daniel there, as well. Now, as she watched, the ranks formed in a semicircle with Ti-sha-wa at its center and Esh-tan's woman at his side. Caroline watched the woman's face as Ti-sha-wa spoke. For the most part, she beamed with pleasure, but when the chief turned to Daniel her face darkened again.

When Ti-sha-wa had finished speaking, the bundles were gathered up, and the tribe moved in procession towards the embankment. Ti-sha-wa led the way, with the woman at his left and Daniel at his right. As they approached her, Caroline got to her feet, wondering if she ought to move. But she didn't know where to move to. So, instead, she stood, her eyes upon the ground. They stopped when they reached her, and Daniel spoke, in his harsh master's voice.

"The chief has offered me the use of his wigwam. You, being my hostage, will sleep there, as well."

"Whatever you like," she murmured, hoisting the heavy pack as Daniel moved on with the chief. Glancing back at the embankment, she saw Hannah trying to make her way up it. Although she carried nothing upon her back, her stomach made her awkward, and she, too, slipped backwards in the mud. Caroline saw Hannah's master catch her by one arm and help her to the top, while a gray-haired woman carried Hetty up. Caroline saw how they waited for Hannah to catch her breath. At least, she thought, turning towards the camp again, at least I will have the assurance of knowing that Hannah is in kind hands.

Daniel stood with Ti-sha-wa before one of the wigwams. The woman stood with them, two children at her side. Caroline stopped before them, standing with her head bowed, as befitted her status.

"The chief's wife is Hoo-tan," Daniel told her. "You will help her in the wigwam for so long as we are here."

Caroline acknowledged the order with a nod of her head, keeping her eyes upon the ground to hide what lay in them. Of course, she realized, now that she saw the truth, looking as much as she did like Esh-tan, Hoo-tan would not be his wife, but rather his relative. His sister, perhaps, she thought with a heavy heart. Hoo-tan, for her part, hardly spared Caroline a glance, turning to follow her husband into the wigwam.

"What shall I do with this pack?" Caroline asked in a low voice when Daniel turned, as well.

"Whose is it?" he asked, looking back at her.

"Esh-tan's," she answered, hardly daring to look up, afraid that he would have her bring it to the brave.

But he wished no such thing. Instead, he said, shrugging, "Leave it on the ground. He will come for it, I am sure." And he followed his hosts into the wigwam, leaving her to make her own way.

Caroline's first impression upon coming into the wigwam was of darkness and overcrowding. Certainly, the interior had hardly enough space for four people and their possessions, let alone for two guests. By the light of the fire that burned in the center of the hut, she picked out a clutter of blankets and implements strewn about the floor, leaving so little room to move about that one could not take two steps without treading upon a bed.

Hoo-tan's thoughts, it seemed, had been close to her own, for now the Indian woman addressed her husband, pointing to her children, then to Caroline, speaking rapidly and harshly. Ti-sha-wa silenced her with a single word, but, though Hoo-tan ceased her protest, Caroline did not miss the look of smoldering hatred that she turned upon her behind her husband's back. Bending down, Hoo-tan pushed the blankets about, opening a new space upon the wigwam's floor. Then she set about the business of putting her children to bed.

"Here." Caroline felt something thrust into her hands and, looking down, saw that they were her and Daniel's blankets. Oppressed as she was by the events of the last half hour, it took her a moment to realize what she was meant to do. Kneeling on the hard earth, she spread the blankets out, trying not to think ahead, to the days to come. She had thought that Esh-tan was her worst enemy, but now she feared that she had found a far more relentless one. How, she wondered despairingly, was she to survive in this dark, smoke-filled space with a woman who despised her? And Daniel, whose very presence hurt like a wound to the heart? That was the very worst pain. The Indians might threaten physical hurt, but they could not match this desolation, a desolation only a broken heart could bring. Despairing, she drew the ends of her blanket up and over her. And yet, even so full of dread, she had only to close her eyes to find sleep, her only comrade, offering a night's escape.

* * *

In all the wigwam, Daniel alone did not sleep. From the shadows of his blanket, he watched Caroline. Her face was streaked with mud, and what he could see of her bodice was filthy. He ached to reach out and draw her into his arms. Earlier, on the far bank, she had told him of her faith in him despite his coldness to her, but now, after he had crushed her plan to escape, he knew that her faith was gone. Now she believed he had betrayed her.

That might help him win Ti-sha-wa's trust, but Daniel knew that he could not survive the change in her. His heart was aching with love and tenderness, but Caroline had avoided his eyes, as she avoided those of her tormentor, Hoo-tan. And, too, he knew that the next time she chanced escape she would not come to him. And that made the danger to her very grave indeed. Watching her from beneath his lashes, Daniel swore to himself that, risk or no risk, he must tell her the truth. He could no longer play at deception; the cost was too high for them both.

Finally, long into the night, he sought the oblivion of sleep himself.

The day that followed resembled the evening past. Daniel ignored Caroline, while Hoo-tan ordered her about. Finally, as the day wore on, Hoo-tan took her out to the woods, where most of the women and children were busy gathering nuts. At first, Caroline was reluctant to go, but, despite her dread of Hoo-tan, the time passed almost pleasantly. For one thing, the weather was fine. The air was crisp with fall's approach, and the sun filtered through the trees, dappling the children playing underfoot. Hetty played among them, her head bent to theirs, as if living among the Indians were the most natural thing in the world.

Hannah was there, as well, working beside the woman with whom Caroline had seen her last night. The woman's face was broad and plain, and her frame was stout. Her eyes, when they met Caroline's, held no hostility. Caroline also noticed that the woman's children looked after Hetty, just as Tom and Elizabeth had done.

As they worked, the women gossiped and sang, giving the endeavor a festive air. At first, Hoo-tan kept close watch over Caroline, but eventually she fell to gossiping with a group of friends, and Caroline gradually made her way towards Hannah, until at last she managed to reach her sister's side.

"How are they treating you?" she murmured, taking care to keep her voice low and her eyes upon the ground.

"Well, very well," Hannah replied, with a look whose sharpness Caroline did not understand until she added, "My mistress, Yum-sa-wek, speaks English very well."

"Oh!" Caroline felt her cheeks color, but Yum-sa-wek's look was benevolent.

"Your baby is behind?" she inquired.

"Behind?" Caroline shook her head uncomprehendingly.

"She means," explained Hannah, "do you have children, too."

"Oh. No." Caroline shook her head.

Yum-sa-wek frowned, clucking her tongue. "You come to my wigwam. I give you medicine."

Caroline glanced at Hannah, who told Yum-sa-wek, "She has no husband. That is why she has no baby."

"Why not?" Yum-sa-wek shook her head. "Master look pretty good. You come to my wigwam. I give you medicine."

"Thank you," muttered Caroline, unable to meet Hannah's eye, for fear of being overwhelmed by hysterical laughter.

"You come to my wigwam," Yum-sa-wek murmured to herself, as Caroline moved away, in Hoo-tan's direction.

In the evening, after the meal, the people gathered in the various wigwams, where the men smoked their pipes and the women played games of chance. Daniel sat at Ti-sha-wa's side, and Caroline managed to slip away before Hoo-tan could call her back. She found Hannah and her mistress watching a group of women playing a game with triangular stones that seemed to be a variation on what she knew as dice. Yum-sa-wek held a clay pipe clenched between her teeth; it bobbed with every word she spoke.

"See, over there?" She gestured through the open door to where a white-haired man sat all alone, slowly beating on a drum. "That is So-ki, the medicine man. He prepares for the hunt."

"For the hunt?" asked Caroline, her gaze sharpening. "When will they be going?"

"With the dawn," said Yum-sa-wek. "Tonight he asks the spirits to show him the way."

Drawing nearer the door, Caroline looked out, wondering how many of the men would go away. She hoped they would all go, and stay away for some time. Perhaps, with just the women there, they could manage to escape, though they would have to cross the river in one of the big canoes. And what of the horses? she wondered, her brow furrowing. She wondered if Daniel would join the men or stay here at the camp. Though it required an effort of will, she hoped that he would go.

The drum So-ki was beating was a wooden hoop strung with a deerskin head across which were stretched two rawhide strings whose vibration produced a buzzing sound over the steady beat. As the night drew onwards, the force of the drumbeats increased and, by ones and twos, the men drew near to it. Watching them by the light of the fire, Caroline realized that they had covered their bodies with fresh war paint.

Now So-ki began singing, in a high, nasal voice.

"He sings to the spirits," Yum-sa-wek explained, joining Caroline in the wigwam's doorway. "He says, 'Storms hearken to the sound of my drum. The wood spirit ceases chopping to listen to my drum. Lightning, thunder, storms, gale, forest spirit, water spirit, whirlwind, spirit of the night and air, are gathered together, listening to my drum!' " Yum-sa-wek nodded. "Come, let us draw near."

They moved towards the fire, where the voice rose and fell with a thin, haunting sound. More men and women gathered, swaying to the eerie cadence. Caroline found herself swaying with the others, and fought against the drum's power with a shudder of revulsion. Presently, So-ki set his drum aside, taking up from the grass beside him what appeared to be a section of the shoulder blade of some large animal. A fire burned at his side. Kneeling before it, he scraped the glowing embers flat, then laid the bone on them.

"What is he doing?" asked Caroline, intrigued despite herself.

"Cracks in bone show So-ki whole country." Yum-sa-wek swept her hand in a circle about them. "Spirits send him a map to know where animals feed."

"Does it really happen?"

"Of course," said Yum-sa-wek, with such perfect conviction that Caroline turned to her.

"How is it that you speak English so well, Yum-sa-wek, when most of the others have hardly a word?"

"My mother's mother was white woman. She was taken up by the Indians when she was a little child. Her parents come, beg chief to give her back, but chief says no, he keep. So she come up with them. When she grow to woman, my grandfather take her for wife."

So-ki was studying the bone with rapt attention. Caroline's eyes met Hannah's over Yum-sa-wek's head. Caroline felt a cold thrill of fear, and she saw Hannah reach out and pull Hetty close to her. This was one more reason why they must get away. She would think of something; she vowed that she would.

After the bone showed So-ki where the animals fed, he returned to his drumming, and the dancing began. The men circled the fire, hopping from side to side, then back and forth, keeping both feet together. Then, breaking their circle, they began a far more elaborate dance that Caroline quickly recognized as a pantomime of the hunt. Striding proudly, they set out on the trail, making their way through the forest until they reached the spot. Then, crouched down upon all fours, they crept forwards silently. When they sprang up, running, Caroline gasped in surprise. Her hands clasped, she watched as they attacked their prey, stabbing and stabbing until it fell dead. She watched their muscles straining as they lifted it onto a brace to bear it proudly back to the waiting camp.

Then it was the women's turn. They moved in a circle as the men had done, some dressed in hide tunics, as they had been before, others wearing girdles sewn with beads or coins that clashed and jangled as they jumped about. Caroline watched the spectacle, entranced, yet, even as her eyes followed the leaping circle, she felt her attention being drawn away.

Looking up, she saw Daniel standing across the circle, his eyes fixed on the dancers, just as hers had been. As she watched, he murmured something to the man beside him, then turned away from the dancers and walked off towards the woods. From the way the man shrugged at Daniel's words, Caroline knew that the man assumed that Daniel was going to relieve himself. She frowned, puzzled. Had he been looking at her, or had she only imagined it? She had felt the pull so strongly that she was almost sure of it. Reason counseled against following, for he had betrayed her repeatedly, but her heart urged her to go. For some minutes, she battled with herself, but finally she gave in.

Checking to be sure that Hoo-tan was still dancing by the fire, she leaned over to Yum-sa-wek, who stood at her side. "Nature calls me to the woods. I will not be long."

"Yes, yes..." Yum-sa-wek nodded, caught up in the dancing, hardly hearing her. With one final look behind her, Caroline moved away.

She forced herself not to rush, in case any eyes were following her, as though she had but one mission in going to the woods, and that the permitted one. But, once she reached the darkness that lay beyond the fire, she quickened her pace, heading in the direction in which Daniel had gone.

She had not gone many paces when a hand grabbed her arm with such abruptness that she would have cried out in surprise, had not his other hand closed over her mouth.

"Don't be scared," he murmured, his lips against her ear. "I only wanted to talk to you alone for a few moments." He waited until she nodded, then took his hand away and turned her around. Even in the darkness, she saw the change in him. Gone was the mask of coldness. This was the Daniel she loved. So strong was her reaction, so powerful the torrent of her relief, that she could scarcely focus on the words he was murmuring.

"There isn't much time," he said. "Not enough to say everything. Ti-sha-wa doesn't trust me. I think that he suspects that we meant to rescue Hannah, despite what I said to him. That's why he wouldn't release you, and why he kept me, as well. I told him that you were my hostage, so I had to act the part. I scolded you at the waterfall because Eshtan had seen. And last night, at the river, I'd seen that it was a trap. If we'd gone for the horses, the trap would have sprung on us."

"Yes, yes..." She nodded, her eyes devouring his face, nourishing herself on the emotions she saw in his eyes. "I had hoped that that was it!"

"Hoped!" His tone was bitter. "Had there been a moment, I would have told you the truth."

"Yes, I know, but now it is all right. Now that I know you were acting, I can stand anything!"

Despite the darkness, he saw her eyes flash with light. Her face was dirty, her hair was tangled and snarled, yet he thought that he had never seen her quite so beautiful as she was now, with all her courage shining in her eyes. Without thinking, he raised his fingers to the last trace of the bruise on her cheek. At his touch, her own hand came up, to rest on his, and her eyes fluttered shut as she held it against her cheek. Time hung suspended. He wanted nothing but to press her close to him.

But time was not suspended. It was passing rapidly, and at any moment someone might come in search of him. "Listen," he whispered, and saw her open her eyes. "The men leave tomorrow on a hunting trip. I must go with them."

"You!" Her eyes widened. "How long?" she asked

"A week? Ten days? The chief will warn Hoo-tan not to be hard on you." He forced himself to speak with conviction, but he felt a sinking within. How could he leave her, after all she had been through? His voice dropping, he said, "No, I shall not go. Instead, we shall leave tonight, but only we two. If we can get across the river, I think we can outrun them."

"But what of Hannah?"

"I will come back for her. I swear to you that I will."

"No." She shook her head. "I can't leave her alone. Once they know that we have gone, they'll guess the whole truth. Perhaps they'll punish her for it— I can't take such a risk. I can stand Hoo-tan, now that we've spoken here. Believe me," she whispered. "Only promise me that you'll come back."

"I will come back."

Footsteps, approaching, rustled the leaves nearby. She felt Daniel's fingers close about her arm, though there was nowhere to run. Face-to-face, they listened as the footsteps advanced. Caroline's heart thundered against her ribs, and she could feel the silence of Daniel's bated breath. Then the footsteps halted, and a tell-tale stream began. A moment later, the footsteps withdrew.

They did not stir, but stayed as they were, standing so close together that she could feel the heat of his breath upon her cheek.

He felt her, as well. Despite the danger of the moment, he felt all the last week's longing rise within his loins. He knew that if he drew her to him she would not protest, that she would meet him caress for caress. But the voice of wisdom ordered that he send her back to the fire before she was missed.

"You must go," he whispered, tightening his grip on her, meaning to turn her in the direction of the camp. But somehow, instead, his touch only drew her nearer until his arms were around her and his lips pressed to hers.

For a full minute, they clung together, their fingers grasping, their lips devouring, their bodies, of their own accord, seeking each other's heat. At last, in desperation, they tore themselves apart.

"I cannot leave you!" he whispered.

"You can, you must!" she said, and, anxious to be gone before her will gave out, she turned back towards the camp.

"Wait!"

Even as she turned away, his voice called her back, and in the next moment she felt the smoothness of metal pressed into her palm. Without looking down, she knew what it was.

"Your knife!" she whispered. "What will you do without it?"

"I will make do," he said. "It will give me comfort to know that you have it. But take care to hide it well, so that none will know. Take it, and go now. Go quickly," he urged, thinking less of discovery than of the limits of his restraint. For a moment more, she lingered; then she turned away, and he heard her light step as she ran through the newly fallen leaves.

Chapter Twelve

The hunters marched in a body to the beach, the women and children following at a respectful distance. Caroline walked behind Hoo-tan, carrying Daniel's pack, trying to keep her thoughts from what these next days would mean. From the look Hoo-tan had turned on her as they had left the wigwam just now, Caroline suspected that Ti-sha-wa had spoken to her of Caroline's treatment in Daniel's absence. The way that Hoo-tan had glowered at her just now made her wish that he had not.

Well, what was done was done. She had endured other hard times, and she would get through these. And better she than Hannah. Her eyes sought her sister, who walked with Yum-sa-wek. She was struck by the irony of the likelihood that Hannah's life with Yum-sa-wek would be more pleasant than life with her own husband, but for the constant strain of captivity. Once again, she recalled what Yum-sa-wek had said last night about her grandmother being taken as a child and adopted by the tribe. No wonder poor Hannah looked so pale and drawn. At least her time for birthing was still more than a month away. Before it came, Daniel would have saved them. She must believe that.

The men righted the canoes, which they had inverted on the beach to keep them dry inside. They carried them to the water and put them in, holding them steady as the women came forwards to deposit the packs. Daniel was in the first canoe, as was the chief. As Caroline slung his pack forward, over the canoe's edge, her body brushed against his, and her eyes came up. Caught off guard, he could not hide what lay in his, and for just a moment she saw both his anxiety and the same desire she had felt last night.

"Do you jostle me?" he snapped.

"I am sorry, master," she muttered, lowering her eyes, but this time, for the first time, without a heavy heart. Knowing that Daniel's feelings towards her had not changed, she could bear his harshness as though it did not exist. She stood in the shallow water, watching through the blur of her unshed tears as the boats pushed off into the river and then slowly turned upstream.

Daniel felt the rush of speed when the canoe was pushed free. It was a moment that had always brought a lifting in his soul. He had felt it when he and Caroline had pushed off a week before, but now the motion only added to his sense of foreboding. Though he added the force of his paddle to the strength of the other men, as the canoe drew forwards, his heart dragged against it, turning back instead, towards land and Caroline.

Last night, for a moment, he had crushed her to his heart, felt the soft fullness of her breasts, the sweetness of her mouth. Had he doubted the place she occupied in his life, that one fleeting, desperate embrace would have stamped the truth on his soul. There had never been a woman like her in his life. She was dearer to him than that life itself. Perhaps too dear, he feared, for to taste her sweetness brought pain and pleasure both.

It galled him to see her living like an animal, in filthy rags, for he longed to see her body draped in the finest furs. He recalled the blue dress she had worn to the party at the fort, and how her eyes had sparkled when he had led her in the gavotte. Then, too, he recalled that light fading before MacKenzie's ruthless remarks. Life had already shown her enough of man's cruelty. It pained him to leave her to face more alone.

The canoe gained the river's middle and turned to the northwest, working against the current, which lapped against its sides. The hunting grounds of this tribe lay on the

iver's northern bank. They would travel one day westward, then hunt back towards the camp. And, if they found
one of the herds that So-ki had divined, they would launch
he canoes in the river again and try a spot farther west.

Turning his head, Daniel saw the women still on the bank,
though the wind, blowing downriver, swept away their calls.
n his memory, he saw again the longing in Caroline's eyes
when she had raised them to his on the beach. The priests of
his childhood had described hell as a deep pit of fiery filth.
But now he understood that hell was not mud and fire; hell
was having to turn away from Caroline's longing eyes. Hell
was the choice between realism and one's heart's desire.

But Caroline was strong. That was the thing to remember, to balance against the pain. Even now, he could see her,
head up, lips drawn scornfully, meeting MacKenzie's sneer-
ng look with one of granite pride. When MacKenzie had
been unwilling to go after his own wife, Caroline had
damned him and struck out alone. As a country girl of
eighteen, she had stood up to her father, and a false lover,
as well, refusing to be stampeded into marriage with a brute.
And, for the next eight years, she had punished herself re-
lentlessly—punished herself far more harshly than Hoo-tan
could do in one week. For all that he might yearn to shield
her from pain, Caroline was able to take care of herself.

The river was shallow through here, for a sandbar rose
from the north bank and sloped towards the south. The
canoes went in single file, skirting the edge of the bar. As
they reentered the deep water, two trout flickered by, and
every man made a mental note of their size and position for
some future foray. They would not stop now to fish, for they
carried two days' supplies, but the location of food was always a matter of the utmost importance.

Two miles past the sandbar were rapids that they could
not run, so they portaged on the south bank, carrying their
packs on their backs and the canoes above their heads. Each
crew worked as one man, moving in unison, their steps so
perfectly synchronized that they could run or walk at will,
and with the precision of a centipede. It was a change for
Daniel, who was used to a solitary life, and, despite his cares

for Caroline, he soon found himself falling into the group's rhythm.

Evening was descending when they reached the tributary along which their path lay, for the bone had shown So-ki many moose in the marsh through which it passed. Pulling the canoes from the water, they ate their meal upon the shore, then lay down on the ground in their blankets for a short night's sleep—all except So-ki, who spent the following hours in communion with the spirits.

The medicine man woke them long before dawn, and they started out, dipping their paddles silently so as to give the moose no alarm. Two miles or so from its mouth, the tributary opened into a fair-sized lake. Its banks were low and marshy and cut by numerous channels. Here the hunters divided, the canoes fanning out across the lake so that each could claim and cover a part of the territory.

Daniel's canoe made its way to the lake's northern bank, entering a channel that was about three feet across. Now, while the others held it steady with their paddles, Ti-sha-wa, who rowed at the bow, lifted a cone made of rolled birch bark that, when blown skillfully, imitated the call of a cow moose. Ti-sha-wa gave two short calls, then lowered the cone. Faintly, from across the lake, came other calls—likely the other hunters, attracting their own prey. Such a superfluity might have scared another species away, but a rutting bull moose would ignore any other sound, so desperate was he to locate the willing cow.

Ti-sha-wa was a good caller. Again and again he raised his cone as the rose-pearl light of the dawn spread over the eastern sky. His calls varied subtly, lamenting one moment, demanding the next. For a time, there was no answer, but then, all at once, they heard the heavy thrashing that could only mean a bull. Smiles curved the lips of the three in the canoe. The chief raised his cone and blew again, most persuasively. Then, lowering it to the water, he filled, then emptied it, holding the tube high in the air in imitation of the expectant urination of the cow in heat.

This was too much for the bull. The water in which they sat quivered as he thrashed his way towards them. The In-

dian in the stern kept the canoe steady with his paddle, and
Daniel and Ti-sha-wa lifted their long spears, poised and
ready to thrust. Guns would bring down this one moose, but
would send any others away, and the meat of a single bull
would hardly sustain the camp.

Then the bull was upon them, scarcely ten feet away, its
massive twelve-pointed antlers reaching eight feet across,
head up, nostrils flaring with enraged passion. Its broad
chest split the water, plowing aside the reeds; it headed
straight for the canoe's side, its antlers lowered now. Ti-sha-
wa brought his spear back, and Daniel did the same. They
released them as one and saw them find their mark. At first,
it seemed that they had no effect, for the moose continued
to charge at their now-undefended flank. Then, just when
it seemed its antlers would pierce the canoe, it stopped its
charge, faltered, then toppled to one side, its huge chest
collapsing in a dying groan.

Slowly, it drifted towards them, still and ponderous as a
great fallen oak, staining the water dark with its spreading
blood. Together, Ti-sha-wa and Daniel looped it with a stout
rope and lashed it to the canoe to haul it to the shore.

It was a huge creature, so heavy that the three of them
together could hardly pull it up. Ti-sha-wa's spear had penetrated the great bull's throat, Daniel's his eye. Either would
have killed him, but Daniel's had been the harder shot. Ti-
sha-wa gazed down silently at the massive corpse for a moment. Then, looking up, he placed his hand upon Daniel's
shoulder.

"You have hunted well," he said, his grip strong. His eyes
added, "You have passed the test."

Daniel stood with the chief, his prize at his feet. His pulses
were still throbbing with the exhilaration of the kill. But, at
Ti-sha-wa's words, his thoughts moved away from it. If he
had earned the chief's trust, now, perhaps, they could break
free—not only Caroline, but also her sister, without whom
she would not leave. He was filled with impatience for the
hunt to be through, so that he could return to Caroline.
Placing his hand on the moose's shaggy head, he dedicated
the kill to her.

* * *

"Ayee!" The shrill voice broke into Caroline's thoughts. Turning from the river, which was empty now of canoes, she brought her wistful eyes to Hoo-tan's outraged ones.

"Ayee!" Hoo-tan screeched again, giving Caroline a shove that almost sent her sprawling to the ground. By pointing and gesturing angrily, Hoo-tan conveyed quite clearly that Caroline had no business loitering on the shore when there was much work to be done.

Caroline's body went rigid. Her first thought was to lash out at Hoo-tan. She was tempted to tell her what she thought of her and her bullying ways, and to remind her of her husband's admonition. How could this brutish woman attack her now, when she was already reeling from Daniel's departure? Hot blood coursed through her veins, and hot words bubbled to her lips. She thought briefly of Daniel's knife, hidden beneath her pallet, and imagined plunging it into Hoo-tan's breast. She felt her nostrils flaring with the satisfaction of the thrust.

But, even as her emotions prompted this wild foolishness, her mind soberly lectured her on reality and risk. Others among the women, Yum-sa-wek in particular, might feel pity for her plight, but they would never openly oppose Hoo-tan. In Daniel's absence, she was entrusted to Hoo-tan's care, and, according to law and habit, each mistress was the sole and absolute arbiter of her own captives' fates. If she were Hoo-tan's captive absolutely, Hoo-tan would be entitled to kill or mutilate her according to nothing more than whim. As her temporary overseer, Hoo-tan was entitled to indulge in a certain degree of abuse. Moreover, Hoo-tan was the wife of Ti-sha-wa, and therefore the first woman in the camp. No woman would consider lightly challenging her behavior with regard to her own affairs. And, until such time as Daniel returned, Caroline was her affair. And, Daniel or no Daniel, were she to pull a knife on Hoo-tan, her life would be forfeit.

Some of the other women had turned at Hoo-tan's shriek, and, from the corner of her eye, Caroline saw Hannah press her hands together in fear. Perhaps she herself was willing to bear the consequences of resistance, but was she also willing to force Hannah to bear witness? How many times had she seen her sister bend to Thomas's will when she herself would have snapped? How often had Hannah saved her from the sting of Thomas's wrath? Resisting Hoo-tan might avenge her own wounded pride, but was that worth the sorrow it would lay on Hannah's heart? How many days could the men be gone? No more than ten, at the most. Ten days was not forever. She could stand ten days. So, forcing her fists open, Caroline bowed her head, quelling the mutiny in her heart to submit to Hoo-tan's will.

For her struggle, she received the reward of a sharp cuff on the side of the head. As she had the first evening, Hoo-tan gestured towards the camp, telling her to get moving without further delay. And this time, her ears ringing, Caroline did as she said.

She reached the wigwam just before Hoo-tan and stood before the door, uncertain of whether she should enter or stay outside. Hoo-tan resolved the dilemma by thrusting two buckets at her with a force that almost sent her sprawling back through the door. Hoo-tan pointed towards the river, and Caroline hurried off.

She spilled some of the water in her hurry to be prompt, but if Hoo-tan noticed, she chose not to comment, pointing directly to the fire and showing by gestures that Caroline should fetch more wood. Again, Caroline did the chore with all dispatch, but when she returned with her arms full Hoo-tan flew into a rage, screaming at her for what seemed like hours before finally thrusting a pile of clothes at her and sending her to the river to launder them.

They were no more than filthy rags. Caroline wondered where Hoo-tan had gotten them, for her and her children's things were the finest in the camp. Dipping the rags into the water, Caroline could not help but wonder if Hoo-tan had borrowed them as a cruelty. Still, she had no choice but to clean them as best she could.

The sun, which had greeted their waking, had long since disappeared, leaving behind a sky piled high with gray clouds, and the wind coming off the river held the promise of frost. Caroline's clothing, already damp from lugging buckets to and fro, became all the more so from her hour's laundering. Kneeling on the sharp stones, she shivered from the cold, scrubbing the rags until her fingers were numb.

She had no idea how long she worked. Little by little, the filth dissolved from the homespun and wool, which took on a semblance of its former shape and shade. When at last she rose to wring and shake them out, she could not help but feel a certain sense of accomplishment at having turned such offal into something of use. When she came up from the river, the camp looked deserted, the women and the children having sought shelter from the day's damp. Plumes of smoke were curling from the roof of every wigwam, and the air smelled of woodsmoke and of cooking food.

After the chill of the river, the warmth of the wigwam made Caroline's eyes tear and burn. At the fire, meat was stewing in a pot. The smell filled her head, for she had not eaten since early that morning. Her eyes carefully downcast, she handed the clean laundry to Hoo-tan, who snatched it away from her without looking and threw it to the ground. Taking a woven basket from a hook on the wall, she handed it to Caroline, explaining by gesture that she must fill it with ground nuts.

"May I eat first?" asked Caroline, pointing to the steaming pot to make herself clear.

A maniacal light filled Hoo-tan's eyes. Without warning, she raised her hand and struck Caroline heavily on the forehead. Her words needed no translation: Did Caroline think she should eat when she gathered no food? Be gone after the ground nuts or be sorry that you stayed! Her head throbbing, the basket beneath her arm, Caroline turned slowly and left the wigwam.

It was colder than before, and a light rain was beginning to fall. The raindrops hit her arms and the back of her neck like needles of ice as she knelt on the wet ground, pulling with one hand while the other dug with a sharpened stick. At first, misery numbed her and she worked automatically, but soon enough her heart thawed and hot tears burned her cheeks.

Then someone spoke her name. Someone was leaning over her.

"Caroline!" Hannah whispered. "Caroline, are you all right?"

"I think so, only bruised—and tired and wet," she said, raising her head to see Hannah and Yum-sa-wek at her side. Together, one on either side, they helped her to her feet and hurried her across the wet ground to Yum-sa-wek's wigwam.

She felt as if she had suddenly entered paradise. Gentle hands stripped her wet clothes from her, rubbed her dry with soft hides, wrapped her in warm wool. She saw Hannah whiten at the sight of her face.

"It's only dirt," she mumbled, smiling apologetically.

"Yes, dear, I know," Hannah replied, dipping a cloth in cool water and laying it over the swelling on her forehead. At the touch of the cloth, Caroline winced.

While Hannah tended to her wounds, Yum-sa-wek fed her broth. Caroline looked from face to face, one light, the other leather-dark, but both sharing the same look of compassion blended with dismay. For the first time, it struck her that Yum-sa-wek's feelings did not come from her white blood, but rather from a humanity that cut through culture and race. Hoo-tan was ruthless, but no more so than Thomas. Indians, like white people, came in all temperaments: angelic and evil and everything in between.

Her eyes dwelling on Hannah, she saw that her sister's face, so often tense and drawn, was calm and unruffled now. So often it had been she who bathed Hannah's brow, but this time, she realized, their roles were reversed. This time, it was Hannah who was caring for her, caring with strength and calmness—not to mention an Indian ally. She had always considered Hannah a weaker being; perhaps she had never allowed for Hannah's inner strength. It was something to think about.

Hannah finished with Caroline's face and turned to her clothes, clucking in dismay at their condition, and Caroline, seeing them spread out in the firelight, realized that they were no better than those she had washed earlier. How could they be, after all, when she had worn them through the wilderness, not to mention the rigors of her three days of camp life?

The fire leapt and flickered when the door was swung back and Hoo-tan appeared, her brows rising as her eyes absorbed the cozy scene within. Yum-sa-wek, rising, spoke appealingly, but Hoo-tan shook her head. Caroline understood, and felt her heart sink—yet it did not fall so low as it had before. Something had changed in the last hour; something in the silent moments she had shared with Hannah and Yum-sa-wek had wrought a change in her, so that now she shared the same strength she had sensed in her sister. Whereas earlier today her choices had seemed to be between open resistance and abject submission, now she saw another way. Drawing herself up from the wigwam floor, she met Hoo-tan's cold gaze with her own steady one.

"I know you," she said. "You are like Edmund Bredon, or Thomas MacKenzie, using your position to frighten the powerless. Well, I am not frightened, though I may be your slave. I will do your bidding, because for a time I must. But I shall not surrender my dignity to you."

She saw Hoo-tan's brows draw down, puzzling over her words. She wondered if the woman would lash out at her, but either her expression stayed Hoo-tan's hand or Hoo-tan had had enough violence for one day. Casting one final glance at the three women, she beckoned to Caroline to follow. Then she turned and left.

"It's all right, Hannah," Caroline said quickly, forestalling her sister's protests. "I don't think she'll do more, and I can stand it if she does. I don't mind anything—except putting my clothes back on, until they're at least dry. If I could borrow the blanket..."

"Yes, take it," Yum-sa-wek said, and, with a quick nod of gratitude, Caroline swept up her clothes and went out into the night.

After that, she and Hoo-tan existed in a state of uneasy truce. Hoo-tan still ordered her about, but she did not starve her, and she refrained from striking her, while Caroline took care not to antagonize the Indian woman. She kept away from Hannah when Hoo-tan was near, and took care even when she was not, lest one of the other women tell tales against her. On the third day after the men left, Hoo-tan presented her with needle and thread and the clothing that she had washed, indicating by gesture that she wished her to sew shirts for her children. Caroline did as she was asked, and, although Hoo-tan offered no thanks when she was through, Caroline could see that she was pleased with the work. She could not help but risk smiling to herself when she recalled her mother's despair over her needlework. All of which went to show that everything is relative.

Moments of humor were rare. Despite the measure of peace she had gathered the first night, still she carried within her a constant gnawing fear. What if Daniel met with some accident on the hunt? Esh-tan and his sister were very much alike—what if the brave had taken his revenge? Of course, Daniel was wise to the tricks of Indians, but still he was outnumbered.

Then, too, there was the worry of Hannah's pregnancy, which became more of a problem with every day that passed. Would she be able to travel when the time came for escape? And what if she was not? Yum-sa-wek's presence was a constant reminder that not all the Indians' prisoners were freed. Although she schooled herself in patience, the days seemed to drag by. One night she dreamed that she grew old with the Indians and, when she died, was buried in an unmarked grave in the woods. It was a sobering thought.

Chapter Thirteen

The loon's call, dividing the early-evening calm, heralded the return of the hunting party. As they had done the night the captives had arrived, the women lit pine torches and went down to the water's edge, calling out their welcome to the approaching canoes.

This time, Caroline and Hannah stood with the welcomers. Hannah's face was swollen with advancing pregnancy, while Caroline's still bore traces of her rough treatment, mingled with a yearning that she could not disguise. Oh, pray God, let him be with them! Let him be there, safe and sound, or I shall surely die! She repeated the words silently again and again as, her hands clasped to her bosom, she watched the boats approach. Head after head she counted, each the color of the night sky. Then, at last, she caught sight of the flickering gleam of gold. He was there! He had come back! Caroline turned away, afraid that the watching women would notice her tears.

But no one was watching her. The very life of the tribe depended upon the success of this hunt, and the winter would be a bleak one if the catch was small. True, the men would go out several times again, but once the spirits had turned against them they were not easily won back. One might read the venture's success in the men's faces—not in their mouths or noses, for a true man fought the urge to smile with his pride—but rather in their eyes. It was too dark by now to see clearly enough, but keen ears listened for how soon the first boat scraped rock. The earlier the scraping, the heavier the load would be.

The first canoe hit the river bottom before it reached the waiting group. Hearing this, they sent up a cheer of praise and thanksgiving. Then they were in the water, pulling the boat ashore. Already the men were describing the greatness of their trophies. There were deer and moose and caribou, sleek and fat for the wintertime. The spirits had been friendly; the spirits had smiled upon them. It was good, agreed the women, nodding and nodding their heads.

Daniel's canoe hit the beach. He jumped out with the others, one hand on the gunwale to pull it ashore, his eyes raking the crowd, looking for Caroline. Then he saw her and felt the tightness drain from his chest. He saw her look at him, then look away again. Guessing at the reason, he, too, turned away, busying himself with some small task of unloading.

The children stood at rapt attention, and the women clucked their tongues, as carcass after carcass was hoisted onto the shore to be received by willing hands. The closeness of the crowd impeded its own progress, but no one minded, for the slowness of the procession only drew out the glory of the hour.

Daniel carried the front end of a stake from which hung the carcass of a caribou, bled but not yet gutted, as was the Indian way. Coming up the embankment, he saw Caroline watching him, her eyes luminous in the light of the torch she held. He meant to pass her, but found that he could not, in part because the parade drew to a halt just then, but also because his own feet refused to move. For a long moment, he stared into her eyes, seeing the longing and the relief there. Then his eyes moved to her forehead, and there he saw the dark smudge of a bruise. He felt his stomach contract, and his two hands tighten, as if about Hoo-tan's neck.

"Ho, brother!" a merry voice called from behind. "Would you have us stand all night?" Once again, the crowd was moving. Daniel forced his eyes away from Caroline as his feet sought a sound purchase in the embankment. Keep your head, he warned himself, the time is drawing near. There will be time later to exact revenge. Whatever has happened to her, she is alive and well. That is the thing to remember. That is the thing that counts.

Caroline turned her head to watch as Daniel passed, noting a marked change in the way the men addressed him. Earlier he had spoken of lacking Ti-sha-wa's trust. It seemed that he had gained it during the course of the hunt. Now, perhaps, they would find the opportunity to escape.

She turned back to the procession, a new ease in her mind, to find Esh-tan standing before her, his eyes proud and dark and arrogant, and full of threat, as well. Facing him, she remembered what she had learned with Hoo-tan, but somehow with Esh-tan her nerve failed her. Although she resisted the urge to turn her head, her whole body was shaking by the time he, too, had passed.

The stakes were hung on trees, where the animals would be gutted. Even their innards would be boiled into soup, for the Indians ate everything. Then the carcasses would be carved and the meat hung up to dry. This catch alone would take them well into the winter months, and they meant to show their gratitude in the joy of their celebration.

They cut the haunches from the largest deer and set them to roasting on a spit. Then drums were brought out, and to their steady beat the warriors danced and chanted the full story of the hunt, with the same abandon with which they had danced a week before. Eyes shone eagerly by the light of the roaring fire, and, throughout the circle, every motion was applauded. The dancing continued until the meat was done. Then Ti-sha-wa accepted the first cut, throwing a piece of fat into the fire in a traditional gesture of thanks, which the spirits accepted with a great burst of flame.

Daniel ate with the men, aware in every instant of Caroline's whereabouts, for all that he kept his eyes from her. And she, too, was fully aware of him as she moved about the fire, carrying food to the men, caught between the great relief of knowing he was well and the building yearning to feel him close to her. All week she had forbidden herself to think of their parting embrace, for fear that it would weaken her defenses against Hoo-tan. But now that he was here and safe, it came flooding back with a force and a vividness that made her breath come fast. Surely, with everyone absorbed in the merrymaking, they would find a moment together during the course of the night. Perhaps this night would give them their chance for escape, for not only was there celebrating, there was drinking, as well.

They had brought out a keg of rum. Caroline recognized it as one of Thomas's, stolen in the raid on the farm. It gave her a perverse pleasure to watch them tap the bung, knowing how very little Thomas liked parting with his things. The rest of the women, however, saw nothing at all that was pleasing.

"It no good," Yum-sa-wek clucked. "Rum poison to Indian man. Turn him to animal." She shook her head, and the other women nodded in agreement.

Yum-sa-wek seemed to be right, for Caroline soon saw that the men used no moderation, swilling the rum like water, becoming by turns silly and boisterous. She saw Esh-tan among them, and her heart sank within her when she recalled the look he had fixed on her earlier. He was bad enough sober; she could well imagine him drunk. She would have to take care to keep out of his path.

But, as if Esh-tan had read her very thoughts, she saw his head come up, his eyes scanning the celebrants and settling upon her. This time she made no effort to challenge his gaze, but rather turned quickly away, looking about for a means of hiding herself from his view. She had seen enough of drunken men to know how their minds worked. Perhaps, if Esh-tan did not see her, he would put her from his mind. She thought briefly of Daniel, and hoped he had not seen the look, for the last thing she desired was a confrontation that would ruin the evening.

A group of women squatted beyond the fire's brightest light, scraping clean the hide of the deer they had feasted upon. Caroline moved towards them unhurriedly. Crouching beside them, she fixed her eyes upon their work, and gradually her heart stopped its thundering to match its beat instead to the rise and fall of the women's hands. One of the women noticed her and passed her a scraping tool, a palm-size disc of stone, the longest edge of which had been well sharpened. Although Caroline had never handled such a tool, she accepted it readily, glad to have something to occupy her hands.

The women sang softly as they worked, matching their song to that being sung at the fire, but singing just behind it. The result was a counterpoint that was hauntingly beautiful. For the first time that evening, Caroline forgot her own concerns, losing herself in the sounds and scents of the firelit night. But her respite was painfully brief, for no sooner had she felt her body relax than it tensed again, and the skin on her neck tingled with the certainty that someone was watching her from behind. And, from the way the women muttered and shook their heads, even before Caroline turned she guessed whom she would find.

It was Esh-tan, his eyes red rimmed from drink, his body swaying slightly above his wide-planted feet. When she rose to face him, she thought that she would faint from the potency of the fumes that enveloped her when he exhaled. He was drunk, there was no doubting it, yet his eyes were not blurred, but rather even more intense than before, and glinting with a madness that brought back all too vividly what had passed between them in the first hours of her captivity.

By habit and by instinct, she kept her eyes on his, and she saw his tongue come out to moisten his dry lips. She shuddered with revulsion at the sight of it.

The women were still muttering, though at the fire, behind her, the singing continued. Had Daniel not noticed what was happening? Had he his back to her, or was she blocked from his view? She wanted to turn away from Esh-tan in order to search for Daniel, but she could not tear her frightened eyes from Esh-tan's gaze.

Something hard lay in her hand. The scraper, she realized, with its sharpened edge. In her mind's eye, she saw herself striking out, bringing it down again and again on Esh-tan's hateful face. She saw the bright blood spurting, and felt its sticky warmth. Her fingers tightened their grip on the rock, even as her mind warned that the vision was a dream. Even if she was lucky enough to manage to strike him once, how could she imagine that he would give her a second chance? His bronzed muscles gleamed in the firelight, and the fresh paint upon his face and chest made him even more awesome. No, it was madness to strike him. Instead, she must turn and flee.

The thought brought action. She turned and took a step towards the fire, where Daniel must be. But Esh-tan was a hunter, trained to track a deer; he moved after her so quickly that it seemed they moved as one. He blocked her escape, seizing her left arm in his well-remembered grip. Without thinking, she raised her right hand and brought the sharpened rock down against his left cheek with all the strength she could summon, and with the force of her fear, as well.

It was her greatest mistake. For a moment, he stood unmoving, his features frozen in astonishment. Frozen as well, Caroline watched the blood brighten the line of the wound. He raised his hand to touch it, then drew it away, gazing with the same expression at the red stain on his fingertips. Run, you must break away! Caroline's mind cried out, but her legs had turned to jelly and would not obey. She watched in horror as fire filled his eyes. His nostrils flaring, he turned his hand to her.

His first blow sent the scraper skidding away on the ground. Again he raised his hand as if he would strike, and, though she sought for courage, instinct made her cringe. But then his eyes flickered and his hand relaxed. Reaching out to her, as he had the first night, he hooked his index finger inside the top of her bodice, as if he would pull her towards him. But he did not pull. Instead, he ran his finger down, inside the edge, tracing the rise of her breast. She felt herself shudder again with revulsion, and saw his lips curl with satisfaction. His finger pressed downwards, pulling against the buttons that held her bodice shut, and she knew that in a moment he would go farther.

But that moment never came. Instead, in a flash of sudden movement, Esh-tan's finger was jerked free and his body spun backwards and into the firelight. She heard his

cry of surprised rage rise to shatter the air; then, where he
had stood before her, Daniel stood instead. For a moment,
his eyes scanned her, as if to assure himself that she had not
been harmed.

Turning back to Esh-tan, he spoke curtly: "*Viens,
cochon.* Come, and prepare to die."

"Oh, *no!*" Caroline whispered, but Daniel did not seem
to hear. He seemed aware of nothing but Esh-tan's gleaming body, which was no longer sprawled out, but rather
coiled like a spring. Then she saw the silver flash in Esh-tan's
hand and realized that he had drawn the knife he wore at his
waist. Daniel's hand went to his waist, as well, and in that
moment Caroline recalled that his knife still lay well hidden
beneath her blanket.

Esh-tan's cry had brought the men from the fire. Caroline heard their murmurs when they saw Daniel had no
knife. Yet no one among them offered to give him one. Instead, they drew in closer, narrowing his maneuvering space,
their faces chiseled, statuelike, by the leaping flames.

Slowly, the two men circled, arms out, bent from the
waist, hands open and moving, like wrestlers seeking a first
grip, except that Esh-tan held the knife. Its blade flashed
bright and silver as he slashed the air with it, his arm describing how Daniel was to die. He had height and weight on
Daniel, but Daniel had a lightness lacking in the bigger man.
And Daniel, too, had all his senses intact. His eyes burned
with blue fire, and his focus was absolute. Esh-tan's eyes
held the hunger of a stalking animal, while Daniel's showed
no appetite save that for the kill. Caroline's lungs emptied
in a long, hissing sigh that disappeared unheeded amidst the
crowd's murmuring.

She had not yet drawn breath when the first strike came.
Esh-tan lashed out with his knife, and red stained Daniel's
right cheek. Caroline's stomach heaved in fear and nausea,
while behind her the crowd shouted its approval of the first
drawing of blood. She heard Esh-tan's satisfied grunt. Only
Daniel made no sound; nor did he show any notice that he
had been hurt.

Having tasted blood, the knife had developed a thirst. Dipping and leaping, it pursued its prey, leaving Daniel no choice but to move where it bade him. Backing around the circle into which the tribe had penned him, he had to pay full heed to the knife, and thus could not watch his feet, although the ground was uneven and strewn with debris. His foot encountered a pile of logs, and, though he stepped aside, the hesitation was enough to provide Esh-tan an opening. Again the knife flashed, this time towards his chest. Caroline heard him grunt and saw his face register pain, even as the red stain appeared on his tunic.

Esh-tan saw, as well, and his eyes opened in exultant glee, as if the sight of the new blood had brought a thirst for still more. His mouth open, he lunged again, this time with his entire body, the knife aimed at Daniel's heart. Daniel saw him coming and managed to spin away, but in so doing his foot caught the edge of the hide that the women had been scraping. Esh-tan stumbled, falling against Daniel's chest. Daniel fought for his balance, but could not maintain it. Down he went, arms flailing, and landed hard on his back, grunting involuntarily, the wind knocked from his lungs.

He lay still for a moment, stunned, but a moment was all that Esh-tan needed to recover. He was already rising, pushing himself up with the flats of his palms, when Daniel hit the ground. Turning, he saw his foe immobilized, and, his lips curling, he raised his hand for the final thrust.

"Dear God, no!" whispered Caroline, through bloodless lips. She watched in horrified fascination as Daniel's hand reached out, groping on the rough ground until his fingers touched a rock. As Esh-tan lunged towards him, he heaved with all his might.

The rock was not heavy, but the aim was true. It caught Esh-tan in the jaw, solid as a well-placed punch, and sent him reeling backwards, sprawling on the ground with the same paralyzing force with which Daniel had gone down. But this time it was Daniel who was on his feet, then down over Esh-tan, one hand clamped on each wrist, fingers digging into muscle, probing deep for nerves, while Esh-tan used his full strength to try to throw him off.

In this, they were evenly matched. Slowly, painfully, Daniel's fingers bore down on muscle and nerve, digging more deeply, until Esh-tan's fingers opened and the knife fell from his grip. For a moment, it lay in the dirt, bright in the firelight. Then, before Daniel could free his fingers to grab it, a foot darted out from behind him, catching the knife on the hilt and sending it skittering away and far beyond his reach. Arms folded, eyes malevolent, Hoo-tan met Daniel's gaze. And, in the same moment, Esh-tan twisted violently, throwing Daniel away from him and coming to his feet.

Esh-tan's hands must still be numb, Caroline thought. Moving back, he shook them, flexing his fingers. Determined to press his advantage for as long as it held, Daniel was up and on him, gripping him from behind, but in the next moment their positions were reversed, and Esh-tan had Daniel's right arm pinned against his back. His other arm clamped firmly around Daniel's chest, he pulled up on the twisted arm until Caroline thought the bones must surely snap.

Daniel's face was twisted with pain. The wound on his chest was bleeding, staining his tunic brown, and rivers of sweat were coursing down his face, mixing with dirt and blood. Slowly, and with great effort, he raised his left hand and foot, and in the same movement he struck with both at once, hitting Esh-tan on the temple and the instep of his foot. The first blow stunned him, and, though he tried to hold on, the second blow finished him. Bellowing in pain, he threw both of his hands in the air. Daniel heaved him back onto the ground. Then, twisting, he was on top of him, straddling his chest as he had before, both hands wrapped around his neck.

Daniel's fingers squeezed again as they had done before. At first, Esh-tan lay quiet, but then the struggle began. Esh-tan's hands rose blindly, his nails raking Daniel's skin; they pushed up against Daniel's chin before settling for his neck. But by then it was too late. Esh-tan's face was a deep red, and his eyes were rolling up in their sockets.

Daniel felt the moment when Esh-tan lost consciousness. He felt the powerful body go limp beneath him. He knew the fight was over, and that he had won. He knew he would prove nothing if he continued to squeeze.

And yet he could not stop. He still seemed to see the expression in Caroline's eyes, and the long bronze finger sliding down over her breast. This man would have to die for what she had endured. He would offer up this Indian as a sacrifice.

And then what? asked his thinking brain, slowly returning to life. Perhaps they will not kill you for taking this man's life, but they will no longer count you among their friends. All the trust you have built up during the course of this last week will have been for naught, and you will destroy the only chance you may have to escape. You will jeopardize the very life that you mean to revenge.

He hated to let go. It took all his will to loosen his grip, and, even when he did so, still he did not rise, but remained crouched over Esh-tan, palms flat in the dirt, bruised ribs heaving with fatigue and nausea.

Someone was raising him. He thought at first that it was Caroline, but the hands were dark.

"You come," muttered Yum-sa-wek. "I see to that cut."

"Caroline," he murmured, too weak to resist.

"She come, too," said Yum-sa-wek. "Think that you can walk?"

He could, but only barely, his feet stumbling on the ground, but now Caroline was with him, supporting him on one side, while the Indian woman supported the other. He tried to see the expression on Caroline's face, but her head was down, and his own was swimming. Then they were past the fire and at the wigwam door. He entered on all fours, collapsing on the first pallet to which he came. Closing his eyes, he lost consciousness momentarily. When he regained it, Caroline was kneeling over him, his left hand between both of hers. She was crying, and her tears wet his fingers as she pressed them to her cheek, then to her breast.

"I thought he would kill you! I thought that you would die! What would I do without you?" She was sobbing, and he could feel her trembling. "Oh, God, what would I do?"

It was indiscreet, he knew, with Yum-sa-wek just behind, and yet he was filled with a longing to draw her down with him and to pillow his aching body against her softness.

"Don't worry." He managed a smile. "It will take more than a drunken Indian to drive me from this life."

"Liquor white man evil," muttered Yum-sa-wek, moving beside Caroline. "Take off this shirt now, see what you need."

Caroline helped Yum-sa-wek remove Daniel's shirt and watched as she bathed the jagged cut. It was deeper than she had thought, and still oozing blood, and dark bruises were already spreading along his arms and chest. Hannah had come in with them, and sat a few feet away, her eyes also on Daniel, her lips moving in prayer. In the corner, in a blanket, lay Hetty and Yum-sa-wek's children, all curled up together, like lion cubs.

When the wound was bathed, Yum-sa-wek smeared it with something that looked like bear grease but smelled of herbs. Producing an old cotton petticoat from a pile against the wall, she tore it into broad strips and bound his chest, protecting the wound with a compress on which she smeared more of the salve. Resting for a moment, she rose with a sigh. "Best I go fetch my man now, or he sleep where he fall." To Caroline, she added, "Best you stay the night here, out of Hoo-tan's way."

"Yes... Thank you," murmured Caroline, wondering how she would ever face Hoo-tan again. Up until this moment, her only thought had been for Daniel's life; now, for the first time, she wondered how the fight would affect their relationship with the tribe. Then, too, with Daniel wounded, they could not think of escape. And, when Esh-tan recovered, would he not want revenge? The flood of new worries threatened to sweep her away, so she forced herself to turn away from them and back to Daniel. The water with which Yum-sa-wek had bathed his wound was stained a dark red from his blood. Emptying the bowl out the wig-wam door, she refilled it with clear water in order to bathe his face.

When the cool rag touched his forehead, his eyes opened into hers.

"Caroline?"

"I'm here." As before, she took his hand, bringing it up to her lips.

"Yes. And your sister?"

"She is here, as well," Caroline replied, glancing to where Hannah still prayed. "Yum-sa-wek has gone to fetch her man."

"Good . . ." His voice died away as his eyelids fluttered down. But in a moment they reopened. "We must leave to-night," he said.

"Tonight!" She stared at him, wondering if he was delirious.

"Yes, tonight," he repeated. "As soon as they are asleep. Mrs. MacKenzie?"

"I am here," Hannah replied, and, turning, Caroline saw the unuttered fear in her eyes.

"You will have to tie a rag around the child's mouth so that she makes no sound."

"But," Caroline protested, "how can you hope to travel in this condition?"

"It is the only way," he said, closing his eyes as he drew in breath. Opening them, he added, "The men will all be too drunk to notice that we've gone, and, with luck, the women will be too busy nursing them. Take my word, I've traveled farther in worse condition." Then, seeing from her expression that she resisted still, he added, "After this, it would be too dangerous to stay."

She had opened her mouth to protest, but now she shut it again. Seeing this, Daniel found her hand with his. "I will do well to sleep for a bit. Can you stay awake?"

"Of course," she said quickly.

"Then wake me in two hours, as soon as the men are asleep."

For a long moment, she watched him. Then she whispered his name: "Daniel?"

His eyes opened.

"Thank you for what you did."

He lay unmoving for a moment. Then he said, "It's over and done. With luck, we will be gone in two hours and never speak of it again." He closed his eyes a second time, and was asleep almost instantly.

"Caroline?" Seeing that Daniel was sleeping, Hannah dared to speak. "Do you think it is possible?"

"Daniel thinks it is," she said, looking down at him. He looked so pale and tired that the sight of him wrung her heart. How could she wake him in two hours, when what he needed was to rest? Then, recalling how he had beaten Eshtan when all had seemed lost, she said, "Yes, I think we can."

"But what if we are recaptured? Things may go even worse for us."

"Yes..." Caroline nodded, though she was thinking to herself that Esh-tan would make things bad enough if they stayed. Seeing Hannah's eyes go to Hetty, asleep with the other little ones, she added, "Remember what Yum-sa-wek said about her grandmother. What if they let you go but keep Hetty back? You don't want her to grow up an Indian."

Hannah gasped. "God save us. All right, then we'll try. And perhaps we may even prevail."

"We will prevail," said Caroline "Now you should sleep, as well. We've only got two hours until it's time to leave. And take Hetty in with you, so we don't wake the other children when it's time to leave."

"Yes..." Hannah's eyes rested on the tangled pile of children. "How do they learn?" she wondered. "What makes them change as they grow?"

"Survival," said Caroline, and she was surprised by the lack of rancor in her voice.

"Daniel." Caroline spoke softly, her fingers pressed lightly to his lips. She saw his eyelids flutter as his body clung to sleep. Then his will triumphed, and his eyes opened into hers. For a moment, he stared at her with an unfocused gaze. Then she saw his eyes clear.

Yum-sa-wek and her husband both slept, he with his head flung back, filling the wigwam with his stentorian snores. In the course of the past two hours, Caroline had started to think that Yum-sa-wek suspected they meant to leave. She was also hoping that Yum-sa-wek would not be held responsible for their escape.

She heard the sharpness of Daniel's breath as he raised himself. His face grew pale, but he did not sink back on the pallet. Behind her, Hannah sat on her sleeping blanket, Hetty stretched out at her side, a band of material fastened across her mouth. Hannah's eyes were enormous, but her mouth was determined. Caroline saw Daniel's gaze linger on her appraisingly, as if he were calculating their chances of success. Then, reaching for his tunic, he tried to draw it on, but this he could not do without Caroline's help—and then she had to struggle to ignore how he flinched with the pain. When it was on, he crawled to the wigwam door. He gazed out for a moment before turning back to tell them with gestures that they should remain where they were while he went out to scout. Not waiting for their agreement, he turned and disappeared.

Caroline sat unmoving. For the past two hours, she had turned away from all her doubts, reminding herself over and over again that she must have faith. But now, with the clear vision of how he had flinched in pain, she could not help but wonder how he would manage to survive the rigors of the next days.

Then he was back again, beckoning them from the door to follow him soundlessly. His eyes, passing Caroline, fell upon the woven container of salve that Yum-sa-wek had used on his wound, and he gestured for her to pass it to him. This she did, and she saw that he put it in his pouch, which he must have retrieved from Ti-sha-wa's wigwam. Then, gesturing for her to carry Hetty in her arms, he turned and withdrew. Putting Hannah before her, Caroline crept out into the night.

Outside, the fire had died down, and the moon was a pale, drifting disc behind the clouds. Some of the women, like Yum-sa-wek, had managed to lead their men to bed, but the rest of the hunters lay where they had fallen, in profound alcoholic sleep. Daniel led the way, with Hannah just behind, carrying the blankets which she had snatched as an afterthought. Caroline brought up the rear, with Hetty in her arms. She saw that Daniel had his rifle again, and that he, too, carried a bundle of blankets upon his back. Then he had not just been scouting, he had been gathering provisions, as well.... She thought with fleeting regret of his knife, still buried in Hoo-tan's floor.

The pebbles on the beach shifted beneath their feet, the sound loud and grating in the stillness of the night. In their haste to begin the celebration, the men had not drawn the canoes up the beach, nor had they turned them upside down. Instead, they had left them at the river's very edge, where they could be pushed out into the current with no trouble at all. Daniel swung his bundle into the nearest one and gestured to Caroline to lay Hetty in it as well. He helped Hannah get in and settled her towards the back, but, when Caroline made to join her, Daniel shook his head.

Leading her by gesture, he had her pull the canoe out until she stood waist-deep in the freezing water. She held the canoe steady while he pulled the others out, tying them together in pairs behind the first. When he had finished, he held up his hand again and, when she nodded, disappeared off towards the camp.

He returned with the horses, whose mouths he had tied with cloth to keep them from whinnying. Their hooves seemed to thunder against the rocky shore. Two of them came docilely, but the third balked, especially when Daniel tried to lead it into the stream. Caroline watched. She was exhausted from worry and lack of sleep, and chilled to the bone, as well. The whole evening had taken on a nightmarish tinge. She wondered how Daniel could fight a horse with a wound in his chest. Beyond that, she could not imagine how they would get across, with the canoes and the horses and no strong paddlers. It all seemed impossible. But she responded swiftly when he spoke to her.

"Get in the front of the canoe. Be ready to grab the lead when I pass it to you. Quickly," he told her, his voice tight with pain.

Caroline moved to obey him, but it was difficult for her to board, for the canoe bobbed on the water, while her wet skirts pulled her down. In the end, it was Hannah who hauled her over the edge, and no sooner had she righted than she felt the lead thrust into her hand. Looking up, she saw that the horses were now in the water, Daniel mounted on the first one, the others tied behind. He had taken off their muzzles so that they could breath, and this seemed to have encouraged the one that had balked before. Urging them forward, he headed farther out into the stream. At first, nothing happened, but then the lead went taut, and in the next moment Caroline felt the canoe begin to move as the horses towed it forward.

The crossing was terrible. Caroline sat immobile, torn between fear for Daniel's safety and fear of discovery. Her body clenched in terror, she kept her eyes fixed ahead, on the small blur of brightness that was Daniel's head against the lead horse's neck, all the time imagining a cry raised from behind as the camp learned of their absence and rushed down to the beach. Her clothes clung to her body like fingers of ice, and she had to clamp her jaw tight to keep her teeth from chattering. And, if she was freezing, how must Daniel feel? Behind her, hands clasped together, Hannah was reciting verses from Exodus.

Despite Hannah's supplications, God did not reach down His rod and part the river for them, but somehow they managed to reach the other side without either cry or light coming from behind. As soon as the canoe touched bottom, Caroline leapt out, holding the lead in her right hand, the boat in her left, afraid to release either for fear of losing them. She looked about for Daniel, her heart in her throat, and in the next moment he was at her side, the water still streaming from his clothes.

"I'll tie the horses. Can you hold the boats?"

"Yes, of course," she said, her voice as breathless as if she had swum the stream. Her whole body was shaking.

"Shall I get out?" Hannah asked, her voice no steadier than Caroline's. Behind her, the rest of the canoes drifted to the shore, jostling against each other with hollow knocks and thuds.

"I guess so," said Caroline, pulling the canoe as far up as she could manage and reaching out to help her sister. Hannah's fingers were as icy as her own.

"Help me pull it up." Daniel appeared on the far side of the canoe, and together he and Caroline hoisted it up onto the shore. The flow of the river brought the others up, as well, drifting in sideways to rock along the edge. Reaching in for the bundle he had set in the canoe, Daniel rummaged in its contents, emerging with a tomahawk. Wading to the last of the bobbing canoes, he raised the ax above his head and brought it down against the side.

Hannah and Caroline watched, huddled on the shore, as Daniel demolished each of the canoes in turn.

"Must you?" asked Caroline, wincing in spite of herself at every blow.

"If I don't, they'll only pull them back again. They'll come across in a raft and be back within minutes. This way, they'll lose time getting everyone across—and they'll take it as bad spirits that all their boats are gone." His words came in brief spurts between blows. Once again, Caroline wondered where he had found the strength. Perhaps the wound was not so bad as she had thought.

But, soon enough, she found reason to think otherwise, for after he struck the last blow his arms dropped abruptly, and had he not caught himself, supported against the canoe, he would have pitched forwards. Before he could draw breath, Caroline was at his side, her arms about him, helping him to shore.

"You have attempted too much. You must rest, at least for a while." She drew him with her towards the shore, but he shook her off.

"No, there is no time."

"But your wound—" she began, but he cut her off.

"I have survived this life ten years without a nursemaid n the woods, and I believe I will survive ten more. If you vill see to your sister, I will untie the horses so that we can >e off before the alarm is given and they come after us."

For one stunned moment, Caroline watched him walk off, tung by the coldness of his tone, and by his words, as well, lthough she knew that both were products of the pain he nust be suffering. Then she shook herself mentally. There vas no place for wounded feelings now; the dangers they vere facing were far more important. So, straightening her houlders, she turned back to the canoe and Hetty and)aniel's bundle, and everything else that remained to do.

Chapter Fourteen

They moved southeast along the river, towards the Connecticut, the hooves of the horses sounding hollowly on the
pebbled shore. They rode in single file, with Daniel at the
front, Hannah in the middle and Caroline at the rear, carrying the still-sleeping Hetty in a blanket sling, as the Indians had done on the trip north. Although Daniel had not
spoken since his last curt words, from the direction he had
taken, it was not hard to guess his plan. They would follow
this river as far as the Connecticut, whose flow would then
direct them south, all the way to Fort Dummer. She saw no
reason why they should not reach the fort, so long as nothing happened to slow their progress.

Already exhausted by the strain and her sleepless night,
she felt her head nodding as she rode along. She was almost drowsing when a splashing brought her awake. Raising her head, she saw that the beach had dwindled to a
narrow strip of tumbled rocks beneath the river's steep
banks. Rather than choose the soft earth of the higher
ground, on which they would leave a clear track, Daniel had
turned to the river, instead, and Hannah, coming after, had
followed his lead. Caroline turned her horse to follow them.
When she saw Daniel circle and start back towards her, she
assumed he meant for her to stop, so that they might converse.

"Keep to the water," he said, bringing his horse flank to
flank with hers. "And take care to avoid the rocks." Then

before she could reply or question, he was off again, no longer headed southeast, but rather towards the north-west—back in the very direction from which they had just come!

"What—" she began, but then she stopped, for Daniel was beyond her range.

"It's to fool the Indians," explained Hannah, who had also turned, and had come even with her. "So they think that we've headed south."

"But won't they see us coming back?"

"Mr. Ledet thinks not. He thinks that they will still be sleeping when we pass, and, even if they are not, the night will cover us. But we must hurry—look, he is already gone."

It was true; Daniel had already vanished into the night, leaving behind only the splashing of his horses' hooves. Hannah moved forwards, leaving Caroline alone, her mind full of questions and doubts. It was all well and good to speak of fooling the tribe, but did not their true advantage lie in speed? If they kept on in this direction, they would be at least a half day ahead, and they were mounted, while the Indians would be on foot. And what if Daniel was mis-taken, and the alarm had already been spread? Caroline opened her mouth to protest, but then she realized that there was no one to hear her words. By now, Hannah was no more visible than Daniel had been. Left with no choice but to follow, she turned her horse upriver again.

Take care to avoid the rocks! It was a fine sentiment, but how was she to avoid something she could not see, for now the moon had sunk down below the hills that hugged the river's western bank, turning the water as pitch-black as the starless sky. And what if her horse did fall? Then they would be minus one of their precious means of transport, and three hours' travel time, as well. Was Daniel in his right mind to think of such a plan? But she had no chance to put the question to him. It took all her skill and courage simply to keep up, and she wondered how Hannah was managing.

They slowed when they reached the stretch of river just opposite the camp, and Caroline held her breath, terrified the sounds of the horses' hooves might cross the wide expanse. She superstitiously kept her eyes averted from the far bank, but, when she dared glance in that direction, she saw no sign of light. Although they kept to the water, they picked up their speed again after they passed the camp. Hetty woke soon after, but Caroline got her back to sleep with a half-whispered lullaby.

The first light was showing when they reached another stream that cut away to the south. Caroline breathed a sigh of relief when they turned into it, but a mile later, when the stream turned west, Daniel did not quit it, but rather forged ahead. Caroline was hoping that it would turn again, but another mile showed that it did not. If anything, it looped up farther towards the north.

What could he be thinking? Caroline wondered in dismay. Why expend so much effort in heading the wrong way, when Daniel was already weakened and Hannah so very pregnant? She racked her brain for an answer, and found but one possibility, a possibility so fantastic that she could no longer hold her peace. She urged her horse forward and into the deeper water, pulling ahead, past Hannah, to where Daniel led the way.

He heard the sound of her horse's splashing hooves and glanced about, frowning. But his disapproval was nothing compared to the pallor of his face. For a moment, she forgot the question that she meant to put to him.

"Yes, what is it?" he asked, turning back to the stream, for he had seen from her reaction that the pain he was in was too obvious. He knew that she meant well, and he doubted that she could understand that the concern that she showed him only made things more difficult. He'd traveled wounded before, traveled farther, and with pain just as bad, and experience had taught him that his body could manage as much as he forced it to. But trying to explain all that to Caroline would only sap his strength. Besides, he suspected that she would not believe what he said.

"Is something wrong?" he asked.

"No, nothing." She shook her head quickly, drawing abreast of him. "I was only wondering about our direction...why we are headed north. I wondered if you were meaning for us to go to—" She stopped, unable after all to speak the name.

Nor was there need to speak it, for Daniel read her thoughts and, despite his discomfort, threw back his head and laughed, though any joy was quickly snatched away in a painful grimace. "To go to Montreal?" he said, and saw her glance away. "So that I can present you to the graves of my ancestors—or did you think I meant to sell you to the governor myself?"

"No!" she gasped, horrified, but then she saw that he was jesting with her.

"No," he said, shaking his head, "we are simply trying to baffle our pursuit."

"But wouldn't it be wiser to try to outrun them?" she replied, at last giving voice to the doubts that had plagued her these past hours. "We must have close to a day's start, and we are mounted besides. Look how quickly we caught them when we were heading north."

"Because they were not expecting pursuit. Have you ever seen an Indian who is making time? He doesn't walk, he runs—for hours at a time. A running man can move faster than a horse in the woods. It wouldn't take them long to catch us once they got across. And they will cross the river, sooner than you think."

"I feared they might have crossed it before we returned," she said, dropping her voice, ashamed of her lack of faith.

But the irritation was gone from Daniel's face when he replied, "The alarm must be given first, and that will not happen until Yum-sa-wek wakes."

Caroline turned curious eyes on him. "You think she will cover for us?"

"Perhaps not cover," he replied, "but sleep soundly, I think. If I am not mistaken, they are just waking now—and it will take some time yet to clear their befuddled brains."

She knew he meant to be comforting, but still she shivered at the thought of the cry the men would send up when they found that their captives had flown. The danger of their situation bore down upon her anew.

"Will they believe that we headed south? That is why we left them the clear track, so they would think that we had."

"That is hard to say," Daniel said. "An *Indian* would not have done so. An Indian would more likely have come in this direction. But an Indian will believe that a white man would not."

"Not even you?" she asked.

"Prejudice runs deep—in both directions." He shrugged as he spoke, and, because her eyes were on him, Caroline saw him flinch with the pain that the movement brought.

"Forgive me," she said quickly, "but I fear for your strength."

"You must not," he said, making his voice as gentle as he dared. "I know how to measure my own strength. I will get you safely home. But, in the meantime, it will not help our cause if your horse slips and falls."

He meant that it was risky for her horse to be in the deeper water into which she had moved when she had come up to him. "Yes, of course." She nodded. "I will fall back now."

She reined in to let him pass, and, as he did so, he turned back to her. "I would not have chosen this course, had I not thought it best. Have faith."

"I do," she said, but she could not help frowning as he turned away. Perhaps he knew his own strength, but still she feared for him—and her frown only deepened when Hannah pulled alongside, her face as pale as Daniel's from the discomfort of the ride.

"Is it very painful?"

"No, not at all," Hannah said. It was clearly untrue. "And I've spoken to the baby about waiting until we are home. Hetty still sleeps?"

"Yes, thank God. I wonder what she can possibly make of all this?"

"It will fade from her mind," said Hannah, "once she is safely home."

Caroline watched her sister pass, wondering if Hannah had noted their direction. Poor Hannah, she thought with a sudden sharp pang. Perhaps Daniel was the best judge of his own limits, but could he judge Hannah's, as well? All this hard traveling could not be good for her—and what would they do if the baby came before they reached the fort? And, even if they reached the fort before the baby came, Hannah's trials would not end then, for she must hear the truth about Thomas there—unless Caroline told her first. But that was an issue to be decided at a later hour. Just now, there were far more urgent matters to consider. Laying the reins on her horse once again, Caroline moved ahead, just as little Hetty squirmed herself awake.

They halted in late afternoon, bone-sore and exhausted, on a flat rock beside the stream. Only Hetty had extra energy; she clambered down the rock to examine a small pool that had collected at its base. Caroline helped Hannah down, then collapsed on the ground, too tired to chew the meat Daniel put in her hand.

"Take it," he commanded, when she shook her head.

"I'll have some later, after I've had a rest."

"You'll have it now. It will keep you warm."

So she took it, too weary to protest, but, as soon as it touched her lips, she wished that she had not. With her other worries, she had not thought of her stomach, but now at once she realized how hungry she was—ravenous enough to gobble up three days' supply. Three days, she thought, dismayed. How will we ever survive? Even if we do fool them with our choice of trail, it will only add extra time to our trek. We were a week coming north. How will we ever feed ourselves in the days to come?

Daniel sat with his back against a tree that grew at the top of the rock. When Caroline approached him, he opened his eyes. She kept hers carefully averted from his bloodstained tunic.

"How is Mrs. MacKenzie?"

"Well enough, I think," she said, and paused. "What if they do follow in this direction? How far will they search?"

"I hope not far enough. As much as they want the ransom, they have to think of their hunt, and there is only so much time they can devote to chasing us. There is more meat to catch, and winter is not far away."

"And how much time is that?" she asked, trying not to think of the prospect of cold weather. So far, they had been lucky in the mildness of the air.

"Not enough, we hope. And, if they come near, we shall hide. I know these woods as well as you know your own garden."

"But do not the Indians know them just as well?"

"No." He shook his head. "Their hunting grounds lie on the river's northern side. They will have spent little time in these parts. Now you must try to get some sleep before we must move again."

"What about you?"

He replied, with a ghost of a smile, "I can sleep and watch at once."

Caroline fell asleep as soon as her eyes closed, to be awakened all too soon. "No, not yet," she protested, and felt Daniel's hand cover her mouth to still her words. The moon had already risen, and it gave them light through the trees, for the night was clear. Though the air was gentle, Caroline shivered with fatigue. Hannah, who lay beside her, sighed in her sleep, and Hetty whimpered.

"Let them rest a bit longer," she whispered, but Daniel shook his head, and, though her whole body protested, she knew that he was right.

"How is your wound?" she asked, but either he did not hear or he chose not to answer, moving away from her to where the horses were tethered in the stream. Caroline watched him, stiff and still stupid with sleep. What would she not give to stay here where she was, clinging to the warmth of her blanket and the transitory comfort of sleep?

She watched, unmoving, as Daniel untied the first horse. Then, leaning forward, she murmured in Hannah's ear.

"Come, sister, it's time to go."

It could not have been past midnight when Daniel had awakened her, for they traveled many hours before the first light broke. In time, the worst of the stiffness left Caroline's bones, but the chill clung to her, and the stupidity, so that even the thought of the Indians no longer struck fear in her heart. Every fiber of her being wanted to be lying down, wrapped in the warm comfort of a goose-down quilt, not jolting along on a horse's back in the wilderness with an injured man and a pregnant woman and almost nothing to eat.

It was worse in the daylight, when Hetty awoke and needed to be coaxed and coddled into not crying when she wanted to be set down. What if the Indians did find them? Caroline wondered now. Could they keep Hetty quiet for as long as they must hide? And what would they do with the horses—and with Hannah, for that matter? You couldn't keep a pregnant woman perched in a tree.

A bit of cold meat and dry corn bread was their morning meal. Hetty, elated to be set on her feet, trotted here and there, picking up pebbles and bits of twig and chattering to herself. Caroline sat with Hannah, paralyzed with fatigue, until she realized that Daniel was not sitting with them. Rousing herself, she looked around, and saw him a short way off. His tunic was drawn up, and he was wrapping his wound again. Rising, she crossed to where he stood, but he had seen her coming, and he turned, pulling down his tunic to hide the dressing from her view. At his feet, she saw the bark container of salve that he had taken from Yum-sa-wek's wigwam. Now he stooped to retrieve it and stow it away in his shoulder pouch.

"I would dress it for you."

"Yes, I know." Even at this moment, with her filthy clothing and her tangled hair, she looked beautiful to him. There was, he suddenly realized, much about women he did not know. He had thought to know their secrets, but now he saw how much he had yet to learn. He knew better than any other what Caroline had endured, and yet she made no complaint for her own comfort. Nor did Mrs. MacKenzie, for whom this must be agony. Even the child adapted, seeking pleasure when she could find it, and distraction when she could not. His heart filled with admiration and with gratitude. He wished he could tell Caroline how he felt, but, battling fatigue and pain, he could find no words.

"Thank you," he said at last, and saw her eyes come up.

"For what?"

"For your offer—and for everything."

"But I have done nothing. I have been a burden to you."

"A burden— Oh, no." He shook his head, for, though he saw how she could think it, he had not felt so.

She started to turn away, but seemed to come to some decision. Turning back, she asked, "Why did you not kill him?"

"Him?" His mind was blank.

"Esh-tan." She winced slightly as she spoke the name. "I thought that you meant to kill him, at the very end. But then you let him go."

"I wanted to," he said slowly. "But I knew I could not. It would have jeopardized our chances of getting away."

"You thought of that, then?" she asked, gazing at him with the same wondering admiration that he had felt just now. He would have stayed there with her, enjoying her company, but his wound was throbbing, and they still had a ways to go.

The day dragged on endlessly, a blur of rocks and water and Hetty's piping voice. Again they stopped when darkness fell and slept through half the night, and again it was Daniel who roused them from their sleep. The third dawn was just breaking when Caroline saw Hannah sway and lean forward against her horse's neck. Forgetting all caution, she cried out in alarm.

"Hannah! Daniel—stop!" Urging her horse forward, she reached Hannah's side before he did, and reached out to hold her sister so that she would not fall. It was not necessary, she realized, so tightly were Hannah's fingers twined into the tangled mane. Hannah's face was ashen, and her jaw was clamped. At the sight of her mother, Hetty began to cry.

"Now, Hetty," said Caroline. "Why are you crying when that big fat robin is laughing at you right now? See him in the tree?" she asked, pointing at random. Then, turning back to Hannah: "When did it start?"

"Not so long," whispered Hannah, her jaw clenching again. "Sometime during the darkness—I'm not exactly sure." Releasing her breath as the pain passed, she smiled an apology.

Caroline looked at Daniel, who had joined them. "We have to stop," she said, wondering if he would protest.

But, instead, he nodded. "Mrs. MacKenzie, do you think you can manage another mile?"

"I can try," whispered Hannah.

"There is a place," he said quickly, before Caroline could protest. "Let us not waste time disputing," he added, taking Hannah's reins and beginning to move again.

It was a long mile. To Caroline, it seemed endless, amusing Hetty and riding at Hannah's side, her own face contorted in sympathy with each new pain. But, somehow, they made it, and then they were on the land, making their way through the forest to what looked like a pile of rocks.

"Here?" she asked, looking about her, when Daniel stopped before the rocks. She dismounted quickly and helped him let Hannah down. Between them, they walked her towards the rocks, and it was not until they had reached it that Caroline saw the opening—or rather glimpsed a shadow, since it was almost hidden by the brush. Holding aside the branches, Daniel led the way, and Caroline, stooping, found herself plunged into inky darkness.

It was like going blind. Overtaxed, her nerves inched towards hysteria, but, well before they reached it, her eyes grew accustomed, and she saw the faint light filtering down from somewhere behind. Then she could see that the cave in which they stood was some ten feet by twelve feet, with a second chamber towards the back. Dry branches had been piled along one wall, perhaps by humans, though the place smelled of animals.

"The blanket," Daniel commanded, nodding towards the sling that Caroline wore. She untied it and laid it on the branches, making a rude bed upon which to lay Hannah.

"Mamma! Mamma!" It was Hetty, still outside the cave. She had not been watching when they had come in, and now she found herself alone and abandoned outside. Caroline went to fetch her, with Daniel close behind.

"Gather wood for the fire," he said. "As much as you possibly can." Collecting the horses' reins, he began moving back towards the stream.

"Where are you going?" she asked.

"To tether them on the far bank, then to wipe away our tracks. Here," he added, drawing a knife from the pouch at his belt and tossing it to her. "Cut some fresh branches from behind the rocks that we can use for a bed."

Caroline stooped to retrieve the knife. "How did you find it?" she asked.

"What—the knife? It's borrowed—permanently," he said, leading the horses away.

Hetty thought wood-gathering great fun after the confinement of the trip, and ran about the clearing, bringing back armloads of twigs. Caroline carried armloads of deadfall into the cave, pausing with each load to kneel at Hannah's side for a moment's reassurance. She was cutting the fresh branches when Daniel returned. He did not stop to greet her, but disappeared into the cave, and by the time she followed, he had the fire lit.

"What if they see the fire?" she asked, looking up at a small chink in the cave's roof, through which the smoke escaped.

"The chances are they won't. Here, help me with the pallet."

She laid down the fresh branches, which they covered with a stout hide that had been in his bundle. Now Caroline saw what else he had carried with him—a bark bucket, and several baskets and bowls, as well as a soft doeskin.

"To wrap the baby," he explained, setting it aside. Taking out another hide, rougher than the first, he added, "And this is for the birth."

To lay beneath Hannah, he meant. Caroline stared at him in bewilderment. "Did you plan on it being like this?" she asked.

"Life in the woods has taught me that it pays to be prepared. Though, of course," he added, unable to resist, "we could have managed with what we found at hand."

Caroline looked about her, trying to imagine what that might have been, but Daniel gave her no time. Telling Hannah that they would be right back, he motioned Caroline outside. He walked a half-dozen paces, then stopped to wait for her. When she reached him, he asked, "What do you know about babies?"

"I've never brought one myself, but I've helped at home," she added, feeling light-headed. He must have seen her eyes roll, for now he gripped her arm.

"This is home now," he said. "And, if you can keep your head, I believe we shall all survive. Can you do that, Caroline?"

For a moment, her dark eyes met his blue-gray ones; then she nodded once. "I'll try," she said.

"Good. Then go back to your sister. I'll be there in a few minutes."

"Yes. Where are you going?"

"To gather what you'll need."

Hannah's pains had worsened before Daniel got back. Caroline had torn a strip from her apron, and was using it to bathe Hannah's face and hands. At home, she would have tied a towel to the end of the bed and given Hannah one end on which to pull against the pains. But here there was no towel to pull, and nothing to tie one to, so Hannah clung to Caroline's hand, squeezing it with such force that Caroline feared that her fingers would break.

She was worried about Hannah. She had been with her when all her babies had been born, and, except for Young Tom, who had been the first, the births had not been hard. But this one, coming early, and after the strain of these last three weeks, seemed to give her more pain than she had had before, and, although she tried to smile, her eyes were filled with fear. Nor did it help that Hetty was right here with them, watching her mother's labor with large, frightened eyes.

"Mamma will be fine." Caroline managed a smile, wondering what could be taking Daniel so long. "She'll give you a new baby, and won't that be fine?"

"Hetty Mamma's baby!" was the whimpered reply.

When Daniel finally ducked through the entrance, Caroline turned to him, relief stark on her face.

He carried a blanket, and he now spread it on the floor. Caroline saw that it contained a hodgepodge of leaves and roots, as well as tufts of thistle fluff, light against the dark. When he had laid the fire, he had put in stones to heat. Now, filling the largest of the baskets from the bark bucket, he added three of the red-hot stones, using two sticks as tongs. The stones hissed when they met the water, and it was not very long before the water began to steam. Pouring some into a bowl, Daniel added some of the leaves, and a bit of root that he had crushed with a stone, and stirred the mixture with his knife. A sharp, pungent aroma filled the cave.

This done, he moved to Hannah's side. "Mrs. Mac-Kenzie? How are you feeling?"

"Oh, it's not so bad," Hannah gasped. "Perhaps it will be another boy.... Thomas will be so pleased." She closed her eyes as a new pain came, and Caroline and Daniel exchanged a wordless look.

When Hannah's eyes reopened, Daniel spoke again. "I'm going to take Hetty outside with me. I've found a bushful of barberries, and a hickory tree besides. I thought we might

pass the time gathering some food. I thought they might
taste good to you after the baby comes.''

"Yes, of course," gasped Hannah. "How very good of
you." Though Caroline, too, recognized the necessity of the
plan, she had to bite her lip to keep from begging him to
stay. As if he understood, she felt his hand rest on her
shoulder when he rose to leave the cave, and the warmth of
it lingered even when he had gone. His wound must be getting better, she thought, relieved, for him to do so much.
Perhaps they would survive after all. If only the baby would
make up its mind to come...

Hannah's breathing changed. The labored breathing
ended, and the fevered panting began. At last! Caroline
thought, releasing Hannah's hand and rising from her knees
to push the blanket back. Pushing up Hannah's skirts she
took the rough hide Daniel had set out and slid it into place.

"It won't be much longer," she said—or thought she
did—and if Hannah answered, she was not aware, her whole
being focused on what was to come.

How long did it take? Caroline could not have said, being
unaware of time—being unaware of anything but the tiny
patch of red that was the first she saw of the new life fighting its way into the world. What words had she spoken? She
had no memory; nor, very likely, had Hannah, to whom the
words had been addressed, urging and exhorting, encour-
aging, threatening, cajoling this scrap of life through the last
triumphant inches of its momentous journey. The world
about them had long since ceased to exist, except for her and
Hannah and the little scrap of red, which in time became a
small head attached to scrawny red shoulders. Then, with a
rush of wetness, the whole of creation was resting in her
hands, red and gnarled and squalling and too slippery to
hold. But, somehow, she managed, dipping the rag in the
warm water and wiping clean the new skin, then laying it on
Hannah's stomach to cut and tie the cord with the knife
Daniel had taken from the tribe. Then she took the doeskin
and wrapped the baby snugly, and when at last she sat back,

she was astonished to find herself in a cave, and not at the farm or in New Haven, or even back in Surrey.

Hannah was speaking, her voice hoarse and faint.

"What is it, sister?"

"A girl. A perfect little girl." Caroline leaned over her to lay the swaddled scrap in Hannah's arms. "A beautiful baby girl."

"She is so tiny." Hannah touched the wrinkled face. "I fear she will not stay with us."

"She will stay!" Caroline snapped back, startled by the sound of her own voice. "She will stay, I swear it. I will not let her go!"

"Yes, of course," murmured Hannah, her face ashen and drained. For a moment, Caroline knelt, looking down at her; then, painfully, she roused herself, for there was still much to be done.

After the dimness of the cave, the sun was blindingly bright. Caroline stood blinking, surprised to find it still high in the sky. Could so much have happened in the short hours since dawn? And what of the Indians? The coming of the baby had pushed all thought of them away, and even now they seemed a threat from another life.

A stirring among the bushes led her to Hetty, who sat cross-legged on the ground before a pile of barberries. At first, she thought that Hetty must be alone, but then she saw Daniel sitting a few yards off against the rocks, his head tilted back, as if he were asleep. But he was not sleeping, for now he looked up.

"There is a new life. A baby girl," she said. For a moment, she stood gazing down at him, but when he opened his arms, she ran to him. The fear, the weariness, the pain, all slipped away, soothed and softened by his warmth. No matter what happened, they were together now. They would save the baby, and they would save themselves. Caroline snuggled closer, feeling the sun on her back, feeling the heat of the sun. And then she realized that they sat in the shade, and that the heat she felt came from no sun, but from Daniel himself.

"You are burning up with fever!" She started up from his embrace, seeing now what she had missed in the brightness of the light: the burning blue-gray eyes, the pallid skin, the damp, matted hair. Without waiting for an answer, she sprang to her feet, half leading and half dragging him back towards the cave.

It was he who reminded her of Hetty, left behind.

"I'll go for her later."

"No, it is not safe—and be sure to bring the berries. Do not leave them behind."

"But you are ill!" she cried, but, because he asked it, she propped him against the rocks and went back for Hetty and the pile of bright berries.

There was no place to lay him but the cold bare floor, but he made no protest as she helped him down. Pointing to the fire, he rasped, "The bowl. Give some to your sister, and then give me the rest."

She did as he said, dipping a measure of the brew he had mixed into a smaller bowl, and holding his head and then Hannah's so that each could drink. By the time she had finished with Hannah and returned to Daniel's side, he was semiconscious, his head thrashing back and forth, muttering in his fever words she could not understand.

Hetty crouched by the fire, playing with the berries. Hannah dozed peacefully, the baby asleep at her side. It had already taken her nipple, and that was a hopeful sign. Everything was hopeful, except for Daniel.

Daniel... She knelt and looked down at him, the hot, hard weight of tears rising in her chest. Oh, Daniel, what will I do if you leave me now? Not just for this one ordeal, but even afterwards. When I rose from bringing the baby, my first thought was of you—of sharing the pleasure with you, of seeking your arms at last. What will become of me, if I lose that embrace? Oh, Daniel, please don't leave me! Don't leave me just yet!

She wanted to hold him, weeping, wanted to wet his tunic with her tears. She wanted to cry out, to pray to God to spare this man she loved. But the time for praying would come soon enough—and, in the meantime, there were other things that she could do for him. She hoped she could do enough. So, steeling her exhausted body, she set to work once more.

The first thing was to get him off the ground. Taking the knife from beside the fire, she rose and left the cave to cut two armloads of fresh branches with which to make him a bed. There weren't enough blankets for her to lay one beneath him. Later she'd wash the rough hide, and he could use that, but for now she would have to leave him on the branches without more. At least that was better than the cold, damp earth.

He was not a big man, yet now he was all deadweight. She struggled, tears of frustration rolling down her cheeks because she knew that she was probably hurting the wound, and yet there was no one to help her, and nothing else to do. When at last she had him settled, she knelt beside him once more. Bracing herself for what she would find, she unlaced the string at his throat and eased off his tunic as gently as she could.

The heat of his fever hit her like a wave, and with it the sickly odor of the festering wound. Although her fingers kept on working, unwrapping the binding about his chest, she felt her stomach sinking, felt herself sinking into stone-cold despair. What if she couldn't save him? What if he'd gone too far? She caught her breath in pure fear as the last strip of cloth came away and she found herself confronting the oozing, inflamed mass that had been his smooth, muscled rib cage only three days before.

Had the wound been this bad during the whole of their trip? She could not imagine so. Instead, she thought it most likely that it had worsened gradually, until, sometime during the past twelve hours, the infection had taken hold. Now the thing was to stop it. But to stop it with what?

At home, she would have known. She was no great healer, but she knew the remedies, both the apothecary's powders and the old country cures. At home, they would have bled him after they'd packed the wound, but here she had nothing, except for Yum-sa-wek's salve, which Daniel had been using to no avail. Despair once more rising within her, she glanced about the cave, her eye falling upon the collection of leaves Daniel had carried in before the baby had come. Then she had assumed that they were to treat Hannah. Now she moved to the pile, her heart nursing a thin flame of hope.

Some were known to her. That root was witch hazel, and here was maidenhair, and, of course, she recognized the leaf of the giant oak. Oak leaves! Yes, now she remembered Daniel packing them on her foot when she had had those blisters, and how quickly they had been cured. Oak leaves, he had said then, will draw out the infection. Snatching up a handful, she turned back to where he lay, but, on second thought, she knelt by the fire instead.

The water that he had heated when he had made the brew was no longer hot. Removing the rocks from the bucket, she returned them to the fire, taking out three more hot ones, which sizzled when she dropped them in. Then, when the water was steaming, she dipped out a cupful and, tearing up the oak leaves, added them one by one, pushing each one down with the knife until they had absorbed most of the hot water.

Daniel started in his sleep, moaning, when she laid the poultice on the wound, and she had to hold him down flat in order to keep him still. Even so, he resisted, until she thought her backbone would snap from the struggle of holding him down. At last he was quiet, and slowly she let him go, leaning back on her knees, massaging the small of her back. But her sense of triumph ended when she saw his face. It was flushed bright with the fever, beaded and running with sweat.

She had been feeding the fire throughout the endless day, and by now the cave was so warm that she was sweating, too, and the water in the bucket was tepid from the heat. She would have to fetch cold water from the stream to bathe him. Rising, she looked about the cave. At some point during her struggles to keep Daniel still, Hetty had given up playing with her berries and crept to her mother's side, and she was sleeping now, curled up against her. Caroline pulled the blanket up over her. Then, taking the bucket, she ducked out of the cave.

Now the sun was gone, though she could not see enough of the sky to guess at the time. The night air was alive with the cries of small animals, and she caught her breath when something scurried by. She tried to pick out her surroundings, her imagination showing her shadows behind every tree. What if the tribe was here, watching her, even now? What if they had smelled the fire, despite Daniel's assurances? Her natural inclination was to turn back to the cave and to wait until morning to go down to the stream.

But she could not wait. Daniel needed the cold water, needed it to live, and if the Indians were watching, then they knew everything, and there was no point in retreating back into the cave. Straightening her shoulders, she hurried to the stream, forcing herself to ignore the skin crawling on her back. She sloshed herself with water as she ran back to the cave, and when she got there her legs were so weak with relief that she sank down on the floor and pressed her palms together until the trembling ceased.

The night was as endless as the day had been. She held Daniel pinned down when he thrashed, and when he did not she bathed him with cool water. At intervals, the baby woke, and she helped Hannah put it to her breast. Twice Hannah was thirsty and called out for a drink. The first time, Caroline brought her water, the second, medicine—the rest of which she poured down Daniel's throat as best she could.

She must have drowsed herself at some point, for Hetty's crying awakened her with a start. A faint light through the smoke hole told of the dawning day. Hannah was awake, too, the baby at her breast, and doing her best to quiet Hetty, who was crying for food.

Food. Sitting up, Caroline pushed her hair back from her face. Daniel was unconscious, still burning with the fever, but at least he had not torn the dressing from the wound. Dipping the rag in the bucket, she wrung it out and laid it on his head. Then she crept towards Daniel's bundle to see what might be left.

The corn bread was gone, but there was a handful of meal, and a bit of meat. These she put together in a bowl, adding water and stones from the fire to bring it to a boil. Seeing the barberries where Hetty had left them by the fire, she added them, as well, stirring with the knife.

"Just a bit more," she told Hetty. "Then we'll have something nice. While we're waiting you can help me fetch water from the stream."

The day was bright and clear, and the air was fresh and bracing after the heat of the cave. They crouched at the stream, and, after Caroline filled the bucket, she washed her face and neck. Hetty performed her own manner of toilet, mainly splashing and play. She toddled along behind Caroline, chattering to the birds who watched the procession with bright-eyed curiosity.

The broth Caroline had concocted tasted peculiar, but Hetty was too hungry to complain. She fed a capful to Hannah, who managed to swallow it, although her face was still etched with weakness and exhaustion. No doubt there were things she might be doing to make Hannah more comfortable, but she would have to do them later. Just now she had no time, not when there was Daniel, in far more desperate need.

Heating more water, she made a new poultice for the wound. She held her breath as she peeled the old one away, but, though the wound seemed unimproved, at least it seemed no worse. He thrashed again at the burning of the hot dressing, and she had to hold him down until he had stopped. Then she crouched over his crude pharmacopoeia, trying to recreate the brew he had made yesterday.

She doubted that she had it, but Hannah said it tasted much the same, so she gave her a cupful and poured one down Daniel's throat. Then, when he was quiet again, she took Hetty back down to the stream, to play on the bank while she laundered the rough hide with plain cold water and sand from the riverbed.

They were just starting back when she recalled the horses. Crossing to the far bank, she heard a nickering and found them where Daniel had tied them, in a small clearing. They had enough grass to last them several days, but they needed water. Untying them, she led them to the stream, and then, when they had drunk, back to the clearing. Turning back to the stream, she thought of the Indians.

Were they headed south? Or had they decided that Daniel was as clever as they? She could smell the woodsmoke from the fire almost to here. If the Indians did come this way, they would be found for certain. But what was the point in worrying, when there was nothing to be done?

A bunch of thistles nodded their dried heads at the clearing's edge. Remembering the baby, she broke a half dozen off and dropped them into her apron in order to carry them back. Retrieving Hetty, she brought her back to the cave, leaving her in the berry bushes while she went to gather wood.

Hannah and the baby waked and slept throughout the day. Daniel thrashed and lay still. Caroline fed them medicine and made a new poultice. She added more berries and meat to the broth, which was their evening meal. She continued bathing Daniel; at one point, she was certain that his fever was starting to drop, but then, five minutes later, he was burning up again. The dim, smoke-filled chamber took on a nightmarish cast, and her thoughts ran together in one muddled hodgepodge, England and New Haven, the farm and the Indian camp.

Esh-tan and Thomas MacKenzie merged into one figure, and then they merged with Edmund. Daniel was fighting him, using neither fists nor knife, but flashing swords instead, diving and parrying, and she was worried for him, worried because she knew that he had no skill, whereas Edmund was accomplished and could run him through. Now Daniel sprang forwards, but Edmund drove him back, his blade flashing upwards, then arcing down towards Daniel's heart. Although she screamed, it was too late. Bright blood spurted out as Edmund withdrew his blade, a bright-red shooting fountain that inundated them all, and she was drowning, drowning, drowning in Daniel's blood.

Blinking, she came awake. The fire had died down, and the cave was almost dark. Something felt peculiar, something clammy and wet—Daniel's blood! She jerked upright, half lost still in the dream. She had dozed off while bathing him, and had slipped to the floor, lying with her head resting in the curve between his shoulder and his neck. Somehow, her fingers had become entwined in his hair—and his hair was soaking, as was his face and his neck. Cold water was running down him, as though it were raining on his head. Confused, she held out one hand, thinking that rain must be leaking through a hole in the rocks. Then, suddenly, her mind cleared, and she understood: it was not rain that ran from him, but good, cool, cleansing sweat! His fever must have broken while she'd slept. Laying her hand on his forehead, she found that it was cool. His cheeks were cool, as well—and his throat, his chest, his hand.

"Oh, Daniel!" she murmured, laying her cheek upon his hand. "Dear Lord, thank you, thank you!" She had remained dry-eyed during this whole ordeal, but, now that it was over, she wept hot tears. They flowed through his open fingers, mingling with his sweat. She wanted to sing, to dance, to cry, to rush out into the cool, fresh night. She wanted to tell the heavens that Daniel would not die!

His first shudder brought her rapture to an end. His whole body was clammy— He would catch a chill! Releasing his fingers, she leapt up to stoke the fire, peeling off his sweat-soaked blanket and replacing it with the hide. Then she heated more water for a fresh poultice. When she took the old one off, she saw that the wound had begun to calm.

She dressed it again and covered him, then sat holding his hand. She would have sat until dawn, gazing down at him, but she was suddenly so tired, she could hardly think. Stretching out beside him, she pulled the hide over her and, laying her head on his shoulder, lapsed into a deep, dreamless sleep.

Chapter Fifteen

Caroline woke during the daylight hours, but Daniel slept on still. She did not try to rouse him, knowing that the rest would do him as much good as any herbal brew. At first she stayed close to him, afraid lest the fever return, but by afternoon she accepted that he would be well. Then she turned to the more urgent business of finding them some food, taking Hetty along to free Hannah and to keep her company.

As Daniel had mentioned, there were hickory nuts lying about by the hundreds on the forest floor. She and Hetty started with them, filling the bark bucket. Hetty sang as she worked and talked back to the birds. Caroline's thoughts followed the labor of her hands. She cataloged the foods they would find close at hand, and the ways in which they could be prepared to be eaten or stored.

Hickory nuts were versatile, for they could be eaten fresh, or dried in the sun outside the cave and ground into flour or meal. And then there were the barberries that Hetty loved so well, and ground nuts in quantity, not to mention small game and fish. She herself had seen several trout in the stream. Perhaps, when Daniel was better—

With a start, she stopped herself. What was she thinking of, planning out her harvest as if this were a permanent home, instead of just a hiding place in which to bide their time until Daniel was recovered and Hannah strong enough to move. What was she thinking of? she wondered, adding another handful of nuts to her store. She had a half bucket, more than enough for now. Rising, she called to Hetty and moved on to the spot where she'd noticed the curling stems that meant ground nuts. Breaking a stick in two and selecting the sharper half, she began digging, as she had in the Indian camp.

Where would they go when they left here, she wondered, resuming the train of her thoughts. Of course to Fort Dummer, but what after that? Not to the farm, for, even if it had somehow survived the fire, she knew that Hannah would never live in it again. Poor Hannah had had enough of wilderness adventure to last her for three lifetimes. Her heart was set on her old home in New Haven.

New Haven. The thought of it pulled Caroline down like a millstone about her neck, as she recalled the bleak and joyless years she had wasted there. Going back to New Haven would be like welcoming her own death. She would rather spend the rest of her days living in this cave than return to New Haven. And yet, she had no choice. Where else did she have to go?

She had dug enough ground nuts to last them through the day, and she'd been gone long enough. Perhaps Daniel had awakened, she thought, with a quickening of her heart. But even the thought of Daniel could not drive the darkness from her thoughts, for she knew that, when their journey ended, she must lose him, too. When he was strong enough to travel they would leave this place, and when they reached Fort Dummer he would bid her farewell. Whatever she felt for him—whatever he might feel for her—she had no more place in his world than he had in hers.

No! her heart cried out. No, it is not possible! How can I give up Daniel, when I have only just found him? How can I have saved his life, only to give him up? Because, the darkness answered, that is the way of the world. What little time you have here is all that remains. See that you use it wisely and well.

With deliberate fingers, she gathered up the nuts and carried them down to the stream to wash off the dirt. As she

watched the water running through her hands, it struck her
ow very much she had learned in these few weeks. Once,
ot so very long ago, this place would have seemed to her
ne great emptiness. Now she saw it so very differently, as
 place to seek shelter and safety and nourishment. And,
oo, she saw it as a place to seek happiness. Rising, she re-
rieved the bucket and Hetty, and, loaded with her bur-
ens, she made her way back to the cave.

Daniel was still sleeping, but Hannah was awake, gazing
t the baby, who suckled at her breast. Hetty crept to her
nother's side to crouch there, one berry-stained finger stuck
n her mouth. As the baby suckled, so Hetty suckled, too,
er small forehead puckered over life's greatest mystery.

"How is the baby?" asked Caroline, kneeling at Hetty's
ide.

"She eats well enough." Hannah's gaze upon the baby
eld pride and sorrow both. "Though she is so tiny she
annot take much. If only we were at home, I believe there
vould be a chance."

Home. Caroline's very soul rebelled against the word.
"This is our home for now," she said, recalling how Daniel
ad spoken the very same words. "It may not be New
Haven, but we've got food to eat and water to drink and fire
o keep us warm. And, if God is willing, we shall all sur-
ive."

"Yes, of course." Hannah smiled for Hetty's benefit, but
er eyes, when they met Caroline's, were full of doubt.

She was thinking of the Indians, Caroline realized, and
he realized with a shock that she had not thought of them
ven once when she had been gathering nuts. Now, with a
hudder, she recalled the noise that Hetty had made, laugh-
ng and chattering to the birds.

"Daniel says that we will be safe," she said firmly. "He
ays that they don't hunt here, and won't know about the
ave. And we left no trail behind that they could follow."

"Yes, perhaps," said Hannah, and she let it go at that.
Hetty was still frowning over her baby sister. Seeing this,

Hannah's eyes softened. "Would you like to touch her?" she asked, and Hetty's head bobbed once. The berry-stained finger slid slowly out to trace the very edge of the curve of one tiny ear. Then it was withdrawn, and plunged once again into the security of her own warm mouth.

Hannah's eyes filled with tears. "I remember how Young Tom did the same thing with Elizabeth. Oh, dear, my poor babies!"

"Hush. Don't worry." Caroline stroked Hannah's arm. "We'll be with them again. How they will love their new sister, Elizabeth especially! What do you think you will call her? Have you got a name?"

"Yes." Hannah nodded. "I shall call her Sarah, after Thomas's mother. Sarah Caroline." She turned her eyes to Caroline but the sight of her sister's tears was more than she could bear. "Oh, my poor sister!" she cried. "How much you have endured! All of Hoo-tan's cruelty, then bringing the baby alone, and Mr. Ledet's illness—and still I add more burdens to those you have carried so long! Oh, how will I ever make it up to you?"

"You!" Caroline stared at her sister, shocked out of her tears. "But, Hannah, you have nothing, *nothing* to make up! Now you rest with the baby, while I make us some food. Come, Hetty, I'll show you how to pick the thistle fluff to pack around little Sarah to keep her dry."

For herself and Hetty she roasted ground nuts among the coals, but Hannah and Daniel needed something gentler, so for them she concocted a gruel of boiled ground nuts and barberries. She supported Hannah in a sitting position while she fed it to her. Then she went to Daniel, to see if he still slept.

She thought he did when she knelt by his side, but, when she laid her hand on his forehead, his eyes opened to her, clear gray and as lucid as a Christmas sky. He did not speak, and neither did she; she stayed as she was for a long, silent moment, feasting upon his gaze. When she took her hand from his forehead, he reached out for it.

"Caroline." His grip was weak, but his fingers were cool.

Gratitude and emotion brought tears to her eyes, but she made her tone light and teasing. "I thought that you were the one who knew his own limits."

"Was I so wrong?" he murmured. "I'm still here, after all."

"Thanks to me," she retorted.

"Yes. Thanks to you," he said.

Even as his eyes held her, blue stole into the gray and she felt herself melting beneath the warmth of his gaze. Tears she had held back rose up hot and strong. Turning away, she said quickly, "I have some food for you. Some gruel made from ground nuts..."

"In a moment," he murmured, hating to let her go, even for an instant, now that he had her again. In his fevered nightmares, time and again, he had reached out for Caroline, only to have her slip beyond his reach. He had lost her in the river, in the woods, and in the camp. He had lost her to Esh-tan in the most terrible dream of all. But that had been the fever, and now he was cool. "How is the baby?" he murmured, before she could rise.

"Small, but she takes milk. Hannah worries for her, but I believe she will survive. When you've finished eating, I'll bring her for you to see."

"Yes... Caroline?"

She could not resist turning at the sound of her name, and then he saw the tears she would have hid from him. Reaching up, he caught one on his fingertip.

"I would hold you to me," he whispered, "and never let you go."

"And open your wound," she managed, "and bring the fever back. Save your strength for swallowing—and you'll soon be strong again."

"Not soon enough," he whispered, as she rose from his side.

As she had done with Hannah, she supported him while he ate.

"Tell me if I hurt you," she said, moving him gingerly, afraid of opening the wound.

"Have you tried spruce boughs?" He smiled and sighed contentedly as her breasts pillowed his head. Despite his weakness, her closeness stirred a flame in him that burned with a purity he had never felt before. He wished he had the strength to turn his body against hers, to slip his arms around her and draw her down with him. He ached to feel the softness of those breasts beneath his lips, to pleasure them to tautness, to give her what he craved.

Too soon, the bowl was empty and her warmth withdrawn. He thought that she might leave him, but instead she lingered at his side, smoothing back his matted hair with her light, cool touch. He felt sleep creeping towards him and fought to hold it back. "I won't be useless forever. I'll get you home safe yet."

"Hush." She laid a quieting finger against his lips and felt them pucker lightly before opening in a sigh. For a moment, her finger lingered, but Daniel was asleep, the ravages of the fever still harsh on the planes of his face, and in the dark smudges in the hollows beneath his eyes.

He was right, she suspected, gazing down at him. Chances were he would mend quickly, though perhaps not quite as quickly as he'd like. The trick with such a fever was in not getting up too soon, but Daniel hardly struck her as one to lie abed. Her lips curled in tender affection as she foresaw the struggle he would likely wage against her to be up and about his business before he was really fit. Her fingers found his forehead, the rough curve of his cheek; her breasts still tingled from his remembered warmth. Shaking her head in wonderment, she tried to recall if she had ever felt as happy as she did now, kneeling in her filthy rags on the dirt of this cave, with nothing for dinner but water and ground nut gruel. She wondered at life's madness, and its logic, as well.

She had guessed right about Daniel's recuperation, but had been wrong about his attitude, for he did not protest her nursing, or insist upon rising too soon, but rather seemed willing to let his body heal as it would. By the second morning he was able to sit up, propped against the cave wall,

and by the third to rise and walk a short distance with her
assistance.

There had still been no sign of the Indians, and, although it was possible that they would yet appear, Daniel
was of the opinion that it was more likely that they would
not. But of course the tribe they had escaped were not the
only Indians in the woods. If this was not their hunting
ground then it belonged to another tribe, who could still
stumble across them.

"If so," Daniel told them, "you will keep silent, and I will
say that you are my French wives."

"What—the both of us?" Caroline arched a brow.

"You think that I'm unworthy?" he asked, with a wink
at Hannah, who could not hide her smile. Hannah still had
trouble rising, even with Caroline's help, but her bleeding
was lessening. The night before last, little Sarah had refused the breast and had fussed until Caroline had begun to
believe that Hannah was right. But then, towards morning,
she had quieted and slept, awakening at midday to suckle
greedily.

Still smiling, Hannah said, "Mr. Ledet, if you get us
home, I'll gladly marry you!"

"I don't know, Mrs. MacKenzie, what your husband
would think of that."

"I trust he'll look kindly on the man who saved our
lives," Hannah returned. Her gaze turned to her children,
and her smile softened.

Daniel, looking up, found Caroline's eyes on him, her
expression reflecting his own troubled thoughts. Sooner or
later, Mrs. MacKenzie would learn why her husband had not
followed her. He and Caroline might spare her, but others
would not be so kind. Such gossip traveled quickly along the
frontier; everyone at Fort Dummer was likely to have heard
by now, and people in Northfield, as well. Of course, Mrs.
MacKenzie was not Caroline, but still there was a limit to
how much one could take. Would she forgive her husband,
and cleave to him still? He couldn't imagine Caroline allowing such a thing.

His eyes, still on Caroline, saw hers fill with wistfulness. For a moment, he wondered at the cause; then, with a shock, he realized exactly what lay ahead. Ever since Caroline's capture, and especially in these past days, his thoughts had been fully occupied with matters of survival. But now, with time for reflection, he could look past this cave and his recovery, even past the long trip south. One day, if their luck held, they would reach the fort—and there their lives would separate, most likely forever.

Where would Caroline go? Not back to MacKenzie's farm, for until the war was done no Englishman would be safe living on the frontier. Most likely they would return directly to New Haven. In time, this whole adventure would fade in their minds, until they could hardly imagine that it had happened to them—that they had been abducted by a tribe of Indians and lived for weeks like animals in a cave. Here in the cave, Caroline might gaze at him with loving eyes, but that love was fragile, tied to circumstance and chance. Once she had time to look back and reflect, most likely she would find her memory of him entwined with ones she'd much rather forget. Mrs. MacKenzie might look out through a rosy haze, but Caroline's own life had made her a realist. Daniel saw the future reflected in her dark, wistful eyes.

Daniel knew his own path, as well. Indeed, he had known it ever since the moment he had risen from Yum-sa-wek's wigwam. The moment he had risen to steal from the sleeping camp, he had branded himself forever an enemy, not only of the Abenaki, but of all the eastern tribes who had sworn allegiance to the French. He would no longer be safe hunting in these woods, but must travel westward, beyond the lands of the Iroquois. On its own, the prospect held a certain promise for him, for the western land represented the new frontier. The war could not last forever, and, when it was done, Englishmen would once more resume their slow push northward. Soon enough, these very woods would echo with the ringing of the ax, as New England farmers cleared away new fields. In a way, Daniel had always in-ended to go west, and he would have gone gladly—but for Caroline.

Caroline. For a moment, the dark eyes held his. Then they turned away as she busied herself at the fire, preparing the evening meal. How many times had he watched a woman cooking thus, and yet never with so overpowering a feeling. Watching her, he wanted to cry out, to weep with love for her, to forswear the future, to blind his eyes to it. He wanted her beside him, her body curved to his, wanted her so badly that he had to close his eyes and turn his head to the wall. In the future, he would lose her, but there was still some time, and he vowed to have it, to share it with her.

The weather, which had been fine, had turned wet again. A light drizzle had been falling when they had awakened the day after Daniel's fever had broken. During the afternoon it had turned into a steady downpour that had continued through the night, running in through every crevice to puddle on the floor. Caroline set the bowls beneath the holes and the bucket outside the entrance, to save herself from the soaking of a trip down to the stream. It was still raining the next morning, but the rain stopped just before noon, and the first bright shaft of sunlight seemed to brighten the entire cave. Caroline, venturing out to replenish their supply of firewood, returned with the announcement that she meant to wash.

"Wash? What?" Daniel's eyes narrowed defensively. He was used to his clothes being washed on his back; as soon as he was well enough, he would see to them in the stream. In the meantime, he meant to keep them where they belonged.

Caroline ignored his tone. "Everything," she said. "Beginning with our clothing—or what is left of it. Then I'll do the blankets, once the clothes are dry. You'll see, you'll feel much better when you're fresh and clean."

Hannah made no objection, but rather turned obediently while Caroline unfastened her dress and eased it from her body, followed by her underclothes, after which Caroline tucked the blanket high and snug about her, building up the fire so that she would not take a chill. Daniel, who had already lost control of his tunic, would have fought for his breeches, but for her determination.

"Which goes to show what happens when a woman runs your life."

"Exactly," she agreed, pulling them off by the bottoms from beneath the blanket. She took them down to the stream, with Hetty trailing behind, and the sun was already sinking by the time that she got back. Again, she built up the fire and spread them out to dry. Then, taking the bucket, she fetched fresh water to heat.

She would have washed Hannah first, but when the water was heated the baby had just begun to nurse, so she carried the bucket to Daniel, setting it on the floor beside his head. Her decision about washing had been impulsive. Standing in the forest, which glittered in the sunlight, freshly washed by the rain, she had felt the great surging joy of survival. They had been hunted, threatened and struck down, but they had battled back, and she wanted to do something to celebrate their victory. Laundering their filthy rags had been easy enough, but until she had knelt by Daniel, rag strips in her hand, she had not really reckoned on all it would involve. At least Hannah's attention was fixed on her own children, so she would be spared the embarrassment of an audience.

An audience besides Daniel, she amended, catching his eye, which was fixed on her with interest, and a twinkle, as well.

"Where do you prefer to begin—with my head, or with my feet?" he asked. Thinking quickly, she opted for the head.

She soon lost her self-consciousness before the challenge of the task, for he bore the accumulation of hard travels, and the illness, as well. She regretted being unable to wash his hair, or to shave his beard, but she did her best with the parts that she could reach. He sat, his side propped against the wall, while she washed his shoulders and back, dipping and redipping the cloth as the layers of filth came away.

Then she shifted him so that his back rested against the stone, while she turned her attention to his neck, shoulders and arms.

She was so caught up in the challenge of reaching clean skin at last that all else slipped her mind until the hand that she was washing turned within her grasp, its fingers encircling her own to raise them to his lips. Then her breath caught in an involuntary gasp, and her eyes, rising quickly, found themselves caught in his gaze. Sharp thrills of pleasure ran down from her fingertips, all down the length of her arm. Beneath her encircled fingers, she felt his lips curl. At last he released her, murmuring, "All right, go ahead."

It was different after that. After that he was no longer simply a challenging task, but a man's body, warm and pulsing with life. After that, he was Daniel, hard muscled and golden skinned. With fingers that seemed to vibrate, she ran the cloth along his chest, taking care to avoid the raw, puckered welt of the wound. She felt his heart quicken, and felt her breath speed up, as well. She gently bathed his ribs until they were shining clean, moving down the plane of his stomach to where the blanket lay, resting lightly upon his lap. His eyes were upon her, and his body was motionless, save for the light shaking that came with each uneven breath. She heard the baby fussing somewhere at the back of her consciousness and remembered Hannah and Hetty, scarcely eight feet away, but even that could not raise her hand from his body, or cease her gentle stroking of him with the cloth.

The force of sensation was overwhelming. She could not tell for sure if her eyes were open or shut, but they must be open, for now she saw a certain stirring beneath the cover on his lap. She could not mistake the proof of his desire, and though with another man she would have felt disgust, this sign of Daniel's longing only quickened her own desire. She let her hand move lower, her heart pounding erratically as she felt his hard muscles convulse. For a dizzying moment, her fingers hovered at the blanket's edge. Then she felt her hand encircled as it had been earlier and divested of the cloth. This time he pressed her palm against his cheek, closing his eyes as his chest contracted in a long, shaken sigh.

"I think I'd better take it from here," he said, releasing her hand. She watched his chest heaving, as if he had run a long way.

Her breathing was also heavy, and the skin of her cheeks was a bright red. For a moment, she knelt unmoving, unable to respond. In her mind, she saw herself sinking forward towards his chest, and felt the warmth and pressure of his fingers in her hair. She heard her own moan of pleasure as his lips parted hers, felt the swelling hardness that took her breath away. The vision was hypnotic. Closer and closer she swayed, uncaring of Hannah so near by, uncaring of the world.

It was Daniel who broke the spell.

"Caroline," he murmured. "Caroline, enough!"

Her eyes were pitch-black as they rose to him. For a moment, they blinked, unfocused. Then she recalled herself.

"Yes, of course," she murmured. "You'll need fresh water, though." And, rocking back on her heels, she rose and moved to the fire.

The next day dawned fair. The clothing she had laid out yesterday had dried overnight. She brought Daniel his breeches and helped Hannah dress.

"And what about my tunic?" he asked, glancing towards the garment in Caroline's hand.

She held it out of reach. "I need to wear something while my own clothes are drying." Before he could answer, she was out the door, calling out to Hetty to come along with her.

Hetty didn't mind parting with her clothes, for the sun was warm on the moss along the bank of the stream. She splashed about happily while Caroline washed their clothes and hung them up to dry—but she raised a mighty protest when it was her turn to be bathed. Caroline, for her part, prayed there were no Indians about, as Hetty's lusty objections shattered the clear autumn air. On Hetty she used not only a rag, but also sand from the stream bed, scrubbing the squirming body until she was satisfied it was clean. Then, setting her on the dry bank, she wrapped her in the tunic, chafing her skin until the warmth returned. Released and once more naked, but this time shining clean, Hetty returned to her playing, while Caroline turned to her own bath.

Giving Hetty strict orders to stay up on the bank, she waded out into midstream, where a pool, deeper than the others, reached almost up to her thighs. How cold the water was! Wherever it touched her body, her skin puckered into gooseflesh, and she quickly lost the inclination to submerge the rest of her—until, hugging herself to keep from shivering, she saw the dirty smudges the water from her fingers had left on her ribs.

How dirty she was! Her whole body was caked with dirt, with layers and layers of filth, and her skin smelled of stale sweat and the smoke of a hundred fires. Her hair, once upon a time her pride and joy, was so caked with grease and dirt that even after she unpinned her braids the coils did not fall free. Instead, she had to force them apart with her fingers. Remembering yesterday how she had swayed towards Daniel's chest, she blushed with humiliation, realizing how she must have looked to him, how dirty and unkempt, in her filthy rags. That was enough inducement. Bracing herself, she plunged in, gasping as the icy waters enveloped her bare skin, snatching the very breath from her lungs in the first few frozen moments.

Reaching down for a handful of sand, she began to scrub her skin, starting with her shoulders and working down her arms. In time, she became accustomed to the water's temperature. Her skin was bright red and tingling from the cold and the friction. She scoured her whole body, right down to the tips of her toes. Then, plunging her head forward, she tackled the masses of her hair.

She stood on the bank afterwards, freshly scrubbed and squeaky-clean, her hair hanging wetly the length of her back. Once more, she gathered it into a hank, and twisted it tightly to drain the water out. Then, shaking the excess moisture from the tips, and from her hands, as well, she moved to where she had hung Daniel's tunic on a tree.

She smiled when it touched her body, all soft and warm from the sun—warm as if from his body, as if it had lain against him. Closing her eyes, she raised the buckskin to her face, inhaling its clean, woodsy odor and the lingering scent of him. Again she remembered how he had looked yesterday, how his skin had rippled beneath her fingers as she had stroked it with the wet cloth. She remembered her own body trembling, the sharp, leaping thrills. She remembered the movement beneath the blanket and felt the breath leave her lungs.

The sun was shining brightly upon her head and her back. She arched towards its good warmth, arched up towards the memory. If only there were no Hannah and no Hetty to hold them back. If only they were once again on their own in the woods. Once again, she remembered the day he had built the canoe, how he had held her and kissed her, and her knees went weak. Each day, his wound was healing further. Soon he would walk on his own, perhaps even tomorrow, or the day after. Perhaps then they would find a place. Perhaps they would find a time. Her heart beating quickly, she moved to the drying clothes, calling out to Hetty not to wander away.

Chapter Sixteen

Daniel and Caroline crouched side by side on a low, flat rock at the edge of the stream. They were facing westward, so that their shadows lay behind them and not across the water, which might alarm the fish. In his right hand, Daniel held a slender shaft of wood to which he had bound his knife in order to make a spear. They hovered motionless, their attention fixed on the three rainbow trout in the pool below. At any other time, Daniel's poised arm would have been like a rock, but today it trembled, because he was still weak. He willed it steady with a quick silent prayer and then, raising it slightly higher, brought it down in a single thrust, grunting at the sparks of pain that shot through his chest.

His eyes remained on the water, watching as the ripples stilled, but Caroline had forgotten the fish and had turned to him instead.

"Daniel, you are hurt!"

He shook his head, feeling a thrill of promise at the sound of his name on her lips. "Only a twinge."

This was their first time alone together since the Indians had captured her. Two nights he had lain awake on his pallet, his body still tingling from the memory of her touch, his heart racing at the undisguised longing that he had seen in her eyes. He had known from her breathing that she was awake, as well, and he had struggled against the desire to reach out across the few feet that separated them. He had not doubted that she would come if he called, yet, despite his yearning, he had not wanted it to happen that way. He had not wanted to take her fumbling in the dark, one ear cocked in case her sister or one of the babies woke. He wanted to join with Caroline in the open and without shame—for her sake, and for his own, as well. So he had quashed desire and turned his face away, and at last he had slumbered, all his dreams about her. And the next morning he had risen, strong in his resolve.

Afraid of a relapse, she had wanted to keep him in, but he had convinced her to let him sit in the sun. She had gone about her tasks, fetching wood and water and what food she could find, while he had amused little Hetty with whatever came to hand. In the afternoon, at his urging, she brought out her sister, as well, laying her on blankets in the warming sun. He had been shocked to see how thin and pale she was.

"She needs meat," he said. "To replace the lost blood."

"We all need meat," Caroline replied. "But isn't it too risky to chance shooting the gun?"

"Then we'll use traps instead. And I'll catch us fish for dinner from the stream." Caroline had protested when he had risen, and indeed he had been shaky in his first few steps. She had hovered over him as he had set the traps, sure he was about to faint, and in fact, when the task was completed, he was ready for a rest.

"You'll fish tomorrow," she had said, leading him back to his pallet as she would have led a small child, clucking at his weakness and bringing him herb tea and hot gruel. But she had been delighted when, this morning, she had found a rabbit in one of the traps. She had gutted it and skinned it and roasted it on sticks, and they had eaten it for breakfast, relishing the change. Then, when they had finished, Caroline had taken Hannah out into the sun and left her with Hetty, and she and Daniel had gone down to the stream.

The fish had vanished, and the knife held nothing but sand. Daniel bent to retrieve it, then stopped.

"What do you see?" asked Caroline, bending forward as well.

Instead of answering, he stepped into the water, bending to dip his hand and coming up with something small and black that he held out to her.

"What is it?"

"An arrowhead. Made of obsidian."

She took it in her fingers, turning it as he spoke.

"In the old days, every warrior carved his own arrow-heads—a skillful hunter could turn out one in just a quarter hour. Then the white man came, with his arrowheads of beaten brass, and what was the purpose in working over stone when one could trade a hide or two for a half-dozen heads? Now the skill is all but lost. Only the very old ones recall." His palm slipped beneath hers, curling her fingers shut about the bit of black rock.

It was the first time they had touched, though, ever since they had left Hannah, Caroline had been conscious of him beyond anything else. Crouched beside him on the rock, she had felt the pull of attraction, electric between them. It had held her spellbound, almost hypnotized, her heartbeat not quickened, but slow and painfully intense. Now, when he touched her, her heart leapt wildly, and her whole body shook. Afraid before such power, she dropped her gaze from his.

"Your knife," she said. "We'd best not chance losing it. Do you think that we have scared the fish away from here?"

"No, they'll come back," he said, continuing to hold her hand. With his free one, he retrieved the spear and laid it on the rock. Then he climbed back up beside her, drawing her up until they stood facing each other, far less than an arm's length apart.

Her eyes were still downcast, but she felt his on her. She resisted a bit longer, more from old habit than from fear. When at last she looked up, she felt her heart stop at the strength of the emotion she found in his gaze.

"Are you afraid, Caroline?" he asked, and, unable to speak, she shook her head once no. For a moment more, he waited; then, still holding her hand, he brought it behind him to lie against his back, pulling them together as his lips sought hers.

She trembled again, more violently, as their lips met and joined, but this time he did not ask her if she shook with fear. Now his hand released hers and moved to her back, and his other sought the soft curve just below her chin, cupping it in order to savor her, then moving around to twine themselves in the soft coils of her hair.

Deeper and deeper his tongue probed, and she welcomed it, opening, as her hand slid down his smooth back to the hard curve of his buttock. She was shaking with desire, with the longing of all these weeks and months, overwhelmed by the knowledge that the obstacles had all been passed and now there was nothing left to hold them back. She opened her lips beneath his, swooning at the pull that seemed to reach deep within her, down to her very soul, and to stoke the fire that had smoldered there so long.

He drank her in. She was like a tonic, sublime and life-giving. He could never have enough. There were not minutes enough in the hour, days enough in the year, for him to touch her, taste her, hold her, as long as he wished. Love and desire transcended time and place; he could take her in the water and never feel the chill. He could take her on this rock, standing where they were. How many days had he watched her, longing and powerless. Now it only increased the pleasure, the thrill, of her touch. His hands slid over her body, over angles and curves, feeling all the beauty, all the promise of what was to come.

The sun, shifting, poured through a space between the trees, bathing their heads in the light, blinding him with brightness, even through his closed lids. At their feet, the water gurgled. They were standing on a rock and, despite the heroism of his avowal, he could not but admit that grass made a softer bed.

She moaned when he pulled away. He smiled at the sound. "Come," he murmured, taking her hand once again. He took the spear, and she held her skirt as they crossed the stream to the opposite bank and made their way through the woods to a small, grassy clearing ringed by graceful birches. Halting within its circle, Daniel turned to her.

Her eyes were the same depthless color they had been when she had bathed his chest, and they stared, wide and unfocused; her breath came through parted lips.

"I want you so much," he whispered. "More than anything in the world. I will never hurt you. I give you my vow on it."

"Yes, I know," she whispered, watching as he raised his hands slowly to the first button of her dress.

He undid them one by one, his breath an uneven counterpoint to the racing of her pulse, quickening at the base of her throat. She stood, rapt and unmoving, and felt the wave of cool air when at last the material parted upon her ragged chemise. She watched as his hands slid inside the open bodice, opening over her shoulders, then down along her bare arms, pushing back the material, easing away the sleeves. As the cool air stroked her back and her shoulders, her breasts hardened and rose.

Daniel saw them move. He felt his pulse responding within his very soul as the darkened circles strained against the cloth, cloth so thin from constant wear as to be almost transparent. He thought briefly of the man who had used her so badly long ago, and for a moment he was distracted by the unfairness of it. He felt a rising anger, but managed to set it aside. That was all history; they had left it far behind. Here there was room for nothing but the joy that they had earned.

She sucked in her breath in a quick gasp when his fingers circled her waist, then released it in a long sigh as his hands slid lightly up over her ribs, his fingertips just grazing the edges of her breasts—and yet that lightest touch sent shivers of sensation through her. His hands slid higher, up the sensitive skin of her arms, which rose of their own volition as he stripped off the chemise. Pulling the garment up over her hands, he tossed it aside. He caught her two wrists before they could fall to her sides and held them raised as he feasted his eyes upon her: the long arms, the slender rib cage, the full, rounded breasts, which seemed to have developed a private yearning of their own.

Caroline tingled for him to touch her, even as the cool air did, to stroke her skin, to mold her body with his caress. And yet, there was a pleasure in the promise of his touch, as well, a building, aching pleasure that started in her loins and ran hot and molten down along her limbs so that his gaze alone made her tremble like a leaf.

Daniel gazed at her in awe. She was so beautiful, still more beautiful than he had imagined, and, unlike other women, she was precious to him, as well. She filled all his senses, and she filled his heart, as well. He was swept away by his desire, and he was humbled by his love. Raising his eyes to hers, he found them no longer dark, but filled with light and sparkle, and as bright as the streaming sun. I love you, her eyes said. There is no room for shame. Releasing her hands, he stripped off his own tunic.

Her brows came down automatically at the sight of his wound, with a concern that might have struck him as maternal yesterday, but that now only added to the moment's excitement.

"It is nothing," he whispered, trembling as her fingertips traced its edge, and he moaned with pleasure when her lips touched his breast.

"Caroline..." he murmured, and felt her lips move against him. Cupping his hands on her shoulders, he pulled her back, not to stop the pleasure, but to seek more of it. Sliding his hands down her arms, he slipped them around her back, pulling her slowly towards him so as to savor fully the first instant in which they touched.

She shivered at the sensation as her nipples grazed his chest and felt him shudder in response. How could this be shameful, this meeting of grace and joy? Shame had to do with something that had happened long ago, something unrelated to Daniel and her. They had left the shame behind them, somewhere to the east. They had come through fire, and this was their reward. She arched with pleasure as she felt him gather her near, curving his arms, his torso, so that they would touch everywhere, each touch a new pleasure, a new source of joy.

Releasing her, he knelt to remove her moccasins, cradling each foot in turn within his open palm, and she discovered that her instep, and even the sole of her foot, felt the fire that was slowly consuming her. Then he unwrapped her leggings so that her skirt hung free, running his hands lightly up her naked legs, turning her love so warm and liquid that she moaned deep in her throat. Her hips, of their own volition, swayed and thrust towards him. His hands cupping her buttocks, he pulled her against him, burying his face in the folds of fabric until she moaned again.

He rose, his hands still pressing her hard against him, so that she felt the throbbing pressure of his desire. Her hips were still moving, and now he moved, as well, his hands on her buttocks governing her rhythm. With every circle, their desire gathered and grew, until Caroline wondered if he had forgotten her skirt and the breeches he still wore.

He had, or had ignored them as the fires had grown, all his senses lost and sated in the firmness of her skin, the exquisite sensation of her breasts against his chest. His wound was throbbing, but he hardly noticed it, forgot the trees, the forest, the sun warm on his back. He forgot everything but Caroline, the taste, the feel of her, and the building passion he had nursed all these long months.

His hands slid from beneath her skirt to the clasp at the waist. For a moment, his fingers fumbled; then they found their prize, and the skirt fell without a rustle to lie in a pool at her feet, a shapeless, ruined flower from which she rose straight and proud.

Despite his desire, Daniel gazed at her nakedness with wondering eyes. "You are beautiful," he whispered aloud for the first time. "I would have loved you regardless, but you are beautiful."

"I am for you," she replied, and watched as the wonder was consumed within the pure blue blaze of his eyes. With shaking fingers, he undid the thong that held his breeches closed.

At the sight of his nakedness, despite herself, Caroline felt fear. The pain she had felt with Edmund—and the pain afterwards—came rushing back to her, cold and inhibiting, and, without intending to, she turned her head away. She felt him pause an instant, but then she felt his hand on hers. Drawing her hand to him, he laid it upon his chest, so that she could feel the familiar beating of his heart.

"Look at me," he murmured. "Tell me what you see."

She turned then, but could not answer, for she lacked the words. Nor did she resist when she felt her hand drawn down, and, in the moment when she touched him, he was beautiful.

Beautiful. He did not rush her, though she could feel him holding back, and in this one kindness she saw the depth of his love. Whatever she had been through, whatever price she had paid, had all been worth it, if she was to be allowed Daniel's love. Releasing him, she raised her hands to his neck, and he drew her closer, until at last they met and she felt the last vestige of cold fear melt away before the purifying flame that leapt between their bodies before they merged into one.

Now there were no boundaries, no spaces to be crossed, nothing to do but to follow the searing, breathless path that twined through her body to his and back again. At first she was conscious of following Daniel's lead; then she was conscious of nothing but where their bodies touched. He led her through bright pathways arcaded in diamonds and gold, through crystal walls that shattered into shooting stars. There was no pain to notice when he entered her, for indeed he had been within her all along.

The sun rose towards its zenith, illuminating the woods, glittering on the water of the clear, cold stream. Nuts fell on dry leaves, and birds called and replied. Daniel cried out her name, and she answered with his.

They lay on the tunic, their skin cool where the air found them, warm where they met. Caroline purred and stretched, and Daniel sighed and smiled.

"Happy?" he murmured.

"How can you ask?" she replied, smiling, as he rose on one elbow. But, even as she spoke, she felt the first shadow cast by the certain knowledge that this could not endure. From Daniel's expression, she knew he had read her thoughts, and she turned her head away, as if she could hide them from him.

She was so beautiful, he thought, his heart aching as if she were not here in his arms, their bodies still supple and warm from lovemaking. Her braids had come loose, and one lay across her breast. She stirred when he bent to kiss it, and her eyes came back to him. She watched as he began to untwine the coils.

"The first time I saw you," he said, his lips curving as he spoke, "there at sunset, on the river bank... I remember that I wondered how your hair would feel—how it would feel on my hand. And then, that first morning, when you let it down..."

At last it was unplaited. He ran his fingers through the thick, silken mass, letting it slide between them and letting it cover his arm. All her life Caroline had been proud of her hair, but not until this moment had she felt its true beauty. She lay back, contented, as he undid the second plait, spreading it about her in a dark, shining cloak, his lips curved in a secret smile that she understood perfectly. For a long while, he had wanted her, and now she was his. There was no point, no purpose, in wondering how long they had. Now they were together; that was all that mattered. There would be time enough for sighing in the years to come.

She smiled up at him. "I would lie here with you forever, but Hannah must be wondering. And then there are those fish..."

"Yes, the fish." He smiled. "We mustn't forget them."

He watched as she replaited her hair. "Why don't you leave it loose?"

"I would, for you," she replied. "But what would Hannah think?"

"That you had taken a lover." Ignoring the half-finished braid, he reached out for her. "Oh, Caroline," he murmured, despite all his resolve. "When I feel you in my arms, I wish I had been the first."

"You were the first," she said. "What happened with the other has nothing to do with us."

"If only things were different. If only—"

"Hush." She laid a finger against his lips. "We are lucky to be here, to be together and alive. Let us be grateful for what we have."

"I am grateful," he said, and, drawing her to him, he kissed her long and deeply.

Caroline would always remember the next five days as the happiest of her life. Each day, she and Daniel managed to steal away for an hour or two of bliss alone together in the woods, while most nights, after Hannah and the children slept, she would steal to his pallet or he to hers, and they would lie together, content simply to feel the beating of each other's heart, the warmth of their embrace. They didn't even mind that they had to catch themselves before they fell asleep so that Hannah would not find them together when the baby woke her in the night.

"I wonder if she knows," Caroline said as she sat on the bank of the stream, watching Daniel crouching in the process of spearing a fish.

Her words broke his concentration. Lowering his arm, he turned. "Has she said anything?"

"No." Caroline shook her head, the smile he loved so much playing on her lips. "But I think that if I were she I surely would have guessed."

"She's wrapped up in the baby."

"Yes . . ." Caroline knew that he was probably right, but she wondered just the same. Feeling the current of attraction that ran between Daniel and herself, she could not imagine Hannah missing it. Then again, perhaps Hannah felt the same about little Sarah. Perhaps she wondered how Caroline could not want to gaze down at the little wonder from sunrise to dark. Still, even if Hannah knew how she felt, Caroline could not imagine kissing Daniel before her. Kissing and holding Daniel were things of sweet intimacy. She enjoyed keeping their secret; it gave them one more thing to share. And, if Hannah did know, she would only worry later on, when they were home and Daniel was gone.

Daniel had been watching her, half following her thoughts. From her face, he knew the moment when she had looked ahead to what the future held. Turning back to the water, he said, "The baby is doing well."

"Yes. And Hannah, too," Caroline answered, leaving the unspoken question hovering between them. Hannah and the baby were both gaining strength, while Daniel's wound was almost completely healed. The weather, though holding fine, was growing colder steadily. The first heavy frost could come any day, as could the first heavy snow. If they were well enough to travel, they were foolish to linger on. Caroline knew this, and knew that Daniel knew it, as well. But not just yet, she protested. Just a few more days. Her eyes upon his bent back, she watched him watch the fish, wondering which of them would find the strength to call the retreat.

In the end, it was neither of them, but rather Hannah, who spoke. It happened one sunny morning, on little Sarah's twelfth day of life. Hannah sat outside the cave with the baby at her breast, while Caroline cracked hickory nuts between two stones. Hetty, crouched a short way off, was picking thistle fluff, adding one pinch to the pile, tossing the next into the air to watch the soft seeds separate as they drifted to earth.

"I wonder what Thomas is thinking," said Hannah, her eyes on the trees opposite. Caroline paused between two nuts, then began working again.

"I'm sure he has faith," she said, with a conviction she did not feel. "Perhaps he has already written to Montreal to see if you and Hetty have been brought there yet."

"Yes, I am sure he has—or even gone himself. But when he finds that we have not . . . Well, no matter, he shall know the truth soon enough."

"Yes, soon enough," Caroline agreed, the words bearing down upon her like a physical weight.

The baby lost the nipple and fussed until Hannah guided her back. For a moment, she watched Caroline, then, clearing her throat, she said, "Have you thought of what you will do once we are safely back?"

"Do?" Caroline repeated, knowing well what she meant, but having no answer to give.

To her surprise, Hannah said, "I meant about Mr. Ledet. That is—"

The rock slipped in Caroline's hand, hitting her thumb. She cried out at the pain, though her heart was hammering not from the bruise but from Hannah's words.

"I'm sorry," said Hannah. "I suppose I should not have asked. If you don't want to discuss it . . ."

"It's just that I thought you didn't know. I thought that with the baby . . ."

At this, Hannah smiled. "I may be deaf and dumb, but I'm not quite blind. Were you worried that I would not approve?"

"I don't know," said Caroline, and she blushed despite herself. "In New Haven they would not."

"But this is not New Haven. Not by a very long shot." Hannah looked about herself. "Has—has he proposed marriage?"

Caroline shook her head. "Nor will he," she said. "His life has no place for such a thing. He cannot abide civilization, and what would be the point of being married to a man one saw but twice a year?"

"People can change."

"Perhaps. But I would never ask such a change from him."

"I see. I am sorry."

"Don't be," said Caroline. "I knew from the beginning. have no regrets."

The baby, her stomach sated, had fallen asleep at last, releasing Hannah's nipple with a milky sigh. Looking down t the peaceful, sleeping face, Caroline felt a pang. Feeling Hannah's gaze upon her, she smiled, and shook her head.

"Well, almost none," she said.

"The time has come to leave."

Caroline's words echoed through the clearing and vanished in the crisp air. Leaving Hannah at the cave, she had come here, intending to gather more nuts to add to their provisions for the long trip home. Daniel had found her sitting on the grass, near the spot where they had lain together on that first day. He had found her staring, her eyes fixed on nothingness, a handful of nuts in her apron, her face full of wistfulness. Hearing him, she had looked up, and then she had spoken those words.

"The time has come to leave."

Although the effort pained him, Daniel nodded his head. "Yes, I know," he answered, and saw her flinch, as if she had been hoping that he might alter the truth. He wished it were within his power, but he knew as well as she that they risked new danger by lingering on at the cave. Even so, had it not been for Mrs. MacKenzie and the children, he would have stayed. When Caroline raised her eyes and smiled, he felt the pain pierce his heart, because she was so courageous, and because he loved her so.

"Mrs. MacKenzie said you were gathering nuts."

"To take with us on the trip. I haven't got very many," she said, showing him her pile.

"No matter," he said, shaking his head. "We'll find more along the trail." He held out his hand for them, and, when he gathered them up, he stowed them in his pouch. Then he reached down for her.

She came to him readily, fitting into his embrace as if she had been born to it. He had never known this with a woman before, this way of being together, this easy naturalness. Sometimes he could not remember the time before they had met. Nor could he imagine his life when she was gone.

"Caroline," he murmured, his lips seeking hers. He felt hers answer as she met him touch for touch, helping him with the buttons, with his own clothing. "You are forward," he said teasingly, and felt her smile against his chest.

"Am I?" she murmured, her lips running over him, over his muscled stomach, and down lower still.

"Caroline, no..."

"Why not?" Her gaze rose, dark and confident.

"Because it is not necessary."

"But I want to," she murmured, and felt his body shudder convulsively beneath her renewed caress. How she would have shuddered in horror at the thought of such intimacy six months ago. She would have denied it to Edmund, even had he circled her finger with a ring. And yet now, with Daniel, it was a thing of love, of pleasure, even of sweetness, and her heartbeat quickened when she felt the pressure of his fingers twined deep within her hair.

His breathing was ragged when he pulled her up. "Oh, God, how I love you!" he whispered, wrapping her in his arms and drawing her down beside him one last time on the grass.

"I think that must be everything," Caroline said to herself, her words echoing blankly through the empty cave. She cast a final glance about her, hating the sight of the dirt floor and the rock wall, bare save for the pile of firewood stacked against the wall. It looked so desolate, as the house in Surrey had looked on their last morning there. It wasn't a question of furniture, but rather of memories—in Surrey they had been bitter, but here they were all sweet. It struck her that she had never known a happier home.

The horses whinnied outside. They were all packed and ready to begin the trip. They had been on the verge of leaving when she had darted back inside, murmuring an excuse about something left behind. She knew neither Daniel nor

Hannah had been fooled in the least, but she could not help
herself—she needed one last look.

Well, this was the last. There was no point in staying on.
She doubted she would ever lay eyes on this cave again, yet
she knew that in the years to come she would think of it
frequently. She had discovered love here, in this unlikely
place.

"Goodbye, home," she murmured, and her words
seemed unnaturally loud. For an instant more, she lingered; then she turned towards the low, slanting entrance for
the very last time.

They moved slowly south. Caroline had wondered if they
would follow the stream, but they left it directly, though
they met another just before nightfall, and thus had water
for their evening and morning meals. She helped Daniel
build a lean-to of branches covered with evergreen boughs;
they built the fire on the open side and slept clustered together for warmth, Caroline between Hannah and Daniel,
Hetty's head on her shoulder. It rained towards morning,
and, though they managed to protect the baby, the rest of
them got wet. Still, they stayed warm with the fire, and the
rain ended just after dawn.

They moved through the woods, following no trail, rely-
ing on Daniel's tracking, based on the sun and the stars.
They saw no sign of other humans, but still Daniel was reluctant to hunt with his gun. They crossed streams frequently, and the second day he caught two fish that they
fried for dinner and ate with hickory nuts. Once, on the
fourth day, they heard something in the woods and took
cover, but it turned out to be a deer. Caroline glanced at
Daniel, wondering if he was tempted to shoot it down.

"There would be little purpose," he said, reading her
thoughts. "For we could carry so little of it. It would be a
waste of life."

He was right, she saw, and it struck her that this was his
world, that he saw the balance within it and took the long
view of things. The thought filled her with a sadness, for it
drew him apart from her. And yet, at the same time, she felt

a part of this world. It was something she had never felt in
New Haven.

On the sixth day, they reached the river that she and
Daniel had crossed coming north and found the bark canoe
where they had hidden it. They crossed in two trips, making camp in the same place where she and Daniel had stayed.
Caroline felt the ghosts of memories everywhere, and she
knew, when she glanced at Daniel, that he felt the same.
Although they had been together constantly since they had
left the cave, they had had hardly a moment alone. Even at
night, they were all too close for any real intimacy. She had
not minded, satisfied to be near him; but here, with all the
memories, she felt the need to store up more for the years to
come. She needed to feel Daniel's arms around her one last
time, and to match her body once again with his.

But time was running out. Two nights later, they slept in
the bend of the Connecticut, which lay one day's journey
north of the Great Meadow. Although she was weary from
traveling, Caroline's sleep was not restful, but rather broken by snatches of dreams. She woke with the first light to
find Daniel watching her. Laying one finger on his lips, he
beckoned for her to rise.

She followed him to a rise overlooking the river and the
mountains beyond. They stood on a stone outcropping,
watching the first rays of the sun paint the land with a vivid
brush. Caroline had been aware of the gradual changing of
the trees, but now she saw the full impact of their splendor,
the gold and orange and vermilion, the bright yellow and
deepest red, laying their brilliant mantle across the rolling
land. There was so very much beauty here, and she owed it
all to him. He had eased away bitterness and guilt and
shame and hate. He had led her from an empty past into this
moment of glory.

"I wish I had a gift to give to you," she said suddenly.

"You have given me a gift," he replied, his eyes meeting
hers.

She knew it was the truth, but even so she protested. "No, something really fine. Something to keep with you, to remind you of me."

"And where would I keep such a thing? In my pouch, perhaps, or wrapped in my blanket?"

He was right, she knew, and yet the truth of it made her sad. These were the last hours; they had almost reached the end.

His hands gripped her shoulders. As always, he had followed her thoughts. "No, Caroline," he murmured. "Not just yet. We still have this day left, still this hour to ourselves."

This time his embrace was rough, with a need and a desperation that found an instant response in her. His lips sought her bare breasts, and she smoothed the way, her nails digging into the hard muscles of his back. The ledge gave them no room on which to lie comfortably; instead of moving, they made love standing up, her legs wrapped around him, her back pressed against the rock, rocking together, beyond all care or restraint, not wanting the ending, and yet unable to hold it back.

Afterwards, they sat side by side on the ledge, his arm around her shoulders, her head resting on him.

"Will we stop at the farm?" she asked, feeling her throat tighten painfully about the word. For all that she knew it must be, she could not imagine a future without him.

Daniel's shoulder moved as he shook his head. "There is no point. I think it would be better if we made straight for the fort. Perhaps we shall have news before then, if we overtake a patrol." Sighing unconsciously, he added, "We should be getting back."

"Yes," Caroline said, but she made no move to rise. "Where will you go when you leave us?"

"To the west," he said.

"But what of the war?" she wondered.

Daniel shrugged in response. "I shall give the war a wide berth. The land is big enough. I will find my place in it." He paused, then added, "And you will return to New Haven?"

"Yes." She looked out over the valley, for she could not look at him. If she did, he would see the longing in her eyes, and it would only make it harder for him to say goodbye.

"I suppose it will be a relief."

"Yes, in a way," she said. She felt the tears welling up and turned her head away.

There was a pause. Then he said, "Will it be a relief?"

She opened her mouth, ready to lie to him, but she shook her head instead. "Not very much," she whispered.

"Caroline," he murmured, in the tone she knew so well. She felt the tears rising, spilling over and down her cheeks. "What would you prefer, then?" he asked, in the same tone.

"Our cave," she whispered, turning back to bury her face in his neck, inhaling the warmth and woodsmoke and pine scent that was him. She felt him press her closer. "Anywhere—with you."

He drew in a long breath and shuddered as he let it out. When he spoke, his voice was even, but she could feel the beating of his heart. "It is a hard life," he said. "No pretty things, few parties, not even a horse to ride. Weeks may pass together before you hear another woman's voice. Perhaps we could stake a claim to land, build a house upon it. But no fields, no farming. I was not born for that. And, if the world drew too near, I'd want to move on again. You know I can't stand—"

"We?" she interrupted, caring for nothing else. "We? Then you would take me along?"

"I would not force you. I would not ask such a thing of you. To give up everything to which you are accustomed. To—"

"I'd give it up," she said. "I'd give it up in a minute. How can you think I would not? Do you think I have not been happy these last weeks with you?"

"With me, yes. But not with life in the woods." Yet, even as he spoke the words, he knew they were no longer true. Again he saw her crouched silently beside the stream, waiting patiently while he speared a fish. He saw her on her knees, digging ground nuts from the earth, saw her barefoot and smiling in the cornfield at the farm. He saw her lips parted as she lay in his arms. He saw her walking with him all the days of his life.

"But what of your sister?" he asked, remembering.

"That is something," she admitted, but thoughtfully, not in defeat. "Before, when we were traveling with the Indians, I vowed that I would tell her the truth about what Thomas did, and I mean to keep that vow. Then, if she wants to stay with him, at least it is her free choice, but if she wishes to break with him I shall do what I can to help. But," she added, looking up, "not at the cost of my own happiness. Nor would she wish it. That much I have learned. Perhaps my parents would take her. That we shall have to see. And, once I have seen her settled, then I will go with you. Will you wait for me?"

"Forever," he replied, catching her hand, which lay in his lap, and pressing it to his lips. "How can you even ask?"

She gazed at him, her eyes shining despite her tears. "I did not know that life could hold such happiness."

"Nor I," he said, his thoughts already moving to the wonders they would share. He would show her the mountains, the valleys and the lakes; they would walk together the trails that once he had walked alone. He, who loved adventure, had found a whole new frontier, and one as full of promise as any he had ever known.

This time, when he murmured that they must get back, Caroline rose without protest or qualm. He helped her from the rock ledge and then kept her hand as they walked through the woods.

"Shall we tell your sister now, or shall we wait?"

"Not yet." Caroline shook her head. "Not until she knows the rest. Do you mind?" she asked.

"Not at all." He smiled. "It is the best secret I have ever kept."

Chapter Seventeen

Private Ever Cheltenham leaned against the rough wood of the fort's parapet, watching the meadow below him turn from gold to shadowed green as the sun reached the horizon and disappeared below the western hills. Ten feet away, his cousin and boyhood companion, Ira Scales, stood with his gun on his shoulder, also watching the end of the day. The sight was beautiful, to be sure, as was the blazing glory of the changing trees, all the deeper and more brilliant for two day's early frost. But, if they had wanted to admire fine sunsets and foliage, Ever and his cousin might have stayed back in Agawam. They had signed up for frontier duty in order to fight Indians, for thrills and real adventure and the chance to be something besides farmers all their lives. They had tramped north with the newly mustered troops, seeing in their minds how the girls would greet them as heroes when they marched home again.

Well, they had been wrong, Ever reflected, shifting the weight of his gun. They'd been at Fort Dummer four months now and hadn't seen a single Indian, except for the old squaw who did their laundry, and even she was half-white and not quite right in the head. Instead, they'd spent the summer chopping wood, hoeing weeds in the garden and tramping aimlessly on patrol, eating indifferent food and sleeping in lumpy beds. At first there had been the relief of local amusements, but, after the raid at the Great Meadow, most of the settlers had gone, including all the pretty girls.

Now they had nothing to look forward to but the winter ahead: five more months of boredom, not to mention the cold and the snow.

They had had one near miss, about a month before, when a war party had attacked MacKenzie's farm, scalping Silas Henry and Ethan Reed and carrying off Mrs. MacKenzie and her sister and the youngest child. When MacKenzie's man had arrived with the news, the men of the garrison had clamored for revenge, but Captain Holcombe, their commander, had refused to give chase, not without reinforcements from Fort Number 4. He'd wasted five precious days sending messages back and forth, and then in the end had decided that they would never catch up.

Never catch up... Humph! Ever spat over the edge of the parapet, watching as his spittle vanished below. He'd have caught up, if they'd given him the chance. He'd have caught the Indians and showed them a thing or two. He was good with a rifle, and better with his fists, and there was nothing he'd like better than to bash in some red man's face. Cowards, that was what they were, huddling here in the fort, tiptoeing along the frontier, likely under the very eyes of savages hiding in the woods. They'd heard of parties raiding to the east and to the west, though ever since MacKenzie's, it had been quiet here.

MacKenzie, Ever thought, spitting again, this time from superstition. According to the story MacKenzie had told, the Indians had taken both the wife and the sister, but Ever had heard the rumor—as they all had—that the sister had been hiding when the raid had come. Afterwards, she'd begged MacKenzie to go after the wife, but he'd been too busy trying to save his precious trees. Well, MacKenzie had been paid back for his greed, crushed by his own timber and drowned in the river. And, as for the sister, according to the tale, she'd been so angry that she'd set off on her own, into the woods, with two days' supplies, and never been heard from since.

A pity, Ever thought, for she'd been a beautiful woman, likely the most beautiful he'd ever seen in his life. Even now, squinting his eyes, he could remember how she'd looked dancing at the party after the fall of Louisbourg. Ever had wanted to dance with her, but he'd been too shy. Too bad, he thought now. It would have been something to think of on an evening like this.

"Hey!" Ira's cry interrupted his ruminations. Opening his eyes, he glanced towards his cousin, who was pointing to the meadow's northern end.

"Who goes there?" Ira added, confused by his excitement, for the only one who heard him was Ever, who made no response, occupied as he was with squinting through the twilight at the distant figures that had just appeared.

There were more than a dozen of them, some mounted and some on foot. They couldn't be Indians, for they wouldn't advance that way, right out in the open for anyone to see.

"Looks like a patrol," said Ira, who had better eyes. "But it's too big for one of ours. Must be from Fort Number 4, on the eastern bank. Wonder what they're doing down here?"

"Maybe escorting more settlers. Maybe a family with pretty daughters," Ever ventured hopefully, but Ira was squinting still.

"Could be you're right," he allowed. "Looks like they've got women and children along. I count two women— Say, isn't that one up front that French fellow, Ledet?"

"The trapper?"

"That's the one. I heard he took off after MacKenzie's wife and his sister-in-law. I'll bet he's brought them back! Wouldn't that be something? I'd better give the word."

"I'll give it," said Ever. "You stay up here." And, before Ira could object, he was off down the narrow stairs, already calling out the news of the party's approach. Maybe he wasn't too late, after all. Maybe he'd have a chance to dance with the sister yet.

Caroline raised her head at the cry from the fort. Her muscles were aching, for they had ridden far today. Tomorrow she'd be sore. Tomorrow, she thought, her heart leaping as her eyes rose to the fort, silhouetted in the dying light. The light picked out the gold of Daniel's hair where he rode just ahead. Still, she had trouble believing that what had happened this morning with Daniel was not just a dream. For the first time in years, the future held out happiness to her; it would take some getting used to, living with such joy.

At her side, Hannah caught her breath. "It seems a miracle," she murmured, lifting her eyes to send a prayer of thanksgiving to God. Only five minutes more of the journey, and then they'd be safe at the fort. Only five minutes, thought Hannah, until she'd have word of Thomas again. Perhaps, she thought, her eyes scaling the stout stockade, Thomas would be waiting there himself.

To her surprise, Hannah frowned as the image of Thomas's heavy-browed face rose up in her mind. Her reunion with Thomas had been her goal all these past anxious weeks, and yet now, at the last moment, she did not feel the joy she had anticipated. Perhaps this was because Thomas was scowling in her mind, and she couldn't make him smile, no matter how hard she tried. She was still weak, and too weary to face his moods. Just the thought of his anger made her shoulders slump. Perhaps it wasn't for Thomas but for home that she yearned, for Young Tom and Elizabeth and all the good, familiar things. In a way, she almost wished that he would not be there, so she wouldn't have to tell him that the baby was another girl.

Perhaps he would not be. The soldiers in their escort hadn't seemed to know. When she'd asked about him, they'd all shook their heads, suddenly tongue-tied—quite a contrast to how they'd been just before, all bubbling over with questions and gossip and news.

They'd met the soldiers just after midday, when the sun had already passed its zenith and was sinking towards the west. Mr. Ledet had just been saying that perhaps they would not reach the fort by that night after all. Hannah had been disappointed, though Caroline hadn't seemed to care.

At the thought of her sister, Hannah glanced at her, wondering at the strange change in her mood. She had seemed downright happy when they had been at the cave, but, once they had started for home, her happiness had ebbed. Hannah couldn't have said that Caroline was sad, especially not compared to how she'd been all these last years. Perhaps wistful was a better word, or even melancholy. But then, this morning, her happiness had returned. Hannah had awakened to the sound of Caroline singing as she heated water for the morning meal. And, each time their eyes had met, Caroline's had shone like the sun. Could Caroline be that happy at the prospect of reaching home? True, she had been through a great deal, but what of Mr. Ledet?

Perhaps, Hannah thought, something had happened between them. Perhaps he had decided to try settling down. He wouldn't have to go so far as New Haven. They could try something more rustic, perhaps a Northfield farm. And then, with the war's conclusion, they could move farther north. Caroline had seemed happy living at the farm. Of course, Hannah would miss having her near, but that did not count as much as Caroline's happiness.

A cry broke Hannah's thoughts, and, turning away from her sister, she saw that they had arrived. The soldier who had been leading her horse drew up on the reins, watching as his sergeant identified them to the watch.

"We are from Fort Number 4. We have two women and two children, captives who have escaped. We found them five miles below the Great Bend. Ledet here rescued them," he added, glancing in Daniel's direction.

"Just a minute," called the watch, withdrawing from the parapet. They heard the request repeated down the stairs and into the yard, and a minute or so later heard the heavy timber bar lifted from the gates.

"We are home," whispered Hannah, tears streaming down her cheeks.

"Welcome home! Congratulations!"

Caroline smiled dazedly at the throng of well-wishers who jostled against the horse, fighting each other for the privilege of helping her to dismount. But where was Daniel? Turning her head, she caught a glimpse of him vanishing to her left, borne off to be questioned by the garrison commander. The fort looked familiar, and yet so different, either much larger or much smaller than she remembered it. She felt as she had felt in New Haven eight years before, arriving in a new land after a long journey by ship.

In the excitement of their entry, her horse and Hannah's had been separated. Looking about, she saw her sister being helped down just now by a man whose massive shoulders stood above the crowd. For a moment, she thought it was Thomas, but the man's hair was light.

"Why, it's William!" she exclaimed. "Why, William is here at the fort!"

One of the soldiers nodded at her words. "Yes, ma'am. He's been here ever since the week after you were took, though the other one went south at least a month ago."

"Jonas," she said, surprised that his name could come to her, when she hadn't given him a thought all these long weeks.

"Yes, ma'am, that's right. But this one wouldn't go. Said he'd stay right here until he knew for sure. He's a good fellow. We'll be sorry to lose him now."

"Yes, William was always good," she murmured, watching him holding Hetty and helping Hannah down. Hannah seemed overjoyed to see William again. Caroline saw her show off the new baby, while Hetty squirmed in his arms. Then Hannah asked him something, and William hesitated. When at last he replied, she saw Hannah's face go white, and saw her sway. By instinct, she leapt forwards, though she could not have reached her in time, and in any case William had an arm around her and was already leading her off to the captain's house.

"What is wrong with Hannah?" she asked. "What could William have told her to make her act that way?"

"Likely breaking the news about MacKenzie's death," said one of the soldiers, drawing a jab in the ribs from one of his comrades.

"Death!" Caroline turned on him so fiercely that he stepped back a pace. "You mean Thomas is dead?"

"Yes, ma'am," the man mumbled. "Two days after the raid. Drowned in the river, trying to rescue his logs. He floated down to where they'd jammed five miles south of here. We told him that it was too risky, but he went anyway. Seems he lost his footing and hit his head as he went down. Probably suffocated trying to come up through the logs. A pity," he said tentatively, his eyes upon Caroline's face.

"Was it?" she replied. Then, excusing herself, she hurried after Hannah to bring her what comfort she could.

They gave Hannah a room upstairs in the captain's house. William carried her up and laid her on the bed. Then he took Hetty while Caroline got Hannah to sleep.

"Caroline?"

"Yes?" She sat beside the bed, wondering if it was unchristian to feel so little remorse. She was sorry for Hannah, but Thomas's fate struck her as no more than he deserved.

"I feel that it is my fault, that he's been punished for my sins."

"That's ridiculous," Caroline said flatly. "You were better to him than any mortal could have been." Or should have been, she added to herself.

Hannah shook her head. "Before, when we were just coming up to the fort, I was wishing that he would not be here. And then, when I saw that he was not and there was William instead, I was glad. I—I was afraid that he would be displeased that Sarah was a girl."

"And likely he would have been," Caroline replied. Then, shaking her head, she added, "Oh, Hannah dear, I know I shouldn't say such things at a time like this, but I'd rather speak ill of the deserving dead than have you suffer like this. Thomas MacKenzie alive was a selfish, bad-tempered brute whose only salvation was having you for a wife. Why, after the raid—'' She stopped herself. What was the point of burdening Hannah with all that now? Instead, she murmured, ''Hannah, he was long dead before you had such thoughts. Perhaps you even sensed it and were trying to steel yourself.''

''Yes, perhaps...'' Hannah sighed. ''William says he will take us to New Haven as soon as we wish. He was only staying here until there was word of us. He has been writing regularly to Tom and Elizabeth.''

''William is a good man.''

''Yes,'' Hannah murmured, her eyelids drifting shut. Almost at once, they opened again. ''You won't leave me alone? I am afraid to sleep alone tonight.''

''I will sleep right here beside you. Now close your eyes and rest, there's a good girl,'' she murmured, as she had years ago, when she and Hannah were children and sharing a common bed.

After Hannah fell asleep, she went downstairs again to see Hetty and William—and Daniel, wherever he'd gone. She wondered if he'd heard yet about Thomas's death. She was still too dizzy from the news to consider what it might mean to them.

William was in the kitchen, said the sentry below, and Daniel was with the commander, recounting their trials. ''He sent word to tell you he'll be spending the night over here—if they sleep at all!'' The sentry shook his head, wondering that she should look so calm. If half of what he'd heard of her travels was true... Held hostage by the savages, and then the escape—not to mention helping her sister give birth in a cave! Women were surprising, so much stronger than they looked.

Caroline thanked the soldier for his news and went off to find William, who was sitting by the fire, Hetty asleep in his arms.

''I gave her a bowl of soup,'' he said, looking down at the rosy cheeks. ''It doesn't seem that the experience has done her much harm. The baby's a beauty, too,'' he added, his eyes gleaming with pride. "I understand you were the midwife."

"Word travels fast." She laughed, sinking down, suddenly exhausted, into a chair opposite him. She looked about the room, thinking how strange it was to be in a house again. For all that she had dreamed about one during the time in the Indian camp, now she found it close, almost oppressive. It was like being in a box.

William saw her looking. "Seems strange to be back, I guess."

"Yes..." She turned to him again. "You've been waiting all this time just to know that we were safe."

He nodded. "Ever since I got back with the milled wheat. I would have gone after you, but there didn't seem a point. Mr. Ledet had already gone, and if he couldn't track you, what chance would I have? So I wrote up to Montreal, to the governor. But of course there's been no word."

"It was so good of you," Caroline said, tears coming to her eyes. "You've done more than anyone else would have done.... I don't know how to thank you."

"I need no thanks for it." He shook his head so emphatically that Hetty stirred in her sleep, mumbling unintelligibly as she snuggled closer into his arms. Caroline watched, a sad smile playing at the corners of her mouth.

"Poor Hannah," she murmured. "I know it is disrespectful, but I hope she will wed again. She deserves a better life than she's had thus far." Her eyes rising to William, she frowned at the look on his face. "William, is there something you haven't told me yet?"

William cleared his throat, and, when he finally spoke, the solemn, almost pained look lingered. "I doubt that I'll ever have what MacKenzie had, but I'm willing to work hard. And Mrs. MacKenzie will have whatever he's left. Of course," he added quickly, "I'm not thinking of that—not for myself, that is. But there are the children. They ought to have the best." He paused, as if he were unsure of how to continue.

"Why, William!" Caroline exclaimed. "You want to marry her!"

At her words, he colored. "I am not worthy, I know—"

"Not worthy? Oh, William! If anyone wasn't worthy, it was Thomas himself! Tell me, have you asked her?"

He looked shocked at the idea. "Not with her just hearing the news of Mr. MacKenzie's death. I thought perhaps later on, after she's back home safe and has seen Elizabeth and Tom...."

"Yes, of course," Caroline agreed, as if what they were discussing were the most logical thing on earth. How much had happened in the past two hours! She felt both exhausted and filled with mad elation. Her impulse was to find Daniel, but she could not very well burst in on the commander's conference with her giddy news.

Hetty stirred again. Rising, Caroline held out her arms for her. "Here, I'll take her up and put her to bed. I told Hannah that I'd stay with her."

"She's heavy," William protested, rising as he spoke. He led the way up the staircase, and Caroline followed him, smiling at the notion that she, who had survived what she had in these last weeks, could not manage to carry Hetty up fifteen wooden steps. Hannah would have a good husband. And so would she! So would she!

As soon as William left, she undressed and climbed into bed. She had thought that her excitement would keep her awake, but sleep overtook her almost immediately.

It was light when she awoke, and the sun was pouring in through the room's single narrow window. Stretching, she found her body a mass of new aches and pains. She blinked, momentarily disoriented, not sure of where she was; then, in a rush, she remembered, and the memory brought her upright in bed.

She was alone in the room. Hannah must be downstairs, and she'd taken Hetty, as well. Hannah, she thought, remembering what William had said last night. Then she thought of Daniel, and all else flew from her mind.

She heard Hannah's and William's voices coming from the kitchen as she hurried downstairs, but she did not stop to greet them, heading instead for the door. She rushed out into the brightness of the parade ground. She paused for a moment, blinking, to accustom her eyes to the light, and would have rushed on again, had not a voice spoken at her back.

"I thought you would never wake."

Daniel! Whirling, she found him lounging on the bench beside the door. The brightness of the sunlight turned his hair to a silver crown.

"And you? Did you sleep?" she asked, aware that she was grinning at him like a fool.

"Well enough," Daniel said, also smiling. He stood and, despite the soldiers milling about the grounds, took her hands in his. "You look well this morning."

"I feel well," she replied. Then, pausing, she said, "Have you heard about Thomas?"

"I heard that he was dead."

"I shouldn't be smiling."

"No, indeed." Daniel shook his head, and that only made her laugh. "I saw your sister just now. She seems to be taking it well."

"Does she? Good. I'm glad. Last night she was feeling shaky...and guilty, as well, I'm afraid. I tried to tell her that it was not her fault." She hesitated, then added, "I didn't tell her what he'd done. I don't think I will now. There isn't any point."

"No," Daniel agreed. A pair of soldiers, passing, bade them good-day, their eyes moving quickly to their joined hands and away again.

Caroline ignored them, her eyes on Daniel still. "And what do you suppose? William told me last night that he wants to marry her!"

"Your sister?"

She nodded. "Yes indeed. The children adore him, and he's so good and kind, and sweet-tempered and honest—all

hat Thomas was not! Oh, Daniel, I can't think of a better
usband for her!''

"And for yourself?" he wondered.

"What do you think?" she asked with a laugh. She pro-
ested, still laughing, when he slipped his arms about her.
'What will the soldiers say?"

"That you'd make a pretty bride. Caroline," he mur-
nured. "Will you marry me?"

"Today," she answered. "Tomorrow. Whenever you
ke."

"Without a pretty bride's gown?"

"With nothing but love."

"Ah," he said, smiling. "That we shall have plenty of!"
And, before the startled soldiers, and in full view of the
vatch, he held her close and kissed her, and she kissed him
back.

* * * * *

**TWO NEW COMPELLING LOVE STORIES
EVERY MONTH!**

Pursuing their passionate dreams against a
backdrop of the past's most colorful and dramatic
moments, our vibrant heroines and dashing heroes
will make history come alive for you.

**HISTORY HAS NEVER BEEN
SO ROMANTIC!**

Six exciting series for you every month... from Harlequin

HARLEQUIN

The series that started it all

Tender, captivating and heartwarming...
love stories that sweep you off to faraway places
and delight you with the magic of love.

◆

Harlequin Presents®

Powerful contemporary love stories...as individual as the women who read them

The No. 1 romance series...
exciting love stories for you, the woman of today...
a rare blend of passion and dramatic realism.

◆

Harlequin Superromance®

It's more than romance... it's Harlequin Superromance

A sophisticated, contemporary romance-fiction
series, providing you with a longer,
more involving read...a richer mix of complex plots,
realism and adventure.

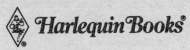